# THE PHOENIX HOST

Book One of the Roanfire Saga

C.K. Miller

Edited by Marissa Gramoll and Melissa Frey

Cover art, layout, and interior graphics by C.K. Miller

www.ckmillerbooks.com
ISBN-13: 978-1-7324544-0-8

To my love.
The man who lifts, supports, and grounds me.
Matt
I love you most.

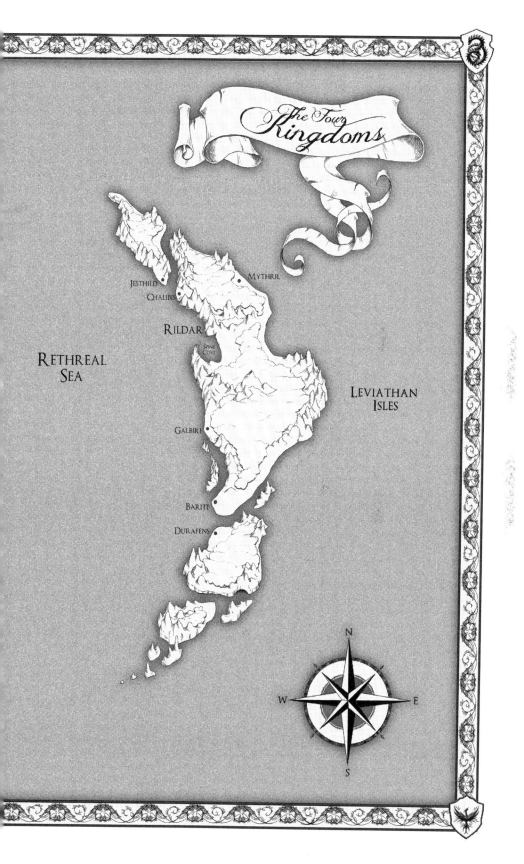

C.K. Miller

# CHAPTER 1

# THE DARAM KEEP

*even ships dotted the horizon like moonlit war-banners. They shouldn't be there. Not this time of night, and especially not in the season of storms.*

*Leaning out the castle window, a woman with flaming red curls squinted at the faint shape of the coiling black symbol painted boldly onto the canvas. They'd materialized from the mist. Somehow, the Leviathan pirates were here.*

*Already, a deafening horn tore through the night like a wounded animal. Torches and lanterns flickered to life across her beloved coastal city below.*

*She leaned back into the tower. "Phoenix help us."*

*Her captain approached with his hand resting on the hilt of his sword, ready for a fight. "Your Majesty? What are your orders?"*

*Her hands curled into fists at her sides. "Prepare the artillery. Ready what ships we can. We've withstood their pitiful attacks for centuries. This is no different."*

*"Yes, Your Majesty." The soldier turned and waved to the others to follow him from the room.*

*A crack vibrated through her chest, ripping through the circular tower as if a brazen warrior had kicked in a wooden door. She spun back to the window, nails scraping the cold stone edge as she leaned out. Orange light flickered on a sleeping ship in the marina.*

*How? The pirate's ships weren't close enough to . . .*

*Oh no. Another ship barreled through the water like a black cloud, so close she could smell the pitch of the flickering torches on* deck and catch glimpses of the blue-painted pirate faces on board. Two dozen flaming harpoons shot forward, orange light streaking across the black water.

They struck the city with a succession of hollow thuds. A dozen buildings blinked with fire. Screams erupted as the acrid stench of smoke rose to the sky. The damaged ship in the marina flared hot, followed by black smoke roiling up the mast and sail.

This couldn't be. They'd never come this close. Her ships were always ready, always watching. Somehow the pirates had slipped through.

Over the haze and rising flames, she narrowed her eyes at strange slender shadows breaking the white line of foam on the beach . . . Longboats.

Ice crept into her blood as the hazy silhouettes of pirates spewed from the slender vessels, already flooding into her city.

Torches and lanterns wormed through the alleyways of her metropolis, heading to the safety of the garrison on the cliff. Her people were coming.

Closing her eyes, she shook her head, and stepped away from the window. There was nothing more she could do. The garrison wasn't meant to withstand an attack like this. It was a watchtower, and because they hadn't seen the ships sooner, the pirates had already breached their greatest defense.

"I can help you."

The words whispered through the tower as if a thousand voices spoke together.

She spun, searching the empty tower for the source. "Who said that?"

Nothing but arched windows stood open to the moon and stars winking through the billowing smoke. A strange warmth grew against her chest. Voices filled her ears as red light bloomed to her face.

"I have the power to save this city," they hummed together.

Her eyes snapped down to her chest. It sounded like the voices were coming from the ruby necklace hanging there. Was it pulsing with a heartbeat? Her heartbeat, she realized. Every frantic beat. Heat soared through her skin.

She jerked the golden chain from her neck, holding the heirloom aloft. Its hazy red glow spread through the tower like sunlight *through smoke.*

*"Do not fear me." The ruby's light throbbed with each word.*

*Startled, the queen dropped the red stone, stumbling away. Crimson sparked as it struck the painted floor with a delicate chink.*

*"What . . . what are you?" she breathed.*

*"I am life," the ruby said. "I am the future and the past. I am as old as Roanfire itself. Your ancestors knew me, worshipped me, loved me. As long as they honored me, I protected them. Alas, I have been forgotten. I've become a trinket, something beautiful to adorn your neck and hand down to your posterity. But I am so much more."*

*A wave of screams drew the queen's gaze back to the burning city.*

*"I can save your people," the ruby continued.*

*"How?" The queen's voice shook. "The city already burns," she said. "The wharf is lost, and the ships are already under Leviathan control."*

*"All I ask in return is a willing sacrifice." The crimson jewel glowed eagerly. "As the phoenix rises from its ashes, so shall I be reborn. My blood flows in your veins. Give yourself to me, and I will save your people."*

*The queen took a step back. "I . . . I don't understand."*

*"You won't survive the night," the ruby said. "Make it a worthwhile cause."*

*The queen's eyes flew wide as she stumbled away from the glowing ruby. "It was you. Oh Phoenix, it was you all along." She clutched her heart. "You . . . you are the reason they—"*

*"They all found safety in me," the ruby said.*

*Eyes wild, the queen's red curls flew around her shoulders as she frantically shook her head. This ruby heirloom wasn't her salvation. It was a curse.*

*"You were born for this purpose." Angry desperation grew in the ruby's voices. "For my rebirth."*

*"No." The queen sprinted for the tower stairs.*

*"A sacrifice must be made!" The voices burned together, roaring like a blacksmith's furnace, heat and light expanding through the tower like a great burst of red sunlight. It consumed everything.*

My eyes flew wide, and my heart walloped against my chest like the flaming harpoons hitting the city. The smell of smoke filled my lungs, a taste of ash coating my tongue.

Were the pirates here?

Hurling the blanket from my legs, I leapt from the upper bunk. My feet hit the floor in a run. Reaching the window, I tore the burlap curtains aside and silvery moonbeams flooded the barracks. A wave of groans erupted from my bunkmates as they rolled their backs to the light.

My breath came hard, fogging the windowpanes as I scanned the sea. Rhythmic swells rushed onto the midnight beach, flowing with a whisper of the shifting tide. Were there ships on the horizon? It was too dark. The line between sky and see blended together.

I lifted my eyes to the watchtower where orange light burned through the row of arched windows around the top. Five soldiers were always assigned to survey the ocean. If there was anything to see, they would find it.

Dropping the curtain, I rubbed the back of my neck, finding cold sweat sticking to my fingers. The dream had been so real. The horn still vibrated in my chest. Smoke still stung my eyes. And the ruby ... its voices hummed through my ears and ran down my spine like ice and fire at the same time.

"Dagger?" My bunkmate and childhood friend, Ropert Saded, propped himself on one elbow. His luscious head of blond locks cascaded down his broad shoulder as he squinted at me. "What in the blazes are you doing?"

I rubbed my trembling hands down my thighs. If I told him a nightmare woke me, I'd never hear the end of it.

"I can't sleep," I said and snatched my oversized tunic and boots from the foot of my bed. I was grateful they required the soldiers to sleep fully clothed. If the pirates attacked, we would be ready. And if I needed an escape from Ropert's questions, even better.

"Where are you going?" he asked.

"To visit Mayama."

"At this hour?"

"Why not? She's awake."

He flopped his compact, muscular frame back onto his pillow, and the entire bunk swayed and creaked under his weight. "Don't blame me if you're too tired to keep up with the drills today."

"Like your snoring hasn't kept me up before," I muttered. Not that his snoring kept me awake. The soft rumble that emanated from the back of his throat was actually soothing to me, though I would never admit it.

He rolled his back to me and let out a soft purr. And just like that, he'd fallen asleep again.

As I slipped out the door, icy air bit my cheeks and stung my lungs. I made my way past the empty training arena—a sizable field of smooth dirt surrounded by a wooden fence. It was strange seeing this place so empty. It would be alive with soldiers in a few hours.

A bulky building stood beside the field with three chimneys stretching to the night. One curled with white smoke, and soft orange light radiated through the windows like a warm embrace. One I could always count on.

I pushed the door open and stepped into the mess hall. "Maya?" I called.

One of the three mammoth ovens was alive with fire. Silhouettes of bowls, canisters, spice jars, and other cooking contraptions lay scattered across the table by the flames. But where was Mayama? She never left the kitchen.

My footfalls echoed through the empty hall. Once again, it was strange with the place so quiet. It was the main hub of Daram, the six long tables and benches barely compensating the troops as we came and went throughout the day.

I pulled a long bench from under her workstation, sat, and stretched my feet to the fire. The smoldering logs popped and cracked, and the vision of the blazing wharf burned behind my eyes.

Why did it bother me so much? It was just a dream.

"Who's there?"

I twisted, spotting the plump cook emerging from her pantry, pointing her wooden mixing spoon at me like a dagger. Firelight fell across her silver hair tucked beneath her white cap. Her little black pearl eyes scowled my direction.

"If you even think of trying to steal from my pantry, you have another thing coming."

"It's just me, Maya."

"Keatep." She lowered her spoon. "Flaming feathers, child. You know better than to startle me like that." She stepped around the table. "My eyesight isn't what it used to be. It's impossible to see in this shadowy pit they call a kitchen."

I braced my elbows against the table. "What were you going to do with that wooden spoon of yours?"

A harsh clap snapped through my ears and then the sting registered in my shoulder.

"Ow!" I rubbed my shoulder.

She waved her spoon at me. "Don't underestimate the damage I can do with this, young lady. I've frightened many a scavenger from the kitchens with it." She sank to the bench beside me. "What brings you here at this hour—or should I use my spoon to shoo you away as well?"

I chuckled. "Do I need a reason to visit my favorite cook?"

"Before dawn?" she asked. "After a grueling day of training? Call me stuffed and buttered, but you should be sleeping, young lady."

My smile dwindled.

"What is it, child?"

I rubbed my palms against my knees. Maybe this was a mistake. It was just a dream, after all. These feelings—and the images—would fade.

"Sweet pea?" Mayama pressed.

Ugh, I might as well get it off my chest. "I had a nightmare," I sighed.

"Ah." She slapped my knee with her hand. Flour flew from her wrists, puffing out in white clouds at the motion. "There is nothing better than working to the sound of a story." She pushed to her feet, setting her spoon on the table.

I swiveled on the bench as she removed the white cloth that draped over the rim of a large bowl, revealing a plump mound of soft white dough.

"Go on. I'm listening," she urged, grabbing a handful of flour. She tossed it across the tabletop and began kneading her dough.

I pinched a sprig of fresh herbs lying on a platter, tearing it apart piece by piece. The sharp scent of rosemary released.

"Well," I began, "there was a seaside keep, much like Daram. But this one stood on cliffs overlooking a city I didn't recognize. The Leviathan pirates attacked."

"Sounds like the typical dream of a soldier," she said.

"It started out that way." I dropped the sprig of rosemary and rubbed my hands on my thighs. "But it changed quickly. I saw everything through the eyes of a queen with flaming red hair. She had a ruby necklace that spoke to her. It said it could save the city, but the queen would have to die."

Mayama's hands slowed.

"You know something about this?" I asked.

"Kea, 'twas no dream you've experienced this night. 'Twas a vision." She resumed kneading. "You witnessed the destruction of the Fold Garrison."

"Fold? The Dead Forest? But that happened . . . how long ago? Three hundred years?"

"Four hundred," she corrected. "And don't you think it's strange that in all that time the forest hasn't regrown?"

I bit my lip. I hadn't thought of it that way before. I knew about the Dead Forest, heard rumors and stories. It was a prime location for ships to anchor, but even the pirates avoided it.

"I do not condone what the pirates have done, or what they stand for," Mayama said, "but I don't blame them for the curse on Fold."

"It makes no difference," I said. "Pirates are pirates. If those vile, foul-smelling, warmongering sea serpents set foot on Roanfirien soil, I will see they met their end."

"As you should, my young soldier." Mayama slipped her beautiful mound of dough on the end of her paddle and glided it into the smoldering baking oven, sealing the black iron door.

My mouth watered. Nobility got the best. Fine-ground wheat molded into the softest, tastiest bread. Mayama had slipped me a slice or two over the years. I could taste it now. Warm and soft, melting against my tongue with a texture too fine to describe. The lousy baker who delivered bread for the soldiers spoiled his wheat with tree bark. I'd found myself chewing on a piece of wood more often than I cared to admit.

Mayama's eyes wrinkled with a smile. "I know that look." She wiped her hands on her apron. "Help me get the kitchen up and running and you'll earn your slice."

I smiled. Soon Mayama's workbench bustled with scullery boys and girls, kneading, butchering, peeling, chopping, and measuring.

Two serving boys waited patiently as Mayama leaned over a pair of identical trays, fussing over the arrangement of cheeses, butters, and jellies, cured ham, and perfectly sliced, beautifully crusted, warm bread. After adding a boiling teakettle and two mugs to the mix, she waved for the young servants to take the meals away.

Satisfied, she straightened, wiping her hands on her apron.

I licked my lips as the trays vanished from the kitchen.

"You didn't think I'd forget you now, did you?" Mayama said as she placed a warm, soft slice of buttered bread in my hand.

Everything in me smiled. I held it to my nose, inhaling. It was heaven, and the soft texture melted as I took a bite.

Mayama chuckled. "With that face, one would think you would rather court a freshly baked loaf of bread than any of the strapping young men in Daram." She wiped the table with a rag. "You and Ropert seem pretty close."

"Maya," I gasped. My bite caught in my throat. "You know better than to suggest that. Courting is forbidden among the soldiers." We were, however, permitted to court other citizens of Daram—not that I had time to frolic about with all my training.

She chuckled again. "You'd best be on your way."

Standing, I turned for the door. "Thank you, Maya. For listening. It helped."

She shook her rag at me. "Hurry now. You'll be late."

Stuffing the remainder of my bread into my mouth, I hustled from the kitchen and met the rest of the soldiers at the training arena.

My muscles locked and the pommel of my sword stopped a finger's width from my opponent's neck. These training exercises were no longer as challenging as they'd once been.

Thomas groaned, as I released my hold on his arm. He rolled his shoulder, nostrils flaring, redness building in his face. Snatching his sword from the ground, he turned to me in a defensive stance. Feathers, he was angry.

I brought my sword up, ready for the next spar.

"Halt!" Commander Holdan's voice carried across the training field.

Soft groans echoed as weapons lowered.

"I see progress." Commander Holdan declared as he pushed off the fence. His hand rested on the pommel of the sword strapped to his hip. "In fact, I think it's time to push you to the next level. You are dismissed for breakfast. Report back when the sun reaches the second tower. I have a new challenge for you."

Soldiers returned their weapons to the shed at the far end of the training arena. The clatter of swords being tossed against each other resonated from the hut. It would take the lower-ranking soldiers forever to clean up the mess. I didn't miss that job.

Ropert approached with his sword perched on his shoulder, his confident stride the result of a victorious spar. "Watch your flank, Thomas," he said to my opponent. "She takes you every time."

Thomas's jaw worked. "I'm trying."

"He's not that bad, Ropert," I said, then turned to Thomas. "You have excellent footwork. You just need to—"

"Don't patronize me," Thomas snapped as he tossed his sword into the hut. Spinning on his heel, he stalked off.

I looked at Ropert. "What did I say?"

"Maybe you should ease up a little." Ropert chuckled. "It's not easy for a man five years your elder to accept you're better than he is."

"Am I supposed to go easy on him? That's not in my blood. I am a Brendagger." I tossed my sword inside, hearing a clatter of metal as it crashed onto the pile. "Not that it means anything."

Ropert's smile faded as his sword followed mine into the shed. "Dagger . . ."

"It's fine," I said. There were days I wished I hadn't taken the name of Brendagger. Master Eamon was a legendary swordsman, unmatched in both swordplay and tact. He'd trained me, drilled me, pushed me harder than Commander Holdan ever did. I loved learning from him. I never knew what to expect. He always kept me on my toes.

But all that changed five years ago when Eamon returned victorious from the battle of Amall. I didn't understand. He'd won. He was a war hero. Yet, he took to the bottle like a parched man in the Tolean desert. He hadn't trained with me since. He barely even looked at me.

Ropert wrapped his arm around my shoulders. "Care to join me for breakfast?"

I gave him a crooked grin. "I've already eaten."

His eyes bulged, his brilliant blue irises glowing like a pure summer sky. "You didn't."

"I did."

He crushed my head under his arm, pinching my ears and cheeks in solid muscle. "And you didn't get any for me?"

My elbow shot back to his sternum. "Ropert. My hair." I squirmed from his grip, pushing the stray auburn strands from my face.

He chuckled, rubbing his chest. "What? You look good."

"Ha." I unraveled my braid. "I hope you find a piece of bark in your bread."

"You're not joining me?" he asked.

"I need a nap. I didn't sleep well."

"Alright then. Just don't sleep through our next training session." He turned, following the rest of the soldiers to the mess hall.

I kept a wary eye over my shoulder. Ropert was notorious for doubling back. He'd stuck my head in a rain barrel just last week, and I had yet to retaliate with something good. Something he'd remember for—

I collided into a solid body.

"Pardon me." The young man's arms shot out, grabbing my shoulders before I fell back. "I wasn't watching where I was going."

I glowered at his chest, searching his tunic for status or insignia. A low-ranking soldier would get a piece of my mind. But nothing indicated he was a soldier. His dark-blue tunic was simple, well-worn, and immaculately tailored to his impressive frame. An innocent smile spread across his lips. Flaming feathers, what was wrong with his eyes?

His right iris shimmered a beautiful hue of azure, like the Rethreal sea on a moonlit night. But his left iris flashed an unnatural tone of emerald, bright and crisp, almost glowing. Two-toned eyes. This man was cursed . . . and breathtaking.

Silky, deep-brown hair fell in loose strands from his warrior's tail, framing his chiseled features and olive skin.

"I . . . I'm sorry." I stepped back, straightening my oversized tunic. My hair. Oh, why did Ropert have to be such a child? It hung in wild brown ripples over my shoulders. Heat burned my cheeks.

What was wrong with me? I'd never been concerned with my appearance before. He was just another man. Just another strapping, young, muscular . . .

"No, no. I should apologize." His voice was like Mayama's bread. "I was admiring the construction of the keep. The towers alone are impressive."

Sunlight flashed across a slender pink scar as he looked up. It slipped from the top of his left cheekbone to his chin. Only a warrior would carry a scar like that.

He looked back at me. Feathers, those eyes.

"I was told Eamon Brendagger lives here in Daram," he said.

Eamon? What did he want with Eamon? "Yes, Eamon is here," I said.

"Do you know where I can find him?"

I tilted my head. This man was poised and fresh, clean-shaven, and sober. If he knew Eamon, he knew him when he was a respected general. Perhaps if Eamon understood this young man was looking for him, he'd wake up.

I couldn't hope too soon.

"He's not . . . he's not in a position to receive visitors at the moment," I said. "Can I give him a message?"

"Tell him Ikane Wulver is here to see him. I'll be staying in town at the Brandywire Inn."

"I will give him your message, Sir Wulver."

"Call me Ikane." He smiled, and my knees grew weak. "And you are?"

"Keatep. Keatep Brendagger. My friends call me Kea."

His mismatched eyes took me in with a new level of curiosity. "Brendagger? What are the odds? I didn't know Eamon had a daughter."

"He took me in when I was an infant."

Ikane's smile flooded with memory, something bittersweet drawing his eyes to a distant place. "He's always had a big heart," he said.

If only he knew that Eamon had left his heart so exposed that his only love was the bottle now.

"I'm glad to have met you, Keatep Brendagger," Ikane said as he bowed to me like I was a high-born lady. "I hope we meet again."

My cheeks were on fire. I didn't know what to say. I wanted to learn more about this handsome young man. But did I dare let him distract me from my training?

He turned away and moved across the training arena with a confident stride. His voice carried as he greeted the soldiers standing guard. One thing was clear: Ikane was a warrior, possibly trained by Master Eamon himself. This would change things.

It had to.

# CHAPTER 2

# MASTER EAMON

I made my very occasional route to Eamon's chambers, climbing stairs to the third level of the keep, home of the higher class where the intricately carved doors took on a new level of expertise. Torches flickered on black iron sconces, their shadows as cold as the surrounding stone.

My stomach tightened with every step.

I stopped by a familiar door, my fists clenching and unclenching.

How long had it been since my last visit? A month?

Gathering a deep breath, I let it out in a long, measured blow, lifted my hand, and knocked.

Shuffling came from behind the door, followed by the soft patter of bare feet.

"I told you t' go 'way." The door flew open to a red-faced Eamon with bloodshot eyes. "Kea." His eyes softened. "I didn't know it was you. Wha' a surprise." He stepped back, clinging to the lever for balance.

Drunk, again.

"Who were you yelling at?" I asked, keeping my voice level.

"Gah. Some errand boy tryin' to get me to take a bath."

He needed it. His hair was tangled to his shoulders, his breath smelled, and old bits of food clung to his uncombed beard.

I stepped into his room, the stench of sweat, wine, and urine thick and putrid. Plum-colored stains littered his unmade bed, clothes lay strewn across the floor, and the washbasin looked like it hadn't been touched in days.

"It couldn't hurt," I muttered, moving to the single window halfway shuttered against the oncoming chill of winter. It was the only means of fresh air in this stuffy space.

Eamon cleared empty bottles from the round table in the center of his room.

"What brings you 'ere? I 'aven't seen you since . . ." He counted his fingers, shrugged, and retrieved a full bottle of red liquid from a shelf. He sighed as his body sank into a chair. "Sit."

I shook my head.

His smile faded.

"Ikane Wulver," I said. "Who is he?"

His body turned to ice, his eyes growing narrow. He pulled the mouth of the bottle toward his lips.

My heart sank with each gulp.

"You can't keep drowning your problems. He knows you from before, doesn't he? He called you 'Master.'"

Eamon lowered the bottle, cupping it in both hands as he glowered at the liquid inside. "There are many young men who wish they knew Master Eamon. They swoon over me like women over pearls." He wiped his mouth with the back of his sleeve. "You should stay away from strangers."

The bottle sloshed as he lifted it to his lips again.

My fists clenched, hope dashing to the filthy floor for the hundredth time. Eamon's bottle was half-empty, and another waited on the shelf.

"I will speak to whomever I please," I said.

He lowered the bottle, red liquid trickling down his beard. "Stay away from him."

I slammed a hand on the table, which sent my palm stinging. "Look at me, Eamon. I am not a child anymore. You've done nothing but rot up here for the past five years, wasting away. Do you know what the soldiers say about you?"

He leapt to his feet. The table tipped, rocking to its side. The bottle hit the floor, amber glass shattering. "You know nothing of what I've been through! Get out!"

I stormed for the door. This was a mistake. It always was. I shouldn't have come.

"He's staying at the Brandywire Inn, not that you care." I yanked the door shut, the slam echoing through the hallway.

Why did I keep trying? It ended like this every time. I wanted to pummel something. Anything.

I slammed my fist into the wall, pain flaring through my knuckles. Why did Eamon have to be so bullheaded? Everything he did reflected on me. I had to work twice as hard to prove myself, and I was exhausted.

I stormed down the stairs, eager to leave the garrison behind.

Outside, Mayama's voice carried through the courtyard. "Make sure those potatoes are cut evenly. Oh, stop your weeping—those onions have nothing on you. How many carrots did you cut? We need twice that many. You, go fetch more rosemary from the garden, and bring some more firewood."

The door opened, and one of her staff members hurried from the building with a basket on her hip.

My feet slowed, heart sinking. She had her own battles to face. I didn't need to bother her with this, too.

But Mayama arched back, squinting through the closing door. "Kea?"

"I'll come back later," I said.

"My eyesight may be waning, but I see a thundercloud over your pretty little head. Get in here."

I pushed through the door.

Her black cauldron bubbled violently over the fire, a warm smell permeating the walls like an embrace I didn't want.

I melted onto a bench.

Mayama joined me, wiping her hands on her apron. "What's wrong, sweet pea?"

"Eamon."

"Ah, your visits have never ended well."

"I don't know why I try."

"Because you care, child." She placed a warm hand on my back.

"I wish I didn't. I keep hoping he will come back, train me again, stand proud." I clutched my fist, knuckles red from striking the wall. "Feathers, I hate wine. Don't bring him any more. Force him to be sober."

"We've tried that already. If you recall, he snuck into the cellar and made a mess."

"At least it would get him out of his room."

Mayama chuckled. "You have become a remarkable woman despite Eamon's choices. You cannot make everything right for others. As hard as you might try, only he can change his mind."

I took a deep breath and let it out harshly, trying to release the negative feelings.

"That's my girl. Now go." Mayama stood. "I have much to do before supper, and I think you have a training session to attend."

"Flaming feathers." I leapt to my feet. "I'm late."

I bolted from the kitchen.

By the time I grabbed a blunt sword from the hut and reached the training arena, the soldiers already stood at attention. My usual spot beside Ropert was taken.

Commander Holdan drifted along the line of soldiers, hands clasped at the small of his back.

Scrambling to the end, I saluted as he reached me.

"Corporal Brendagger." He kept his eyes on the sea. "Tardiness will not be tolerated, even if this is your first offense. You are to report for formation fifteen minutes early for the next fortnight and assist with the stowing of weapons."

My heart sank, remembering the way swords piled up inside the weapons hut. "Yes, sir."

Commander Holdan turned to the rest of his squadron. "Soldiers. It is my privilege to inform you that in two months' time, Prince Sander Noirfonika will finally accept his place as the King of Roanfire."

Quiet murmurs broke out among the soldiers. It was about time. King Myron had been frail for months now, and the prince had been ready to take the throne for years.

Commander Holdan continued. "In honor of this, Duke Adair has invited all within Daram to join them in celebrating the annual Harvest Festival. We have a fortnight to prepare for the event. You will each receive your assignments in assisting the caravan regulations and providing the security of the guests.

"Today will be our final sparring session until the end of the Harvest Festival. Now." Holdan turned away, moving to the center of the arena. "You will train with the combatant to your right. I will not match strength nor size, skill nor weapon."

The stout soldier beside me was at least three inches shorter than I was but higher ranking. Tup Grompel's prematurely graying hair easily deceived one to his age. However, he was anything but old. He was one of the best.

Commander Holdan paced before us. "You will each draw a circle on the ground large enough that you can both stand an arm's length away from each other. You will try to force your opponent out of the circle, and you will continue this drill until I see fit. Understood?"

"Yes, sir!" our voices boomed in unison.

"Begin."

We gathered in scattered pairs across the training ground.

Tup spun his battle-axe as I drew a circle in the dirt with the tip of my sword.

"It's about time I put you in your place, Brendagger," Tup said. "You've been taking it easy, picking on the weaker soldiers."

I blinked. What did he just say? I wasn't trying to ease my way to the next level. I fought harder than anyone here.

"Thomas isn't weak," I said.

"I didn't say he was." Tup stepped inside the circle, scrutinizing it. "A little uneven."

He was asking for it. "It'll do." I took my stance, my teeth gnashing together.

He set his feet, bending his knees. "Ready?"

I gave him one nod.

He roared as he lunged, slashing upward. I parried, the sound of steel on steel grinding through the arena. I spun my blade around his—a move, if done right, that always worked. By dragging my opponent's weapon to the side, I could open them to a solid elbow strike.

The hook of Tup's axe interrupted the smooth glide of my sword. Tup slammed his weapon into the dirt. My neck snapped back. The shaft of his axe flew toward my face.

Dropping my sword, I arched back, stumbling out of the circle.

Tup huffed. "You see?"

What just happened? I wasn't as skilled as Tup, but had he been right? Had I really been choosing easy targets to make myself look better?

I bounded back into the circle, snatching my sword from the

ground.

He came at me.

As I raised my sword to block him, I felt him try to catch my blade. I'd be a fool if I let him do that twice.

I spun, my sword slipping from his axe.

He shifted his grip, push dragging forward, and solid wood slammed against my shoulder. Numbing lightning raced clear to the tips of my fingers. My sword dropped. My chest hit the ground, and dust swirled, obscuring the rough circle I'd drawn in the dirt.

I wasn't out yet.

Grabbing my sword, I rolled onto my back.

Silver winked above my head. Tup's axe froze inches from my nose.

A death blow.

He stepped back. "You are an embarrassment to the Brendagger name."

My fist crushed the hilt of my sword, energy surging through my blood. Red spots blurred my vision. He'd gone too far.

"You think less of me than that drunkard?" I leapt to my feet.

He brought up his axe, his eyes growing wide as my blunt edge bit deep into the wooden shaft. As I jerked his axe away, my elbow raced for his face, and the impact rippled up my arm. Tup stumbled out of the circle, red dripping from his nose onto his tunic.

Silence stretched across the field as sparring sessions paused.

Breathing hard, I searched the training field for Commander Holdan. His chin rose as our eyes met, and I knew this disruption was going to add to my tardiness penalty.

But it didn't matter. I'd take whatever punishment he gave me. I was done. I didn't have to prove myself to anyone, least of all Tup.

I tossed the tangled sword and axe at Tup's feet, turned on my heel, and stormed from the training field. My fists tightened. I'd stop if Commander Holdan ordered it. No matter how angry I was, I would obey.

But he did not call my name.

At the edge of the arena, I slumped against the rough bark of a tree, watching as the soldiers resumed their sparring sessions.

Commander Holdan checked on Tup, testing his nose for signs of a break.

Was I really considered the worthless daughter of a drunk? I worked harder than any soldier here. I trained longer, I knew how to use almost every weapon, and I stayed ahead in every competition. Commander Holdan knew this. He'd even said that this was my first tardy offense. I had never been late before—not until Ikane arrived. Not until Eamon threw me from his chambers . . . again.

I shouldn't have visited him. None of this would have happened.

The sparring session ended. Soldiers returned their weapons to the hut—a mess I would need to clean up later.

I bit my cheek as Tup approached. Blood stained the front of his tunic, and the bridge of his nose was purple.

"Brendagger?" he asked.

I looked away.

"Forgive me. I should not have compared you to Eamon that way."

I swallowed hard. "Is that how everyone thinks of me?"

"It's hard to live up to a legend."

"I'm not Eamon."

"I know."

Ropert stalked up to us as if he hadn't noticed the scene I'd made earlier. I knew he had. He noticed everything.

"Commander Holdan had it in for me today," he said. "Try fighting against a spear in that paltry circle. Let me tell you, I'm going to look like a plump purple prune tomorrow." He rolled his shoulder, exaggerating a wince.

I smiled in spite of myself. How did Ropert always manage to lighten the mood?

"You've sustained a decent mark on your head," Tup said. "Perhaps you should see the healer."

"I'll be fine after a hot meal." Ropert extended a hand to me, helping me from the ground. "Let's eat."

"Brendagger," Commander Holdan called from the training field.

Closing my eyes, I gathered a deep breath. Right. I had work to do. "I'll catch up later, Ropert."

He gave me a quick tap under my chin. "Stay strong."

Commander Holdan stood in the center of the training field, hands folded on the pommel of his broadsword. The crease between his brows deepened as I approached.

"I do not condone your behavior this afternoon."

"Yes, sir." I wanted to glance down at my boots, but Ropert's little tap lingered under my chin. I squared my shoulders instead.

"Nor do I condone what Tup Grompel said." His voice was softer, almost fatherly. "You realize his taunting was a tactic. Words can inflict damage on your opponent. Rage will blind them, as it did you. They will make poor judgments or doubt their ability."

"Yes, sir."

"You are skilled with the sword; no one can say otherwise. But you must learn to use your temper to your advantage. Do you understand?"

"Yes, sir."

"Now." He handed his sword to me. "Don't you have some weapons to clean up?"

# CHAPTER 3

# TWIN SWORDS

*T*he fortnight passed swiftly, and my days were spent monitoring the merchants and guests gushing into Daram City for the Harvest Festival. The docks brimmed with ships as merchants brought their wares by boat. Daram had never been so vibrant.

On the night before the Harvest Festival, I returned to the garrison, feet aching, back sore, and throat dry. Soldiers raided the kitchen for whatever food they could find, and Mayama chased a few from her pantry who tried to steal from her dwindling supply of apples.

So much commotion. All I wanted was a bit of silence.

I snagged a wedge of bread and cheese and slipped outside. Sinking beside a rain barrel, I tucked my legs against my chest, watching moonlight dance on the broken surface of the Rethreal Sea.

Scattered flashes of silver looked like spinning daggers. The ocean breeze felt touched with a hint of ice against my cheek.

My skin prickled. The first frost would come tonight.

"You've been busy."

I turned. A figure stepped into the light spilling from the open kitchen door. Why was he so gorgeous?

"Ikane," I said.

"No, don't get up." He sat down beside me, his shoulder brushing against mine. "You look exhausted."

I leaned my head against the wall. "I am."

"Were you able to give my message to Master Eamon?"

I closed my eyes. "He hasn't contacted you yet, has he?"

Ikane shook his head.

"Eamon hasn't been the same since returning from the battle of Amall."

"Oh?"

"He is a drunkard." The word tasted bitter coming from my lips, like I was betraying him somehow. "The Brendagger name is not as chivalrous as it once was."

"You place too much value on his name. Brendagger or not, you have incredible skill."

"The soldiers seem to think differently." I tore off a piece of bread and stuffed it in my mouth.

"Have you ever sparred against twin blades?" he asked.

Twin blades? I hadn't done that before. "No."

"Would you care to spar with me?"

Eamon's warning flashed through my mind. Ikane commanded flawless posture, his stance that of a man extensively trained in battle. It was the way Eamon used to stand.

But what did Eamon care? I'd enjoy a challenge. Besides, it gave me an excuse to see Ikane's beautiful, strange eyes again.

"I'd like that."

He stood, offering me his hand. "Tomorrow then?"

His grip was firm, his skin warm. Something raced through my chest, a spark unlike anything I'd felt before. I didn't want to let go. But I had to before I started blushing again.

"It'll have to be before the sun peaks. I have a full day scheduled tomorrow," I said.

"I look forward to it." He gave me an elegant bow and slipped into the night.

*"Phoenix, give us strength," she breathed.*

*Torches and lanterns flickered to life as far as she could see as her beloved coastal city woke to the deafening sound of a horn tearing through the night.*

"Your Majesty? What are your orders?" Her captain approached.

Tearing her eyes from the scene, she faced him. "Prepare the artillery. Do not let them take the wharf."

"Yes, Your Majesty." He saluted crisply, turned, and escorted the rest of her soldiers from the room.

Heart pounding, she turned back to the window.

Bang.

The sound rumbled through the tower, vibrating against her chest. Fire erupted on a sleeping ship in the marina, dark smoke roiling up the mast and sails, illuminating the forms of shadows swarming along the docks.

They were coming from the ships, slipping toward her beloved city like arrows. Fire ignited in a building along the dock, then another. Streams of torchlight wormed through the streets, heading for the safety of the garrison on the cliff.

Warmth expanded against her chest, a strange red light blooming to her face.

"I can help you." A thousand voices filled her ears. "I have the power to save this city."

The ruby necklace lying against her chest burned and pulsed with every frantic beat of her heart. The queen jerked the golden chain from her neck, dropping the ruby. Crimson sparked as it struck the painted limestone floor.

"What . . . what is the meaning of this?"

"I am as old as Roanfire itself," the voices said. "I can save your people. All I ask in return is a willing sacrifice." The crimson jewel glowed eagerly. "As the Phoenix rises from its ashes, so shall I be reborn. My blood flows in your veins, as you are a daughter of the Phoenix. Give yourself to me, and I will save your people."

The queen took a step back, her brows furrowing.

"You won't survive the night," they said. "Make your death worthwhile."

"You've taken them all," the queen said. "You . . . you are a curse."

"You were born for this purpose. For my rebirth."

The queen sprinted for the tower stairs.

"A sacrifice must be made." The voices burned together, heat and light expanding through the tower like a great burst of red sunlight, consuming everything in its path.

I sat upright, heart slamming against my ribs.

The dream again? That was three times this week, and each one grew deeper and more intense. The horn, the pirates, the screaming.

I rubbed my face, pushing my hair back. Morning light seeped through the curtains.

The spar.

I unpacked the woolen cloak from the bottom of my trunk, the dream pushed away by the thought of seeing Ikane again. Something about facing two swords sent adrenaline racing through my blood.

The first rays of sunlight spread over the sea, touching the thin clouds with pink as I reached the training arena.

My breath plumed. Frost glistened on the wooden fence, and the smooth surface of the training grounds shimmered white. Even the weapons hut was a shade lighter.

I slipped inside. Swords, axes, knives, shields, and spears hung neatly along the walls, as they should be. I'd arranged them that way last night.

Reaching for a staff, I slid it from its perch on the wall. It was balanced and light—wielding this weapon was like a dance, and fluidity was needed. I'd tested my skill with the staff a few months ago, but Eamon's voice pushed into my head as I considered it. *A staff is useless against a sword,* he'd said.

I scoffed. What did he know? He hadn't set foot on the training ground since . . .

I returned it to its place and grabbed the long sword.

"Choosing your weapon?"

I whirled. "Feathers. Don't sneak up on me like that."

"Sorry." Ikane brushed the staff with the tips of his fingers. "I've only seen you use the sword. You hold the staff like it was meant for you."

He drew his short swords from the double scabbards at his back, holding them as if they were an extension of his arms. He shifted his grip, handing one to me. It was a stunning weapon, forged of black steel, the blade polished like the surface of midnight water. A snake-like body coiled to the pommel, and a serpent's head arched over the end with three thick horns protruding like barbs.

*Strange choice of ornamentation.* "A Leviathan?" I asked.

"I want to show them who is superior on the battlefield," he said. "What better way than to wield their mascot against them?"

I returned it to him. "I've never seen its equal."

"Weapons reflect their master." He stepped back. Steel blurred around his body, a soft whistle filling the air as his swords spun and danced.

He was fast. I would need to watch out for that.

He lowered his swords. "As a boy, I fought with two sticks. Eamon knew these would be the right weapons in my hands."

"Eamon trained you?"

"I was fourteen when we met. A boy with cursed eyes and a chip on his shoulder." A crooked smile tugged on his lips. "I guess he saw something in me."

"Where did you meet?"

"In Amall."

I knew it. "Five years ago?" I asked.

"More like six. I trained with him for a solid year. He was incredible." We moved outside. "He treated his men with respect, and they respected him. He never used his title or status to gain. He listened. He instructed. He chastised when necessary, but not without encouragement. I saw men changed under his command. *I* changed. I wished to be as strong someday . . ." His voice trailed off. A breath later, he squared his shoulders. "It seems we've both had the honor of being tutored by Master Eamon Brendagger. Let's see what we remember."

We took our positions on the training field. He gave me a nod.

I parried his first strike. The force of his blow rippled through my arms. Black steel split the air again, flashing at my face. I parried once more.

Too fast. He was too fast. I couldn't counter.

He stepped away, moving in a defensive circle. "You've good reflexes."

"And you strike like a cobra from the Tolean desert." I shook my tingling hands one at a time. He had full control of this spar already. This would be worse than my spar with Tup if I didn't change something.

I lunged, hitting his shielding blade down. His second weapon flashed. Dancing to the side, my sword slammed into his, catching his cross guard. I pushed against his forearm, pulling my sword back. A soft grunt escaped his throat as his wrist bent back. His sword dropped.

He stumbled away, brows furrowed. "You're holding out on me."

I stepped back, allowing him to retrieve his weapon, heart pounding. It was luck. That's all. I couldn't have orchestrated that disarm if I'd tried.

He lunged. The grinding noise of our weapons echoed through the training arena as they spun, hit, and deflected. He stepped to the side, his first sword hitting my blade down. The second followed with such a blow, my neck snapped back.

His black boots skipped behind me.

No, no, no. I'd neglected the first rule of combat: Never let your opponent get behind you.

I dropped, his sword hissing above my head.

Was he *trying* to kill me?

My legs pushed forward, keeping my body beneath his arms. Driving my elbow into his solar plexus, the air whooshed from his lungs.

Black flashed for my torso as he stumbled back. I brought my sword up, keeping it tight to my forearm. *Clang.* A sting sliced through my wrist.

This was getting out of hand. I should've insisted on using blunt swords.

Ikane leapt back. "I'm sorry." His chest heaved. "Are you alright?"

"What are you trying to do? Kill me?" A clean cut ran through my forearm. Red stained the edges of my sleeve. "I think we're done."

"Giving up that easily?"

Ever since Eamon stopped tutoring me, I'd stopped growing as a fighter. I couldn't do this. "You've already won."

"Not by my standards," he said. "I haven't disarmed you yet."

"You nearly dismembered me."

He shrugged one shoulder. "I knew you'd avoid it."

He had more confidence in me than I had in myself.

I brought my sword up slowly, holding the grip with both hands. He was too fast. His swords were solid extensions of his arms—even with the added range of my weapon, I could not breach his defenses.

But every weapon had a weakness as did the one wielding it. Eamon had reminded me of that many times. Ikane had used his upper-body speed to keep me at bay, but how deft were his legs?

"Alright. One more time," I said.

Ikane grinned.

I charged. His black weapons came up, ready to deflect. His blades sliced air as I dropped to my knees, folded my shoulder under my body, and rolled behind him. Eyes wide, he spun, swords racing to defend himself.

I could've sliced his arm clean off, but I twisted my blade at the last second, catching his forearm with the flat edge. Metal rippled as it struck bone.

Ikane grunted. His sword dropped. Stumbling back, he cradled his arm against his chest.

My breath came fast. "Done now?"

The muscles in his jaw tightened. His nostrils flared. Brows narrowing, he glanced up.

I stepped back.

His eye. What was wrong with his eye? The green one smoldered like fire.

He moved like water, snatching his fallen sword from the ground. Black steel flickered.

Parry. Move. Parry.

My bones rattled with the strength of each strike, threatening to tear my sword from my hands. Each resonating clash ignited a new flash in his eye.

"I yield." I retreated.

He followed. Lightning-fast metal twisted and dashed inches from my face. My arms burned. I couldn't keep this up. He was going to cut me to ribbons.

"Ikane. I yield."

*Stay away from him.* Eamon's voice rang through my skull. I should have listened.

My hands cramped. "Ikane!"

My back hit the wall of the weapons hut. I had nowhere to go.

"Ikane!" My teeth clenched, eyes scrunching tight.

Silence filled the arena. The blades stopped coming.

I opened one eye.

His swords were locked over my throat, my upright sword the only thing keeping his blades from cutting my skin.

Ikane's breath was hot against my forehead. "Impressive."

What . . . ? Where was the green smolder in his eye? I *had* seen it, hadn't I? Or had I been imagining things?

"No one has ever managed that," he said as he released me.

Letting out a shaky breath, I slid down the side of the hut. My arms burned, and my hands throbbed with new blisters.

Lonely clapping drew my attention to the training field. Commander Holdan stepped from a crowd of soldiers.

We had sparred clear into the regular training session of the day. Soldiers joined his applause.

This couldn't be happening. They had seen my disgrace for the second time in less than a month.

Using the wall for support, I stood and saluted. My shoulders ached.

Ikane sheathed his swords at his back, barely winded. "She is an exceptional warrior."

"As are you, young man." Commander Holdan appraised Ikane with an awed respect I rarely witnessed. "Would you consider joining us? We could use a skilled fighter in our ranks. Perhaps you could teach these fledglings a thing or two. You will have bedding, a roof over your head, and meals provided. What more could a man want?"

Ikane smiled, shaking his head. He cradled his arm to his chest. "Thank you for the offer, but I have other obligations."

Commander Holdan's shoulders dropped. "I understand."

"But I would enjoy drilling with the soldiers this morning," Ikane said.

Commander Holdan clapped Ikane on the shoulder. "Give them a taste of what you've given Corporal Brendagger. And you." He looked at me. "You had best see the healer. Report back when you're done."

Ikane gave me an apologetic smile.

There was something off about him, and Eamon knew it.

# CHAPTER 4

# HARVEST FESTIVAL

*I*kane didn't miss a beat. He followed the drills, moved with accuracy, and shamefully outpaced us. He wasn't normal.

There had been a green shimmer in his eye. I knew it. But no matter how much I searched, there was no evidence of it.

After Commander Holdan dismissed us, I slumped against the large oak tree on the edge of the arena, watching the younger students practice their weapons skills. Ikane mingled with the soldiers on the other end—even Ropert was there. *Traitor.* Ikane had made an impression while I sank lower in the invisible hierarchy of the soldiers.

Ikane must have felt my gaze. He glanced my direction.

I didn't look away. No matter how dangerously handsome he was, I would not be intimidated.

"Look, there is that man with the two-colored eyes."

Three boys and a young girl hung on the fence nearby, pointing to Ikane.

"The one with two swords?" asked another.

The girl jumped from the fence. "I heard he bested one of our finest soldiers this morning."

My fists tightened.

"I would love to see him spar with my trainer," she added.

"Now *that* would be a fight," the third student chimed in.

I drew my knees up. Ikane would crush him.

"Go ask him to spar with your teacher," the girl urged, shunting her friend toward Ikane. He hesitated a moment then squared his shoulders and sprinted away. The other boy approached his instructor.

Only seconds after the boy had reached him, Ikane glanced at his suggested opponent. He looked at me again then nodded to the boy.

Why did he look to me? It was like . . . like he was seeking my approval, making sure I was watching.

Whooping with excitement, the boy joined his friends on the fence. Ikane stepped onto the training ground, drawing his weapons.

His blades flashed sunlight. He knew them. Their weight, their balance, the exact extension they lent his arms. He held one near his hip and the other above his head with the blade sloping toward his opponent's face.

With a shout, the battle began.

Metal rang. Cheering and wagers on who would win erupted through the crowd. Ikane's strokes were powerful and quick, without flaw. The instructor fell back, clumsy compared to Ikane's precision. Students and soldiers hollered with exhilaration at every hit the instructor inflicted on Ikane.

Yet the true expert was already obvious.

I'd fought that? I'd deflected those blows with only a scratch to show for it?

Ikane trapped the instructor's swords, thrusting them at his face. Only a trained eye could see the way he hooked his boot around the instructor's ankle. The instructor landed hard on his back, a streak of red appearing on his brow.

Cheers died.

Seagull cries and rushing waves filled the silence.

Ikane could have easily killed the instructor, and everyone knew it.

"You are a worthy opponent," Ikane said, lowering his swords. He extended his hand to the instructor.

"Your style is . . . unique." The instructor tested his forehead for blood once on his feet. "Where did you say you were from?"

"Amall."

The instructor nodded, muttering something about seeing a

medic, and turned away.

My breath emerged in a harsh puff. I needed to speak with Eamon. I needed to understand what I was dealing with.

No. Eamon had said all he was going to on this matter.

Standing, I dusted off my trousers and headed to the warm kitchen, hoping for Mayama's hot soup and advice.

"Kea."

I glanced over my shoulder, seeing Ikane jog toward me. My heart rate quickened as I watched his eye for the glow. Nothing.

"The soldier I just challenged was defeated within seconds," Ikane said.

"You don't need to gloat about it."

He chuckled. "No. That's not what I meant. I accepted the spar to show you how incredibly well you held your ground. In fact, I couldn't disarm you."

Now that he mentioned it, I hadn't let go of my sword, despite sweat and pain. Even the group of young students had called me "one of the best." Perhaps I *was* being too hard on myself.

I nodded to his forearm. "Are you alright? I felt that blow."

"I can't even feel it anymore. You?" He jerked his chin to my bandaged arm.

"I didn't need sutures." I shrugged.

His face darkened. "You saw it," he whispered. "I saw the fear in your eyes."

I bit my lip, my heartrate increasing at the memory. "Are you . . . are you cursed?"

He said nothing for the space of three breaths. "I am."

"Is that why you've come to find Eamon?"

His jaw tightened. "Eamon needs our help. Perhaps, if we work together, we'll have a better chance—"

"I am done wasting my time with him," I said, pushing through the door to the mess hall, a hundred conversations rebounding off the musky stone walls. The rich herbs in Mayama's soup barely masked the smell of body odor and mead.

Ikane handed me a bowl. We filled our trays with thick soup and bread. Ikane sat across from me at a table, toying with the steaming chunks of potato that were too hot to eat.

"Ikane?"

He glanced up.

"Why didn't your eye flare when you were sparring with the instructor?"

Ikane broke off a piece of his hard bread, dipping it into the soup's broth. "It only flares when I get irritated," he said, stuffing the saturated bread into his mouth. "You disarmed me. Twice. *That* really irritated me."

I swallowed hard, watching his green eye. Still nothing.

Ikane surveyed the crowded kitchen. "Daram's army is inspiring. It's refreshing to see as many female soldiers as men."

"Daram is harsh—it has made all of us resilient," I said. "And most female soldiers are archers. You see Valine over there?" I pointed my spoon toward a soldier with long, unruly brown curls sitting on a bench just across from us. "She's doubtless the best archer in all of Roanfire. I can't hit a target worth anything. I'm one of only a few close-combat female soldiers here."

"And a good one, too," he said.

My cheeks flushed.

"Kea!" Ropert's voice roared over the clattering dishes and conversation. He beckoned to me, motioning to the doors.

Another assignment.

I dunked the rest of my bread into my soup, soaking up the rich flavor. "Will I see you at the Harvest Festival tomorrow?"

"I don't intend to miss it," he said.

"Good." I took a big bite of the bread, swinging my legs over the bench. "I'll see you then."

I had to push through the congested mess hall to reach Ropert. "We've been ordered to return to the barracks," he said. "The seamstress has delivered our new uniforms for the Harvest Festival."

"And this couldn't have waited until after I finished my meal?" I held up my soggy piece of bread.

He grabbed my wrist and took a gigantic bite right from my hand.

"Ropert!"

He sidestepped my punch, snickering around cheeks as full as a greedy chipmunk's.

*Let the games begin.*

I stuffed the rest into my mouth and darted toward the barracks. Ropert took the challenge and sprinted after me, knocking a soldier off-balance on the way.

His legs might have been longer, but mine were quicker. I barreled through the door of the barracks just as Ropert lunged for the collar of my shirt. We collided into our bunk, breathless and snickering with half-eaten food crumbling from our mouths.

"One of these days, I'll catch you," Ropert huffed.

I wiped crumbs from my chin. "Doubtful. You're getting slower."

He laughed.

I found my new uniform folded on my pillow. Daram's crest, a silver sea lion surrounded by an artistic weave of white threads, sat over the left shoulder.

Ropert lifted his, scrutinizing the gray-blue fabric. He frowned. "It's too small. My arms alone will bust the seams."

"It's all the food you're stealing," I said, unfolding my uniform.

What in the name of the Phoenix was this? It unraveled clear to the floor. A full-length dress? Slits climbed to the hips in a poor attempt to free leg movement. "How do they expect me to fight in this? Look."

Ropert tilted his head. "It's rather fetching."

I punched his shoulder. "I need practical, not fetching. No doubt Duchess Caitelyn had a say in the design."

Ropert pulled his old tunic off, his cotton undershirt covering his muscular frame. "Your spar with Ikane was something. What do you make of him? His skill was remarkable. I've never seen anyone move so fast. But there is something about his eyes."

I straightened my undershirt. "You saw it?"

"Saw what?"

My shoulders dropped. The last thing I needed was for him to think I was going mad.

"Nothing," I mumbled, grabbing my new uniform and pulling it over my head. "He seems genuine enough."

We struggled to fit the new uniforms to our bodies. I was not accustomed to the snug feeling around my waist, and Ropert could barely move his arms. Annoyed, he flexed his torso. The sounds of seams popping and fabric rending filled the barracks.

His smile was childish but triumphant. "That's better."

I laughed. "Don't let the seamstress see what you did."

"I won't."

Hundreds of elegantly dressed guests crowded the Great Hall. Some danced to the sprightly tunes of minstrels, others sang. But most stood along the walls, enjoying Mayama's lavish meal that was spread across three tables.

Roasts were decorated with parsley and radish. Baked squash, corn, potatoes, beets, and carrots glistened with butter and herbs. Fig and pear tarts, almond cakes, custard pies, and fritter apple rings dotted the table with golden-brown crusts.

"Mayama's outdone herself." Ropert's bright blue eyes bulged, fixated on the spread.

The music shifted. I recognized the tune.

"This is one of my favorites." I grabbed Ropert's arm. "Come on. One dance before you stuff your face."

"Fine," he groaned.

We linked arms in the center of the Great Hall, joining a wide circle of blue-uniformed soldiers. Clearly, I wasn't the only one who enjoyed the fast-paced rhythm and stomping steps. Our boots slammed into the scented rushes strewn across the floor, echoing like drums. The walls spun.

One final foot stomp thundered through the Great Hall, and the music stopped.

Breathless, I cheered and clapped with the crowd.

Ropert moved toward the festive meal. "Now?" he begged.

"Go on. I'm going to dance a bit longer."

"You'll miss out on the pastries," he said. "Those always go first."

"Grab one for me, then."

Three dances later, winded and hot, I searched for Ropert. His strawberry-blond hair towered above a swarm of young ladies. Some giggled, batting eyelashes, others flipped flawlessly curled locks, and one brushed her fingers against his arm. He flinched as if she had just swiped a knife against his skin.

Stifling a laugh, I pushed through the elegantly dressed ladies.

"There you are." I slipped my arm through Ropert's, earning dagger-like glares from the women. "Did you fetch me the pastry I asked for?"

Ropert's face turned a new shade of red. "What are you doing?" he hissed through his teeth.

"Saving you," I whispered back.

He swallowed hard, pulling an apple fritter from his pocket. "Last one, just for you."

Three ladies turned on their heels.

"You know me so well. These are my favorite." I took a bite, taking the extra time to run my tongue along my lips until the last persistent damsel rolled her eyes and left.

Ropert and I snickered through our noses.

"When are you going to learn to stand up for yourself, Ropert?" I asked. "Especially with the ladies."

"I try. Really, I do. I just get so flustered. They are so delicate. I'm worried I'm going to break them. Unlike you. I thought—"

An impeccably dressed man stumbled into us. His drink spilled down the front of my new uniform, the sour fruity smell making my stomach flip.

Wine.

He laughed, shaking the foul liquid from his hand. "Pardon. I didn't—"

I shoved him away, causing him to spill more of his vile red drink onto the floor.

"Easy, Dagger," Ropert warned.

He was right. I was a soldier of Daram, and treating a citizen this way would earn me punishment.

"I need air," I said. I turned, pushing through guests, not caring where my elbows landed.

Outside, crisp air drove the bitter smells and boisterous sounds of the celebration away. My fists unclenched as I inhaled the breath of the sea, listening to the distant crash of waves on the shore.

My second breath filled with the smell of wine wafting up from my uniform.

I hurried to the rain barrels sitting beside the wall, dousing the maroon splotches of wine with bitterly icy water. My skin prickled, but the smell remained.

Why did this vile stuff even exist?

I jerked my belt off, leaning my sword against the rain barrels. Even if I got the smell out, the brand-new uniform was ruined. I pulled it over my head, shivering as the chill hit my damp cotton shirt.

A pair of familiar voices reached my ears, coming from just around the corner. Curious, I rolled my uniform into a ball and listened.

"I've come to you for help. What more would you have me do to pay penance for my heritage?"

Was that Ikane?

Doubly curious, I peered around the corner to see Eamon stagger to his feet. Of course, he would come from his chambers if there was a celebration. Anything to justify his need for drink.

Ikane stood before him. His eye . . . it was *glowing*.

Eamon shunted Ikane in the shoulder with one hand, a bottle of wine in the other. But his movement was sloppy, and Ikane shrugged him off.

"Go home, boy. You'll find no help here." Eamon staggered past Ikane, raising his bottle to his lips.

"This is beyond you and me, Eamon. Roanfire needs you, and you know it."

Eamon ignored him.

Ikane grabbed his shoulder, his eye flashing. "Eamon."

The older man paused for the space of a breath. "Get your hand off me, boy." It was the clearest, most deliberate speech I had heard from Eamon in years.

"Not until you hear me out," Ikane said.

The bottle of wine slipped from his hand. He seized Ikane's wrist, twisting it. Ikane let out a small grunt as his arm rolled behind his back. Eamon shoved him to the wall, pinning him against it.

"Leave Daram, you hear? Leave," Eamon said through his teeth. "Or the next time I see those mismatched eyes of yours, I will claw them out with my bare fingers."

Eamon shoved Ikane away then bent down and retrieved his glugging bottle of wine. Half its contents glistened on the cobbled road.

"What a waste," he grumbled, swaying upright. He jerked a finger at Ikane. "And stay away from Kea. She doesn't need any more trouble in her life."

Ikane rubbed his shoulder, the green spark in his eye fading. I knew the look. It was hope dashing to the ground, a wish crushed under a boot.

Eamon tipped his head back, ready to gulp down the rest of the bottle's contents, but his bloodshot eyes found me. He paused, eyes growing hard once more.

"The same goes for you, young lady. Stay away from him."

Ikane's eyes shot up, finding me.

I expected to see sorrow in his expression—or anger—but I glimpsed something very different there. Worry?

Eamon stumbled over to me and jabbed his finger into my shoulder. "I mean it. Stay away."

His breath reeked.

Bumping his shoulder into mine, he pushed into the festivities of the keep.

I hugged my soiled uniform to my chest, eyes staring at the ground. "I'm sorry, Ikane," I whispered. "I . . . I came outside, and when I heard your voices . . . there's no excuse. I should not have been eavesdropping."

Ikane rolled his shoulder experimentally and winced.

"Are you alright?" I asked.

"Even as a drunk, Eamon can best me." He massaged his shoulder. "He's stubborn, but he may just get his wish. I have to go."

I didn't want him to leave. "Don't let him chase you away."

"I never intended to stay long," he said. "I have business in Meldron. And I need to make it there before the winter storms set in."

I understood, but I still hated the thought. "What happened between you and Eamon? Why does he hate you so much?"

Ikane's eye darkened. "You'll have to ask him that."

Trying to get that out of Eamon would be like trying to pull a pronged arrow from a wound. "I don't care what Eamon says. I hope we meet again."

His brows furrowed with a sweet smile. "As do I, Keatep Brendagger. I've genuinely enjoyed your company." He rested a hand on my shoulder, squeezing lightly. "Look after Eamon for me, will you? A drunkard he may be, but he is still a friend and mentor."

"I will."

# CHAPTER 5

# NOSEBLEEDS

*I* *can help you."* The sound was otherworldly, whispers of a thousand voices mingling together, humming through my ears. *"I have the power to save this city."*

*Heat radiated against my heart, red light blossoming to my eyes. What was . . . ?*

*The small ruby dangling on my chest glowed, growing hotter. I tore it away, the cord biting the back of my neck. The ruby sat in my palm, redness filling the tower like sunlight through smoke.*

*This couldn't be happening. This wasn't real.*

*I dropped the ruby.*

*Crimson sparked as it struck the painted limestone floor.*

*The voices were in my head. They heard my thoughts.*

*"I am as old as Roanfire itself. Your ancestors knew me, worshipped me, loved me. Alas, I have been forgotten. I've become a trinket, something beautiful to adorn your neck. But I am so much more."*

*"No . . ."*

*Run. Come on. Move. Why wasn't I moving?*

*". . . is a willing sacrifice."* The jewel glowed brighter, more eager. *"As the Phoenix rises from its ashes, so shall I be reborn."*

*"No, leave me alone."*

*"You were born for this purpose. For my rebirth."*

*Go, now, go! My feet finally moved.*

*"A sacrifice must be made!"*

*The ruby's brilliance ignited, heat pouring from it like an explosion from a blacksmith's furnace.*

*Brittle heat ate at my bones, tearing through my body.*

*I was on fire. I couldn't breathe.*

*Phoenix help me. My mouth was open. Why couldn't I breathe?*

The smoke released. My lungs pulled at cool air, chest heaving. The heat faded like the glow of iron doused in quenching oil.

Skin damp with sweat, I sat up. My head ached. Something warm trickled from my nose, and I wiped it with the back of my wrist. A red line streaked across my skin. Blood.

I'd thought the dream felt real before. But this? This was more than I could handle.

I slipped from my bed and opened the door. Icy air struck my damp skin, a chill racing up my spine as I closed it behind me.

I thought I understood the burning pain the queen endured. I thought I knew the fire. I was wrong. In all my years as a soldier, the bruises, the breaks, the sutures—they all paled in comparison.

Sagging against the wall of the barracks, I stared at the moon, bright and round and cool. Silver light struck every feathery splinter of frost. Ocean waves crested with white, yet red still burned behind my eyelids. Heat still threatened to overtake me.

The door creaked open.

"Dagger?" Ropert stepped outside, rubbing his shoulders, his breath puffing. "Are you alright?"

I nodded quickly. "I . . . I'm fine. I just need a minute. Go back to bed."

He closed the door softly. "Don't think I haven't noticed. This is the fourth time in a fortnight that I've heard you whimper in your sleep." His bright blue eyes flashed in the moonlight, brows furrowing. "Your nose . . ."

I sniffed, pressing the sleeve of my shirt against it. "It's just a dream. Just a dream." But no matter how many times I repeated it, I didn't believe it. This was more.

"Dreams don't cause nosebleeds," he said. He leaned against the wall beside me. "Tell me."

"Now? It's the middle of the night. And it's freezing out here."

He folded his arms across his chest, settling deeper. He wasn't going to let it go.

I pushed off the wall. "It's nothing. Come on, Ropert. Let's just go back to bed."

His lips pursed, and he tilted his head at me. "Tell me."

I tested my nose. The bleeding had stopped. "I'm fine, Ropert. Really."

"Dagger." His voice was firm and weighty, unlike his usual self. This meant something to him. He was worried.

I settled back against the wall, touching his warm shoulder. "Mayama says it is a vision depicting the fall of the Fold Garrison. I see a queen watching the Leviathan pirates destroy her city. She wears a ruby necklace. It glows and speaks to her." I paused, searching his eyes for a spark of mischief. If he was going to make light of the dream, this would be the place. A talking ruby? Even I thought it was ludicrous.

"Go on," he said.

Really? He wasn't going to mock my dream?

I swallowed, rubbing my hands together. "The ruby says it can save Fold, but only if the queen sacrifices herself to it. When she refuses, the ruby flares brighter than the sun . . . and burns her from the inside out."

He grimaced.

"I know," I whispered, hugging my shoulders.

"But that doesn't explain this." Ropert tapped my nose with a finger.

I closed my eyes, still seeing red. "This one was different. I am usually a spectator. I just watch. But tonight, I *was* the queen." Spasms ran through my body. "I felt everything. Her fear, her worry, the fire. Feathers, the fire. It was unlike anything I've ever experienced."

"And this dream repeats?"

I nodded. "Mayama thinks it's a vision, that I am witnessing history."

"I don't remember any historical mention of a talking ruby."

There it was. "I knew you wouldn't believe me," I said, pushing away from the wall. "Just go back to bed."

"Dagger, wait." He grabbed my elbow. "I didn't mean it like that. You're tired. Your performance is wavering. You're getting slower, and I'm worried about you." His grip eased. "This nightmare, vision, or whatever it is, is really taking a toll on you."

I pressed my palm against my forehead, wishing I could push the dream out of my mind. "I just want it to stop."

"I'll always be here for you, Dagger," he said. "Whatever you need."

"You're going to regret saying that. Sleep deprivation does not look good on you."

He waved me off. "What are you talking about? I can go for weeks without sleep."

"I don't want to see that." I opened the door to the barracks.

"Good." He yawned. "Because I'm exhausted, and it's freezing out here."

The barracks door opened just as I stuffed my feet into my boots. The silhouette of a short man squinted at a small piece of parchment. The modest feather protruding from his hat identified him as one of the keep's servants.

"Commander Valine Coro." His voice carried through the barracks, louder than I thought a man of his age could manage. "Sergeant Fortin Gray and Corporals Ropert Saded and Keatep Brendagger. You've been summoned to Duchess Caitelyn's quarters immediately."

The duchess? I grabbed my cloak.

Ropert followed, struggling to buckle his sword-belt around his waist. Commander Valine Coro, the best archer in Roanfire, smoothed her unruly brown hair away from her face. The older soldier with graying hair, aptly named Sergeant Fortin Gray, followed.

We trailed the servant into the keep and up several flights of stairs to the third floor, the same floor as Eamon's room. My jaw tightened as we walked past his door.

Three doors further, the servant stopped, straightened his coat and hat, and knocked.

The door creaked open, warm light spilling into the hallway.

"The soldiers, as requested," he said.

A young maiden opened the door wider. "Come in."

We filed into a candlelit chamber smelling of roses and honey. Tapestries detailing the beauty and elegance of court covered the walls. Plush carpeting concealed the stone floor, and an enormous bed with four intricately carved posts dominated a corner. Deep velvet curtains draped seamlessly over the bedding. Small tables and shelving cluttered with plants, paintings, literature, and jewels crowded the room, barely leaving space for the three chairs and single table in the center.

Amid all the jewels and royal finery sat Duchess Caitelyn, clothed in an embroidered robe of pink silk and lace. Another maidservant brushed her long, dark hair but stopped at a delicate gesture from the noblewoman.

The manservant stepped forward, bowing. "My lady, may I present Commander Valine Coro."

Valine did not salute as I expected her to. Instead, she bowed gracefully. Where had she learned that?

"Sergeant Fortin Gray."

Fortin stepped forward as he was announced and saluted.

The servant waved to Ropert. "Corporal Ropert Saded."

Ropert stepped forward, saluted, and then bowed.

"And Corporal Keatep Brendagger."

I stepped forward. Should I bow? Salute? Curtsy? Better to stick with what I knew. I pressed my fist against my chest, bowing my head.

"Thank you, Jasper. You may leave." Duchess Caitelyn rose from her seat as the door closed behind him. She laced her fingers together and approached Valine, her dress rippling like water in a pastel sunset. Without a shift or twitch in her expression, she scrutinized Fortin and Ropert. Her long, dark lashes blinked as her gaze fell on me.

"So you are the famed Keatep Brendagger, daughter of the once extraordinary Master Eamon."

Once extraordinary? He might have been a drunk, but that changed nothing he'd done for Roanfire in the past. He was a hero. I hoped my anger didn't show.

"I expect great things from you," she said as she returned to her seat, flipping her long hair over the back of the chair. Her maidservant resumed combing her already gleaming locks.

"As you know, Prince Sander's coronation is in less than a month. Due to the uncertainty of the raids along the coast, even for this special occasion, I cannot leave. I have chosen you to escort my niece, Lady Serah, to Meldron. She will represent Daram at the prince's coronation."

Meldron? My eyes darted to Ropert, but he obediently ignored me.

"You will leave tomorrow at dawn. I've arranged for Commander Holdan to excuse you from your duties today. That should be ample time to get your affairs in order. You shall not be returning until late spring." She lifted a scroll from a nearby table. "I have painstakingly written out every detail of your journey to Meldron. If I receive anything but a pleasing report from my niece, you will regret the day you called yourself soldiers."

Valine bowed. "You will not be disappointed, my lady."

"The courts in Meldron are brutal. I will not have Daram represented as a barbaric province. Lieutenant Coro, you are to train these unrefined corporals in the conduct of high society during your journey." Caitelyn's eyes narrowed at us. Or was it me? Yes, she was definitely glowering at me.

"Yes, my lady." Valine bowed again.

"Meet Lady Serah in the courtyard when the sun reaches the first tower tomorrow morning. Do not keep her waiting." She motioned to the maidservant.

The girl opened the door, and we slipped out.

The door clicked shut.

"Can you believe it?" Ropert's eyes were wide. "We actually get to attend the coronation. *Attend.*"

"Only if I can get you to bow without looking like a stiff board," Valine said. "You two need work."

"We're quick studies," Ropert said.

She turned on her heel. "We shall see."

# CHAPTER 6

# FOUR-HUNDRED YEARS

*S*oldiers crowded tables in the mess hall, a hundred conversations echoing off the walls.

"Get out!" Mayama's voice boomed above the noise. She waved her ladle at a soldier who managed to look innocent and offended at the same time.

The soldier was Corporal Mordak, a tall man with wild hair and an entitled attitude. I'd put him in his place a time or two. It looked like he needed a reminder.

Mayama wedged her short, round body between him and a young serving girl who hugged her shoulders, cowering.

"If you even look at her again, I shall see you court-martialed. And I can assure you, the duchess and I agree completely on this matter," Mayama snapped.

Mordak's mouth clamped shut, his fists curling at his sides. He looked over Mayama's head at the cowering girl. "It was a harmless little kiss."

"Out!" Mayama jabbed at the door with her spoon.

"You heard her, Mordak." I folded my arms across my chest. "Out."

His jaw worked, a vein popping on his forehead. Growling, he stormed away.

Mayama straightened her apron. "Really," she huffed. Turning to the girl, her face softened. "Go tend the herb garden for a bit, dear. No one should bother you there."

The girl slipped out the back.

Mayama turned to her workbench, aimlessly moving bowls around. "Just because courting is forbidden between soldiers does not give them the right to harass my aides. The soldiers need time to fraternize, get all that energy out. This isn't healthy."

"It's just Mordak. I can take care of him for you." I winked.

She smiled. "Doesn't your next drill begin shortly? You'd best be eatin' something."

"Actually, I came to say goodbye."

She stopped. "Oh?"

"They've assigned me to escort Lady Serah to Meldron for the coronation. I leave tomorrow."

She embraced me with her short, chubby arms. "Daram will be a dismal place without you, child."

My chin rested on the top of her linen hat that smelled of sage and onion. "I'll miss you, too, Mayama. I wanted to see you first, but I'm going to say goodbye to Eamon."

"Wait here a moment." She hurried away, returning with an amber bottle in hand.

Was that wine? What was she thinking?

She held it out to me.

"I thought we'd try one last thing," she said. "He may respond to the drink differently if you present it to him."

That was the last thing I wanted to do. I'd stolen Eamon's wine bottles before. He sniffed them out like a bloodhound. Pouring them out his window hadn't yielded any better results.

I sighed. Whatever I did now couldn't make things worse.

My fingers turned to ice as they gripped the neck, years of bitterness weighing it down.

Mayama petted my arm. "Don't lose hope, child."

A loud crash came from the pantry, and Mayama's eyes rose to heaven. "What in the blazing feathers is going on today? Take care, sweet pea. Be safe. And come home soon."

That was it.

Our farewell had been that simple. I would be gone for three months, but I had never left the Daram keep for more than two nights. It would be strange to not have Mayama there. She was the closest thing I had to a mother.

Clutching the bottle, I entered the keep's dark hallway. The sloshing made my stomach roll. This was madness. Eamon wouldn't think twice if I gave it to him. He'd lick wine off the floor if that was what it took.

Perhaps leaving was exactly what I needed. Knowing he was in the keep hindered my growth. I was always wishing, always hoping he'd emerge sober with his sword in hand, ready to push me to my limits.

"... before the raids begin again. I can't hold them off much longer, Eamon. I need your help. I don't know what else I can do."

I knew the voice floating down the hallway. Ikane? Again? What was he still doing here?

Light spilled from Eamon's slightly open door.

"Why do you do this to me?" Ikane asked. "What did I do wrong, Eamon? Why do this to Kea?"

"Oh, now you're bringin' 'er into this?" Eamon's voice slurred. "She 'as accepted me for wha' I've become. I 'ave a headache. Get out."

I inched toward the door.

"She's given up on you. Did you know that? She's hurting. You treat her like the mud on your boots. By the name of whatever element you choose, Eamon, she bears your name. Calls you master, guardian, father. For what? What if she were to die tomorrow? Would you even care?"

The harsh bang of something hit the floor. Probably Eamon's chair. "Get out! You have no right to accuse me of such heartlessness!"

I sagged against the wall. *Oh, Ikane. Just let it be.*

"You took care of me, Eamon. You saved me. Now you're losing her."

Glass shattered. Another bottle.

"I am not your father, boy! I am not 'er father either. Stop lookin' to me like I am. I can't . . ." Eamon's voice broke.

Was that a sob?

"Go home, boy. You will find no help 'ere."

"You know what will happen to me if I do." Ikane's voice was low.

"I. Don't. Care."

The door opened. Ikane stepped out, face downcast, shoulders drooping. It was a feeling I knew well.

53

"Ikane?"

He jumped. "Kea." He glanced around, green eye flashing. "How much did you hear?"

"I thought you were gone."

"How. Much. Did. You. Hear?" His hands shot up, grabbing my shoulders, driving me against the wall. Feathers, he was fast. My heart thundered. Twice now I'd eavesdropped, violating his trust.

His eye flashed like otherworldly magic, ready to tear me apart. I reached for my sword.

He grabbed my wrist, pinning it against the wall. His breath trembled hot on my forehead. He was shaking, but it wasn't irritation in his eye. It was fear.

"You were only trying to help Eamon," I said.

He slammed me against the wall, the glass bottle clinking as it struck stone. "You're not answering my question. What did you hear?"

"Feathers, Ikane. What's wrong with you?"

His eyes danced between mine, flashing between sky and meadow. He swallowed hard, lips moving.

Maybe I *had* missed something in their conversation. Some secret he kept. Something festering deeper than an infected wound.

His head dropped. "I'm sorry." He turned away, pinching the bridge of his nose. "I'm not myself today. What are you doing here?"

I held up the bottle of wine from Mayama. "Trying something different."

He blinked at the bottle. The green spark was gone, replaced by a sadness deeper than a well.

"You were right. He's hopeless. I thought I'd give him one more chance. I . . . I shouldn't have."

I stepped from the wall. "I'm glad you did."

He shook his head. "It would've saved me a headache and three silver bits if I had left yesterday."

"When do you leave?" I asked.

"Tomorrow morning."

Something sparked in my chest again.

"I leave tomorrow as well. I've been assigned to escort Lady Serah to Meldron for the prince's coronation. I came to bid Eamon farewell."

A smile tugged on his lips, the depression lifting from his face. "Perhaps we will travel together."

What was wrong with me? He just drove me against the wall. He had secrets. He was strong and fast and dangerous.

Maybe that was what I found so appealing.

"I'd like that," I said.

"No." Eamon glowered from his door with a pair of bloodshot eyes shooting flaming arrows at Ikane. "I told you to stay away from her."

I folded my arms across my chest, the wine bottle hanging by my hip. "You forsook all right to be my guardian when you took to the bottle, Eamon. I will only obey when you no longer drink."

Eamon's mouth clamped shut.

This was different. I expected him to lash out, take the bottle, and barricade himself in his room.

Instead, he dragged a hand down his face. "Get in here, Kea."

"I'll talk to you later," I said to Ikane and stepped into Eamon's room.

Closing the door, he rested his forehead against it, shoulders drooping as if boulders weighed them down. "I don't know what sort of fate has brought you two together, but I caution you to go your own way, Kea. Ikane is dangerous."

My jaw tightened. I'd already faced Ikane with his glowing green eye. I'd held my own against his strength and speed. "I can take care of myself," I said.

Eamon turned to me, his face filled with so much emotion, so much pleading. He really meant it. He really didn't want me associating with Ikane.

"Keatep. For your own good, stay away from him."

Squaring my shoulders, I set the fresh bottle of wine on his table. "You know my terms."

He looked at the new wine. A growl vibrated from the back of his throat. "You are as shrewd as your father."

My father? He had never spoken of him. Never made the slightest remark to indicate that he was alive.

"What?"

Face turning heavenward, he closed his eyes.

"Eamon?" I pressed.

His bloodshot eyes fell upon the wine bottle. He reached for it.

I grabbed his wrist. "My father is alive, isn't he? Who is he? Why did he give me up?"

Eamon shook his head. "I . . . I can't."

"Tell me."

"It isn't that simple."

"It's not that complicated, either."

He twisted his wrist from my grip. "Once I reveal his name to you, you'll become a target. There are many who want to harm your father. You will never see yourself as a simple soldier again. Your life will never be the same. Is that what you want?"

I swallowed. Maybe I was being too rash. I'd lived all my life here in Daram. I was a good soldier. I had everything I needed. Was I willing to risk it falling apart? I'd made it this far without knowing who my father was. What would it matter now?

I had to know. Anyone would be a better guardian than this drunk.

"Who is he?" I pressed.

Eamon closed his eyes, taking a deep breath of the rancid air in his chamber. He knelt by the beat-up trunk at the foot of his bed and opened the lid. Reaching as deep as the chest allowed, he retrieved an old piece of parchment. It was stained with age and burnt in a corner. He held it out to me.

"Here. This will tell you what you want to know."

The paper felt heavy in my hands but fragile, the creases worn as if it had been read countless times.

How would knowing change so much? It's not like I was going to seek my real father out and ask him to take me back. I was old enough to take care of myself. I'd been on my own for the past five years, anyway.

I unfolded the letter. Faded ink stared back at me.

*General Eamon Brendagger,*

*I do not know whom else I can trust with my son's illegitimate child. Her very existence is a threat to the union with the Glacial Empire. Yet she is the first female heir born to the throne of Roanfire in over four hundred years. I cannot bring myself to end her life. She is of great worth to Roanfire.*

*Take her, and raise her as your own. I am certain that she will*

*come to learn of her true purpose in time. Prepare her. Teach her.
She may be the key to ending all strife between the four kingdoms.*
*King Myron Noirfonika*

The parchment trembled, letters blurring.

What was this? King Myron? The Glacial Empire? How was I a threat? First female heir in four hundred years?

I looked at Eamon.

"I had just been promoted to general when you were left on my doorstep," he said. "We took you in without question. You were a gift from the Phoenix, an answer to my dear Veronika's prayers. In our three years of marriage, we could not have children of our own." His knees cracked as he rose from the floor, righted the overturned chair, and sat at the table. "When you were six, King Myron ordered that you be trained as a soldier. It was the last thing we wanted."

I swallowed, images flashing through my mind. A woman with beautiful thick lashes crying. Eamon's strong hand steering me away from a cottage. The smell of the barracks. The girls and boys fighting over bunks.

It was when I first met Ropert, a boy taller and broader than the others but just as terrified of the new phase in our lives. We became inseparable.

"Veronika tried to visit you. Do you remember?"

I bit my lip. "I remember a woman with dark hair showing a little babe to me. She had a beautiful smile."

Eamon's eyes shone. "Our son. You were eleven when he was born. You'll also remember I was called to bring reinforcements to the coast of Amall three months after his birth." His eyes fell on the wine bottle, sunlight lancing through the amber glass. "I was gone too long."

Why hadn't I seen it before? I had been too young, too self-centered, too naïve to understand. Eamon had been in Amall for an entire year, fighting off raid after raid from the Leviathan pirates, all while his little family remained here in Daram. Just before his return, Daram was attacked.

It all made sense.

"The Leviathan pirates killed them, didn't they?"

A tear streaked down Eamon's cheek.

I set the letter on the table. It didn't matter who my actual father was anymore. All that mattered was Eamon, the father I already had. The past five years of anger and resentment faded like fog in the warming sun.

I pushed the bottle under his nose. "I'm sorry."

He pushed it away. "I choose you. Take the bottle. You deserve better."

"Eamon, it's al—"

"Travel safely to Meldron. Stay away from Ikane, and I will be sober when you return."

Dazed, my fingers curled around the cold neck of the bottle. "Farewell, Eamon." I slipped out the door.

Now, what to do about Ikane?

Every part of me believed Eamon would choose the bottle. Was I ready to uphold my end of the bargain? It's not like I had control over which road Ikane took to Meldron. We were bound to cross paths.

I supposed I'd let fate decide.

# CHAPTER 7

# LADY SERAH

*S*unlight streaked through the white smoke billowing from the numberless chimney stacks on the garrison's tiled rooftops. Clouds puffed from our horse's nostrils. Frost coated everything from the doors and window frames to the trees and shrubbery.

Where was she? My cheeks and nose burned with cold. The sun had passed the tallest tower ages ago.

I rubbed my hands together, stomping my feet. I could've drilled this morning. At least that would've kept me warm.

"She's here," Ropert said.

Half a dozen servants led ten heavily packed horses into the courtyard. We stood at attention as a beautiful young maiden with golden-red hair drew near. She couldn't have been older than fourteen. She pulled her heavy, fur-lined cloak around her shoulders, inspecting us with large, brown eyes. I saw a strong resemblance to Duchess Caitelyn in them.

She pursed her painted lips. "These are the soldiers?" She turned to an older servant with snow-white hair, disappointment ringing in her voice. She glowered at Valine. "Look at them. Her hair looks like straw."

She scowled at Fortin. "And how old is this one? Seventy? His belly rumples his uniform. And this one is as slim as a willow tree. Can she even wield a sword?"

I tried to keep my jaw from clenching. I wasn't a statue to be altered at her pleasure. What did my leanness matter? I could wield a sword with the best and outrun half of Daram's troops. She obviously mistook my thinness for weakness. *Just wait,* I thought. *When it comes to battle, I'll show you.*

"And this one . . ." Her eyes lifted to Ropert's tall frame. Her jaw eased, and she tapped her lips with a finger. "This one will do nicely. What is his name?"

"That is Corporal Ropert Saded, my lady," the white-haired servant said.

"He's perfect. But the others . . ." She threw up her hands. "What was my aunt thinking?"

"Lady Serah, my dear, these soldiers are the finest in Daram. Duchess Caitelyn would give you nothing but the best," the servant assured her.

"I suppose they will have to do." She stole another glance at Ropert before climbing into the saddle of her white mare.

I nudged Ropert in the ribs. "She fancies you."

"She's a child," he whispered. "Her affection will fade."

Our small entourage meandered toward the wharf on the northeastern side of Daram City. Thirteen ships moored near the pier with masts soaring to the cloudless sky, boasting white sails waiting to catch the wind. The docks already bustled with sailors and merchants, thanks to Lady Serah's tardiness. We dodged wooden carts clattering down the cobblestone street and damp-skinned workers carrying barrels and crates on shoulders.

We neared a smaller vessel anchored just beyond a large stack of crates. It was breathtaking.

What it lacked in size, it boasted in workmanship. Her masts were constructed of thick, white oak with carvings of the sea embedded in the timber. The main body, fashioned of slender planks, alternated in color from white oak to black walnut. A beautiful sculpture sat on the bow, carved to form the head of a mighty sea lion, Daram's mascot. Perfect black paint surrounded by a border of bright silver formed the letters of her name: the *Otaridae*.

A broad-shouldered man with a rounded belly accompanied by a stout-looking woman strode down the plank, meeting our party at the dock.

"Welcome aboard the *Otaridae*, Lady Serah." The man's graying hair and beard complemented the robust way he moved. His voice was rough and powerful, perfect for shouting commands at his crew. "I am Captain Rawing. We will launch in a few minutes. This is my first mate, Piper." He placed his large hand on the stout woman's shoulder.

Lady Serah adjusted her hood. "Can we please get out of this wind?"

What was she talking about? There was barely a breeze.

Captain Rawing's suntanned skin wrinkled around his eyes. "Of course, my lady. If you would follow me. Piper, please settle the others below."

Lady Serah trailed after the captain, her white-haired servant following.

"Brendagger, get my things. Lady Serah should not be left without a bodyguard," Valine said, hurrying after them.

"A ship is no place for idleness," Piper said, leading us across the deck toward the stern, our boots thudding against the planks. We passed an open hatch in the center of the ship. Horses shifted in pens below. "It is up to you how much of the smell you can tolerate. It is your responsibility to clean up after the horses."

She descended through a second hatch toward our accommodations directly beside the stables. The smell of horse already filled the hull.

"There are buckets and shovels secured to the wall over there." Piper turned on her heel. "Stow your gear well before we launch. You don't want things falling on your toes once she takes off." She disappeared up the stairs.

Ropert eyed the slender bunks along the walls, stacked three high, then examined his shoulders. "This will not be comfortable."

"You can have the top," I offered, dropping Valine's bag on the opposite bunk. "It looks like it has a little more room."

"I don't think it will matter."

"Fortin! Saded! Brendagger!" Valine's voice boomed down the hatch.

Fortin shot up from making his bed on the middle bunk, hitting his head. He cursed under his breath. "What?"

"Lady Serah wants to speak with us."

"Now?"

"Now."

I stuffed my bag in a net hanging from the rafters and shoved Valine's in a cubby. We followed Fortin to the deck.

Now there was wind enough for Lady Serah to complain about. Thick ropes swayed across the railing, reaching high to the crow's nest. Sailors clung to the rigging and yards, awaiting the order to unfurl the sails.

Valine knocked on the captain's cabin door. The white-haired servant opened it.

Compared to our accommodations below, the cabin was a palace, constructed of white oak and adorned with willowy carvings and graceful curves. Lady Serah sat on a bench filled with varying shades of blue pillows stretching across the wide expanse of windows at her back. Through the framed glass panes, another grand ship bobbed in the water.

"For the love of the Phoenix," Lady Serah groaned. "You all look like drowned rats. Your hair is unkempt, your faces are smudged, and your uniforms look like they haven't been washed in a month."

I'd barely had this new uniform for a week. I'd even managed to get the wine stain out of it.

"Lady Se—"

The click of Serah's fingers broke Valine off. "No excuses."

I stiffened. She must have stepped in something rotten this morning.

"You soldiers are all alike." Lady Serah drifted to the table holding a bowl filled with red grapes, pears, and apples. She opened the bottle of wine standing beside it and filled a goblet. "You don't think for yourselves. It is unappealing how you simply bend to every command. I am a lady of the court. I will not have barbarians standing about dumbly waiting for an order."

She swirled her goblet, sauntering to Ropert. A dangerously sweet smile pulled on her lips. She rose on her toes, and her hand flashed, striking his cheek. Not a drop spilled from her goblet. "For the love of the Phoenix, shave that atrocious red fuzz from your face."

Feathers, his face. I'd never seen him so stunned.

I pinched my lips tight. I shouldn't laugh. But a snort burst from my nose.

Lady Serah whirled to me. "You. Stop tromping about like an ogre. Pull your shoulders back, and hold your head up." Her hand rose.

Was she going to slap me, too? I braced for a strike.

She pressed a finger under my chin instead, forcing my head up. "Have you no pride? Wash your face, and run a comb through that tangled mess you call hair."

She turned to Fortin. "And you . . . I don't even know where to begin." She took a long drink. "What was my aunt thinking? This will be a disaster. I need bodyguards that have been properly educated and groomed. I can give you fine clothing and have my servants polish you to perfection, but it won't do any good unless you behave like refined folk. I can't possibly fix this before we reach Meldron."

"That is why I am here, my lady." Valine gracefully slid one of her feet back, pinched the long tails of her new uniform, and spread it wide as if she wore the finest gown in Roanfire.

Lady Serah arched an eyebrow over the rim of her goblet. "You think you can do it?"

"I know I can," Valine said.

"We must do something about your hair. The appearance of a wild mare is unacceptable."

"Yes, my lady."

Serah took a sip of her wine, turning to the windows. "I have ordered new clothing for all of you. You will be dressed in the height of fashion." She settled into the cushioned bay window. "I will keep the new clothing in my possession, lest you soil them before we reach Meldron." She waved a hand. "You are dismissed."

I bowed, following the others from the cabin, the chilly air warmer than Serah's presence. I sighed as the door closed.

Ropert leaned close to me. "She's a jackanapes giglet if I ever saw one."

I laughed.

Valine's stern look made me bite my lip.

"You'd best learn to like her," I whispered back. "We're stuck with this 'giglet' for the next three weeks, at least."

"Maybe we can get her to Meldron in a fortnight instead," Ropert said.

I laughed again.

Sailors hoisted the anchor, loosened the lines, and unfurled the sails. They expertly maneuvered the ship around fishing vessels and into the wide canal.

I stood at the bow, clinging to the railing, my stomach fluttering as the ship's nose rose and fell. The main sail dropped, a gust snapping it tight, driving the ship forward with a notable lurch.

Wind rushed through my hair, tearing loose strands from my braid. It felt like freedom. Water rushed beneath the ship as if it were flying. The air blew sharp and cool. The sun fell warm on my shoulders.

"Do you smell that?" Ikane slipped beside me, his eyes on the horizon. His deep-brown hair blew from his face, revealing his chiseled features. He looked younger somehow, like he felt the same freedom I did.

I gathered a deep breath of crisp air, closing my eyes. "It smells like liberation."

Ikane leaned on the railing, lacing his fingers together. "I was practically born on the water. Nothing can compare."

The ship plowed through a rough swell, making my legs buckle. I grasped the railing tighter. "Is your father a merchant?"

He shook his head. "He *was* an aristocrat. He died many years ago. My brothers manage his fleet now."

"How many brothers do you have?"

"Six."

My brows rose. "And where do you fit in?"

He chuckled. "I am the youngest."

"Are they the ones holding off the Leviathans?"

He raised an eyebrow at me.

"I'm sorry. I know I shouldn't have eavesdropped, but you told Eamon they were holding off the Leviathans. This is beyond him. This is a matter for the king. Roanfire should leap at the chance to help defend Amall."

"Amall?"

"Isn't that where they are stationed?"

"I . . . well . . . I wouldn't call them heroes."

"Dagger!" Ropert peeped from the hatch. "Valine has ordered us below."

I pushed from the railing. "If you don't ask the king for help, then I will."

Ikane smiled. Feathers, he was handsome. "Go on, Brendagger. They're waitin' for ya."

I hurried toward the hatch, his smooth tenor voice lingering in my ear. The subtle way he rolled his *r*'s was like a purr. Had he always spoken that way? My feet slowed. I glanced over my shoulder, but he was already gone. I'd have to pay attention to that in our next conversation.

The ship rocked to the side as I descended the stairs. My boot slipped, my heel striking hard on the next step.

Ropert's arm shot out. "Careful."

"Thanks." I found my footing and straightened my uniform.

He moaned softly, sagging against a beam. He looked pale. Perhaps it was just the poor lighting down here. The smell—a mixture of body odor and horse—didn't help, either.

"Are you alright?" I asked him. "You don't look good."

He held his stomach. "I don't feel so good." He sat on the bottom step. "It must have been something I ate."

"Now that you are all here," Valine started, perching on a nearby bunk, "let's get to work." Her hair sat in a rigid bun at the back of her head, an attempt to smooth her unruly curls. Brown wisps escaped the confinement, casting her head in a halo. Her wild hair suited her far better.

Fortin slumped on the bunk closest to her, folding his arms across his chest. "Let's get this over with."

Valine stood, bracing herself on the bunks. "How does one properly address a nobleman?"

"You need to be more specific," Ropert said. "Are we addressing the prince, a duke, or a lord?"

"Very good, Ropert." Valine smiled. "That determines how one addresses a noble. However, what if you do not know their title?"

Ropert opened his mouth. He froze, lips going white. He bolted up the stairs.

"Ropert?" I sprinted after him.

He hung over the railing, heaving into the water. His shoulders trembled.

"What's wrong?" Valine called up the stairs.

"He's seasick," I called back.

Valine groaned. "It will take a miracle to have you all trained in time at this rate."

Ropert heaved into the water. When his body finished, he slumped against the railing, his glazed eyes staring at the dry land only a boat ride away.

"How long are we traveling by ship again?"

"It's two days to Gimath," I said. "And from there it's another two days to Bakka."

He whimpered, dragging his fingers through his flaxen curls, pulling them from his warrior's tail. "I'd rather run barefoot on thorns the whole way. Do you think Lady Serah would consider traveling on foot to Bakka instead?"

"Can you really see that woman traveling a dusty road instead of sitting in the captain's luxury cabin?"

"No."

I pressed a hand to his back. "Try to get some rest, Ropert. Your stomach is empty."

"I can't. Feathers, Dagger. I am no good as a bodyguard like this." He slumped to the deck, leaning against the balusters. "I'd be better off disembarking in Gimath and meeting you in Bakka."

He was right.

"Seasick?" Ikane approached. He sank to the deck beside Ropert, casually swinging his legs through the railing.

Ropert let out a short groan.

"Here." Ikane opened the flap on his belt pouch. He pulled a little sack from it, dropping it in Ropert's hand. "It is a blend of ginger, peppermint, and fenugreek made specifically for settling the stomach."

"I don't want to take it if you need it."

"I'm not the one who is seasick. You need it more than I do. Simply brew it like tea. And for your sake, I'd make it strong."

Ropert clutched the little sack to his stomach like a treasure. "Thank you." He gripped the handrail, pulling himself to his feet. As soon as he stood, his face turned a new shade of white. Arching over the water, he heaved again.

I'd never seen him so sick. The sooner we could get the herbs in him, the better. "The cook should have warm water. I'll go fetch some."

"It's alright." Ropert wiped his mouth with the back of his wrist. "I'll do it." He stumbled in the direction of the galley.

"I hope it helps," Ikane called.

Ropert waved without looking back.

"I'm worried about him." I sat down beside Ikane, leaning against the railing.

Ikane struck the hull with his heels. "He's not built for the sea."

"Maybe I should speak with Lady Serah, see if she'll allow him to disembark."

"Wait and see if the herbs help first."

That was a sound idea. No need to upset the lady without good cause. She might be small and young, but she was as aggressive as a cornered cat. At least Ropert held her fancy. That was an advantage.

"Thank you for your help."

"Don't thank me yet. The herbs don't work for everyone." Ikane leaned back on his hands, his gaze fixed on the horizon. Vibrant orange sunlight touched the graying outline of the shore causing the white foam on the water to burst into flame—orange and red, like fire, glowed like the ruby from my nightmares.

I squeezed my eyes shut. I didn't want to dream tonight.

"Are you feeling alright?" Ikane asked.

I opened my eyes, avoiding the sparks on the waves. "I'm fine. Tell me. What is Amall like? I've never been to that end of Roanfire before. I imagine it's like Daram."

The wind caught the soft, dark strands of hair too short for him to keep bound in his warrior's tail. "Amall is very unlike Daram. Cliffs surround the cove, allowing the ships to dock in a very sheltered marina. It is cold and almost always rains. The terrain is harsh, the trees are thick, and sharp rocks tear through even the most durable boats."

There it was. The subtle roll of his *r*. I could listen to him speak all day.

"Sounds . . . lovely," I said.

"In a way, it is. There is a rugged beauty you can't find anywhere else."

Why wasn't he rolling his *r*'s now?

"And your brothers?" I asked.

He gave me a crooked smile. "You cunning little soldier. Still trying to get me to talk about them, aren't ya?"

"Can you blame me? If there's a chance they could fight off the Leviathan pirates, we should help them. Eamon may not be compelled to make the right choice, but I am a Brendagger. I could go in his stead."

"Oh, Little Brendagger." His smile was tinged with sadness as he gazed at the sun fading on the black horizon. The sky darkened to red and violet. "How would someone like me even get close to the king? Eamon was my only hope."

"Lady Serah." I tucked my legs under me and stood. "She'll address Prince Sander during the coronation. She could put in a word for you."

He pushed to his feet. "You have such a fighting spirit, Kea."

His smile was perfect. His eyes were like gems in the fading light.

I cleared my throat. "I should probably check on Ropert. And where is Valine?" I scanned the deck. "She should have been back ages ago."

"Kea? Can I meet you here tomorrow, same time?"

"I'd like that." The words slipped out before I could think. This was exactly what Eamon didn't want me to do. But Eamon wasn't here.

I liked Ikane. And what Eamon didn't know couldn't hurt him.

Ropert snored softly on the top bunk, a slight flush touching his cheeks. The herbs were working. Color had returned to his lips.

I jumped from the bunks, turning to Fortin who sat cross-legged on the floor. He glanced up from his woodworking project.

"He just fell asleep. It's about time, too. I couldn't take his groaning anymore." He blew shavings from the mutilated piece of wood in his hand, inspecting it briefly.

"Have you heard from Valine?"

He shook his head, setting his knife back to the wood. "As far as I know, she's still with Lady Serah."

That was odd. None of us enjoyed Lady Serah's criticism. "I should see what's keeping her."

Returning to the deck, I glanced at the railing where I left Ikane. He wasn't there.

Sailors' shouts blended with the distinct sound of giggling as I neared the captain's cabin. I peered through the small round window to see Valine and Lady Serah sitting at the table. A grand meal was splayed out before them, mostly eaten.

I knocked.

"Enter." Lady Serah's voice was tinged with laughter.

I stepped inside. Why was she grinning at me? Valine was, too, her cheeks rosy.

The smell of wine made everything clear.

"Brendagger," Valine said. "What is it?"

"Commander." I saluted. "I was worried when you did not return."

"That may have been my fault," Lady Serah said. "I needed to do something about her hair. Look at it now. It's shining like gold."

Valine's curls had been tamed into perfect glossy ringlets, a waste of time and energy. Valine was a soldier. It would be a mess by morning, not to mention how badly the wind would destroy it.

Lady Serah set her goblet on the table. "Come here."

Her demanding tone made me comply. I closed the door and stepped closer, onion and rosemary wafting from the remains of roasted poultry.

"You have very delicate features." Serah placed a finger against her lips.

I bit my tongue; she'd scrutinized me once before. I didn't need it again.

"And you've a very flattering figure beneath that burlap sack my aunt claims is a uniform."

"Don't let that fool you," Valine warned. "Brendagger is a force on the battlefield."

Serah didn't seem to care. "Let your hair out."

I swallowed hard. The last thing I wanted was for her to mess with my hair the way she had with Valine's. But she was a lady and my superior, so I pulled the cord from the end of my braid, unraveling my auburn strands.

Lady Serah sauntered around me, running her fingers through it. My soldier's instincts were to turn and face her. I hated having someone behind me.

"Lovely," she whispered. "Simply divine. Do you know you have a reddish glow beneath all this dirt? All it needs is . . ." She pulled. "Yes. That's it. The simpler the better for you. Oh, and the brown dress I picked out for you will be stunning with your skin tone."

She released my hair like she'd released me from an arm bar. She took her seat at the table again.

"Is Ropert feeling any better?" Valine asked.

"Ropert?" Lady Serah's eyes widened. "What do you mean? What happened?"

"He's seasick," I said. I should ask now. She was already concerned for him. I could draw on that, get him off the ship. But what if she refused? I had to make her think it was her idea. "He feels terrible that he cannot perform his duties as a bodyguard in this state."

Serah leaned back in her chair. "The poor man."

"He's not built for the sea, my lady. He's looking forward to a reprieve when we stop in Gimath."

Serah tipped her head. "Gimath. Yes. We could rest there a day or two . . ."

"That isn't possible, my lady," Valine said. "Duchess Caitelyn's schedule is very rigid. If we miss one checkpoint, delays will compound on the rest of our journey."

For the first time, Lady Serah seemed human, her eyes downcast with an emotion of helplessness. She ran her finger along the rim of her goblet.

"A single rider could make the journey from Gimath to Bakka in the same time it would take us to reach Bakka by boat," I said.

A light sparked in her eyes, and she straightened.

*Yes, she took the bait.*

"He can ride," she said. "We will drop him off in Gimath, and he can meet us in Bakka. He should be able to handle that."

"He will be forever in your debt." I bowed.

Serah's smile vanished. She rounded on Valine. "You still haven't taught her how to bow properly."

"It's a work in progress." Valine made it sound like I was at fault. Between Ropert being sick and Lady Serah fussing over her hair, Valine hadn't found the time.

I pushed my hair behind my shoulders. "I will work on it, my lady."

"See that you do. Now off with you. Give Ropert the good news, and wish him well for me." Serah waved me off.

"I will, my lady," I said. Ropert would be elated.

"Brendagger," Valine called after me. "The hull stinks. I expect you to have shoveled out the horse pens before bed."

Of course. I would clean the stalls while she sat here and dined on herb-roasted poultry and wine. Maybe I would shove a horse apple under her mattress. Then she'd really have a smell to complain about.

# CHAPTER 8

# STARS

*F*ire snaked through my bones, coiling and tightening, threatening to shatter them. Heat roiled through my skull, blistering coals burning behind my eyes. My lungs seized.

*Breathe. I needed to breathe. The heat, the pain, it suffocated me.*

*No. I needed to wake up.*

*Wake up. Wake up.*

Wake up.

My eyes opened.

I gasped.

The heat in my bones vanished like I'd been submerged in a river of ice-cold water. A dull ring pulsed through my ears, muffling the sounds of the water striking the hull. I slipped from the narrow bunk, my knees buckling as I hit the floor with a solid thunk.

I needed air. The heat, the smoke, the fire, the screaming still tore through my senses.

Staggering up the stairs, I shouldered the hatch open. A soothing breeze struck my face, filled with life and movement. I crossed to the railing and sagged against it. Something warm trickled from my nose, a dark drop falling into the water below.

Why? Why did this dream keep haunting me? It had to stop.

"Brendagger?"

The muffled sound in my ears made it hard to decipher where Ikane's smooth voice had come from. I scanned the deck, and the light of a few torches flickered against his dark shape lying on a cluster of crates.

He sat up, rubbing his eyes. "What's wrong?"

"What . . . what are you doing out here?"

His boots made a soft thump on the deck as he slipped from the crates, pulling his heavy cloak with him. "Sleeping. I don't do well in confined spaces. Besides, it's a fraction of the cost."

He sounded like he was speaking to me from across the ship. I rubbed my ears, wishing the muted sensation would ebb.

"Kea . . ." Ikane's brows furrowed. He took my hand, turning it over. "Is that blood?"

Jerking my hand from his, I turned away. The tips of my fingers were coated with something sticky and almost black. My ears? I touched them again. First my nose, and now this? What was happening to me?

My heart thundered through my skull. This nightmare was out of control.

Something brushed against my shoulders. I jumped.

"Easy." Ikane draped his cloak around me. "You're trembling."

"You're not going to ask what happened?"

He leaned against the railing beside me. "Whatever you are going through, it seems to have startled you as much as it did me. You'll tell me if it's what you want. I won't pry. But I am here for you." He sounded closer now, almost normal.

Gathering a shaky breath, I pulled his cloak tight. It still held his warmth and smelled of sun, sea, and steel.

The waves lapped against the hull, starlight dancing on the black water. There was no fire here. Only water, a cool breeze to soothe my fears, and a friend to help shoulder the burden.

"Does the captain approve of you sleeping on those crates? Don't you get in the way of the sailors doing their job?"

"Not at all. The captain has actually offered me a permanent job as one of the crew. I wish I could accept, but I just can't. Not with everything going on with my brothers . . ."

I grinned. "You brought them up, not me."

He chuckled, pushing off the railing. "Come. I want to show you something." He took my hand, his skin warm, his grip strong.

He pulled me to the crates. I climbed up beside him as he laid back, lacing his fingers behind his head.

"Look."

I followed his gaze to the sky. Thousands of stars sparkled above us like a beautiful, surreal blanket, stretching on to the black horizon. All my life I had seen the same constellations and patterns in Daram's sky, but there was something vastly different about the stars glistening over the water. They seemed bigger somehow, like I could reach out and touch them.

"They never change," he said. "Every night they burn, constant and strong. I never feel lost when I see them. They will always guide me home." There was the accent again, sort of musical.

I laid beside him. "Ikane?"

He hummed.

"Thank you."

He smiled, closing his eyes.

What had the stars seen? A thousand seasons, a thousand lives, a thousand stories? Each one held a secret. Each one burning like the other, yet individual and unique. They knew everything. If only they could speak.

Stars trapped behind my eyelids. I didn't need to sleep. I just needed the stars.

I pried my eyes open. The stars winked with a pale blue hue touching the horizon. Dawn?

I sat up. Had I actually spent the night out here?

Ikane lay beside me, his chest rising and falling with each deep breath filling his lungs. His face was so peaceful, so perfect. How could Eamon say he was dangerous? Ikane was the kindest man I knew.

Pulling his cloak from my shoulders, I draped it over him. He deserved better, no matter what Eamon said. Ikane was a man worthy of my friendship and more.

I forced myself to turn away, slip from the crates, and climb back into the stodgy belly of the ship.

My muscles strained under Ropert's weight as we staggered down the gangway. His breathing was heavy and labored, his face as white as the foam on the waves.

He swayed as our boots hit solid ground.

"Hold a moment." He put a hand to his forehead, scrunching his eyes shut.

"Dizzy again?" I asked.

"I can't tell up from down," he groaned.

"Bring him here." Valine waved to a stack of nearby crates.

He sank down, stretching his legs. "I'm sorry."

"You're lucky Lady Serah fancies you." Valine crossed her arms. "And save your apologies. This isn't something you can control. What you *can* control, however, is meeting us in Bakka in two days."

"Don't you dare be late," Fortin said, shoving Applewood's reins into Ropert's hand. The horse pushed her brown nose into Ropert's shoulder, searching for the usual apple slice he gave her.

He pushed her nose away. "I won't."

Fortin turned on his heel, marching back up the gangway. Why in the blazes was he so sour? If he wanted to ride instead of staying aboard the ship, he should have said something.

"I don't mean to cause trouble," Ropert said.

"Don't fret, it's not you." Valine waved him off. "His wife was about to deliver their third child when we were given this assignment. He is going to miss the birth."

Fortin's pettish walk suddenly looked different. It was the lonely walk of someone who'd left loved ones behind. Someone who wanted nothing more than to go home and protect his family. The wood he'd been whittling must have been a toy for the little one, something to make him feel closer.

"Come, Brendagger. We're on a tight schedule." Valine turned back to the ship.

"Dagger. Will you give this back to Ikane for me?" He handed me the little herb sack. "I hope to never need them again."

I gripped the herbs tightly. "Are you sure you're going to be alright? I can ask to come with you."

He gave me a brief smile. "I'm going to miss you, too. Don't worry. I'll be there before the ship docks."

Ropert and I had never been apart more than a day. We were one. Even Commander Holdan had to separate us during sparring sessions. We flowed too well. There was no challenge. Flaming feathers, what if I had another nightmare? He wouldn't be there to . . .

Ikane. Ikane had been there for me last night. I would be alright. Just for two nights.

"I wager the *Otaridae* will reach port before you do," I said.

Ropert grinned. "I'll take that wager. Ten copper?"

"Twenty."

"Brendagger," Valine called from the ship's deck. "The captain is ready to cast off."

I gave Ropert a slug in the shoulder. "Be safe," I said then sprinted up the gangway.

Over the next two days, I spent my mornings being reprimanded for bowing too stiffly, slouching, or addressing a noble in the wrong way. Fortin didn't fare any better. We stretched Valine's patience.

By noon, she dismissed us with orders to muck out the stables. I ended up doing it myself while Fortin worked on his whittling project. Knowing his story, I didn't mind.

Ikane and I sparred the first evening, accumulating a crowd of cheering sailors and bored passengers.

On the second evening, Ikane was already waiting for me by the stern with an eager-looking crowd.

Ikane broke away. "They're asking if we plan to spar again tonight."

The bruises he gave me yesterday protested, but I hadn't been this challenged since Eamon had locked himself in his room. "Have they placed their bets?"

"You know they have." He grinned. "All on me."

"We shall see."

We took our positions on deck, swords drawn. My heart

rammed against my ribcage, waiting for him to make the first move.

Black steel streaked for me. His blows thundered through my arms as I parried, falling back. The crowd parted as Ikane herded me to the ship's edge. Not again. I stepped to the side, ducking under a swing. Bringing my elbow up, I struck, hitting a nerve in his arm. His sword dropped, a hollow thud echoing across the deck.

He leapt back. Jumping onto the railing, he clung to ropes for balance. I struck at his legs, but he blocked. His sword arched, racing for my head, whistling past my ear.

I stumbled back. That was too close.

Coiling a rope around his wrist, he pushed off the railing and flew across the deck. The crowd cheered as he dropped to the other side, landing firmly. He turned to me, flashed a smile, and gave me a mock bow.

This man was something else.

I had to be faster. I rushed forward, and he stepped aside, smooth as a water skipper, parrying my blade. Something pulled on my ankle. Glancing down, a brown rope coiled around my boot.

Ikane stepped back, jerking his end. The rope tightened, my leg lurching from under me. The world shifted as I hit the planks. Pain flared through my hip and elbow.

Laughter erupted from the sailors and passengers.

This was mortifying.

Ikane stepped over me, extending a hand. "Not bad."

"Not bad?" I grabbed his wrist. "Eamon would be ashamed."

Ikane hauled me to my feet. "Don't even think that. Eamon has been the only person to ever best me. You have potential."

"Come with us to Meldron. Valine would approve. We could spar along the way. You can teach me."

His face looked pained. "I can't tell you how much I would like that. But I have an errand in Bakka that will take a few days to complete. You are on a tight schedule. You can't wait for me."

I sheathed my sword. "Promise me I will see you at the coronation."

"I wouldn't miss the chance to see the outcome of Valine's tutoring." He winked.

"Don't remind me." I laughed. "After this, I vow to do nothing save fight for my kingdom. All this prancing about is making me feel like a show pony."

"Help! Someone, help!"

The cry came from the captain's cabin.

Lady Serah!

I sprinted across the deck, shoving sailors aside.

The old servant with snow-white hair stumbled through the cabin door. Eyes wide and face whiter than Ropert's, he collapsed against the main mast. "She's dead." His voice shook with sobs. "Lady Serah is dead."

I drew my sword as Ikane skidded to a halt beside me.

"Stay with him."

Ikane moved to the old man as I stepped into the cabin. A pungent metallic scent made my stomach flip. The beautiful Lady Serah lay beside the overturned table, her pale blue dress stained red. A maidservant slumped in a corner, wedged between the wall and a chair. Red trailed down the side of her face. Bloody footprints scattered throughout the cabin, evidence of a fight. Where was Valine?

A familiar mess of curls peeked out from behind the captain's desk.

"Valine!" I sprinted to her, my knees slamming into the floor. Phoenix feathers, please, please, please be all right. I heaved her shoulder, turning her limp body onto her back. Oh, so much blood.

She inhaled. A deep, deathly rattle sprung from her chest.

"Valine." My voice was barely audible, but I meant to shout. "Hold on, Valine. I've got you." Dropping my sword, I held her shoulders. I needed help. I couldn't do this alone.

Curious passengers pressed their faces through the door.

"Someone fetch the surgeon! Hurry!"

Something cold and wet pressed against my hand. Valine's bloodstained fingers struggled to grip mine.

"Hang on, Valine. Help is coming."

"He . . . got . . . away," she choked. Blood appeared on her lips. She tried to swallow.

Heat burned behind my eyes. She would not make it. "Who did this?"

She coughed, blood bubbling from her lips. "Pi . . . rate."

That single word burned fear and hatred into my heart. They would pay. I would wipe every single one of them from the face of the four kingdoms.

"Commander?" Fortin knelt beside us, his usual monotone voice resonating with fear. He took her other hand in his.

She coughed again, blood dribbling down her cheek. Her glassy, pale eyes looked through me like she saw something beyond the wooden ceiling of the cabin. The creases in her forehead and brows softened. Her grip eased, slipping from my hand.

I bowed my head. Commander Valine Coro was dead.

I should have been more attentive. Ikane had turned my head. I shouldn't have been sparring with him. I should have been here, watching over Lady Serah, doing the job I was assigned to do.

The Leviathan pirate was here somewhere. We were hours from port. We had to anchor the ship, lock it down, find the killer before he got away.

I looked at Fortin. He was in charge now. "Sergeant?"

He reverently set Valine's hand on her chest, his eyes shimmering.

We didn't have time for tears. The killer would go free if we didn't stop the ship.

Grabbing my sword, I stood. My feet moved, bringing me closer to the door, yet everything felt distant. The waves, the hushed voices of passengers, the seagulls crying overhead, the sails snapping in the wind.

The white-haired servant sat on the ground, knees up, face buried in his hands. Ikane crouched beside him, a hand on his shoulder. They both glanced up as I approached.

"Please. Tell me you know who did this," the old man said.

"Did you see anyone?" I asked. "Anything out of the ordinary? Someone watching through the window?"

He shook his head, closing his eyes. "Lady Serah dismissed me. I went below to find something to eat, and when I returned . . ." Tears flooded his eyes.

"Where is the captain?" Fortin emerged from the cabin, his face grim.

"Here." Captain Rawing stepped from the crowd.

"Anchor the ship," Fortin said.

"I beg your pardon?"

"Someone aboard this ship has killed a lady, a soldier, and a maidservant of Daram. Catching this assassin is our priority. Lock down all lifeboats, and post your most trusted crew members as watchmen." He scanned the passengers and crew with deliberate intent. "No one is exempt from investigation."

I scanned the crowd, searching for blood on clothing, a tear in a shirt, a recent scratch on a face, a bruise, fidgeting, or a wrong smile. Nothing.

"You heard the sergeant," Captain Rawing said. "All passengers are to go below deck. Crew, weigh anchor then present yourself for investigation."

The crowd dispersed.

Ikane stood as the old man followed the passengers below.

"Fortin," I moved closer, keeping my voice low. "Valine said it was a pirate. We are looking for a Leviathan."

Fortin stiffened. "Are you sure?"

I nodded once.

"Sir." Ikane approached. "I'd like to offer my help."

Fortin scanned Ikane with sad eyes, as if watching Valine die had drained his own life away. "You are the warrior who bested Brendagger back in Daram."

"Aye, sir. My name is Ikane."

Fortin sighed. "We need all the help we can get."

# CHAPTER 9

# THE HANDPRINT

*T*he ship bobbed in the water like some forgotten leaf on a placid lake. Lantern light flickered against faces, making all of them look guilty as we searched clothing for bloodstains, checked arms and necks for defensive wounds, and watched for unusual behavior. Each individual deemed clear found a position on deck to wait out the search.

My eyelids burned.

Night had fallen hours ago. The stars shimmering in the beautiful blanket of sky felt more distant than they had the night before. We should have made port by now, should be settled into warm beds at an inn somewhere in Bakka. Poor Ropert would be worried.

Fortin rubbed his face as the last passenger joined the crowd. Nothing pointed to any of them. He rose from the barrel he'd been sitting on. "Captain Rawing? Can I count on you to keep everyone here while we search below?"

The captain nodded and gave orders to a few crew members to take up posts.

Fortin turned to me and Ikane. "Come."

We followed Fortin into the stuffy hold.

Rummaging through beds, bags, and trunks, I searched for weapons, torn clothing, anything suspicious. I was so tired. It would be easy to miss something. Still, I dug through a rancid-smelling trunk on one end of the cabin, finding only dirty clothes and a few dishes with food caked onto them.

"Sir." Ikane called from the other end.

I joined Fortin at the row of bunks.

Ikane pointed to the middle bunk. A bloody handprint stained the woodwork.

"Whose bunk is this?" Fortin asked.

Something wasn't right.

This bunk belonged to Lady Serah's personal aid, the old man with the white hair. He couldn't have subdued all three women, especially not Valine. His hands were knobby with arthritis. He walked like his hips had been fused, and the way he had wept . . . it wasn't him.

"Brendagger?" Fortin said. "Whose bunk is this?"

"Lady Serah's personal aide's, sir. But I don't think—"

Fortin rummaged through the bedclothes. He froze with his hand under the pillow then withdrew a knife. If the weapon had been used to murder those three women, there was no evidence of it. The knife was polished to perfection.

"Find the servant, and arrest him," Fortin said.

"Sir. Something is not right."

"Of course it isn't," he snapped. "Commander Coro is dead, and our charge has been assassinated. We have failed this mission. The evidence points to whomever owns this bunk, and if it is the old man, then so be it."

"But Valine said it was a pirate."

He dragged a hand down his face. "Who's to say that the old man *isn't* a pirate?"

"Fortin. He's not—"

"I am Sergeant Fortin Gray, your superior. You will do as I say."

I clamped my mouth shut. He was exhausted and frustrated, just as I was. Nothing I said would change his mind.

He gathered a deep breath. "Let's get this over with. I've had enough of this blasted vessel." He pushed past me, his boots thumping on the wooden stairs.

How could he let this go? Maybe it didn't matter to him, as long as there was someone to blame. As long as he could go home—if we even had a home to go back to. Duchess Caitelyn would have our heads for allowing her niece to die like this. Failing to apprehend the true killer would result in losing

83

everything I'd worked for.

I turned to Ikane. "Something isn't right."

"I—"

"Brendagger," Fortin commanded from the stairs.

Jaw tight, I followed him onto the deck. All eyes turned to us as we approached the old man, the innocent old man. His eyes were swollen and red, dry tears streaking his wrinkled cheeks. This was wrong.

"What is your name, servant?" Fortin asked.

"Illorce Maque, sir."

Fortin produced the knife, holding it in his palm for the old man to see. "Illorce, can you tell me how the murder weapon came to be in your bunk?"

Illorce's white brows knit. "I've never seen that knife before. You don't think . . . I would never . . ." He fell back.

"There is a bloody handprint on your bunk." Fortin stashed the weapon in his belt. "The knife was hidden under your bedding, and you were the last person to see her alive."

"Yes," Illorce said. "Alive. She was alive, laughing and making merry when I left."

Fortin waved for me to come forward.

My fists tightened, feet sealed to the floor.

"Brendagger!"

I was ashamed to be a soldier of Daram. This was not how justice was served. I couldn't bear to look at the old man as I moved forward.

"Illorce Maque, you are under arrest for the murder of Lady Serah of Daram," Fortin said. "You will be escorted to the nearest station where you will be tried before the council."

"I didn't do it." Illorce's voice quivered.

Fortin grabbed the man's shoulders, turning him about. He pulled his hands back, waiting for me to bind his wrists. Those frail, thin, ancient wrists. The small finger on his left hand curled in with arthritis.

I would not do this.

"Brendagger." Fortin glowered at me, the torchlight flickering across his face, making his expression dangerous.

If I couldn't keep this man from being arrested, then I would treat him with dignity. I took Illorce by the arm. "I'll take him. You deal with the passengers."

Fortin watched me for a moment. "Put him in a stall. That'll hold him until we can get him to the prison in Bakka."

My teeth ground together as I nodded. "Come." I steered Illorce to the hatch.

"I didn't do it. Serah was like a daughter to me." He pulled against me.

I jerked him close. "I believe you," I whispered.

He blinked at me.

"I don't know how I am going to prove it, but I am going to try."

He sniffed. "Phoenix bless you."

"Hush." I glanced over my shoulder. Fortin had his back turned to me, speaking with Captain Rawing. "Let's get you below. We can speak more there."

Illorce took the stairs one at a time into the hull. We moved past the bunks to the stables. The horses snorted as we passed. The last stall was where Ropert's horse, Applewood, had been. "This one is clean, and there is fresh hay."

He stepped inside, sinking to the pile of straw in the corner. "Someone has framed me."

I crouched before him. "Did you see anyone loitering outside the cabin? Watching Lady Serah as we boarded the ship? Did anyone pay her special interest?"

Pain returned to his face. "She's been in the cabin since she boarded. She hasn't even stepped out for air."

I rubbed my jaw. "Try to think. We don't have much time." I had to get back to Fortin before he grew suspicious. Conversations and noises filled the hull as passengers were released. Small crowds gathered near the stable entrance, curious eyes peering in.

"Kea?"

I jumped, whirling to face Ikane who stood just outside the stable. "Feathers, Ikane." I brushed loose strands that had fallen from my braid out of my face.

Ikane looked over his shoulder. "What are you doing?" he whispered.

I waved him inside. "Will you help me?"

"With what?"

"Illorce didn't do it. Can you imagine him taking on Valine, a seasoned warrior? The true killer is still out there. I need to convince Fortin."

"How?"

I bit my lip. I needed solid evidence, something Fortin could see with his own eyes. My mind reflected on everything I had seen: the footprints of blood, the knife wounds in Valine's chest, the bloody handprint on Illorce's bunk.

My head shot up. "The handprint. Illorce has a crooked little finger on his left hand. If we compare it to the handprint, it won't match up."

The ship lurched. I stumbled, catching myself on Ikane's rock-solid form.

"We'd best hurry," he said. "The ship is moving again."

We helped Illorce to his feet.

Illorce trailed me through the crowded hull, keeping his head lowered. Passengers pushed the small separation curtains aside, scowling at him from their bunks. Hushed accusations flowed between them. How could they be so quick to judge an old man they didn't know?

Lantern light flickered against the bunks at the far end. I squinted at the spot where I had seen the handprint, trying to discern wood from fabric in the deep shadows. My heart raced. Where was the handprint? I knew I had seen it.

"Where is it?" Ikane asked.

I touched the wood, gliding my fingers across the frame, hoping to feel a difference in texture. Nothing. It was just wood. Dropping my hand, I stepped back. How could it be gone?

Illorce patted my arm. "You tried."

Heavy footfalls thumped down the wooden stairs. I cringed, facing the hatch. I had nothing to show for my insubordination.

"What in the name of the Phoenix are you doing?" Fortin stormed toward us.

Ikane moved. I grabbed his arm, shaking my head. This was my battle.

"Why is the prisoner out here? Unbound?" Fortin asked.

"Why is the handprint gone?"

"Should we have left it there as a beacon of Lady Serah's murder?"

"It was evidence," I said. "It would have sealed this man's innocence."

"Or his guilt," he snapped, the icy sting of his spittle hitting my cheek. He jabbed a finger into my shoulder, the force so hard I stumbled into the stack of bunks behind me. "How many times must I remind you? I am your superior officer."

So much pain burned in his dark eyes.

"Superior or not, we cannot condemn an innocent man. And we cannot let a murderer go free. He couldn't have fought off Valine, and you know it."

"What would you have me do? Anchor the ship? Go through every passenger again? Spend another day on this miserable contraption with three dead bodies?"

"If that's what it takes," I said. "Fortin. We are all tired. We all need sleep. Have Captain Rawing anchor the ship and post lookouts for the night. Our eyes and minds will be fresh and sharp in the morning. But if we dock now, the killer will go free."

His eyes dashed to Illorce, his frown deepening. "We already have our killer."

"Fortin, pl—"

"I am Sergeant Gray to you." He stood taller than I'd ever seen, his face growing hard. "Defy me again, and I will have you stripped of all rank within Daram's militia. Do you understand?"

My mouth clamped shut.

"Do you understand?!"

"Yes, sir."

Satisfied, Fortin grabbed Illorce by the arm and shoved him through the narrow row of bunks. Illorce's legs buckled. He stumbled, barely catching himself against the wood.

Ikane's face grew dark as Fortin hauled the old man away. "It isn't right."

My jaw was aching from clenching so much. "No. It isn't."

"I need you to pen a letter to Duchess Caitelyn." Fortin dropped a blank sheet of parchment on my lap as I sat on my bunk. "She needs to know what happened. Ask her what she wants us to do. Do we come home, wait, or press on? We will stay in Bakka 'til we hear from her."

Just because I was the one with the best penmanship didn't mean I was his personal scribe, but I could use this to my advantage. I could voice my doubts in the letter, describe his disregard for evidence and practicality.

But what good would it do? The killer, whomever he was, had made a clean escape. Besides, it would ruin Fortin. I couldn't do that to him. Not when he had a family to feed.

"Anything else?" I tried to keep the bitterness from my voice.

I didn't think his face could look any more like stone. "Anything else, what?"

I was too tired to argue. "Anything else, *sir*?"

"That's better. And no." He turned away.

Letter finished and saddlebags packed, I escaped the confines of the hull. Sailors shouted from the rigging, and the mainsail curled up to the yard as orange morning light ignited the ship in gold. Had I really been up all night? It was a nightmare, almost worse than the dream of the ruby.

The city of Bakka loomed behind dozens of trading vessels sitting beside the docks. Birds soared between the masts, and smoke curled to the pastel sky.

"Did you sleep at all?" Ikane slipped into his typical position beside me, his elbows on the railing, fingers laced together.

"I may never get to see Meldron." I dropped my head. "I can see it now: the daughter of Master Eamon Brendagger mucking out stables for the rest of her life."

"Don't be so hard on yourself." He wrapped his arm around my shoulders, pulling me against his solid frame. "You did everything you could."

I could stay here forever. His embrace was like a feather blanket, a warm fire, a sweet slice of bread from Mayama's kitchen.

"You are going to do amazing things, Little Brendagger." His breath was warm, like a summer wind, and smelled of herbs. "Stay true to who you are."

The *Otaridae* eased beside the pier, its hull hitting the bumpers. Ikane's grip tightened, his legs bracing for both of us. A flutter ignited in my chest. He was so close, so strong, so wonderful. I didn't understand Eamon. Everything about Ikane was genuine.

A scraping noise echoed through the entire ship as sailors and dockworkers pulled the ramp into position.

"Ikane," Piper said. "We could use an extra hand."

His arms fell away, and I felt like I'd lost a vital piece of armor.

"Aye," he called to her. He turned back to me. "I hope I see you at the coronation. But if not, may I call on you in Daram?"

Me? My heart raced, the fluttering in my chest near bursting. "I would like that." But then the fluttering fell away like a rain-soaked butterfly, and my face fell. "But . . . Eamon. I shouldn't even be talking to you."

"He wouldn't need to know."

I smiled.

"Until then, Little Brendagger." He bowed and hurried to help the crew.

Passengers eagerly disembarked. The true killer blended in with them, escaping justice. The question remained: Why? Why did a Leviathan pirate assassinate Lady Serah?

She was a lady, a noble, an aristocrat, someone with influence, but she was so young and obsessed with appearances. She wasn't a threat to anyone, least of all the pirates.

I tried to watch for anyone suspicious, but my eyes were too heavy, my mind too exhausted. I had done all I could.

"Come on, Brendagger." Fortin stepped beside me, his bag on his shoulder.

I hefted my own pack, following him down the ramp.

"Dagger! Fortin!" A familiar voice called from the wharf. A head of strawberry-blond hair towered above the crowd. He waved.

Ropert. If only he had been there. He would have understood. He would have stood up to Fortin. He would have . . . he would have been too sick to help with anything. Nothing would have been different.

"What happened?" he asked as we stepped from the gangway. "I expected the *Otaridae* to be here last night. Where is Valine and Lady Serah?" He stood on his toes, looking over the throng even though he was tall enough to see over the entire crowd.

"I'm going to deliver the letter," Fortin said. He turned down the narrow street, slipping between the towering buildings.

My eyes burned. How I hated him. He always took the easy route. I had mucked out the stables during the entire voyage, sought the true killer, prepared the bodies, and wrote the letter, and now he left me to tell Ropert about our failures.

Ropert's brows furrowed as he stared down at me. "Dagger?"

I swallowed. "Lady Serah and Valine were murdered."

His eyes widened. "What? How?"

"It's all wrong." I rubbed my eyes. "Her servant was framed. He didn't do it—I know he didn't. He's too old and frail. I tried, Ropert. Fortin just wouldn't listen. I couldn't . . . I needed you."

He wrapped his arms around me. "I'm here now. We'll sort this out. Let me see what I can do. I've rented a room at the Brawny Boar Inn for the night. Go. Rest. You look like you've been up all night."

"I have."

"Then get some sleep. I'll be back when I have information." He hurried up the plank.

# CHAPTER 10

# FIREBALM

*A*n errand boy stood at the door waving a large scroll with a pale-blue wax seal. The message from Duchess Caitelyn.

I rose from the bed as Fortin snatched it and pushed the door shut. The boy stuck his foot in the way.

Fortin's eyes narrowed at him. "What?"

The boy blinked up at him with large, innocent eyes, holding out a hand.

Ropert stepped forward, placed a coin in the boy's palm, and ruffled his hair. "Don't spend it all in one place."

Smiling, the boy darted away.

Fortin broke the wax seal, paused, and thrust the scroll at me. "Read it. I am not as fluent with my letters as you are."

Of course. If anything was even remotely challenging, he found someone else to do it. It's no wonder he took so long to become a sergeant.

Sinking back to the bed, I unrolled it and tilted it toward the light of the fire. This couldn't be from Duchess Caitelyn; her penmanship was flawless. Why were the letters so uneven and smeared, as if written in desperate haste? This couldn't be good.

I cleared my throat.

*To the escort of the deceased Lady Serah,*

I cringed at the title she gave us.

*I cannot even express my outrage, grief, and heartache. You have failed. I trusted you. I would strip every one of you of rank, give you each a hundred lashes, and let you molder in the pillory for a week if I thought it would ease my pain.*

*It is unfathomable that you would even consider Illorce Maque as Lady Serah's assassin. It sickens me to the core. He rocked Serah as an infant, held her hand as she took her first steps, and walked beside her as she learned to ride a horse. He was like a father to her.*

*Release him at once and see that he receives your utmost respect and care.*

*Daram is under siege from the Leviathan pirates. We have never experienced an attack such as this. I cannot send a new representative, and because we are in dire need of support, I am forced to turn to a crude alternative.*

*Master Eamon Brendagger was once a highly respected soldier. His daughter, Corporal Brendagger, will now represent Daram at the coronation.*

I glanced up. Ropert and Fortin watched me with raised brows.
This nightmare was getting worse and worse.
"Is there more?" Fortin asked.
I swallowed, looking back at the smudged ink.

*You will address her as Lady Brendagger from now until you return to Daram.*

*I do not have time to reorganize your travel itinerary. Do the best you can with what I have already planned for my Serah.*

*Illorce Maque is a loyal servant. Instruct him to tutor Lady Brendagger. The courts of Meldron can be ghastly and manipulative; it is imperative that she make a good impression. Daram needs help.*

My hand crumpled the edge of the letter. The word "help" called to me like a battle cry. I itched to grab my sword and race back to Daram to defend it.

*Sergeant Fortin Gray, I'm sure you are in agony awaiting news of your wife and child. And as much as I would relish making you suffer from the unknown, I shall have mercy and ease your mind. You are the proud father of a new, healthy baby girl. Your wife and children are well and safe within the walls of Daram.*

Fortin's shoulders eased. The dark tension I thought permanent to his face faded away.

*Know this, all of you shall not go unpunished when you return.*
*Duchess Caitelyn of Daram*

I lowered the scroll. The fire snapped and cracked.

At least Duchess Caitelyn knew I was right. Illorce was innocent.

But represent Daram? As a lady? Me? This wasn't what I signed up for.

Fortin rubbed his temples, turning to the fire.

I set the letter on the bed and stood. "I am going to get Illorce."

Fortin nodded numbly. "Take Ropert with you."

Bakka's prison was dank, cold, and exposed. The windows were nothing but iron bars, allowing the freezing air of oncoming winter to penetrate the stone inside.

The guard on duty unlocked the door to the servant's cell. Illorce lay on a bed of filthy hay with chains on his wrists and ankles.

What did they think he would do? Fight his way out? He was an old man.

Illorce barely moved as the guard produced a key and unlocked the shackles on his wrists and ankles. The iron fell away, exposing raw, oozing skin.

Four days.

Illorce had suffered in this smelly, cold, infected pit for four days, all because Fortin was too lazy to find the true killer.

Kneeling beside him, I touched his cheek. He was burning.

"Illorce?" I asked.

His eyes fluttered. "Corporal . . . Brendagger?" His voice cracked.

"Duchess Caitelyn has ordered your release."

He shuddered. "Phoenix bless you, child."

Ropert helped Illorce to his feet. "He needs a healer. Go. I'll take him back to the inn."

I hurried to the main road running through the heart of Bakka. Tucked into the tightly mashed row of timber-framed buildings hung a small wooden sign: *The Healing Arts of Cheraric*. An absurd number of charms hung behind the little window, obstructing my view.

I knocked on the door.

"Just a moment," an old voice said.

I tapped my boot on the cobblestone road. Illorce needed help now. There was no telling what Duchess Caitelyn would do to us if he died, too.

An elderly man with a long, graying beard opened the door. He held a mug in his hand, steam curling from the brown liquid. A wave of potent herbs wafted against my nose.

"Yes?" he asked. He was missing a tooth.

"Are you Cheraric, the healer?"

"It's what the sign says. And you are?"

"Corporal Brendagger from Daram. I have a friend who needs help. He has a fever and infected lacerations on his wrists and ankles."

The old healer placed the mug on his small, round table. A fresh loaf of bread sat on a platter with an arrangement of cheeses and meats spread between two plates. A few bites were missing from each.

I'd interrupted his meal. Whoever his guest was must have stepped out.

"Grab my satchel there, will you?" Cheraric pointed to a large leather bag sitting under the charm-filled window laden with dried herbs, vials, and bandages. "He has an open injury, you say?"

"Multiple." I hefted his bag.

"Let me fetch something from the back. Wait here." He slipped behind a thick gray curtain at the far wall. Hushed arguing exploded behind it. The conversation cut short as the healer emerged.

"Don't wait for me." Cheraric called over his shoulder to whomever was behind the curtain. "Eat up, and be on your way. We are counting on you."

I bit my lip. "I can wait if you need—"

"No, no," he clucked and steered me toward the door. "It is only a guest. He has work to do, and so do I."

I guided Cheraric through the bustling streets to the Brawny Boar Inn.

Ropert opened the door. "What took you so long?"

"How is he?" I asked.

"Ill, but in good spirits. He's already threatened Fortin twice."

Cheraric moved to Illorce's bedside. "Not feeling very well, are we?"

"Not at all." Illorce didn't take his glassy eyes off Fortin, who sat on the windowsill, looking small.

Cheraric placed a hand on Illorce's forehead, humming to himself. Taking the old man's arm, he checked his pulse. He scrutinized the raw skin then turned to Illorce's legs. Moving his patient's trousers up to expose the red lacerations on his ankles, Cheraric uncovered a gash on his right leg.

"You were right to fetch me," the healer said. "The infection is causing the fever. Extremely dangerous."

"Will he be alright?" Fortin asked.

Cheraric reached into his satchel, withdrawing a small wooden box. "I am a healer, not a miracle worker. It takes time for a body to heal, and only time will tell. He is old, but I can see a fire in him."

The scent of burnt cinnamon filled the air as he opened the container. An unusual brown-red salve shimmered with golden flecks.

"This will help."

Producing a small wooden spoon, he dipped it into the ointment. With one swift swipe, he smeared the iridescent salve over the gash.

Illorce jerked his leg, yelping. Despite his fever, he bolted upright, clawing at the wound.

"Don't let him touch it," Cheraric said.

I grabbed Illorce by the arm. Ropert seized the other.

"What sort of healing is this?" Fortin pushed himself from the window.

Cheraric held up his hand. "Just a moment."

Illorce was stronger than I expected, muscles straining to wipe the ointment from his skin. Tears burned his eyes.

Suddenly, his body slumped. His head lulled to his chest. Ropert and I eased him onto the pillow, his breathing deep in sleep.

"There." Cheraric pulled linen bandaging from his bag and began wrapping Illorce's leg.

"What did you just do?" Fortin demanded.

"It was necessary to burn out the infection," Cheraric said. "I find it much more humane than leeching or cauterizing, don't you think? The ointment is of my own making. I call it Firebalm."

I brushed Illorce's white hair from his forehead. "He's still burning."

"Yes, yes. His fever will need to run its course. But because of my Firebalm, it should be gone by morning. Just let the man rest."

Fortin folded his arms across his chest.

"I am accustomed to your skepticism," Cheraric said, "but I shall make a believer of you yet. See how the servant fares in the morning. If he is still ill, this young soldier knows where to find me." He motioned to me. "And just because I have such faith in my secret concoction, I shall give you a small amount. As a gift."

Fortin's arms unfolded. "Very well. How much do we owe you?"

Cheraric handed Fortin a small, round container. "Three silvers."

Fortin withdrew the coins from his purse, slapping them into Cheraric's hand. "It had better work."

"I appreciate your business." Cheraric tucked the money into his coat. He turned to me. "Dear young soldier, would you mind terribly escorting me back to my home? Carrying my bag is rather taxing on my old body."

I nodded, gathering his things.

The charms in his window swayed as if someone had been watching for us as we neared his home.

"Thank you. I can take my bag from here." Cheraric pulled the strap from my shoulder.

"I'm sorry to have kept your guest waiting."

"Don't you fret now. The boy has much to learn, and willfulness is one of his shortcomings. This was a moral lesson for him."

"Thank you for your help."

He tipped his head to me. "It's what I do."

With a blanket wrapped around my shoulders, I knelt beside Illorce's bed and dipped a rag into the washbasin. He must have been a handsome man in his youth. Even now, his well-formed nose and jawline could not be concealed by his wrinkling skin. His white hair swept back from his brow, and his silvery beard was meticulously groomed.

How could Fortin ever see a killer in him?

Dropping the rag into the water, I rested my head on my arms, watching him sleep. The gentle rise and fall of his chest, the puff of his lips as he breathed out. He couldn't die. Our lives depended on it. Our *futures* depended on it.

A hand rested on my head. I sat upright, my neck aching.

Had I fallen asleep? I rubbed my eyes.

"Did you sleep well, child?" Illorce asked from where he was propped up in the bed. His eyes looked bright, even in the hazy morning light shining through the tattered curtains.

I touched his forehead. He was cool—the fever had broken. The old healer's Firebalm really was potent. "Your fever is gone. How are you feeling?"

"Unusually well." He moved the blanket from his legs. "In fact, my arthritis isn't bothering me today. I feel as sprightly as I did in my youth." He moved his hands experimentally, his crooked finger moving easily. He smiled. "I could run like a hunted stag and not be weary. I must have the name of that healer."

I stood. *He* may feel young and sprightly, but I ached. Sleeping hunched over the edge of the bed made me age. "His name is Cheraric. He gave us some of his Firebalm."

An overbearing tingling raced through my left foot, prickling needles intensifying as blood flowed back into my limb. I stomped my foot against the floor.

Ropert leapt from his bed, fists up, eyes searching the room.

Finding no danger, he lowered his guard. He tilted his head at my tapping foot, his forehead creasing. "What are you doing?"

I massaged my thigh as the tingling worsened. "My leg fell asleep."

Ropert rubbed his face. He moved to the window, throwing the curtains wide. Light filled the room.

Fortin groaned, rolling over in the third bed.

Illorce stood, straightening his tunic. Looking at his rumpled, filthy appearance, he sighed. "I need to bathe. And I need fresh clothing."

Fortin's eyes opened at the sound of Illorce's voice. "It worked?"

Illorce folded his arms across his chest. "Indeed, it did. I suggest you get your idle, stewed-prune backside out of that bed. We need to secure passage on the ferry to Shard."

I glanced over at Ropert. I would not make him get on a ship again.

"Come on now. The day is half gone, and we have time to make up." Illorce snatched the blanket from Fortin. "I'll not have Lady Brendagger late for the coronation, you hear?"

Flaming feathers, Illorce was worse than Lady Serah. This was going to be very entertaining.

Fortin sat upright. "Uh, yes. Yes, of course. Brendagger, ready the horses."

Illorce cleared his throat. "*Lady* Brendagger should ready the horses?"

Fortin paused from stuffing his feet into his boots. "Right. Ropert, you ready the horses. I'll pack."

"What about breakfast?" Ropert asked.

Fortin groaned.

# CHAPTER 11

# HONEYBEE

"What is the secret to looking your best?" Illorce asked.

"Always carry a comb up your sleeve, and wash your face," I said.

"Good. And when do you rise from a bow to the king, queen, or archduke?"

"When given permission."

"Do you thank a servant for their service?"

"You needn't express gratitude. It is their duty to serve you."

"Very good. And is it proper to ask a noble for directions?"

"Ask nothing of a noble that a servant can do."

Illorce smiled. "You've come far in the last three days. All that remains is to have you look the part. We'll save that for when we reach Toltak. This does not mean you can let the dirt build up under your nails. I expect regular bathing."

"We're here." Fortin leaned against the short railing of the sailboat's stern, pointing through the bend in the trees.

The city of Shard stood on the edge of the Karn River, timber-framed buildings sloping over the water as if admiring their own reflections. Rowboats, sailboats, and rafts littered the banks, and music carried across the water.

"Do you see Ropert?" I rose from the crate, standing on my toes.

"That could be him." Fortin squinted at a tall figure near an open dock.

The boat drew nearer, the tall figure's strawberry-blond hair, broad shoulders, and crystalline blue eyes becoming clearer. He waved to us.

Something released in my chest, something so tight that I hadn't taken a full breath since boarding this sailboat three days ago. After what happened to Valine and Lady Serah, the thought of leaving him, even for a minute, sent my heart racing.

He caught the line tossed to him, securing the little boat to the dock. "It's about time."

Fortin and Illorce led our horses down the ramp, walking through the merchant-filled streets. Some displayed typical necessities like pottery, tools, saddlery, and fabric. Others brimmed with a fresh catch of fish and clams, juicy cabbages, or pickled beets.

An intricately decorated bird cage embedded with emeralds and sapphires sat on a table surrounded by exotic items. The little bird tilted its head at me.

I'd never seen colors so vibrant. Its feathers burned orange and yellow like a sunset. Long tail plumes trailed from its back, tipped with a blue more vibrant than sapphire.

"Beautiful, no?" the merchant asked in a heavy accent. "I give you bird for bargain. Sweet, sweet songs it makes."

The man smiled, his teeth contrasting with his dark skin. A white cloth draped over his head, secured with a band across his brow.

What in the name of the Phoenix was a Tolean doing in Roanfire? The beautiful bird suddenly looked frightened and starved, caged like the slaves in the desert kingdom. Just because we had a peace treaty with Toleah didn't mean they could flaunt their ways here in Roanfire.

"Come on, Dagger." Ropert took my arm, steering me away. "Take your hand off your sword. You wouldn't want to undo that in one afternoon, would you?"

I hadn't realized . . . I pried my fingers away. "No."

"Come on. We shouldn't leave Fortin and Illorce alone together."

Reaching the edge of the city, we mounted our horses, following the well-traveled road to the city of Toltak. The aspens lining the road were thick. Black-and-white trunks reached to the sky, casting long shadows on the road. Their golden leaves spun in the gentle breeze, sunlight sparking across them like tiny, polished shields.

Fortin turned in his saddle. "We're making good time. We should reach Toltak in the next three days. We can cut our rest there short to make up for lost time."

"And rush the delicate process of transforming her into a lady?" Illorce asked. "One can't simply bathe, put on perfume and a lovely dress, and be presentable. She needs oils to rejuvenate her skin. A massage to relax her shoulders and that tense crease in her brow. She needs her nails filed and shaped, not to mention those callouses on her hands. Her hair should gleam, falling over her shoulders in perfectly shaped curls. This—"

"Alright!" Fortin snapped. "We'll stay the three days."

The thought of arriving in Toltak suddenly terrified me. I glanced over at Ropert, but his eyes were fixed on the road ahead. Mine shifted to take in the forest surrounding us.

Up ahead, I saw a merchant wagon laying on its side, woven baskets, candles, honeycombs, and pots of honey spilled across the road and into the trees. A middle-aged man in a long, gray tunic rose from his crouched position beside the broken wheel.

Fortin and Illorce rode by.

But Ropert pulled on Applewood's reins. "It looks like you could use some assistance."

Ah, my dear Ropert. Always willing to lend a hand.

I pulled Gossamer to a halt.

The merchant's eyes widened. "Yes. Oh, yes. I would be forever grateful."

Fortin turned around, brows narrowing.

"What do you think you are doing?" Illorce's face was stern. "We don't have time for this."

Ropert already had one foot on the ground.

I slipped from my saddle. "Isn't it our duty to help those in need?"

"Not when we are on a crucial assignment," Fortin said.

"It shouldn't take long if we work together."

Fortin eyed the fallen wagon. A girl, not much older than ten years of age, emerged from behind the disaster, her arms filled with loose merchandise. Her cheeks were flushed, and her forehead glistened with perspiration. She tucked a stray piece of hair behind her ear, flashing a red stain on her sleeve. She was injured.

"Papa?" she said, her voice uncertain as she watched us.

The merchant put his arm around the girl's shoulders. "Menora, these soldiers have offered to help us. We may just make it home in time for supper."

A growl rumbled through Fortin's throat as he slipped from his saddle. "We can spare a few minutes."

"I advise against this," Illorce said. "This is not what a lady would do. Get back on your horse, Keatep Brendagger."

I had done everything Illorce had asked. I'd recited his rules until I was blue in the face. I'd pranced like a pony on the swaying deck of a sailboat, trying to perfect my curtsy and improve my posture. The least he could do was allow me to spare a few minutes to help this merchant and feel useful again.

"Illorce?" I folded my arms across my chest. "I am Lady Brendagger, am I not?"

"Yes, you are. And we must be going."

"And as a lady, I say we stop and help these people."

His jaw tightened.

Grabbing a basket, I shoved loose items into it. "Come on, Illorce. The sooner we get this done, the sooner we can be on our way."

"Duchess Caitelyn will hear about this." He swung his leg over the saddle.

"What's the damage?" Ropert pushed his sleeves up to his elbows as he knelt beside the merchant, eying the broken wheel.

"It split where it connects to the axle," the merchant said. "I have a spare, but it's trapped under the wagon."

"Papa?" Menora looked at her father. She coughed, the sound like the barking sea lions on Daram's shores. She clutched her abdomen as the fit overtook her.

The merchant patted her hair. "We'll get you home tonight, honeybee." Then he turned his attention to Ropert and the broken wheel.

I set my basket down. "I have a linctus tincture. It would help ease that cough."

Menora's glassy brown eyes struggled to stay open. "You should stay away." Her little voice was raspy from her illness. "You could get sick, too. This fever is bad. Papa says I've had it too long."

I crouched to her level. "I'm not afraid of getting sick. You need rest and medicine."

Menora coughed into her elbow, beginning another fit. "I'm a good helper." She sounded disappointed in herself. "I can weed, milk the cow, feed the chickens, gather wax and honey from our honeybees, and take care of my brothers. Mama is going to have another baby, so she needs me to be strong."

"And you will be." I steered her to the other side of the road where our horses were waiting. She cradled her arm.

"Are you hurt?"

She pulled up her sleeve. A cut stretched from her wrist to her elbow. The red I had seen earlier was blood. Something shiny coated the wound.

"It happened when the wagon tipped over," she said.

"What's that?" I motioned to the glossy film on her skin.

"Honey," she said. "It heals everything."

Illorce filled baskets, his hands working swiftly, his legs easily crouching and standing. The Firebalm had done that. Perhaps it could help Menora, too.

A cracking noise split the trees. I glanced at the wagon as Ropert gripped the undercarriage, lifting the entire corner. His face grew red, and his legs trembled as he waited for Fortin and the merchant to release the broken wheel from the axle.

Menora's eyes bulged. "He's strong."

"You should see him in battle," I said.

Menora sank against a boulder nearby, hunching as another coughing fit overtook her.

Gossamer snorted, shaking his head. I patted his neck. "It's alright, boy. We'll be on our way again soon."

"I'm glad you stopped," Menora whispered. "The others didn't want to help Papa because of me. They said that I would make them sick. I tried to help Papa. I really did."

"Others?" I rummaged through my pack for my healing kit.

"The other merchants," Menora said. "We were traveling in a big group. Papa says it's safer that way. But they left us behind when I got sick. They were afraid."

I knelt beside her. "It's not your fault."

She coughed again.

The horses snorted, ears flicking back. Something was bothering them. I stood, eyeing the shadows between the trees. It couldn't be the girl's coughing. Our warhorses were trained to ignore the loudest cries.

Something moved in the corner of my vision.

"Look out!" Menora shrieked.

The glint of sharp metal sped for my chest from behind a tree. My feet moved to the side, hand grabbing the attacker by the wrist. My fist rammed against the back of the woman's elbow. A loud snap followed. She howled as I wrung the knife from her limp hand and cracked my elbow into the side of her head.

Rocking sideways, her body hit the ground with a solid thump. She stopped moving.

She was filthy, her face painted with black-and-white stripes to blend in to her surroundings.

"Help!" Menora screamed.

I spun finding another black-and-white painted bandit, this one male, dragging her from the rock. She pummeled his arm with frail fists.

"Ambush!" I cried.

Gripping the knife, I barreled forward, driving into Menora's attacker, plunging the blade into the man's thigh. He roared.

Menora slipped away as I drove him into the trunk of an aspen tree, knocking a shower of golden leaves over us.

He grabbed my tunic and raised his fist, aiming for my face.

I slammed my elbow into his nose instead. His head rebounded off the tree trunk. Another deluge of golden-brown leaves spun to the ground as he sank to the earth with a broken nose and the knife still in his leg.

Gasping, I grabbed Menora's hand, rushing for the safety my party.

I paused.

Fortin wrestled a bandit to the ground while Ropert swung his broadsword at a woman who parried with her own rusty sword. She had talent. They all did, albeit coarse talent.

"Honeybee!"

The voice came from behind the wagon.

"Go." I shoved the girl toward her father. She ducked under the wagon and out of sight.

Another cry broke through the chaos.

I whirled to Illorce. Two bandits stood over him, pounding into him with crude wooden clubs. How cowardly could these bandits be? Two against an old man? They wouldn't get away with this.

Sprinting with my head down, I drove my shoulder full force into the bandit's back. He pitched forward with a cry, landing on his hands and knees beside Illorce.

The second bandit swung at me, his club hitting my ribs. A bolt of pain shot through my torso, knocking all air from my lungs. His boot struck the back of my knee. I hit the dirt.

I couldn't breathe.

Another burst of pain slammed into my side. I was faster than this, better than this. *Come on, move. Ignore the pain.*

I rolled. The club hit the dusty road with a shallow thud beside my head. I kicked his knee. *Snap.* He roared as his leg buckled.

Where was the other—

The second club slammed into my shoulder, white sparks flying through my brain. Lightning shot through my collarbone and arm. Phoenix help me, I couldn't breathe. My eyes blurred. The figure before me raised the club high. I had to move.

A blur crashed into the bandit. Ropert. Thank the Phoenix. Ropert bashed his elbow into the assailant's ribs, and the man dropped his club, stumbling away. Ropert's broadsword flashed at him. "Get out of here!" he roared.

The golden aspen leaves blurred and twisted overhead, turning into one solid yellow cloud. Pain flared through my ribs with each shallow gasp of breath.

"Dagger?" Ropert stood over me.

"Are . . . they . . . gone? Are we . . . are we safe?"

He dropped to his knees. "Where are you hurt?"

Perhaps holding my ribs would ease the pain. My shoulder screamed. This would set my training back by weeks.

"My ribs . . ." I gasped. "Is . . . is Illorce alright?"

Ropert glanced over his shoulder. "How is he?"

"It's not good," Fortin said, crouching over the elderly servant. "We need a healer. Feathers, we can't move him all the way back to Shard."

"There is a cottage near here," the merchant said. "A healer lives there. But I warn you, she is the magic-wielding type."

"Will you take us there?" Fortin asked.

Ropert sheathed his sword and took my hand. "Can you get up?"

I held my side. "Help . . . me."

He took hold of my elbow, hauling me to my feet. Everything spun: the trees, the horses, the wagon, the people. Blackness encroached on my vision like night coming too soon. I clung to Ropert's arm.

"Hold on, Dagger." Ropert slipped his arm under my knees, lifting me from the ground, then he called out, "Brendagger's hurt."

"Charred rachis," Fortin said. "Get her in the wagon with Illorce."

"You'll be alright." Ropert slipped my body onto the wagon bed. "We'll get you help."

Setting my teeth, I shifted to the side, making room for Illorce. Blood leaked from a gash on his brow, clotting into his white hair. His cheek and nose were already turning purple. I cringed at his unnaturally twisted leg.

"Menora?" I asked.

"She's alright," the merchant said, climbing into the driver's box. The girl clambered up beside him.

"Brendagger?" Fortin's head appeared over the edge of the wagon bed. "You did well. You took out three thugs on your own, and without the use of your sword. Master Eamon would be proud."

"I would have . . . taken them all out . . . if only . . . if only I hadn't left my sword . . . attached to Gossamer's saddle," I said between labored breaths.

Fortin turned to the others. "Let's go. She's pale. It's only a matter of time before she goes into shock. Ropert, ride beside the wagon and monitor Illorce and Brendagger."

"Yes, sir." Ropert mounted his horse.

The wagon lurched forward, turning into the trees. The wheels pitched and jolted over the uneven terrain—I'd be better off walking. Darkness encroached on my vision until I could barely see Ropert's solid frame riding beside us.

Another bump jolted the wagon and the world faded away.

# CHAPTER 12

# THE WARDENT'S CABIN

*hips crested the horizon. A tidal wave of flames and billowing smoke encased Fold City. People fled to the keep.*

*The crimson jewel around my neck flared, hot embers burning into flesh. "I have been waiting for you, daughter of the Phoenix. You do not realize the pleasure it gives me to know that my time is finally at hand."*

*"What?" The queen's lips moved, but they were my words.*

*"Yes, Phoenix Daughter," the voices said. "We shall meet shortly."*

*Burning crawled through my bones, fusing with my blood, tearing through my skin.*

A cry tore from my throat, eyes flying wide to darkness. The fire smoldering in my bones dulled as the dream disappeared.

Sweat clung to my neck, my hair clinging to skin. I needed air. I needed these suffocating blankets off. Why couldn't I move? It hurt to breathe.

"There, there. Calm yourself, child," an old woman's voice came from the other side of the darkened cabin and behind a wall. Light flickered through the doorway. Something scraped against wooden floorboards followed by a limping *thump, thump, thump* as a humpbacked old woman appeared holding a wiry cane in one hand and a candle in the other. Her silvery hair was drawn back into a loose bun at the back of her head. Something about her seemed familiar.

Her knees cracked as she knelt on the floor beside me.

"Was it a dream?" She set the candle beside my pillow, touching my forehead with the back of her aged hand.

I didn't want to talk about it. All I wanted was these suffocating blankets off. I pushed at them with my good arm.

"Hold on, dear." She reached into her apron, withdrawing a scrap of linen. "Your nose is bleeding."

I took the cloth, holding it under my nose. "Who are you?"

"I am Faslight." She tipped her head, flashing a toothless smile. "Oh, come now. You don't actually believe the rumor of the little old witch at the edge of the forest, do you?"

"I'm not sure what to believe."

"You are honest. I like that."

"Where are my companions?"

"Asleep in my stable. My cabin isn't big enough to house all of you. But I kept the old man with me as well."

"Illorce? Where is he?"

She gestured to my right. I strained to see the corner of the room, finding a narrow wooden bed covered by a patchwork quilt. The shadowy outline of a figure slept inside.

"Don't move. You have two cracked ribs. I've set your shoulder and placed my knitbone salve on your bruises to help speed recovery."

I flopped my head on the makeshift pillow, trying to push the blankets below my waist. "It's hot in here."

Faslight touched her withered palm to my forehead. "You've no fever. Are you in much pain?"

The ache in my ribs was growing as the burn in my bones faded. "I've been better."

She took the candle in her trembling hand, leaned heavily on her cane, and stood. "I'll make you some tea." She hobbled around the corner, disappearing into the next room.

"It was quite the sight when your comrades arrived." She continued speaking. "I've never had so many soldiers at my door. I must confess, I was rather alarmed at first. I thought perhaps the townsfolk had finally lost all common sense and sent the soldiers on a witch hunt." Dishes clattered. The gentle sound of water filling a cup flowed with her words. "The beekeeper and his daughter didn't stay long. Some people let fear drive them mad." She hobbled back into the room with a steaming mug in her hand.

"*Are* you a witch?

"Why? Are you afraid?"

Nothing about her alarmed me. Not even her toothless smile or humped back. Her eyes were like dark pearls, a genuine warmth radiating from them.

"No," I said.

"You are wiser than most." She sank to her knees again. "Drink this."

I propped myself up on the wall, taking the mug from her trembling hand. "Will Illorce be alright?"

Faslight sighed. "I've never seen so many broken bones. His right knee is shattered. He has a broken ankle and elbow, three cracked ribs, and a fractured skull. Old he may be, but his bones are unusually brittle."

"He's been through a lot on this journey." I tipped the mug to my lips. Bitterness sucked all moisture from my tongue, even with the thick essence of honey behind it. I pulled it away, grimacing. "This is terrible."

"Bitter herbs make preeminent healers. Drink, and go back to sleep. 'Tis the middle of the night, and you need rest," she said. "Oh, don't look at me that way. My herbs will not go to waste simply because you disapprove of the taste. They are cultivated through hard work and love. Now drink."

Opening my throat and tipping my head back, I swallowed, trying to avoid the herbs lingering on my tongue.

"There." She took the empty mug. "Go to sleep. I shall re-dress your bruises in the morning." She rose, hobbled around the corner, and extinguished the candle.

I liked her, despite her lack of tea-making skills.

Chirping rang through the cabin, the laughter of winter birds urging me to rise. I blinked, finding myself on a makeshift bed on the floor. Light spilled from an open window above my head, sparkling with particles of dust.

The cabin seemed larger in the daylight with sturdy log walls, a braided rug, a quiet fireplace, and row upon row of drying herbs hanging from the rafters. Across the way, the foot of a bed protruded from behind a curtain.

Illorce. Bandages covered his legs, both bound in splints. How had it come to this? How many more times would I fail Duchess Caitelyn?

The dreams were bad enough, and the nosebleeds certainly weren't normal. Did last night really happen? Did the crimson jewel address me directly? It felt like it, like I was no longer watching but living it.

"I'd like to see her, please." Ropert's voice came from the open doorway at the foot of my bed.

"She needs rest," Faslight said.

I needed Ropert now more than ever. "I'm awake," I said. "Please, let him come."

"Seems like she's fond of you." Faslight peered around the corner. She had the greenest eyes, like blades of spring grass.

Ropert towered behind her, his brow creased with worry. "Feathers, Dagger. You scared me." He slipped past Faslight, kneeling on the braided rug, taking my hand. "You look terrible."

"I look better than you did on the *Otaridae*."

He chuckled. "I'm sure you're right." He turned to Faslight. "How can we ever repay all you have done?"

"Don't you fret, young man." She folded both hands over the head of her cane. "I sent the sergeant to market for me. That he's not a witch will guarantee he gets the items I need. And just in time—I was nearly out of wheat and cheese for the winter." She turned for the door. "Now then. You should eat while you can. Young man, would you be so kind to help me prepare a meal?"

"I'll be back." Ropert rose, disappearing around the corner with her. Their voices chatted softly, dishes rattled, and water sloshed.

"Ho there, Faslight?" Fortin's gravelly voice came from beyond the cabin walls. A door opened.

"Come in. Ah, thank you. Put the items over there on the table, will you?" Faslight said. "I'm making barley stew with root vegetables. It should be ready shortly."

Something thumped on wood.

"Is Brendagger awake yet?" Fortin asked.

"She is," Ropert said. "She's doing well."

"Good. I'll saddle the horses; you help her pack. We'll leave right after breakfast." The door closed after him.

"Brendagger? As in Keatep Brendagger?" Faslight shuffled around the corner, her small green eyes scanning my features intently. "Are you Eamon's ward? Of Daram?"

"Yes." I struggled to prop myself up against the wall. Why was she asking?

"Mayama mentioned you in her letters."

"You know Mayama?"

"She is my younger sister. She says that you've been experiencing nightmares of late. Is that what last night was about?"

Mayama never told me she had a sister.

"Food is ready." Ropert carried a tray into the room. Four bowls curled with steam and rich fragrance. He sat cross-legged beside me, handing me a bowl. "Mayama's sister, eh? If your food is any good, I'll believe you."

Faslight's cane shot up faster than I thought possible, striking Ropert's arm.

He flinched and laughed. "Well, that hurts just as bad as Mayama's spoon."

"Ropert, don't make me laugh." I hugged my side.

"Is he always this clever?" Faslight asked me.

"He seems to think so."

"Good." Her face went grave. "You will need his joy by your side. I know who you are, child, and I do not envy the challenge you face."

I lowered my spoon. Ropert blinked at her.

"King Myron knew it," Faslight said. "That is why you still live. The dreams you are experiencing now will only grow worse unless you find a way to stop them."

Ropert paused mid-bite, blue eyes dashing between us. "What is she talking about, Dagger?"

She knew. She knew everything.

"How? How do I stop the nightmare?"

Faslight sank to her knees. Laying her cane on the ground, she took a bowl from the tray. Her silvery hair glistened in the sunlight streaming through the window. "The White Wardent. Only he will know how to help you."

"The White Wardent?" Ropert lowered his spoon. "He is a myth."

Faslight shrugged. "Some say he is. Others say he is real."

"If he *is* real, where do I find him?" I asked.

Faslight spooned a bite into her toothless mouth. "That is the riddle, isn't it?"

I stared at my soup, plump kernels of barley swirling in the amber broth. What did she know? We'd only just met. She knew nothing about my nightmares.

But she knew about King Myron. She knew he spared me for a reason. If she knew, did that mean Mayama knew as well? Is that why she said the dream was a vision?

Maybe she *did* know something. Maybe I should take her warning about the dream seriously.

I touched my ear, remembering the blood and the ringing on the *Otaridae*. It was the worst episode I'd experienced.

"Ropert?" Fortin peered around the corner. "The horses are—" His eyes hardened at our little picnic on the braided rug. "I told you to help her pack. We don't have time for a leisurely breakfast. Get up. It's bad enough we have to leave Illorce behind. Duchess Caitelyn is going to have our heads even if we get Brendagger to Meldron on time."

Faslight set her bowl down. "Keatep would benefit from a day or two of rest."

Fortin pinched the bridge of his nose. "We can't . . . we just can't."

"It's alright, Fortin. I won't slow us down," I said.

"Brave little lass." Faslight patted my knee. "I will give you an herbal tea to help with the pain. And I will show Ropert how to dress your bruises." She waved to Fortin. "Come eat, sergeant. You won't get far on an empty stomach."

Fortin reluctantly joined us on the floor.

"Oh." Faslight swallowed a bite. "I noticed a scar on the servant's leg. A recent one. Who cared for that injury?"

"A healer in Bakka," Ropert said through a mouthful of stew. "He has a miracle balm that took his infection away overnight."

"Miracle balm?"

"I used it last night." Fortin touched his forehead. "You can't even tell bandits attacked me. I would've used it on Brendagger and Illorce, but I don't think it heals bones."

"May I see it?" Faslight asked.

Fortin withdrew the small box from his belt pouch.

Faslight opened the lid, sniffing the contents. She tipped it to the light streaming through the window. Her eyes widened. "By the burning feathers of the Phoenix, he used *this* on the manservant?"

Fortin's brows creased. "Yes?"

She slammed the lid shut. "This is desecration to the purity of the elements." She grabbed her cane, hauling herself to her feet. "There is firesprite dust in here. Any true healer knows firedust should never be placed on an open wound. The clubs of your attackers did not shatter Illorce's bones." She shook the box. "This. This did it. Firedust in the blood makes bones as brittle as dry wood in summer sun."

Fortin looked pale.

"What was the healer's name?"

"Cheraric," I said.

"And they have the nerve to call me a witch." Faslight's jaw set. "Come with me, sergeant. We need to get you an antidote as soon as possible. Sprites help me, I just hope I'm not too late for Illorce."

# CHAPTER 13

# GREEN LIGHT

aslight waved from her cabin door, her hunched back preventing her from raising her hand above her shoulder. Mayama's sister or not, I liked her.

With my arm bound to my chest and Faslight's pain-numbing herbs in my blood, I led Gossamer through the trees.

They thinned as we neared the road where we'd been ambushed the day before. Autumn leaves swept across it, guided by the bitter wind. It tasted of snow.

"Do you smell that?" Ropert asked.

"I do." Fortin mounted his horse, pulling his cloak tight. "Make haste."

Gossamer's saddle towered beside me. I couldn't climb that, not with my ribs. He was bred for war, with hooves as large as Mayama's serving platters and legs as thick as the trunk of a seven-year-old oak tree.

"Come on." Ropert came to my side.

Gripping the saddle horn, I set my knee in his hands, bracing for the pain.

"Three, two, one." He lifted.

My chest screamed as I swung my leg across Gossamer's back.

"Are you alright?"

I nodded, waiting for the pain to ease.

Ropert held on to Gossamer's bridle. "If riding becomes too painful, let me know. I'll walk with you all the way to Meldron if needed."

I twisted the reins around my hand once. "It won't come to that."

He smiled, patting Gossamer's neck. "If you say so."

He mounted Applewood.

I kicked Gossamer's sides, and the massive warhorse jolted forward. Thundering jars rippled up my spine as his hoofs connected with the road. It was tolerable, for now. But what would I feel once her herbs wore off?

The icy wind bit at my cheeks and fingers, sunlight fading as clouds rolled across the sky. How could I have let this happen? We were perilously close to failing Duchess Caitelyn completely. Lady Serah, our ward, assassinated. Valine, our commander, murdered. Illorce, my tutor, debilitated. If I didn't make it to Meldron in time, who would represent Daram? Who would inform King Myron of the Leviathan raid on Roanfire's shores?

Was I capable of representing Daram as a lady? I had so much more to learn from Illorce. What was I supposed to say to King Myron and Prince Sander when the time came? Damn the Leviathan pirates. Lady Serah was supposed to do this, not me.

Gossamer's hoof slipped on a rock. My muscles tightened, searching for balance. Feathers, it hurt. I pulled Gossamer to a halt.

"Dagger?" Ropert stopped beside me.

The herbs weren't working anymore. "I can't . . ."

"Fortin," Ropert said, dismounting.

Fortin pulled his horse around as Ropert helped me from Gossamer's back.

"What are you doing? We don't have time for this." He gestured to the clouds.

"I just need a minute," I said.

"Walking will add another seven days to our journey, and at your pace, perhaps even a fortnight. You must ride."

"She said she needed a minute," Ropert snapped.

Fortin stiffened.

"I'll ride. I promise we will make it," I said. "Just let me walk for a while."

The muscles in Fortin's jaw tightened as he watched Ropert. "Don't speak to me like that again, you hear?"

Ropert's fists clenched. "Yes, sir."

Fortin turned his horse about and trotted ahead.

"That cumberwo—"

"Hush, Ropert. You've angered him enough."

Ropert grabbed our horses' reins, leading them down the road. "You are Lady Brendagger now. You outrank both of us. If you need to take a minute, he shouldn't question that."

"Ropert, the mission is priority. We have failed Duchess Caitelyn three times over. I will get to Meldron before the prince's coronation. And if that means galloping across Roanfire, so be it."

I ducked into my hood, hiding my face from the sharp ice crystals flurrying across the road. Sunlight faded behind fields harvested clean, dried sheaves of wheat and squash vines trembling in the breeze.

A thick cluster of pine trees swayed ahead. Blast these broken ribs. I wanted to spur Gossamer into their thick, green, comforting shelter.

Fortin dismounted, leading his horse into the trees.

"I think I see the remains of a campfire," Ropert said.

Thank the Phoenix. In the center of the shielding canopy of evergreens stood a ring of charred stones.

"We'll camp here." Fortin loosened the girth of his saddle. "Brendagger? Do you feel well enough to start a fire?"

What did he just say? Was he asking? Maybe I'd heard him wrong. It was an order, wasn't it? "Sir?"

"Don't think I didn't hear you two." He pulled my pack from Gossamer's saddle. "I'm only trying to make sure we don't fail Duchess Caitelyn again, you understand? If you really need rest, you shouldn't have to use your new status as a lady to get it. I will try to be more understanding in the future."

"I . . . uh, thank you, sir."

"So, the fire?"

The idea of bending down to pick up firewood sent tremors through my ribcage. "I think I'd be better off brushing the horses."

Fortin pulled a brush from his saddlebag. "Ropert, get the fire going. It's getting dark."

Ropert rolled his eyes at me. "Yes, sir."

With the horses groomed and settled at the edge of the campsite, I moved to the fire. Crackling flames and white smoke lifted to the darkening sky, the stars winking overhead. They seemed so far away. They had been so close on the ship.

"Here." Ropert handed me a steaming mug, the bitter scent indicating Faslight's herbs.

I sat on the log nearby, the warmth of the fire soaking into my knees.

"Dagger?" Ropert prodded at the flames. "What did Faslight mean when she spoke of King Myron? That he is the reason you are alive?"

Why did she have to open her mouth in front of him? For the past seventeen years, I knew nothing about my father. Within a matter of weeks, it seemed everyone knew.

I told Ropert everything. We had no secrets from each other. But this? I had to keep this quiet.

"I'm not sure what she was talking about." I took a sip of the tea. It scalded my tongue. Setting the mug aside, I reached for my waterskin. I just needed to cool it enough to drink.

Why did everything have to be so difficult with one arm? I held my waterskin between my knees, fighting with the cork. Everything was a challenge. Even pouring the cold water into my mug ended with a puddle at my feet.

Fortin dropped extra wood beside the ring, dusting his hands off. "There isn't much to scavenge. We'll have to keep the fire short tonight." He sank to the log beside me. "The stretch ahead is without shelter. We cannot travel the same pace we did today."

I lowered the cooled drink from my lips. "I understand."

Ropert distributed our rations of dried meat and bread. "How far to Toltak from here?"

Fortin set his mug at his feet then pulled a folded piece of paper from his belt pouch. A small brown stain glared at me from the corner as he unfolded it—Lieutenant Coro's blood. A frown tugged at his lips. "Two days on horseback. Three on foot. And four if it snows."

Curse those bandits. I didn't have a choice. "Let's just hope Faslight's herbs are up for the challenge."

"You can't rely on that, Dagger," Ropert said.

"Do you see another option?"

Ropert ran a hand through his hair. "No."

"We'll brew a large pot in the morning, fill my waterskin with it, and I can drink—"

What was that? Something moved in the trees.

"What is it?" Ropert followed my gaze, his sword hissing gently from its scabbard.

Fortin stood.

I pulled my knife from my boot. Bandits, again? Was it the same group that had attacked us before? A speck of glowing green light moved toward us.

"Who's there?" Fortin said. "Show yourself."

"I mean you no harm." The voice was smooth and strong, ringing with familiarity. "I only wish to share your fire."

The tall, lean figure stepped into the firelight with raised hands.

"Ikane." I lowered my knife. "What are you doing here? You should be halfway to Meldron by now."

"So should you." He dropped his pack by the fire, eyeing my bandaged torso. "What happened?"

"Nothing Dagger couldn't handle," Ropert said, lowering his sword. He and Ikane clasped hands. "You should have seen her. She took out three brutes with her bare hands."

Ikane's brows rose. "Really?"

"He's exaggerating," I said. "I had a knife."

Ikane chuckled.

"Thank you again for your assistance on the *Otaridae*." Fortin extended a hand. "It's a pleasure to see you again."

"Likewise," Ikane said. "Seeing as we are both headed the same direction, might I join your company? I'd be happy to lend a hand."

Did he just motion to me? I wasn't useless.

"Are you on foot?" Fortin glanced over Ikane's shoulder.

"I'm not keen on horses," Ikane said. "Extra food, extra gear, extra worry. Besides, I can travel as fast on foot as any horse."

Ropert folded his arms across his chest. "I'd like to see you outrun one."

Ikane arched an eyebrow. "Is that a challenge?"

"We can't afford any more delays." Fortin tossed another log on the fire. "Unless you truly can outpace a horse, I must insist that we part ways."

"Don't you worry about me," Ikane said, stretching his hands to the fire, sinking to his knees beside it.

Fortin rubbed his face. "I'm going to bed. Ropert, you take first watch tonight, and I'll take second."

Did they all think I was incapable of anything?

"I can take first watch," Ikane offered. "I have yet to eat my supper."

"Do what you will." Fortin waved a hand at him. "Ropert, come help me shift the bedrolls to make room for our guest."

Ropert followed.

"I don't need a tent," Ikane said.

If they heard him, they didn't indicate it.

Ikane shrugged, adding a fresh log to the fire. The smoldering coals broke under the weight, sending sparks into the sky.

He looked at me. His eyes. How could I have forgotten the way they made me feel, like I stood on an open meadow of wildflowers with little white clouds moving across the sky?

"You're quiet," he said.

Tucking my knife back into my boot, I sank beside the fire. "I'm not helpless."

"I didn't say you were."

I gave him a firm, disappointed look.

"Alright. I may have insinuated that you need assistance, but it was only to convince him to let me stay."

"Shrewd," I said.

"I bought something for you in Bakka." Ikane rummaged through his pack. Pulling a small brown sack from his bag, he handed it to me. "I know someone who has dabbled in the healing arts. I asked him for a formula against your nightmares. He's uncertain it will help, but I thought it was worth a try."

"I . . . I don't know what to say." He thought of me. Me. A simple soldier from Daram.

"What do you say I brew you a cup?"

# CHAPTER 14

# A RACE

*H*er legs burned. Stinging tore through her lungs. She looked over her shoulder, wind whipping her red curls, stirring up ash. Black smoke billowed from the garrison, choking out the moon and stars. Fold was gone.

*A whisper hung in the wind. Run. Don't stop. Run.*

*An unseen force barreled into her from behind. Her body pitched forward, her head striking the rough bark of a tree. Red spots flashed across her vision. She sank to her hands, fingers digging into the decaying leaves.*

*The ruby. How could the ruby have so much power? Everything pointed to the cursed heirloom. All the deaths. How had she not seen this?*

*She staggered to her feet. Fire danced from the tallest tower of the stronghold. Let the ruby burn. Let it die here with Fold.*

*"You force my hand." The voices clashed together.*

*Thunder rolled through the trees as a violet light burst from the tower. It expanded like candlelight, filling an empty room. Rending noises tore through the trees, like some gigantic beast was barreling its way toward her.*

*What was happening?*

*Birds scattered to the sky. The light struck their wings. They screamed, their limp bodies plummeting to the earth.*

*A rabbit sprinted past her legs. Three squirrels leapt from branch to branch overhead. A deer raced for her, its large black eyes wide.*

*All running as though hunted by a pack of ravenous wolves.*

*The light. She had to flee the light.*

*She spun, sprinting after the deer.*

*The violet light struck like a thousand arrows, burrowing into her memories. It caught hold of her mind, tearing through every thought and wish, every dream and desire. It pierced her heart, feasting on life and love.*

*Her scream cut through the wind and groaning forest.*

*"You. Are. Mine."*

*The light recoiled into the tower.*

*All lay silent—no chatter of birds, no buzzing insects, no wind. Shriveled, brittle leaves rained from the trees.*

*Dead. Everything was dead.*

"Kea." Ikane shook my shoulder. "Kea, wake up. You're dreaming. Wake up."

My eyes burst wide to the darkened tent. Ikane's green eye glowed at me.

The jewel, the tiny trinket no bigger than my pinky nail, had eradicated an entire forest. It devoured the queen. It drank the life from everything—every blade of grass, every bush, every insect, rodent, and forest creature. The very breath of the forest, drained. A dry, brittle wasteland: the Dead Forest.

Mayama was right. The Leviathan pirates were not the cause of the lifelessness of the Dead Forest. The jewel was.

I sat up. What did any of this have to do with me? These nightmares had to stop.

"Hush, Kea. Breathe. Just take a deep breath." Ikane stroked my hair.

So much death. Everything, even the wind, gone.

"I'm so sorry," Ikane whispered. "I thought the herbs would help."

He was alive. He was here, breathing, talking, moving.

Fortin? I turned to his sleeping form beside Ikane. His chest rose and fell with breath.

What about Ropert?

Ignoring the sting in my ribs, I pushed the tent flap aside. Ropert's silhouette sat by the fire, his back to me. His broad shoulders rolled in the familiar motion of polishing his sword. His breath plumed. Life.

I dropped the flap, swallowing hard. Why did I feel so dry inside, like the jewel had ripped parts of my existence away? I looked at Ikane. "Why me?"

He wrapped his arms around me. It didn't matter that he touched a bruise or held too tight. I needed to feel his warmth and strength. I needed something to still my trembling.

I turned into his shoulder, smelling campfire and leather on his skin. His heartbeat thrummed, solid, predictable, and real.

"I'm sorry." Ikane brushed my hair from my face. The weight of his cheek on my head was like an extra embrace, as if he wanted to curl himself around me and shield me from this nightmare. "We won't use those herbs again."

I half sobbed, half laughed. It wasn't the herbs.

The dream was trying to tell me something, but what? I had to make them stop. They brought out my weakest moments, exposing me for the coward I feared I was.

Faslight said they would only get worse. These nightmares would destroy me.

"Kea?" Ikane pulled away. "It's time to relieve Ropert."

I gathered a shaky breath. I had to be strong. I couldn't let a dream keep me from my duties.

"I can stay up with you, if you'd like?"

How I wanted to take him up on that offer, but he'd already volunteered for the first shift. "You need your rest. I'll be alright." I grabbed my boots, stuffing my feet into them.

His hand grabbed mine, firm, warm, and kind. "I'm always here for you. You know that, right?"

"I do." I grabbed my cloak, pushing the tent flap aside. "Get some rest."

Years of wagons and teams of horses traveling down the road had etched permanent grooves into the dirt. Open fields, glistening gold in the warm sunlight, stretched to either side while small smatterings of trees broke up the landscape.

Ikane kept pace beside me. His cheeks were flushed, and short strands of dark hair brushed across his forehead. He kept up with Fortin's pace well, even when he pushed. But Fortin was going too fast again, and my ribs were screaming at me to stop.

"Fortin. Slow down."

He glanced over his shoulder. "I told Ikane I wouldn't go any slower. I haven't changed pace for the past hour."

"My ribs."

"Faslight's herbs must be wearing off," Ropert said from behind.

Already? I pulled Gossamer to a halt. Ikane helped me dismount as Ropert brought me the waterskin with Faslight's herbs. It was light and deflated. Had I really consumed that much?

I took several large gulps. "Let's keep moving. I'll walk until the herbs take effect."

Ikane fell into step beside me. Ropert took the rear, holding the reins for Applewood and Gossamer.

"Kea?" Ikane's voice was timid and hushed.

I looked at him.

He swallowed. "Are you ever going to tell me what you dream about? I don't intend to pressure you, but I'm worried. Dreams don't cause nosebleeds. It seems to be something more."

I stared at my boots. I was worried, too. "I don't think there is anything you can do."

"I'd still like to know."

I pulled my cloak tighter around me. "It's a nightmare about the day the Leviathan pirates destroyed Fold. The day the Dead Forest was born."

He tipped his head. "And it repeats?"

"It's been shifting of late." The voices of the jewel rang through my head. *We shall meet shortly.*

Something cold raced down my spine. It had been speaking to me, not the queen. "I'd rather not talk about it."

Ikane nodded. "Your gait is steadier. And you are picking up pace."

My ribs barely hurt. Faslight's herbs were working.

Ikane helped me mount.

"Ready to be left in the dust?" Ropert asked.

"You haven't lost me yet." Ikane patted my leg. "I told you, I'm as fast as any horse."

"I don't see why you two can't settle this debate right now." I shifted in my seat. "I wager ten coppers Ropert bests you."

"I'm hurt." Ikane unclasped his cloak, draping it over my legs with a wink.

Ropert grinned. "Let's do this. To that small grove of trees up ahead."

Ropert's suggested target was a half mile away. A suitable distance.

Ikane jumped up and down, loosening his muscles. He planted his feet, eyes set on his objective. "Alright."

"Dagger, will you do the honors?"

Excitement tingled through my chest. "Three, two, one." I flashed him a crooked smile. "Go!"

Ropert hollered, spurring Applewood forward.

Ikane's soft leather boots hit the ground, his body surging ahead. Feathers, he was fast. He and Applewood flew past Fortin. His horse jerked its head.

"What in the . . .?" Fortin whirled. "What is this?"

I urged Gossamer beside him. "A race." Ikane was actually ahead. His legs moved as fast as he swung his swords. Ropert lowered his body, and his horse gained speed, closing the gap. Ikane wasn't exaggerating when he said he could keep up. It was unheard of.

"You're riding well." Fortin scanned my posture. "Shall we pick up the pace?"

I spurred Gossamer to a gentle trot. The pain in my side increased to a tolerable ache. Perhaps I could encourage Gossamer into a canter.

Fortin glanced over his shoulder. I'd heard it, too: the galloping of hoofbeats. It wasn't coming from Ropert's horse but from behind us.

I turned, spotting six figures on horseback.

Fortin's eyes narrowed. Hoods and masks covered their faces, concealing any distinct features of the horsemen. They passed through the shadow of trees, sunlight glinting on their ready weapons. Bandits.

"Go, Brendagger. Go." Fortin drew his sword. "Get to Ropert and Ikane!"

My heels dug into Gossamer's belly. I leaned forward, ignoring the tenderness in my side. His massive hooves thundered against the road. I was in no condition to fight. If the bandits reached me, my career as a soldier of Daram would meet its end.

Fortin galloped behind me.

Ikane and Ropert, clearly seeing the danger, raced back to us. Had they already reached the tree line? I'd missed who won.

"Brendagger!" Fortin growled.

Curse my ribs. I was holding back. Gossamer was faster than this.

Ropert veered to the side, allowing Fortin and I to gallop ahead. Drawing his sword, he pulled Applewood around, bringing up the rear.

Ikane drew his swords from his back, black steel flashing. A subtle green glow ignited in his eye. Why wasn't he turning around? He barreled past Gossamer. Did he think he could take on all six horsemen alone?

"Ikane! Stop!" I pulled back on the reins. Gossamer's hooves locked in place, nearly sending me from the saddle.

Ikane planted his feet in the road, swords spanning the width as the riders drew near. The leader held a sword aloft, sunlight flashing across his polished blade.

This wasn't a bandit. None of them were. They weren't covered in dirt, wearing tattered clothing, or wielding tarnished weapons. They wore fine leathers and thick clothing. These were mercenaries.

"Ikane!" Fortin jerked his horse's reins. "Come on."

"We can't outrun them," Ikane called over his shoulder.

The first rider galloped straight for him. His sword flew at Ikane's head. Ikane crouched, parrying the blow with one sword, the sound of grinding steel cutting the air. Twisting his core, his twin weapon whipped around, slashing into the stirrup and the raider's calf. The man cried out as the saddle slipped from the horse's back. The horse danced away.

The second horseman flew at Ikane, her sword arching down at an angle impossible to dodge. He was going to get himself killed.

I reached for my boot knife. Pain flared as I leaned down. Charred rachis! These broken ribs. I was useless.

Ikane twisted, somehow slipping between the sword and the horse. His weapons arched like black lightning under the horse's belly. The animal screamed. Stumbling, the horse fell to its side, crushing the raider's leg. The horse rocked to its feet, leaving its rider on the ground, and fled the scene. The mercenary lay still.

Ropert brought Applewood around as the remaining mercenaries pulled their mounts to a halt.

"Leave now." Ikane raised his swords. Blood streaked the black metal, and a flash of green reflected on the blades.

They dismounted. The first raider Ikane had knocked from his horse staggered to his companions. They weren't going to leave. This was a fight to the death.

Ropert and Fortin charged in as the mercenaries converged on Ikane. Ropert's broadsword flew at their heads. Three stumbled back as Applewood stormed at them, one catching his heel on a tuft of grass.

How could I help? I was useless and in pain. Gossamer tossed his head and stomped his hooves, the war breed in him eager to engage.

The tallest of the mercenaries lunged for Ikane, swinging his axe as fast as Ikane moved his swords. Ikane dodged a cleaving blow. He lurched forward, both swords racing for his attacker's head. The man ducked. His axe moved for Ikane's legs, a perfect hooking maneuver.

"Ikane!" I screamed. "Move your feet!"

The curve of the axe caught the back of Ikane's ankle. The man jerked, but Ikane's drop was controlled and balanced. He made it look easy, like gliding through water. The axe slipped from his boot as he rolled backward then jumped to his feet.

Ikane's swords flashed, his feet danced, and his strokes were strong and solid. But the tall, battle-axe-wielding mercenary was driving him back, herding him into a small stand of trees.

A cry tore the air, jerking my attention to Ropert as he pulled his sword from the shoulder of one of his opponents. The man dropped. Two raiders raced for Applewood from the other side, weapons ready to cut her.

"Ropert! On your left!"

He whirled, sword slashing, deflecting their blades. Applewood flinched as a knife grazed her neck, throwing Ropert off-balance. The mercenaries seized his arm, dragging him from her back. He crashed to the ground.

*Move, Ropert. Move.* I had to help. I couldn't sit here and watch my friends die. Blast my ribs. I drew my knife from my boot.

Ropert blocked a blow with his leather armguard. Jerking to the side, another sword plunged into the dirt where his head had been. He kicked, hitting the knee of the nearest mercenary. The man's leg buckled. Crying out, he collapsed.

The final mercenary raised his sword. It came down like a boulder. Metal clashed against metal as Ropert's sword caught it. The force slammed his shoulders into the road, his head rocking back. He kicked. His attacker leapt out of range.

Fortin swung at him, metal ringing through the air as the mercenary engaged.

Ropert rolled to his feet, blood leaking from his wrist. He flexed his hand, scanning the scene for Applewood.

The mercenary laying behind him moved. The glint of a knife flashed in his hand. Ropert's broad back was a perfect target.

"Ropert!" I raised my knife. With every ounce of energy remaining in my body, I hurled the weapon at the raider's back. It sank deep between his shoulder blades.

Ropert whirled. The man dropped to his knees then fell forward at Ropert's feet.

Ropert's face paled at seeing the knife protruding from the man's back. He exhaled a shaky breath.

The man with the battle-axe came running from the trees. "Retreat!" He swung up to his horse and turned it about. Three wounded mercenaries shuffled to their mounts, leaving two comrades dead in the road.

Ikane staggered from the trees. His eye burned like green fire. Jaw clenched, he tromped through the brown grass toward us, sporting a new bruise on his cheek. "Is everyone alright?"

Fortin motioned to Ropert's arm where blood curled up the sleeve of his uniform. "We should look at that."

"Later." Ropert wiped his broadsword clean on the dead raider's clothing. "We need to get out of here. It is a miracle those mercenaries didn't use arrows to pick us off."

Fortin knelt by a mercenary, rolling the man over, removing the mask. "Phoenix feathers," he breathed.

"What?" Ropert asked.

"This man was on the ship." Fortin looked at me. "I investigated him myself."

Something in my chest tightened. If he killed Lady Serah, that meant they had come for me. But why? What did the Leviathans have to gain by doing this? "Is he a pirate? Does he have the tattoo?"

Fortin checked the man's arms. "Here." He pushed the man's sleeve up, revealing the black tattoo of the Leviathan crest.

"Was the other mercenary on the ship, too? The woman?"

Fortin scrutinized the second body. "I can't say I remember her. But I remember the man."

"Filthy pirates." Ropert's eyes bored into the backs of the fleeing mercenaries, now specks of black on the road. "They were after Kea, weren't they?"

Fortin stood, dusting his hands off. "It seems so."

"We'd best get moving." Ikane slipped his swords back into their sheathes at his back. His eye continued to smolder, his brows tight.

"Ikane?" I asked.

His lips trembled. "I'll be alright. I just need a minute." He turned away.

Fortin sifted through the man's pockets. He withdrew a handful of coins, a comb, a talisman of some sort, a sack of herbs, a whetstone, a tin of linseed oil, and a cloth for polishing his weapons. His saddlebag held a week's worth of rations, a waterskin, a change of clothes, and a finely spun bedroll—of a quality the soldiers of Daram didn't receive.

Ropert approached the abandoned horse standing in the field. The animal was smaller than Gossamer but looked strong. A minor cut ran along its belly where Ikane had severed the stirrup, but other than that, the creature was unharmed and calm.

Ropert led her to Ikane. "Here. She's yours."

Ikane blinked at him, the burn in his eye fading.

"You're fast, I'll give you that. But I don't think you can keep that pace in a marathon."

Ikane took the reins, watching the horse's large, black eyes.

"You *can* ride, can't you?" Fortin asked, mounting his own horse.

"Not bareback."

Ropert clapped Ikane on the shoulder. "So there *is* something you can't do." He took the reins. "I'll ride this horse. You can ride

128

Applewood."

Ikane stiffly approached Ropert's horse.

"Relax, Ikane. She's gentle," Ropert said.

He placed his boot in the stirrup. Was he really that inept?

"Use the other foot," I suggested.

"It's been a while." He switched feet, heaving himself into the saddle. He clutched the horn as Applewood shifted under his weight.

Ropert chuckled. "You hang tight now."

Ikane shot him a glare.

We moved forward.

"So who won the race?" I asked.

Ropert and Ikane grinned at each other like mischievous errand boys.

"I say we keep her guessing," Ikane said.

# CHAPTER 15

# TOLTAK

Fortin turned his horse into a sizable collection of trees off the road. All my muscles overcompensated for the pain in my ribs as Gossamer stepped onto the uneven terrain.

Faslight's herbs had faded hours ago. With the sunlight waning, cold sank deeper, burrowing into my bones.

We'd made excellent progress. By tomorrow afternoon, we would be sitting by a crackling fire in one of Toltak's finest inns, sipping on a warm stew after a soak in a hot bath. And sleeping in a bed. A clean, soft bed with an actual pillow.

Ikane looked over his shoulder, watching the road as he followed Fortin into the trees.

"Anything?" Ropert asked.

Ikane shook his head and swung from the saddle. His legs buckled as he hit the ground.

Ropert chuckled. "It's not the same as running, is it?"

"Stop harassing him." I slapped Ropert's shoulder as he helped me from Gossamer's back. It felt wonderful to stand on solid ground, to stop the continual swaying and jolting. Now if only I could stop shivering.

Fortin tugged the tent from his horse's back. "Brendagger's right. We don't want to lose the extra help, especially now."

"He knows it's all in jest, don't you, Ikane?"

"I'm not going anywhere," Ikane said.

"Not on a horse, you're not."

I shot Ropert a glare.

"Alright, alright." Ropert raised his hands. "I couldn't help it."

"Ropert, get the horses settled," Fortin said. "Ikane, start the fire. Brendagger, brush the horses."

"Aye, sir." Ikane disappeared into the trees.

"At least someone here respects authority," Fortin said. He turned away, searching for a spot of ground that wasn't occupied by too many dead branches and rocks.

"Did you see that?" Ropert jerked the saddle girth loose. "He just ordered Ikane to make a fire. He's not a soldier. And you? Lady Brendagger. He just *ordered* you to brush the horses. You pushed hard today. You should be resting." He pulled the saddle from Gossamer's back. "If Illorce were here, he would—" He sucked air through his teeth, dropping the saddle, clutching his wrist.

"Let me see that." I took his arm. A deep slash cut into his armguard, dried blood crusting over the leather. I unbuckled his guard, peeling it away from his bloodstained wrist. What a fool. He should have let me tend to this hours ago.

"It's not as bad as it looks," he said.

"You always say that." I pinched his sleeve, peeling it from his skin. A bleeding gash ran across the back of his wrist. "You tore it open when you lifted the saddle. You're going to need sutures."

"I'll make you tea if you stitch it up." He winked.

"Get me out of this sling first." I unclasped my cloak, draping it over Gossamer's back.

Ropert undid the knot on my shoulder. The bandaging fell away, freeing my ribcage and arm. My muscles sighed, lungs eager to expand. A stab hit my side.

No deep breaths for a while then.

I pulled my cloak from Gossamer's back. "My healer's kit is in the right saddlebag."

Ropert crouched, digging into my bag. "I'll meet you by the fire."

Ikane emerged from the trees as I moved to the log sitting by the empty firepit. He dropped his bundle of wood beside me. "Done already?" He glanced at the horses.

"Ropert's arm needs tending first."

Green flashed in Ikane's eye as he watched Ropert tip the mouth of his waterskin over the bleeding gash in his arm.

"It's not your fault," I whispered. "He's alright, and so are you. I was worried when you were driven into the trees."

"So was I." Crouching, he tossed thin strips of tinder into the ring of scorched stones. "We shouldn't have raced. It was foolish and childish."

"You couldn't have known. Don't blame yourself."

He rubbed his face, dragging his fingers through his hair. "They were waiting. As soon as they saw the opportunity, they struck."

He was right. That was how I would have handled the situation if I were hunting someone, waiting until they let their guard down, until they separated, making them easier targets. "The question is, why? Why did they kill Lady Serah? Why are they after me? What could they possibly gain from this?"

Ikane looked away, his eye sparking again. He struck the flint with such force it caught instantly. Orange licked up the brown grass, a thin trail of smoke rising to the sky. "Why, indeed."

Ropert settled beside me, handing me the healing kit, a leather scroll holding vials, bandages, and other tools for emergencies. "And how did they know Dagger is Daram's representative?" he asked. "She still wears her uniform. We've said nothing aloud nor made any indication that Kea is the new representative."

"Someone must be feeding them information." Ikane placed more logs over the growing flame.

I rolled the kit open. The only thread was black and coarse, meant for closing up a gash much deeper than this, but it would have to do. Choosing the smallest needle, I threaded it by the light of the meager sunlight. Ropert rested his arm across my lap.

"Ready?" I asked.

He looked away, setting his jaw. He made no sound as the needle pierced his skin.

"Daram will be regarded as pretentious, haughty, and insolent if it is not represented." Fortin joined our circle, distributing our cold supper.

"But Duchess Caitelyn said Daram is under attack," I said. "Surely the king would understand our situation."

"It doesn't matter. We must get you to Meldron, Kea. I've a feeling you represent more than just Daram."

I was up for the challenge. My home needed me, Mayama and Eamon, too. I had failed no assignment before . . . before this one. I would not be the one who blundered our last stretch.

Ikane leaned back on his heels. "I'll take first watch tonight."

"I'll take second shift." Fortin's voice was tinged with annoyance. "Since no one woke me for my turn last night."

"We had to curb your sour attitude," Ropert mumbled.

I pulled the last suture through Ropert's skin, tugging a little harder than necessary. His constant impudence could cost him, even if we didn't have Duchess Caitelyn breathing down our necks.

"Done. Now where is that tea you promised?"

*The wind stood still. A suffocating, stagnant mist hung in the air like smoke over a destroyed city. Brown leaves spun to the lifeless underbrush, coating the earth with a blanket of death.*

*Nothing moved. Nothing breathed. Everything was drained of life and color save the entanglement of red curls lying at the base of a tree.*

*The voices from the crimson heirloom hummed through the thick air. "My time will come. One day, I will claim my birthright. You were a fool not to see how glorious you could have become."*

The air was too thick. It sat in my throat like dirt eroding into my lungs. Breathe, feathers, breathe. It didn't matter how much my ribs ached. I needed air, the flow of wind, the motion of life.

My lungs opened.

Oh, how I hated these dreams. Faslight was right. They were getting worse—deeper, darker, more isolated to the desires of the ruby.

Why was it so quiet? I should hear the crackling of a fire, Ropert's or Ikane's breathing, an owl or a wolf.

Ropert lay to my right, curled onto his side. I touched his back; it was warm and solid, moving with breath. Ikane lay on my left, his face turned to the sky, his chest rising and falling.

I crawled from my bedroll, opening the tent flap. Beautiful

white clusters of snow drifted through the trees like stars falling from heaven. A layer of white covered Fortin's shoulders as he sat by the fire, carving away on the same piece of wood that he had been for the past three weeks.

"Kea?"

I glanced over at Ikane.

He propped himself on his elbows. "Is everything alright?"

"I didn't mean to wake you." I slipped back into my bedroll, resting my head on my lumpy, makeshift pillow. I just wanted to sleep. A dreamless, restful slumber where nothing happened.

Ikane rolled onto his side, tucking an arm under his head. "Was it the dream again?"

Yes. The dream. The nightmare that deepened every night. The dream that would break me if I didn't stop it.

Something warm touched my hand under the blankets. Ikane's calloused fingers squeezed mine, his warmth rushing up my arm, spreading into my chest with a cure more potent than Faslight's herbs. My body melted as though I rested on the softest feather bed.

I squeezed his hand, closing my eyes. This was what I needed. He was here. He was full of life and love.

Every worry in my mind slipped into darkness.

"This is it." Fortin's eyes flashed between Duchess Caitelyn's letter in his hand and the wooden sign hanging above the door. The Moonlight Shield Inn. He folded the letter, tucking it into his pocket. "There is a stable over there. Get the horses settled. Brendagger and I will secure our rooms."

"Rooms?" Ikane asked.

Fortin's hand paused on the lever, his breath pluming. "Yes, rooms. You want to sleep in a bed tonight, don't you? Out of this snow?" He gestured to the ankle-deep whiteness around our feet.

"Aye. But with mercenaries on our tail, do you think it's safe to leave Kea alone?"

How incompetent did he think I was? I may have a few bruises and cracked ribs, but that didn't mean I couldn't defend myself.

Fortin eyed me. "You're right. We'd best stay together. Tend the horses, and meet us inside." He opened the door.

Warmth spilled into the street, the smell of sage and rosemary wafting from the inn. Firelight flickered across the whitewashed walls and stone fireplace set in the corner. Polished tables stood in organized rows of two decorated with blue runners trimmed with white and brown. Individual chairs with intricately carved backs stood around them. Even the wooden beams reaching to the ceiling were carved and polished. I'd never seen an inn so fine.

Where were the backless stools and benches? Where were the tables battered from years of use? Where were the stains on the walls and floor?

"Is this the right place?" I whispered.

Fortin shrugged. "Remember, this was originally for Lady Serah." He stepped inside, stomping the snow off his boots.

A richly dressed man and woman looked up from their meal, annoyance plain on their faces.

Fortin shut the door after me.

"Can I help you?" A thin woman appeared from the back, wiping her hands on her crisp apron. She was as pristine as the inn, her brown hair bound back in a silky braid with a face as cold as the snow outside.

"We'd like a room for the night," Fortin said.

She scanned his uniform, the snow on his shoulders, his disheveled hair and beard. "You realize the Moonlight Shield is not a place for soldiers. The Heavy Mallet Tavern down the road might be more suited to your needs."

"We are the representatives from Daram. Duchess Caitelyn has ordered rooms here."

"Ah." The woman's icy exterior melted. "You are here with Lady Serah then. Yes. I have four rooms set aside for her." She turned, waving for us to follow her up the stairs.

"We only need one," Fortin said.

She stopped.

"Lady Serah isn't here. This is Lady Brendagger." Fortin took my arm, pulling me forward. "She has been sent in her stead."

The ice returned. "Do you take me for a fool?"

Fortin's brows furrowed.

"Get out of my inn." She pointed to the door.

It was my uniform. She saw me as a soldier, not a lady. A lady wouldn't tolerate this treatment. I had to be like Lady Serah.

I straightened my shoulders, bruises aching. "I have been dragged through snow and mud for the past three days. I've endured two bandit attacks. Just look at my arm. This uniform I wear is for my protection, a decoy. I shouldn't have to explain myself to you. Now show me to my room where I can bathe and get out of this wretched costume."

She took a step back. Fortin's eyes widened.

"I . . . I apologize. I did not realize."

"Obviously."

"Come with me." She led us up the stairs and down a hallway. She opened a door. "This room is the largest."

Two sizable beds sat on either corner of the room, the frames carved with the same beautiful patterns as the chairs downstairs. The quilts were exquisite with soft blue, white, and brown patterns. A massive fireplace stood between them, decorated with evergreen boughs and thick cream candles. Dried bundles of white roses hung on the wall.

"Will it do?"

I eyed Fortin. There were only two beds. Where would Ikane and Ropert sleep? Was it really necessary to stay in one room? The mercenaries wouldn't come here, would they?

Fortin moved to the only window, shaking the frame.

"It's locked for the winter," the innkeeper said.

He pressed his forehead against the panes, looking down. "This should do. No one should be able to climb."

The innkeeper bowed her head to me. "I will see to your bath straightaway." She ducked outside.

"That was an impressive performance." Fortin smiled for the first time.

"I just did what Lady Serah would do."

"You will do an excellent job representing Daram."

*Everything burned. Smoke filled my lungs, thick and suffocating.*

My eyes flew wide. I inhaled, the gasp louder than intended.

Shadows danced across the walls, the orange glow from the fire searing the nightmare into my brain.

This had to stop.

*Phoenix, please, make it stop.*

The room blurred. Hot tears streaked down my cheeks. I sat up, fists pushing the moisture away. What did Faslight say? I had to find the White Wardent, even if he was a myth.

"Kea?" Ikane's shadow rose from his bedding at the foot of my bed. He perched on the edge, his hand finding mine. His strong, warm, solid hand. "It's alright. It's just a dream."

I sniffed. Why did I have to cry? I never cried.

Ikane's grip loosened.

"Don't let go." I held him tighter.

"Your nose. Just let me get a towel."

He moved to the washbasin, grabbed the towel, and returned. I pressed the cloth against my nose, clutching his hand again. The heat in my bones vanished, cold seeping through every pore in my skin.

"I can't take this anymore." My voice shook, broken with sobs. "These nightmares need to stop."

Ikane's arms wrapped around me. "I want to help, Kea. Just tell me what to do."

"I don't know." I buried my face in his shoulder, tears flowing like a stormy downpour. "I don't know."

"It's alright. I'm here. If holding your hand is all I can do, then that's what I'll do."

Soft white lace drifted from the dense clouds above, alighting on our shoulders and heads until a thick layer of snow stuck to our cloaks and hoods. It was beautiful. Flurries coasted onto

Gossamer's black mane like stars in the night sky.

Ikane rode beside me, his back straight, his body moving with the palomino's strides. He'd come a long way in the past four days.

"Are you going to keep her?"

He blinked at me, snow falling from his mottled charcoal hood. "What?"

"The mare?"

"Oh." He patted her neck. "I'm not sure yet."

"You should name her."

"Wouldn't that confirm I was keeping her?"

"Maybe. She has a sweet personality. You could do—" I cried out as the sound of rending flesh and fabric cut the air and a sharp sting raced up my left shoulder. I dropped the reins, grabbing my arm.

An arrow wobbled ahead, piercing the snow beside Fortin's horse. This couldn't be good.

Ikane cursed under his breath. "Fortin!" He slipped from the palomino's back, swords hissing from their scabbards. "Behind us!"

Glancing over my shoulder, I saw an archer standing beside the tree line, a familiar mask hiding his features. Four more mercenaries appeared, one of them limping, black marks against the snow-covered woods.

Applewood danced around as Ropert drew his sword, spurring her toward the mercenaries. Fortin directed his horse in a tight circle to flank our attackers.

I would not sit idle this time. I reached for my sword, but an odd sensation radiated through my arm. Why wouldn't my fingers grip? Tingling moved toward my chest. The snow, trees, and galloping horses spun. I clutched Gossamer's saddle. What was wrong with me?

"Kea." Ikane dropped his swords, catching my shoulders as I slipped. He guided me to the snow. "What's wrong?" His hands moved across my body, searching. His green eye flashed as he surveyed my shoulder.

"What is it?" I asked. "Why am I so . . . so dizzy?"

He sniffed my wound.

Was he actually trying to detect poison?

He ripped the sleeve of my soldier's uniform from my shoulder. "No, no, no." He pressed his mouth against my skin, sucking hard.

He spit my blood into the snow.

I should be worried. This wasn't good. My heart fluttered in my chest like the beautiful white lace swirling in a dreamlike dance around us. The feathered crystals kissed my cheeks and eyelashes. My breath plumed. I should be cold, shouldn't I?

The ache in my side was gone. My eyes fluttered.

A shadow encroached on my vision, ugly and dark. Something silver and hard rose above Ikane's head. I knew I knew what it was, but I couldn't recall the name. It was sharp, curved, and dangerous. Why couldn't I think?

An axe.

"Ikane!"

He whirled. His hands caught the axe by the neck. The attacker thrust a knee into Ikane's chest, and Ikane rocked backward.

The world spun, everything blurring into white. Was this how I was going to die? Less than a day's ride from Meldron? Out in the cold?

Ikane grunted as his body spun, landing on his hands and knees, back exposed to the mercenary standing above him.

I kicked, hitting the man in the knee. The corners of my vision darkened as the axe came down.

Ikane rolled, black steel flashing up. The man roared, stumbling back, blood dripping from his fingers.

Everything spun. Trees blanketed with snow, reaching to the frosty sky, spiraled into a blur. The ringing of weapons dulled.

I couldn't sleep. Not now.

Against my wishes, my eyes closed, and all sound dulled. Then it faded away completely.

# CHAPTER 16

# THE LEVIATHAN PIRATE

Crust clung to my eyelids. My tongue felt thick and dry, too parched to wet my burning lips.

I tried to swallow, and thorns pushed against my throat. Every joint ached, every muscle was locked tight. A dull throb nettled my forehead.

"Kea." Ikane's voice was soft and filled with relief. The bed creaked, and the blankets pulled as he sat on the edge. His fingers brushed my hair from my forehead. "How are you feeling? Can you move?"

How could he expect me to move with the weight of a thousand blankets holding me down?

He took my hand in his. "Just squeeze my fingers, Kea."

I would if he would get these suffocating blankets off me.

"That's it." He sighed. "The arrow was laced with wolfsbane. Fortunately, it only grazed your skin. You wouldn't have survived otherwise."

My eyes fluttered. The light from the roaring fireplace cast flickering shadows across his features. His green eye smoldered, his cheek sporting a bruise.

"What . . . what happened?"

Ikane scrunched his eyes shut, jaw tightening. "Ropert is alright, but Fortin . . . Fortin isn't doin' well. Those vipers severed his leg clean off. He's bein' tended to at Meldron's Healin' Billet."

The poison must have been messing with my ears. His accent

was thicker.

Meldron? Were we here? Fortin. How could this have happened to him? He didn't deserve this.

The door creaked open.

"Blessed Phoenix, you're awake!" Ropert bolted to my side, a light sprinkle of snow covering his shoulders and hair. A red streak lanced across his forehead, and his jaw swelled with a purple welt.

He took my hand, and his cold fingers stung my skin. "We did it, Dagger. We're in Meldron—and with four days to spare. You should have ample time to heal before the big event."

I wanted to sleep for a week.

"I should let Fortin know you're alright." Ropert stood. "It would put his mind at ease."

"How is he?" I struggled to form the words.

"As long as he doesn't develop sepsis, he should recover. At least that's what the healers have told me. I know little about these things." Ropert moved to the door. "Watch her closely, Ikane. The tall one got away."

"I will. And Ropert?" Ikane asked, changing the subject. "I underestimated you. Would you like to spar with me sometime?"

Ropert's face split into a lopsided grin. "This afternoon?"

Ikane laughed. "You don't want to rupture your sutures. Take this time to recover. I'll only face you at your best."

"Very well. But the moment these sutures come out, we will spar."

Didn't they remember what happened the last time they challenged one another? I pushed the blankets from my chest with a huff. "Give it a rest."

"You are the one who needs rest." Ropert opened the door. "Watch her, Ikane. I'm not convinced this is over."

Ikane nodded. "Kea is safe with me."

Why was it so hard to move? Just trying to sit up was like dragging myself from a pit of mud.

"Hold on, Kea." Ikane slipped a hand under my back, helping me sit. "You've got to take it easy."

"I ache all over."

With his help, I swung my legs over the edge of the bed. Heaviness filled my skull, and the room swayed as if I were on a ship.

"Easy." Ikane held my shoulders. "It's the poison. You've been given an antidote, but it'll take some time before you're back on your feet."

"How much time?"

"A week or two." He sank onto the bed beside me. He looked as heavy as I felt, his shoulders sagging like a man who'd lost everything in the world. His eye smoldered constantly, like the last coal in a firepit refusing to die.

"What's wrong?"

He leaned forward, hiding his face in his hands. "I wish I could have done more."

I touched his shoulder; his muscles were like iron. "We owe you everything."

He dropped his hands, his enchanted eyes locking onto mine as his dark hair fell across his forehead. "You're looking at me like a hero. I don't deserve it."

"I don't care what you think."

He smiled. "Are you hungry?"

"Feathers, yes."

"Then let's get you some food."

Ropert pushed the door open with his back, carrying a tray laden with three steaming bowls of soup and large slabs of bread. "Supper." He grinned.

My stomach growled as the smell of venison, carrots, and potato filled the room.

Ikane carried the small table from the wall and set it beside the bed. I pulled a bowl to me, scooping up a mouthful. Heat scorched my tongue, but it was good. Rich with flavor, it washed away the thick dryness in my throat. I grabbed a slice of fresh rye bread.

Ropert sank onto the bed beside me. "Fortin says we should present ourselves at the castle as soon as possible. We were supposed to be here three days ago . . . something about a week's buffer before the big event?" He dipped his bread in his bowl. "I don't understand these proceedings."

My body shivered at the thought of arriving at court, of trying to stand proud amid prying eyes of nobles. I wasn't ready—Illorce had had so much more to teach me.

And I was still recovering from the aftermath of being poisoned. Even now, the room spun. I didn't have the energy to act like Lady Serah. Not yet. "One more day. Please."

"That's what I said." Ropert winked.

Ikane leaned back in his chair. "If it would help, I would be honored to accompany you."

"I don't see why not," Ropert said. "I'll have to ask Fortin first, just as a formality, but I'm sure he'll be as grateful for your offer as I am."

Ikane nodded.

I swallowed my mouthful. This next phase of our mission was going to be the hardest of all.

"Where did the clothes end up?" Ropert asked. "The ones Lady Serah said she ordered before we left?"

Ikane slipped from his chair, moved to our saddlebags sitting against the wall, and opened one that was stuffed to bursting. He withdrew soft-edged packages wrapped in brown paper and tossed them onto the bed beside me.

Two had my name written on them. The others were for Ropert and Fortin.

I unwrapped both of mine quickly. The gowns were stunning.

One was a beautiful earthy green, the shade of moss that hugged the stone walls of the Daram keep. The other was the color of autumn leaves with a golden-brown trim. But both had strings designed to lace up the sleeves and cinch the waist. I wouldn't be able to dress myself with broken ribs.

"Can't I just wear my tunic and trousers?" I asked.

Ropert looked at Ikane. "I suppose . . ."

But Ikane shook his head. "It wouldn't be proper."

"I wish Illorce were here." I grabbed the brown dress, remembering the way Lady Serah had gushed over the idea of me wearing it.

"I'll need a bath before I dare try it on," I said.

Ropert sniffed the air by my shoulder and dramatically wrinkled his nose. "I concur."

I wanted to ram my fist into his shoulder, but I didn't quite have the energy for that. Yet. "You should talk. I could smell you from outside." In all honesty, he didn't smell that bad.

Ropert chuckled and set his bowl on the table. "I'll walk you to the baths, Kea." He extended his elbow to me. "I'll visit with Fortin in the meantime and ask him about your offer, Ikane."

My legs shook as I rose with Ropert.

Ikane opened the door for us. "I'll fetch you in an hour. The warm water will do you good."

With the copper-red dress draped over my arm, Ropert escorted me from the room and into a beautiful hallway lined with narrow tables topped with painted vases holding stunning flower arrangements. Decorative sconces hung on the walls. This place was even more immaculate than the Moonlight Shield Inn in Toltak.

We came upon the stairs. The brilliantly carved railing was as smooth as a polished sword and glided under my hand like silk.

"This isn't the castle, is it?" I asked.

Ropert chuckled. "No. This is the Belcourt Inn."

We reached the main floor, an open space filled with round tables covered in white tablecloths and flowery centerpieces. A chandelier, blazing with a dozen candles, cast a crisp reflection on the waxed floorboards.

Ropert steered me to a polished counter standing beside the most immaculate hearth I'd ever seen. "Do you think you can manage from here?" he asked.

I slipped my arm from his. "Thank you, Ropert."

"Enjoy your bath." He stole away.

The woman behind the counter looked up as I approached, her hand flying to her chest. "Lady Brendagger? You're awake. I was worried. You were so pale when they brought you in. How are you feeling?"

I would never get used to being called "Lady Brendagger." "I'm on the mend."

She smiled warmly, her cheeks growing rounder. "What wonderful news. And what might I do for you?"

"Can you direct me to the baths?"

"Ah, yes. There is nothing more healing to the body and soul than a hot bath." She opened a ledger behind the desk, grabbed a quill, and dipped it in her inkwell. "I can have a fresh tub ready for you in an hour. Would you like rose or lavender as your choice of fragrance?"

Wait, what? Was she saying that I would have my own private bath with fresh, clean water? Back in Daram, I'd never had that luxury. All the soldiers used the community bathhouse, and it was a mad rush to be the first to use the freshly heated tubs.

The woman suddenly looked worried. "If those fragrances don't suit you, we also have clove, rosemary, or sandalwood."

"I . . . uh, rosemary is fine."

"A wonderful choice for this time of year. Very warming." She jotted the name of the herb in her book. "There." She tapped the tip of her quill against the paper as though she was placing the final addition to a delicate creation. "I shall come fetch you when your bath is ready."

I turned around, the massive dining room looking like the Great Hall of the Daram keep with elegantly dressed patrons sharing meals. A woman eyed me over the rim of her goblet, making me painfully aware of my appearance.

I couldn't stay here in my trousers and untucked shirt.

The stairs towered beside me, looming like a mountain. I'd sent Ropert away too soon.

Legs shaking, I gripped the smooth railing and climbed one careful step at a time. Halfway up, everything blurred. I paused, clinging to the railing. I'd never felt so helpless.

Reaching our room, I opened the door.

Ikane whirled from the washbasin, eyes wide, a knife frozen by his soap-splotched jaw. His bare chest was solid muscle, and pale scars scattered across his smooth, suntanned skin. He was the most . . .

Wait. Was I hallucinating? Was the poison that strong? A black image glared at me from his muscled shoulder: a tattoo, the same one I'd seen on the arm of the mercenary.

I took a step back.

Ikane held his hands up, fingers lose on his knife, eyes pleading. "Kea. I . . . I can explain."

I shook my head. A pirate? My Ikane. The man who made me smile, comforted me, fought with me, held my hand at night. He was a Leviathan pirate?

Eamon knew. That was why he told me to stay away. He knew what Ikane really was.

My stomach curdled as if it were filled with spoiled milk.

"You're . . . you're a pirate." The word stung my lips, tearing through my heart like the bite of his Leviathan-decorated swords. How had I been so blind?

"Kea, please." He took a step forward.

"Stay away from me." I staggered back into the hallway.

He lunged forward, his knife thudding against the floor at the same time his hand pinched my wrist. His speed was uncanny. My neck snapped forward as he jerked me back into the room.

My ribs screamed as I stumbled against the bed frame, dropping the gown.

He slammed the door. "Kea, please." He turned to me with hands raised, and his eyes found mine, the unnatural green one burning like fire. "I am on your side. You must believe me."

I held my ribs, my breaths coming shallow and hard, my heartbeats aching. "You're one of them." He even talked like them. The soft roll of his r's, the occasional drop of a syllable at the end of a word. The Leviathans spoke that way. He didn't even try to hide it anymore.

He took a step forward.

"Don't." The back of my knees hit the bed frame. Every instinct told me to fight, to grab my sword sitting by the fireplace, to run it through his heart.

He followed my gaze, his brows furrowing. "I don't want to fight you, Kea."

"You should have thought of that before you killed Lady Serah." I sprang for my sword, fingers just about to curl around the hilt when my arm jerked back. How in the blazes had he crossed the room so quickly? He was more than a Leviathan.

And more than I could handle on my own, even without broken ribs.

"Help! Some—"

His hand flew over my mouth, slamming my head against his chest, cutting off my cry.

"I didn't kill her." His breath was hot against my cheek, his arms solid cords around mine. He was going to crack another rib.

My scream pushed against his fingers, sounding like a pathetic screech.

"Stop fighting, Kea. You're going to hurt yourself."

My heel ground into his toes, and I slammed a fist back. It struck the soft part of his thigh.

I was aiming for his crotch.

He shook me hard. "Listen to me. I didn't kill Lady Serah. And I wasn't lying when I said I needed Eamon's help. Scales, Kea. I need you to believe me."

Tears streaked down my cheeks, sliding to his fingers. Oh, how I wanted to believe him. I'd opened my heart too much, despite Eamon's warning.

On top of that, he was stronger and faster, and I was at a disadvantage. There was no point in fighting him like this. So I forced myself to be still.

Slowly, he moved his hand from my mouth.

"You," I began, "are a Leviathan pirate."

"That does not define who I am." His grip eased cautiously from my ribs.

"Then what are you doing in Roanfire? Why are you here?"

"I came to warn Eamon. My brothers have been planning an attack for two years now, putting the pieces into place—one Roanfire has never seen before. They've already set things in motion, beginning with Daram."

I stiffened. "The Leviathans are attacking my home, and you want me to believe you're not a part of it?"

Ikane spun me around, driving me against the wall, pinning my shoulders. "I warned him! Scales, Kea. I was there to warn him. He knew, and he ignored it." His eye burned. "You can't turn this on me. I defied my brothers. I did what I could to save Daram."

His brothers? They led the attack? They owned the fleet? The knife in my heart twisted. He wasn't just a pirate.

"Your name isn't Wulver." I spat his traitorous alias. "You're an Ormand brother. A Leviathan prince." I shunted him back.

How could he do this to me?

His handsome face and perfect physique blurred as new tears burned my eyes. "You've lied to me about everything. Is your name even Ikane?"

"I never meant for things to go this far. I care for you too much—"

"Don't." I shut my eyes. I couldn't listen to another word. He was breaking my heart. "Eamon was right. I should have listened to him. He was a fool for not turning you in."

Pain filled his eyes, his blue and green irises fracturing into a thousand shimmering pieces. "Kea . . ."

"Go. Just get your things, and go."

He dragged his shirt from the back of the chair and pulled it over his torso, hiding the horrible twisting serpents on his shoulder. With minty soap still on his jaw, he shoved his belongings into his bag. "You're letting me go. Why?" he asked, hefting his bag onto his shoulder and throwing his cloak over his arm. "You'd be a hero for turning me in."

"Don't tempt me." I swiped at the tears on my cheeks, hoping he didn't see them, and marched for the door. Why was I doing this? Why was I gambling with my future for the life of a Leviathan prince, our sworn enemy?

"I am not what you think." His voice was soft, pleading for understanding. His green eye flickered like a candle in the wind, showing the rush of too many emotions to control.

I couldn't keep looking at him. My gaze dropped to the floor as I opened the door. "Leave."

He stepped closer, his soft leather boots stopping right in front of me.

"Kea . . ." His calloused hand touched my chin, lifting my head, forcing my eyes to his. Couldn't he see how much I hurt already?

He leaned closer.

I couldn't . . . this was . . .

He closed the distance, his lips pressing against mine.

Oh, the heat of his skin, the love and passion burning behind his kiss. The overpowering scent of mint flooded my nose. My eyes closed, tears clinging to my lashes, the world falling away.

I loved him.

Why did it feel so right and wrong at the same time? He was a Leviathan prince. I was sworn to protect Roanfire against his kind. This was treason.

My fists clenched. I should have listened to Eamon. He tried to protect me from this, and I ignored him. Never again. I was a soldier. I was loyal and obedient.

I broke the kiss with a jerk, a cold emptiness filling the space between us, and wiped at the minty soap clinging to my cheek. How dare he!

My fist flew at his face, pain flaring through my knuckles as they struck his jaw. His head rocked to the side, and his body spun into the bed, the entire frame screeching across the floor.

I fought against the tears threatening to surface. "So help me, if I ever see you again, I *will* turn you in." I stormed from the room.

I was no better than Eamon for letting him go.

The innkeeper laced the infuriating strings of the copper-red gown to my waist and arms. She combed through my wet hair, manipulating it into a long, elegant twist over my shoulder.

Numbly, I climbed the staircase to the rented room.

I paused by the door, focusing on the grains of wood. If there was any trace of him, I would break. Why did it hurt so much?

My hand hung on the lever, the latch clicking.

Ropert rose from the chair, dressed in a new deep-blue tunic with thick brown trousers, probably from Lady Serah's stash. He had groomed, leaving his signature growth of red beard at the bottom of his chin.

"Flaming feathers, Dagger." His eyes scanned my frame. "Is that really you? You look . . . beautiful. I mean, you've always been pretty, but now you actually look like a woman."

I closed the door.

"What? No comeback?"

"No." I stuffed my dirty clothes into my bag.

Ropert's brows furrowed. "Where is Ikane?"

"He left."

"What did you do?"

I whirled on him. "Why is it instantly my fault?"

Ropert straightened, his face losing all trace of humor. I couldn't do anything right today.

"I'm sorry, Ropert. I didn't mean it like that."

He rubbed the back of his neck. "So . . . when will he be coming back?"

"He won't be." I returned to my task of packing.

"What do you mean, he won't be back? I was counting on him, Kea. Fortin was relieved when I asked. Lady Serah left for Meldron with four of Daram's finest soldiers, and you have one. I can't do this alone."

My jaw tightened, hands curling into fists. He was forgetting that I was a soldier, too.

"Dagger? What's going on with you?"

"We don't need Ikane. I can take care of myself."

"You can barely stand on your own. What happened? Did he hurt you?"

"We're going to the castle today." I grabbed the green dress from the bed, stuffing it into my bag.

I'd never lied to Ropert before. But if he knew who Ikane truly was, he would be compelled to turn him over to the Phoenix soldiers.

The memory of Ikane's lips against mine—tender, true, and pure—was burned into my mind. He'd meant no harm. He'd done everything in his power to help us get this far. He'd even tried to warn Eamon.

But a Leviathan pirate . . . And not just a pirate, but a prince. A man with power and authority. Had I done the right thing?

"Flaming feathers," Ropert breathed. "He kissed you, didn't he?"

My cheeks burned, and my stomach rolled.

Ropert groaned. "That isn't fair, Dagger. He's my friend, too. You can't simply send him away for overstepping his bounds. I'll talk with him. We need him."

I slammed my bag onto the bed. "He's not a soldier!"

Ropert stiffened.

My heart sank lower. We'd argued before, but never like this. I was making a mess of everything.

Holding my ribs, I turned to the window, watching the blurry outlines of people hurrying through the street. Ikane could be among them.

Ropert stepped beside me. "You've fallen in love with him, haven't you? And you're scared."

I bit my lip.

"I understand. We've worked hard to get where we are. Our lives have been dedicated to Roanfire. We've sacrificed our most intimate desires to rise in rank. You don't see me gallivanting through the streets at night with a beautiful girl in my arms, either. I can't afford the distraction."

"Then you understand why I need to let him go."

"I understand, but I don't agree. Could you please endure him a little longer, just until we return to Daram?" He looked at me with his bright blue eyes, tilting his head like he so often did to get me to break.

Not this time. "No."

Ropert huffed, running a hand through his luscious head of golden hair. "I'm afraid you don't really have a choice. Fortin wants this." He moved to the door. "I am going to find Ikane and bring him back. We'll go to the castle as soon as I return."

"Ropert."

"Lock the door after me, and open for no one." He slipped out the door.

My nails dug into my ribs, irritating the bruises. If Ikane knew what was good for him, he'd make himself scarce.

# CHAPTER 17

# MELDRON

ight snow whispered across the cobblestone road. Timber-framed buildings leaned into the street like giants, blocking the sunlight.

The road opened to a bright market square teeming with merchants and patrons, and I felt every one of my bruises when an elbow and basket carelessly flew my direction. Brightly colored canvas tents stretched over wares displayed in permanent structures, and tables, carts, and wagons filled with the autumn harvest were scattered throughout. Children laughed, darting between them in a game of tag.

A giant fountain stood in the center of the market square, ice-cold water spewing from a gilded statue of a phoenix. Ice clung to the stone in twisted, beautiful shapes, dripping down the gracefully arched neck of Roanfire's emblem.

A child darted into my path. I planted my feet, sucking air through my teeth as every muscle tensed. Another child gave chase, both running to the crenelated curtain walls dominating the side of the market.

There it was. The Meldron castle.

Five whitewashed towers soared behind it, red-tiled spires piercing the gray clouds. The largest of the turrets boasted a dozen arched windows.

Daram's keep was no match for this magnificent fortress.

Ropert and I halted before the gold-plated gates at the north end of the market square. Another fountain stood in the heart of the courtyard, this one comprising three firebirds holding up a massive stone saucer with their wings. Icicles dripped from the bowl like an array of crystal swords.

I steeled myself, ignoring the sluggishness seeping through every muscle. It was time for me to be Lady Brendagger.

A Phoenix soldier stepped forward. I'd always dreamed of seeing the crimson uniform up close. His breastplate and helmet were plated with gold, depicting the burning feathers of the Phoenix. A large golden brooch adorned with the crest of Meldron held his crimson cloak in place.

"State your business." His voice was monotone and bored.

I straightened my shoulders. "I am Lady Brendagger, here on behalf of Duchess Caitelyn of Daram."

The soldier's eyes narrowed. "I was told Lady Serah, niece to Duchess Caitelyn, would represent Daram."

I glanced at Ropert. The soldier didn't look like a patient man, and I had a lot to explain.

"Lady Brendagger." Another soldier appeared. The red feathers on her helmet swayed as she bowed her head to me. "We received word from Duchess Caitelyn; you are expected. Please pardon Corporal Haden. Clearly, he missed the message being relayed."

Corporal Haden shifted nervously under her scowl.

"I shall send for your greeting party at once." She jerked her head at the other soldier, wordlessly assigning him to the menial task of errand boy.

"Yes, Captain Fora." He hurried toward the castle.

"Please, come in." Captain Fora opened the gate for us.

I shivered. Lady Serah's taste in gowns was not conducive for warmth. My cloak was warmer than the dress, and I hugged it tighter. My ribs ached.

Corporal Haden returned with a middle-aged woman. Her face seemed pleasant, and the simple green gown she wore complemented her brown hair. Five stablehands and three maidservants followed.

"Dear me." The woman's voice was low and strong but very delightful. "I was informed that we would greet a party of three." She stood on her toes, searching over our heads.

"We were ambushed on the road from Toltak," Ropert said.

"Oh, you poor child." She put her arms around me, rubbing my shoulders. I cringed as her hand pressed against the healing arrow wound. "I am Adalyah. Duchess Caitelyn and I have been working closely to see to your needs. I will be your lady's maid during your stay. You needn't worry about a thing."

She steered me across the courtyard. A middle-aged man stood at the top of the magnificent staircase to my right, watching us, twisting a ring on his finger. His flaming red hair and beard were immaculately groomed, and gold and rubies embellished his blue velvet tunic. A white collar with ruffles floundered down his rounded chest. His cloak appeared to have enough fabric to warm three men. It draped across his shoulders and over one arm.

"Who is that man?" I asked Adalyah.

"You do not know?" She gasped. "That is Archduke Goldest, cousin to Prince Sander. You shall meet with him soon enough."

I swallowed hard. I didn't want to meet him. Something about him intimidated me.

We approached a side door embedded in the wall. Adalyah opened it, leading us through several corridors and passageways more twisted and confusing than Daram keep's. The marble hallways were bare of any rugs or tapestries but were so meticulously polished I could see my reflection on the walls and floor. Servants scuttled on important errands, and flames of evenly spaced sconces flickered in the rush of bodies.

Reaching the end of a long, barren hallway, we climbed a spiral staircase. Halfway up, my head felt light. The poison.

Ropert caught my elbow. "Are you alright?" he whispered.

I shook my head, trying to clear it. "I'll be fine."

We pushed on.

Reaching the third floor, Adalyah stopped by a door lining the hallway. She produced a key from under the folds of her green velvet dress. A rush of warm air hit my face as the door swung open.

"Flaming feathers," I breathed.

Every inch of plaster upon the walls had been painted with vibrant colors, depicting a beautiful scene of courtship in summer. Green-and-gold tasseled curtains hung over a writing desk standing under two arched windows. Two chests, a hanging closet, a dressing screen, and a full-length mirror stood nearby. A bed dominated an entire wall.

*Five soldiers could sleep in that.*

Honey-colored drapes reached the ceiling on the corner bedposts, and half a dozen pillows sat at the head. A feathered quilt with an intricate pattern of flowers spread across the mattress.

Ropert pressed a hand against my back, urging me inside.

The roaring fireplace with a beautifully carved mantle stood across from this colossal bedstead. Here, a stately cushioned sofa and armchair faced the warmth of the fire.

"Will this suit my lady?" Adalyah asked.

I approached the window, opening it a crack to see outside, trying to hide my awe. I had to be like Lady Serah.

The castle gardens were directly below, surrounded by a wall built too high to scale. A parched fountain stood amidst dehydrated rosebushes and trees.

"I think it will do fine."

Adalyah nodded. "The stablehands will bring your luggage to your room. Duchess Caitelyn was most insistent that a new gown be tailored for you immediately. I shall fetch the seamstress. We only have three days before the coronation."

I caressed the softest fabric I had ever donned alongside my hip. Certainly, the gown I wore would suffice.

"As for you." Adalyah took on a less formal tone, addressing Ropert. "As the bodyguard of Lady Brendagger, you will be in the smaller room adjoining hers. Follow me."

Ropert nodded politely and trailed after her.

I closed the window, grateful to be alone as I unclasped my cloak and let it fall to the floor. All this for me. This room alone could house a third of Daram's soldiers.

I sat on the edge of the bed and lay back.

Daram. My home. Under attack by the Leviathan pirates. The honey-colored canopy suddenly swarmed with the black crest of the pirates like a sail on one of their ships.

I squeezed my eyes shut, rolling onto my side, a tear sliding onto the plush comforter. I missed my home. I missed Mayama. I even missed Eamon.

*Red heat blistered through every bone, muscle, and tissue. Burning scorched my eyes. Hot coals pushed into my mouth. My lungs screamed for air.*

*"We will meet soon."*

I bolted upright, gasping, inhaling until the raging fire ebbed to a bearable smolder. A warm trickle of blood slipped from my nose to my lips. My ears rang, which could only mean one thing.

I reached up. Pulling my hand away, red glistened on the tips of my fingers.

This had gone on long enough.

A drop of red splattered onto my lap. Not the dress. Illorce would march across Roanfire on splinted legs and cuff me if he knew what I'd done.

Something bumped through my ears. A knock, maybe? It was too hard to tell through the ringing.

Cupping my nose, I slipped from the bed, hurrying to the washbasin. I grabbed the towel.

The knock sounded again.

"Who is it?"

"It's Ropert."

"Come in."

Ropert opened the door. "It isn't fair." He waved a hand across the expanse of my chamber. "My room is as crammed as the barracks back home and just as dingy. They gave me a servant's nook . . . Dagger?" He shut the door, coming to my side. "Your nose."

Blood gushed even as I pushed the soaking towel against my face. I leaned over the washbasin.

"Did you dream again? Were you sleeping?" Ropert found another towel and switched out the saturated one.

Why wouldn't it stop? The redness kept pouring, pooling in my mouth. I spat, splattering the edges of the porcelain washbasin with red.

Ropert helped me hold the towel, pinching the bridge of my nose, rubbing my back. "You can't keep going like this."

"I know." My voice sounded nasally and broken.

"Faslight said the dreams would get worse."

"They are."

"What are you going to do?"

"Look for the White Wardent." I moved the towel—the bleeding had eased. Moistening another towel with clean water, I washed the blood from my face and hands. Then I tried scrubbing the drop from the fabric of my dress. At least I was wearing red.

"Where will you start? I mean, no one has heard or seen anything of him. Everything about the White Wardent is in myth, legend, and nursery rhymes."

"Then that's where I have to start." I grabbed my cloak from the floor. "We need to go to the library."

"Now?"

"Meldron has the largest library in Roanfire."

"Yes, but you need rest. Maybe even a surgeon."

"A surgeon can't help with this."

"I suppose . . . Have you any idea where the library might be?"

"No." I moved to the door, opening it, looking down both ends of the long, empty hallway lined with doors. Which way had Adalyah brought us?

Ropert locked the door, tucking the key into his pocket. "After you, my lady."

I randomly chose a direction.

I found a spiraling staircase at the end of the hallway. We descended three flights. We found the cellar, peered into rooms I was sure we should not be entering, and discovered a back door to the castle gardens below my bedroom window. Where was everyone? Were there no servants here to ask for directions? Maybe we were on the wrong floor.

Rising to another level, we came upon a long hallway, a balcony with open arches. A man stood tall and important as he spoke to a page in a guarded whisper.

Finally. Someone to ask for directions.

We drew closer. It was the overdressed archduke.

The page scampered away.

"Ah, Lady Brendagger, I presume." He turned to us with a forced smile.

"Your Grace." I bowed, and Ropert saluted. It felt strange not to salute with him. I would have preferred it, seeing as I was to remain with my knees bent and head lowered until he asked me to rise.

"How are you enjoying your stay in Meldron?" He wandered to the balcony, twisting a ring on his finger. His eyes swept across the red-tiled rooftops peeping over the curtain walls. "'Tis a beautiful city, is it not?"

"I haven't had the chance to see much of it yet." Well, he was a pompous blighter. Making conversation while my legs trembled in a half-crouched position.

He tipped his head to the side. "You may rise. Tell me, how is the sergeant? Fortin Grey. I hear he lost one of his legs to a bandit attack. Terrible thing, that."

I eyed Ropert, desperately wanting his support. But he kept his mouth clamped shut, standing with his hands clasped at the small of his back in a soldier's quiet stance. It was so much easier being like Lady Serah when I knew I ranked higher than the person I was speaking with. But here? This man was second to the king.

My heart throbbed beneath my ribs. "His recovery is going well, thanks to Meldron's exceptional healers."

The archduke approached, his blue eyes looking down his nose as he scrutinized me, and I knew he meant to make me feel small. He wasn't a short man.

"Your journey here was surely a tiresome one. Why not go back to your chambers and rest? Surely everything there is to your satisfaction."

I would not be intimidated, nor would I risk his wrath. I drew my shoulders back, softening my face despite the ache in my ribs. "I have heard many great things about Meldron's library. I am eager to see it."

"Ah, yes. We have the finest library in Roanfire. I shall not keep you then. Enjoy your visit."

I bowed again as he went on his way.

Ropert leaned in. "Why didn't you ask him how to get out of here?"

"Because Illorce told me I should ask nothing of a noble that a servant could do. Something about it being offensive to their title."

Ropert rubbed the back of his neck. "I'd make a complete fool of myself."

A maidservant emerged from a room, a tray of empty dishes in her hands.

"Excuse me," Ropert said to her. "Can you tell us how to get out of the castle?"

She blinked, bowing her head to me. "The quickest way is through the servants' passageways."

Ropert sighed. "Will you show us?"

She nodded, leading us down a spiral stairway, through another hallway, and down a narrow corridor to the left. Smells arose from the kitchens. She pointed to a small door at the end.

"That door will take you to the courtyard."

"Many thanks," Ropert said.

We slipped outside into the wintery afternoon. The guards saluted us as we stepped through the gates into the market square.

Ropert scanned the bustling market. Vendors called out, waving merchandise in the air. Patrons moved from stall to stall. Children ran between them. A dog barked. "Are you sure you want to do this today?"

A tall building stood beyond the icy fountain, the word *Library* engraved in the stone above the two massive entry doors. How could I have missed this? We'd walked right past it.

"There." I moved closer, weaving in and out of the crowd. Six stained glass windows flanked the doors, depicting who I assumed were great scholars and scribes from ages past.

The stained glass creation on the right portrayed a strange fair-skinned young man with white hair and piercing amber eyes. He held a book and a quill made from the feather of a swan.

The window beside him boasted red colors.

My feet stopped.

The woman's flaming hair cascaded down her shoulders. A ruby necklace hung from her neck, her curls almost hiding it. Her sapphire eyes bored into me like she knew.

She knew.

"Dagger? Are you alright?" Ropert paused on the wide stairs leading to the doors.

"Look." My breath plumed in the frigid air. "Look at the necklace."

He followed my gaze. "The ruby. From your nightmare?"

Hope fluttered in my chest. "We're in the right place."

Ropert rubbed his hands together, laced his fingers, and stretched. "Well, then, we have work to do." He opened one of the large doors.

"You don't have to help me." I stepped inside. "I know you haven't learned letters." My voice echoed through the expansive chamber within, and several patrons glanced from their books with irritated expressions.

The place smelled of leather and wood, smoke and earth. A massive stone fireplace stood at the far end of the room flanked by deep mahogany shelving reaching clear to the vaulted ceiling. Ladders and stepping stools scattered across the rows of bookcases. Colorful light filtered through the windows, dusting everything in rainbow hues.

"Welcome to Meldron Library." A woman greeted us in a hushed tone. Her graying hair was pulled back into a tight bun, making her eyes slant. She motioned her ink-stained fingers to a table standing beside the door. An enormous book, a bottle of ink, and a quill sat upon it.

"You are free to look through any of the books made available to you. We only ask that you sign your name in our guest book."

I signed our names.

"Is there anything in particular you are searching for?" the librarian asked.

"Anything about the White Wardent."

She arched one eyebrow. "The White Wardent?"

I knew I should have kept my mouth shut.

She tapped a finger against her lips. "The historical section, maybe? Just over there. You can't miss it."

"Thank you."

Ropert followed me between the scattered tables and chairs. I ran my fingers along the leather-bound spines. Each book contained secrets, answers, neglected history. There had to be something here.

I pulled a book from the shelf, flipping through the pages. There were so many. Where was I to begin? Even the librarian wasn't sure. I slipped the book back into its place.

"How can I help?" Ropert asked. He looked as lost as I felt.

Maybe I was searching for the wrong thing. Maybe I needed to start with something simpler, like the destruction of Fold. Or the ruby heirloom.

I grabbed another book, skimming the first page. *Roanfire's Territories*. A possibility. I tucked the book under my arm and stole another.

"Who taught you to read?" Ropert pulled a chair from a nearby table and sank into it. "I don't remember you being tutored."

"Mayama taught me." I set two books on the table. "When I first came to Daram, she sat with me in the evenings after supper."

"When I went out to roughhouse." Ropert shook his head, as if he regretted passing up on the opportunity.

"I can teach you. When we return to Daram."

"It's too late for me."

"It's never too late. We can start now." I added a third book to my growing pile, opened it, and pointed to the word *Roanfire*. "Look for this word."

He leaned forward, studying the black letters. "Alright." He set his palms on the table, stood, and went to work.

The table was stacked with books. Ropert flipped through them, his eyes red from scanning the letters for his assigned word. I read everything he pointed out to me. Roanfire's trade routes, treaties with Toleah and the Glacial Empire. The shift from our nomadic ancestors to the civilization of a monarchy. I read of famines, wars with Toleah, and the Leviathan pirates. The discovery of Glacier Lake's rich soil, and the marble quarry of Pedre.

Where were the books on Fold? The Dead Forest? The Leviathans? Not even a hint of the White Wardent appeared in anything. Perhaps he was just a legend, a fantastical being created for children.

Ropert's hand squeezed my arm.

I pried my eyes from the book, blinking at him.

"The library is closing."

Already? I'd just started. The librarian stood by the door, checking names in her ledger as patrons slipped out.

I rubbed my eyes. "I suppose we can come back tomorrow." I stood, my legs aching. The room spun. I gripped the edge of the table.

"Dagger?" Ropert took my arm.

"I'm alright."

He guided me to the doors. "You really should have tried to rest today."

"I did." I tapped the side of my nose, reminding him of what happened every time I closed my eyes.

He pursed his lips.

I had to find something. Anything. One of these days, my lungs wouldn't open. The fire would roast me from the inside out.

# CHAPTER 18

# QUEEN DAMITA

*T*he door creaked. I opened one eye, the light from Adalyah's candle casting long shadows across the furniture. She waved two maidservants into the room. One rushed to build up the fire while the other arranged a tray of breakfast items on the small table.

No dream? A full night without the nightmare burning through my mind? I felt renewed, energized, like I could take on the entire court of Meldron.

Adalyah moved to the arched windows, pulling the curtains aside. A hazy orange glow fell across the furniture. Outside, thick clusters of snow whirled in the wind.

I sat up.

Adalyah's hand flew to her chest. "Forgive us, my lady. We didn't mean to wake you." She frantically waved the maidservants from the room.

"It's alright." I was accustomed to early mornings and hard drills. This would give me more time to scour the library for information on the White Wardent.

Slipping from the bed, I moved to the breakfast tray. All this? For me? It was just like the trays Mayama made for the duke and duchess in Daram. Fresh baked bread, warm butter, raspberry spread, and cheese decorated with sprigs of thyme. Peppermint leaves swirled in the mug, the invigorating steam rising in the sunlight.

Sinking to the chair by the fire, I slathered a slice of bread with the raspberry spread. "I'd like to visit the library again. Do you know when it opens?"

Adalyah straightened the blankets on my bed. "You have an appointment with the seamstress today, my lady."

I paused mid-bite. "Oh, right."

"But she is an early riser. I don't think you will wait long. You should have plenty of time this afternoon." She moved to the door. "Enjoy your breakfast, my lady. I will return shortly to help you dress."

"No need. Thank you, Adalyah."

Her hand paused on the door.

How could I be so careless? *You needn't express gratitude. It is their duty to serve you.* Illorce had drilled that into me over and over.

Adalyah graciously ignored my blunder, bowed her head, and opened the door. "Sir Ropert. Good morning."

"Is Lady Brendagger awake?"

"Come in, Ropert," I said.

He slipped inside, and Adalyah closed the door.

Rubbing his shoulders, he joined me by the fire. "My room is freezing. Flaming feathers, Dagger. Is that your breakfast?"

"Well, it sure isn't yours."

He snatched a slice of bread and dug into the cheese. "I could get used to this."

A harsh knock sounded on the door, impatient and quick.

"Enter."

A meaty woman with a prominent scowl pushed into the room, Adalyah on her heels. Needles stuck in the collar of her blouse, and a measuring tape hung across the back of her neck. Another maidservant followed, carrying a stool.

The seamstress waved to the maidservant, who placed the stool in the center of the open floor. "I am Seamstress Shima. This is Molly, my apprentice. Your bodyguard is welcome to stay, but privacy is not my concern. I have two days to finish this dress, so I shall be quick and to the point."

Ropert looked at me with pity, the bread and cheese bulging in his cheek. "I'll return when you're done." He slipped outside.

If only I could go with him.

"Up, up, now." Seamstress Shima clapped her hands at me.

I rose, stepping onto the stool.

"Hold out your arms." She slipped the measuring tape from her neck and wrapped it around my waist. She mumbled a number to her apprentice, who wrote the figure in a tiny leather-bound book.

The measuring tape felt violating as it moved to my hips, bust, shoulders, and arms. Did she have to pull so tight? Especially around my ribs?

"You understand, Duchess Caitelyn should have ordered this gown months ago. I have no choice but to use a ready-made dress and tailor it to you." She swung her measuring tape over her neck. "Off now."

I stepped down, and Molly snatched up the stool.

"Questions?"

"I . . . uh . . ."

"No? Alright then. We shall return on the morrow for a fitting." Shima opened the door, rushed Molly out, and shut it behind her.

Why did I suddenly feel like an abandoned puppy? I had to get out of here. I didn't need help to get dressed, though it would have made the task of cinching the ribbons easier.

The sooner I could get to the library, the better. There was so much work to do. Hopefully, the librarian didn't clean up the stacks of books Ropert and I had worked so hard to find.

I trudged across the courtyard in ankle-deep snow through the market square. The stained glass creation of the queen from my dreams beckoned me to discover her secrets, while the crimson curse hanging about her neck dared me to try.

I would figure this out.

Pushing through the doors, I dusted the snow from my shoulders, signed the ledger, and homed in on the area Ropert and I had been combing through the night before. All the books remained, organized by not-yet-read to possibilities to unhelpful. At least three dozen books were piled here, and in reading most of those, I'd found nothing.

Draping my cloak over a chair, I turned back to the shelves. How many had I passed over that could contain what I needed? Their leather-bound covers were hiding the truth.

I pulled a thin, greenish book from the shelf: *The Leaves of Havenglow, a Tale of Destruction.* The title didn't sound promising, but neither did the others. I flipped it open.

*Havenglow. The forest of plenty. The shore of our fathers. The heart of Roanfire. In a single night, it came to ruin. I shall tell you how.*

I sank to a chair and continued reading.

*Some will say that I lie, that what I say cannot be true. All because Fold was obliterated and no one lived to tell the tale. What I write may not be believed, but it is history. A history that should not be forgotten.*

It couldn't be. Had I found it? I set the book on the table, slid my chair in, and leaned forward.

The author described the city of Fold exactly how I'd seen it in my dreams. The way the garrison stood on the cliffs overlooking the sea, the road winding down to the wharf, the ships bobbing in the water. They described their queen, a wise and fair ruler, with hair as red as fire and eyes as blue as the sea. Queen Damita. At least I had a name for her now.

Then the Leviathans appeared. They ravaged the shore, set fire to the ships, and stormed the garrison. But it lacked the horror I experienced in my dreams.

A violet light burst from the tallest tower.

I turned the page.

*It destroyed everything. The woods. The Leviathan pirates. The people. The animals.*

*But how did I survive? How was I able to see it?*

*I was a boy, hunting in the woods the night the Leviathans attacked. When I saw the smoke and the fire glowing through the trees, I climbed.*

*The light from the tower didn't reach me. If it had, this tale would be lost. I would have died along with the woods of Havenglow.*

*This is how the Dead Forest was born.*

*Beware. Fold is cursed.*

That was it? I leaned back, staring at the black ink and the empty last page. Mayama was right; my dream was a vision. But this book had given me no real answers. It had only confirmed what I already knew.

I slammed the book closed.

"Might I help you find something?"

My eyes shot up to the librarian.

"You've torn this section apart." She nodded to the stacks of books on the table.

"I'm not really sure *what* I am looking for." I rubbed the bridge of my nose. "Have you heard of a crimson jewel, a ruby, that was an heirloom to the Noirfonika family? Like the one on the stained glass image of Queen Damita there?" I pointed to the window.

She studied the image that she had probably seen every day and tipped her head as if she had never noticed the jewel before. "I have not."

I slumped in the chair, ribs aching.

She tipped her head, tapping her chin with a finger. "How is your penmanship?"

"I wouldn't consider myself a scribe, but I have considerable skill with letters."

"Come with me."

What was she up to? I gathered my cloak, following her to the back of the library. She collected a candelabra from a nearby table and stopped at a wrought iron door.

"Some of these documents were retrieved from the Fold Garrison after it was destroyed."

My heart thundered, my chest tightening. *Please, please, please, let there be answers behind this door.*

Keys jangled at her waist. The lock clicked, and she pushed it open on hinges creaking with age and neglect.

Candlelight fell across shelves lined with grit and cobwebs. Scrolls and documents, yellowed with age, looked ready to crumble at the slightest touch. A table stood against an empty wall holding scraps of cloth, a vial of oil, an inkwell and quill, and a large, blank-paged book.

The librarian set the candelabra on the table. "You may look through these on one condition."

My fingers ached to unravel them. "Anything."

She pulled an old, battered scroll from a shelf and set it on the table. Gently opening the flask of oil, she tipped it onto the cloth, saturating the edge. The smell was revolting.

"Dab the oil on the parchment just like so." She touched the fabric to the edge of the scroll. The parched paper drank deeply of the liquid, becoming pliable again. She opened the scroll an inch at a time. "Too little oil, and the paper will break. Too much, and the ink on the document will bleed. This is a task normally given to an experienced scribe, but I have not found the time. These have sat here unread for centuries." She looked over the shelves. "Who knows what mysteries they contain."

My hands shook.

"Your task will be to transcribe what you find in these scrolls into this book." She gestured to the open book on the table.

I pushed my sleeves up to my elbows. I was ready.

She smiled. "Let me fetch you an apron. You don't want to get ink on that beautiful dress."

*My lovely Elenara,*

*What joy you bring to my weak heart. Your cherubic smile and flawless laughter have brought many smiles to my face during the four years I have been blessed to hold you in my arms.*

*My heart aches that I shall not see you blossom into womanhood, for I have taken ill, and no healer or physician can determine the cause for my weakness. Every day, I grow more faint and pale. I can no longer walk with you through the beautiful gardens and catch the butterflies that you so love. I know I must soon be brought down to the grave.*

*My sweet daughter, although I may be gone from this world when you should fully understand this letter, know that I am with you always.*

*This inheritance was given to me by my mother, and to her by her mother. It has been in the Noirfonika family for years beyond count, and I leave this legacy with you.*

*As my mother carried this ruby about her neck, I felt her near. I pray to the Phoenix that you too shall feel my love as you wear this treasure.*

*Let the crimson of this ruby remind you every day that I love you. Take care, my beautiful daughter.*

*With all my love,*
*Your mother, Queen Oleah of Roanfire*

This was it. This was the ruby of my nightmares. But what did it mean? This letter revealed nothing I hadn't already suspected.

I scrutinized my writing, re-reading the letter. A gift given out of love? But it had destroyed Queen Damita. It devoured her, an entire city, a forest.

There had to be more.

I turned, facing the shelf littered with scrolls. It was here somewhere.

Carefully, I set the scroll aside and reached for another. Following the same cautious procedure, I discovered a boring document chronicling the first encounters with the Glacial Empire.

Before I dove into another, the librarian returned, informing me that the library was closing.

"Can I come back tomorrow?" I asked.

"Oh, yes, please. I think you've missed your calling as a scribe. Your penmanship is excellent." She handed me the key to this chamber filled with treasures and answers.

I would spend all day here tomorrow.

Ink stains and the smell of oil lingered on my fingers as I made my way back to the castle. The clouds darkened as the sun disappeared, the temperature dropping. My stomach grumbled. I hadn't eaten since breakfast.

As I opened the door to the elegantly furnished room, I saw Ropert stop by the fireplace. What was he doing in here? And had he been pacing?

He glared at me, his blue eyes igniting. "Where have you been? I've been searching everywhere for you!"

I closed my eyes. I shouldn't have left the castle without him. I had been so eager to escape after the visit from Shima, I'd completely forgotten I *needed* a bodyguard.

"I was at the library."

"For the sake of the Phoenix, Dagger—you can't go alone!" He threw his hands up. "Have you any idea how I would look if anyone discovered that Lady Brendagger was out in the city without her bodyguard? And what if you'd been attacked? A mercenary is still out there."

"I am a soldier. I can fight."

"Not in your condition. Your broken ribs and the aftermath of the poison has left you weak. You couldn't lift your sword if you wanted to."

How dare he say that! I wasn't helpless. I glared back at him. "I've been poked, prodded, and thoroughly invaded with no regard to my privacy. I needed to get out."

Ropert exhaled through his teeth. Turning to the fire, he stared at it for a long while. "Our arguing is getting nowhere," he said. "Can we agree to never leave each other again?"

I swallowed my anger; this was my fault. I'd made the mistake. "Alright."

He sank to a chair, pushing the tray of supper in my direction, but I was uninterested. Strange how a sour attitude ruined a good meal.

"This came from Duchess Caitelyn today. Fortin read it to me." He pulled a scroll from his belt.

Not another letter. My eyes ached. I didn't want to—couldn't— read another word. Still, I set the bowl down and opened the scroll.

*Lady Brendagger,*

*I am relieved to hear that you have arrived safely in Meldron and that all is well with Ropert. My heart aches to hear of Illorce's illness. He is a good man. And it is terribly unfortunate that Sergeant Fortin has taken such a devastating blow.*

*In this letter, you will find a message to recite to Prince Sander Noirfonika when you are announced at the coronation. Please be sure that you have every word memorized.*

*It grieves me to tell you that Daram is under full siege by the Leviathan pirates. We have lost many good soldiers. Commander Holdan is among the fallen.*

*We have taken refuge in the inner fortification. I plead with you to confer with our new king and beg him for help.*

*Make haste. Our lives depend on you.*

*Duchess of Daram, Caitelyn*

I looked at Ropert, something raw and scratchy invading my throat.

He nodded gravely.

Holdan? Commander Holdan was dead? The duchess had mentioned the siege in her last letter, but I did not realize the situation was this dire.

Ikane knew this would happen.

Was Mayama alright? And what had become of Eamon? Had he been killed in one of his drunken stupors? I had abandoned my home in its most critical hour.

Ikane. May he rot on the sea floor in a grave of ships.

I let him go. I should have turned him over to the Phoenix soldiers the moment I found out, but I let him go.

I stood. "We need to go back. We need to help them."

"What can two soldiers do?" Ropert asked. "As exceptional as we are, we need an army. The duchess is right. You must ask the new king for aid at the coronation. We can do so much more from here."

My legs ached to move, to run, to fly all the way back to Daram, but pacing in front of the fireplace was all I could do. "The coronation isn't until the day after tomorrow. Daram could fall by then. Something must be done now. Adalyah!"

She appeared instantly.

"I must speak with Prince Sander straightaway. How do I go about getting an audience?" I didn't care if I sounded rude or naïve. Daram needed help, and I would do anything to defend it.

Her brows furrowed. "Forgive me, my lady. But all audiences with the prince have been postponed until after the coronation. No one—"

"What of the archduke? Daram is under siege, and it is about to give way to the Leviathan pirates. Roanfire will be exposed."

Adalyah swallowed.

"Please."

"I . . . I will see what I can do."

"Thank you." I bit my lip. I wasn't good at this. I'd thanked her again.

"Shall I help you prepare for bed?" she asked. "We have lavender scrubs that promote good sleep, and one hundred brush strokes through the hair will make it shine with health."

I blinked at her. Beauty and sleep were the farthest things from my mind.

Ropert patted my shoulder, moving to the door. "She would like that," he told Adalyah then walked to his own chamber to sleep.

"I suppose . . ."

# CHAPTER 19

# FIGHTING ON TWO FRONTS

Each candle Adalyah extinguished plunged the room further and further into darkness until the only light emanated from the glowing fire in the hearth, crackling and spitting with life. Just like the ruby in my nightmares.

She slipped outside and closed the door.

Rolling over, I tucked my hands under my chin, the smell of oil lingering on my fingers. Would I dream tonight? Would I wake with fire and smoke curling in my lungs?

I scrunched my eyes shut, the stained glass window of Queen Damita and the ruby burning behind my eyelids.

Why did this happen to me? I was just a soldier, and it was all I'd ever wanted to be. I had no desire for more.

I had to end this nightmare. Tomorrow, I would lock myself in the little room in the back of the library. The answers were there.

Rolling onto my back, the words of King Myron's letter to Eamon ran through my mind.

*I cannot bring myself to end her life. She is of great worth to Roanfire.*

And Faslight. She said King Myron knew of my value to his kingdom. It was why I still lived.

But why? Because of the stone? What did it have to do with me?

I rolled to my side again.

Maybe King Myron would have answers. But would he see me? He was old and frail. Some even said his mind wasn't as clear as it had been the year before. Would he even remember sending a baby halfway across Roanfire, leaving her on a young general's doorstep?

Perhaps he would remember but deny it. He said I was a threat to the union with the Glacial Empire. The Glacial princess was here now, the bride-to-be for Prince Sander. I could ruin everything—

A cold hand pressed against my mouth.

My eyes flew open, and my hands shot up, grabbing the shadow's solid arm.

"Kea," a smooth voice whispered. Green light burned beneath its hood where its left eye should be. "Please be still."

Ikane pushed the hood from his head, his hair flowing free, wild. He was as handsome as the day we first met. Stubble covered his jaw, vacant where the scar trailed along the side of his cheek.

What was he doing here?

I jerked his hand from my mouth. "How did you get in here?" Why was I whispering? He was a pirate, a traitor. I needed to turn him in. I should be screaming at the top of my lungs.

He jerked his head to the window. It hadn't been open before. He'd climbed the wall? Three stories up?

"I warned you what I would do if I ever saw you again." I sat up.

"The Leviathans have made their move." He stood, pacing beside my bed. "I don't know what to do. I am powerless against them."

"You are their prince." I slipped from the bed, eyeing the door. He was fast—I had to be discreet. If I made him think I was just stocking the fire, I could get closer. "Just tell them to stop."

"Don't you think I would have done that if I could?" He tore his hands through his hair. "I have six brothers, Kea. All princes, just like me. It is not up to one. The majority rules. I have one brother on my side. One." He whirled in his pacing, turning his back to me.

Now.

I sprinted for the door.

His grip pinched. My body jerked back. His hand curled around my throat, driving me backward. My spine hit the bedpost, my head jarring at the impact. Was I that weak? Why couldn't I defend myself against him? His skill, his speed, his strength . . . they were unmatched.

"Why do you keep making me do this?" His green eye flared dangerously. "Listen to me. Lady Serah's assassination, the two attacks on the road to Meldron, my brother did it. Because *I* refused. I am not your enemy. Why can't you see that?"

Air moved through my nose, rapid and shaky.

"He meant to kill you, Kea. I did everything in my power to protect you." His grip softened, his eye losing its brilliant smolder.

"Why?" The word shot through my teeth. He was toying with my mind, drawing on my heart. It was what an enemy would do.

"Daram is the smallest of the coastal strongholds. If the Leviathans could breach it, they would have access to Roanfire from both land and sea. They could flank the other fortifications and launch a full invasion."

He let me pull his hand from my throat. "What does that have to do with Lady Serah? What does that have to do with my assassination?"

"You're intelligent, Kea. Why do you think? What is happening to Daram right now?"

I swallowed, wishing with all my heart I could go back and defend it.

"They need help. Do you think King Myron would send aid if no one from Daram came to respect his son at his coronation? It's a slap in the face. It is treason. Daram would be abandoned and left to its own devices."

"King Myron knows Daram is too vital in keeping you rats from invading."

His eyes closed, his face contorting as if I'd stabbed him in the chest. He turned away. "Daram is lost."

"Don't say that."

He buried his face in his hands. Did he really hurt that much over this? He almost looked like he was telling the truth.

He leaned heavily on the mantelpiece, the fire illuminating his frame. "I don't know what to do." His head dropped. "I . . . I have been ordered to assassinate Prince Sander."

I blinked. What did he just say? "You wouldn't."

"I don't have a choice."

"There is always a choice."

He slammed his palm on the mantle, green eye flaring. "I have one brother on my side, Kea. *One*. They will kill him if I refuse to do this."

"Your own brothers would stoop to blackmail you?"

"It's the bane of being royal."

This had gone on long enough. I had to put an end to this. I inched toward my sword that was leaning against the desk by the window. He saw the move. His eyes tracked clean, falling on my weapon. He made no move to stop me.

"What do I do? Do I kill Prince Sander and spare my brother? Or do I refuse and spare Roanfire . . . and you?"

Me? How dare he make this about me. He had no right. He died the day I found the vile crest on his shoulder.

"Daram will prevail. It has withstood centuries of onslaught from your kind. And when I return, I will see that it will withstand centuries more." My hand was inches from the hilt.

"You can't go back to Daram," he said.

I grabbed my sword. Why did it feel so heavy? Had I become that weak? Was the poison affecting me that much?

I took it in both hands, pointing it at his throat. "Daram is my home."

"If you return, you *will* die."

"Then so be it." My arms burned, my sword trembling.

Ikane calmly pushed the tip of my sword to the side. "I can't lose you both." His eyes shimmered. "If you stay in Meldron, I will spare Prince Sander. But if you return to Daram, I will complete my errand."

He was making me sacrifice my home for the life of Prince Sander.

Something coiled around my chest, squeezing my heart. He was killing me all over again. My hands tightened on the hilt. Everything blurred, my eyes burning.

My sword raced for his chest.

Ikane slipped aside, trapping the blade under his arm, pinning my hand. Pain shot up my wrist as he twisted. The sword dropped.

My fist flew at his jaw. He caught my hand. I was too weak, too slow, too gullible. A sob escaped, my chest too tight to hold it in as I struggled to pull away. His arms encircled me, pinning me against his solid chest.

"I am so sorry, Little Brendagger." His breath was hot against my hair.

I wanted to dig my nails into his skin, squeeze until his bones cracked. Oh, why did he have to be a Leviathan? Why were we destined to be enemies?

Tears burned down my cheeks. "I will kill you."

His arms jerked as he pulled something from his belt. His grip around me eased, and I looked down. He held a knife between us. "I can't keep fighting on two fronts. My brothers hate me. You and Eamon despise me because I am one of them. I have no place to go, nowhere to make a stand. All I want is peace, and I can't even manage that."

My eyes dashed from the blade to his face. Was that an actual tear streaking down his scarred cheek?

"Overlook this mark on my shoulder, or end it now."

Why did this hurt so much? He fought to defend me, lying the entire time. He defied his blood. He willingly sacrificed the life of his one loyal brother to save Roanfire.

He was a Leviathan who cared. I couldn't let him go, but neither could I accept him.

I pulled away, clawing my own shoulders, staring at the floor. "Leave."

"Please, don't go back to Daram."

"I said 'leave'!"

He pulled his mottled gray hood over his head, his green eye glowing faintly within the shadows. Sheathing the dagger in his belt, he moved to the open window. Was he actually going down the same way he came up?

He stepped onto the desk, swinging his legs over the ledge, and glanced over his shoulder. "Stay in Meldron."

A fresh wave of tears burned my eyes. How was it possible to love and hate someone so much? "Go."

He jumped.

Was he trying to kill himself? I lunged for the window, leaning out. A shadow plunged down the side of the castle. He landed, a thick snowbank piled against the wall breaking his fall. Rolling forward, he leapt to his feet.

He glanced up.

I ducked back into the room, face burning. I should have known. Leviathans had skeletons of steel. He could have jumped from four stories and not shattered a bone.

Closing the window, I latched it and drew the curtains.

I had to help Daram, but Ropert was right; I could do more from here.

And now I had no choice.

"Dagger? What are you still doing in bed?" Ropert shook my shoulder.

I groaned, rolled over, and pulled the blanket from my face.

His brows furrowed. "You've been crying." He eased onto the edge of the bed. "You never cry."

"I'll be fine."

He placed a warm hand on my shoulder. "I'm worried, too, so let's make ourselves useful. King Myron will send an army, and we will return roaring like lions at those blasted pirates." He slapped my leg. "We need to rebuild your strength. Get up, and get dressed. I'll be back in five minutes."

We sparred in the courtyard, each motion taking so much more energy from me than it should have. I could barely support my sword. After only a few brief minutes, I was panting through my aching ribs, begging for a respite.

"We have a lot of work ahead of us." Ropert sheathed his sword.

"It's the poison. Ikane said—" What was I doing talking about him?

"What did Ikane say?"

"I don't want to talk about it."

"You brought it up."

"He said it would take up to two weeks to clear my system. There. Are you happy?"

He opened the door to my room. "That wasn't so hard, was it?"

A man stood by the fireplace, his opulent clothing fighting for attention with his jewels and trinkets. His flaming red hair and beard grew brighter by the light of the fire.

"Archduke Goldest." I bowed. I should have been more careful with my choice of wardrobe. Shirt and trousers were not a lady's proper attire. And my boots were muddy.

He twisted a ring on his finger, stepping around the armchair. "I was informed that you had an urgent matter to take to the king concerning Daram. How desperate is the situation? I don't wish to bother my uncle with superfluous issues, now of all times."

"Daram is about to fall, Your Grace. I hoped to wait and address Prince Sander at the coronation tomorrow evening, but Daram could be lost by then. Duchess Caitelyn has informed me that the soldiers have barricaded themselves in the inner fort. If we do not reclaim the Daram keep, the Leviathans will have free rein over the entire southern half of Roanfire." My legs shook. He still hadn't asked me to rise.

Goldest stroked his ringed fingers over his perfectly groomed beard. "That seems urgent enough. I will speak to King Myron. But I am afraid I will not have the chance to do so until this evening."

"Thank you for taking the time to see me, Your Grace."

He walked to the door and stopped. "Lady Brendagger. Next time you beg for an audience, do not keep me waiting."

"Yes, Your Grace." My face burned.

The door closed.

I stood upright, swallowing hard.

"He has a way of making you feel as small as a mouse within the claws of a cat," Adalyah said.

"I had another description in mind." Ropert moved to the fire. "But that works, too."

Adalyah turned to me. "You are not a typical noblewoman. You bow with the rigidity of a soldier, and you allow me to state my opinions of a man third in line to the throne of Roanfire without reprimand."

Oh, feathers.

"Don't you worry about me. I think we need more nobles like you. But I do suggest that you learn to curtsy a little more fluidly. I'd be happy to help you rehearse."

"Later." I set my sword on the desk. "I need to get back to the library."

"Let's get you dressed first."

My fingers ached as I pulled an old journal with a cracked spine from the dusty shelf. I'd worked for the better part of the day and uncovered nothing. Perhaps I'd found everything there was to find?

I set the book on the table, stretched my neck, and opened it. Pages spilled lose.

*Journal of Yotherna, the White Wardent.*

My heart thumped. The White Wardent? The myth that everyone believed was only a fictional character? His words stared at me, open, ready to be read.

*King Leonard's daughter, at the tender age of three, perished but a moment ago. I can no longer stand by and watch.*

*I am ashamed. I should not have forged the jewel for Queen Rion. I knew I was tampering with magic that should have been left untouched. I thought I was doing the right thing. The Phoenix Stone was supposed to bring power to the Noirfonika family.*

*She promised me she would do as I instructed. But greed always leaves one wanting more. It never satisfies.*

*She has not kept her promise. She has become impatient and rash and has tainted my creation so that it is now a curse to her lineage. Those of her heritage that receive this heirloom are dying far too young.*

*Due to her nature of corrupting magic, she shall emerge from her jewel not as a glorious phoenix of light and power, but as a foul curse upon Roanfire, suffocating all life with her gluttonous lust for it.*

*The Phoenix Stone must be destroyed.*

*I wish I could do it. Undo what I should not have done.*

*But it falls on the ones cursed by its greed. Only two daughters of the Noirfonika lineage remain: Queen Moriah and Princess Damita. If they fail, I will have no choice but to cause the line of the Noirfonika family to become barren of female inheritance.*

*I pray it will not come to that.*

That was the end of his journal entry for that date, but it picked up again ten years later.

*Queen Moriah has failed. Rion claimed her life the moment she discovered my treachery. The Phoenix Stone has been passed on to the innocent Princess Damita. She knows nothing of the curse, and I could not meet with her. I fear it will be too late by the time I make the journey to Fold for her coronation.*

*Yet I hold great hope for her, for she is a resilient woman. She may yet be the one to destroy the curse.*

*But she cannot do it alone. The four kingdoms must unite with her to completely rid the land of the effects of my foolish deed. I have determined the keys for her success and have given my report to Emperor Skarand of the Glacial Empire for safekeeping. He has been charged with . . .*

The writing became illegible. I was forced to skip to the next lines that I could make out, dated one month later.

*Fold has been crushed by the Leviathan pirates, and the newly crowned Queen Damita has been found dead in the Woods of Havenglow.*

*There is nothing more I can do.*

*This is but a taste of what she will bring if she channels her rebirth.*

*Now I must administer the potion to King Tallone to ensure that no more daughters are born heirs to Rion's serial madness. I simply cannot risk another child being slaughtered by her greed.*

*My plan is not foolproof. Given time, Rion may yet rise from the ashes.*

I set the quill on the desk, leaning back in the chair. My hands shook. My nose burned the way it did after a nightmare.

It all made sense, Eamon's note from King Myron. I was heir to this curse, the first daughter of Roanfire in four hundred years. I had to do this? I had to destroy something that powerful? Something the White Wardent had created—

Wait. I scanned the document again, checking the timeline. I hadn't made an error. The White Wardent, Yotherna, had forged the Phoenix Stone *and* had lived to witness the destruction of the Fold Garrison. That meant he was at least six hundred eighty-seven years of age when he had last written in this book. He wouldn't be alive now. That would make him nearly two thousand years old.

A soft knock pulled me back to the room. Ropert leaned in. When did he leave?

"Dagger. We have a situation. Seamstress Shima is waiting in your room."

I stood, grabbing my cloak from the back of the chair. "She should have specified a time. I can't sit around all day waiting."

"Hurry. We don't have time for setbacks. The coronation is tomorrow."

I followed him from the library and back to the castle, my mind reeling over the information I'd stumbled across.

Faslight said things would get worse, much worse. The Phoenix Stone was a curse, and it was only just awakening.

# CHAPTER 20

# THE CORONATION

Adalyah's hand swirled through the water, the smell of rosemary and lavender rising from the steam in the large wooden tub. Serving boys dumped the last of their buckets into it as a lady's maid draped a heavy towel over the rim.

"Nothing like a nice, hot bath before a coronation." Adalyah winked. "Take your time. I'll return in an hour to help you dress."

When the water became tepid and my fingers shriveled to raisins, I climbed out, wrapping the thick towel around my body.

A knock sounded on the door. Adalyah was right on time.

"Enter."

The door opened. Seamstress Shima bolted into the room. She glanced at me. "Good. You've bathed."

Molly entered, carrying a gown the color of a blue summer sky. It shimmered like water, rippling white and silver.

Shima set her hands on her hips. "And where is Adalyah?"

"I'm right here." Adalyah rushed inside, closing the door softly.

"Over here." Shima stood by the full-length mirror in the corner, handing me a white shift. "Put this on."

I squirmed and tugged at the silky fabric over my damp skin.

"The dress." Shima snapped her fingers. Molly brought the dress forward, and all three ladies helped slip the heavy gown over my head.

Shima tugged the cords hard. It crushed my ribs, agitating the bruises. "Not so tight."

"Pain is the price of beauty," she said.

She was going to break my ribs all over again. The last thing I needed was to pass out while addressing the new king. "Loosen it."

"But—"

"Loosen it."

Shima sighed. "As you wish."

The tightness eased.

She stepped back, scrutinizing her work.

"It is another masterpiece, mistress Shima." Molly smoothed the wide skirt, revealing gathered sections adorned with silver embellishments.

"Well?" Shima asked expectantly.

I glanced at my reflection. This was not me. My skin glowed with the cultivated oils in the soaps. And where did these curves come from?

The wide neckline, embellished with silver flowers, drew attention to my collarbone. Dangling sleeves trailed from my elbows to the ground. It was the most beautiful and uncomfortable thing I'd ever donned.

"It's lovely."

"It helps when the woman wearing it is just as stunning." Shima smiled, smoothing an invisible wrinkle, gazing at my visage in the mirror. "We must be off. We have three more fittings before the hour is over. Come, Molly."

They bustled from the chamber, closing the door.

Adalyah waved me to the desk, pulling the chair out. "Of all the ladies I've waited on, none have looked as lovely as you do now."

"I feel . . . exposed." I tugged on the neckline, trying to bring it higher.

Adalyah ran her fingers through my damp hair.

Hours had passed by the time Adalyah finished braiding, coiling, and twisting ribbons and pearls into my hair. She turned her attention to my face, producing a pale powder for my nose and some sort of vibrant red ointment for my lips. They felt heavy and sticky.

She picked up a charcoal stick, moving it to my eyes.

"No more." I stood. "That's enough."

"Trust me. It will bring out the blue in your eyes."

"Dagger?" Ropert called through the door.

Thank the Phoenix he was here. "Come in."

"The guests are starting to—" He froze in the doorway, bright blue eyes staring.

Was this my Ropert? His boots and leather belt shined with polish. The crest of Daram sat proudly on his shoulder, his military badges gleaming against the pale blue of his tunic.

Why couldn't I wear something like that?

Adalyah tugged my arm. "It is time."

I moved to Ropert. "Well?"

"I . . . uh . . . you look . . ." He cleared his throat, shaking his head. "You look good. Very regal." He held his arm out.

My hand trembled as it slipped through his elbow. "Don't leave my side," I whispered.

"Never." He led me into the hallway bursting with light. Extra candles had been lit for this special occasion. Music and voices echoed through the corridor.

My feet stopped just outside the doors. An annoyed couple pushed by us.

"What's wrong?" Ropert asked.

"I just need a minute." I tried to gather a deep breath, but the gown restricted the movement. I rubbed my sweating palms on my thighs. Darn this dress. It was too slick to do any good.

I'd dreamed of meeting Prince Sander for so long. He was a legend among the soldiers. An idol.

He was my father.

I swallowed, the realization weighing on every part of my body. What if I said something wrong? What if I offended him? Did he even know who I was?

"Come on, Dagger." Ropert tightened his arm, pulling me closer. "You can do this."

We stepped through the doors.

Nobles, dressed in their finest attire, filled the room with a myriad of colors and jewels. Gilded chandeliers hung from the vaulted ceiling, illuminating the room like the sun on a bright summer day. Marble stairs covered with a majestic red carpet flowed to the floor like a waterfall.

At the other end of the room stood a dais with two golden thrones. Two figures sat there. One was a woman in a white dress. And the other . . .

My breath caught. It was him.

My heart thundered as we waited in the reception line, sweat growing under my arms. Duchess Caitelyn's carefully constructed letter ran through my head faster than a charging brigade.

Prince Sander smiled, greeting everyone with the dignity of a king. His deep-auburn hair contrasted beautifully with the golden crown upon his brow. His russet beard was neatly trimmed close to his face, and his broad shoulders rivaled Ropert's, filling his crimson tunic.

Each step forward made my heart thunder to a new level. I was going to make a fool of myself.

"Name and province?" a man with impeccable posture asked.

"Lady Brendagger of Daram." My mouth was dry.

The man turned and announced my arrival.

Prince Sander's head snapped up. It was almost imperceptible, but his shoulders tensed. Was he threatened by me?

I saw myself in him—the wide forehead, the slender nose, the high cheekbones.

Ropert released my arm and stepped back. I suddenly felt abandoned.

Trembling, I spread the skirt wide, slipping one leg behind the other. "Prince Sander. Princess Lonacheska."

"Welcome, Lady Brendagger." His voice was clear and powerful, resonating throughout the chamber. He waved a hand, granting me permission to rise.

My foot slipped. Hopefully, no one noticed.

What was I supposed to say? Oh, Caitelyn's letter.

"Duke Adair and Duchess Caitelyn send their deepest regrets for not being able to attend this historic occasion." My voice shook with every beat of my heart. "They hope that by defending the coast from the Leviathan pirates, they can show their undying loyalty and respect. Please accept their highest compliments as they protect and serve their future king."

There was a pause. Had I recited her words properly?

"They will be sorely missed this evening," he said.

The Glacial princess smiled. Her flawless skin glowed against her white-gold hair, shimmering like sunbeams down her spine. Her amber eyes flickered with sunlight against her white gown. Although slender, she looked as sturdy as the icy mountains themselves.

"Please enjoy yourself this evening, Lady Brendagger." Her voice was deeper than I expected but musical and clear.

The next nobleman was announced.

That was it, the end of the conversation. Something nagged for me to stay, to plead Daram's situation right now. Why wait? There would be no better time than this.

Ropert took my arm.

It was better this way. The last thing Duchess Caitelyn wanted was for me to deviate from her instructions. My fingers dug into Ropert's skin as he escorted me from the dais. My legs wobbled, like I had been running this entire time. Slipping into the crowd, I sagged against him, all strength drained.

"You did beautifully." He patted my hand.

"Next time, you do it."

He chuckled.

The music grew livelier. Prince Sander stood, offering Princess Lonacheska his hand. They descended the stairs in perfect harmony. He took her in his arms in the middle of the Great Hall, leading her in a dance. Something shone in his eyes—he cared for her. It wasn't just an act for the people. The love he had for this woman was genuine.

My heart flipped. If she knew about me . . .

The Great Hall swarmed with dancers, Prince Sander and Princess Lonacheska blurring between them.

None of that mattered. Daram needed help. The archduke should have gotten back to me by now. I combed through the mingling couples for his opulent attire.

I was looking at Prince Sander again. My *father*. He was so poised, so proper, so handsome. Was he looking at me? A nobleman stepped between us.

I was imagining things. *Focus, Kea. You have a job to do.*

There. The archduke stood by a bunch of well-dressed courtiers. He was clothed finer than the prince, boasting jewels and lace ruffles around his collar and the cuffs of his sleeves.

"Wait here, Ropert," I said, pushing through the throng.

Archduke Goldest bade farewell to his friends, snaking off to another area of the room.

He saw me. I knew he had. He was avoiding me on purpose.

The clergyman's staff pounded against the stone floor, minstrels and guests silencing.

"Prince Sander Noirfonika," he called out. "Come forward."

Prince Sander ascended the stairs stoically. Reaching the man with the golden staff, he halted. Another man, garbed in rich red velvet and gold, appeared at the head of the stairs behind the man with the staff.

King Myron.

I had never seen the king in person, but given his opulent dress and the magnificent crown on his brow, this man couldn't be anyone else. His bearing was not the ideal of stately grace. The pallor of his skin was nearly as white as his hair, resembling freshly fallen snow. His back hunched, and his knees trembled under the weight of his aged body. It was a miracle he hobbled to the clergyman's side.

Prince Sander bowed to the king. My grandfather. The man who sent me away.

"My son," Myron began, his voice barely audible. "Today I am passing on the responsibility of protecting and governing Roanfire." He broke into a horrid coughing fit.

A servant appeared, steadying the old man. At a nod from the king, the clergyman continued in his stead.

"You have proven yourself ready to receive this burden. As many of the court will attest, you have demonstrated great loyalty for the welfare of the kingdom and have been righteous and just in all your dealings. You have adhered to the laws of the kingdom, tempered justice with mercy. Above all, you have dedicated your life in the defense of our coasts. This day, the people have spoken."

King Myron stepped forward with the aid of the servant. The clergyman took the crown from King Myron's head and held it before Prince Sander.

"Do you swear to keep peace in accordance with the principles of the Phoenix and the people?"

"I solemnly swear," Prince Sander said.

The clergyman placed the crown on his head.

Next, the clergyman removed the heavy cloak from the frail king's shoulders and held it before Prince Sander. "Will you keep all the domains rightful and rule with compassion and truth?"

"I solemnly swear."

The clergyman placed the heavy cloak on Prince Sander's broad shoulders. Then he took the scepter from King Myron's hand.

"Do you swear to defend Roanfire in justice and mercy?"

"I solemnly swear."

The scepter was placed in his hand.

Last, a sword was brought forward by another servant, lying on a red pillow that had a golden tassel on each corner. The clergyman raised the sword high.

"The people have spoken. Rise, King of Roanfire, and tend to your subjects."

The crowd cheered as the new king humbly rose to his feet, received the sword from the clergyman, and turned to his people. Ropert hollered, raising his fist high.

I blinked. This was the time to show my pride. I tried to cheer, but it came out weak and pathetic.

Sander looked at his bride who smiled proudly at him. His face was grave. He raised a hand for silence. The room grew still.

"I pledge, this day and forevermore, to uphold the same values of my father, King Myron." He used the same booming voice he had earlier, and the sound rippled through my chest. "In addition to his achievement of building our great economy, I will unite us with the Glacial Empire and provide law and order among all the people of Roanfire. I vow to not only protect and defend the land the same way my father has, but to utterly subjugate the entire race of the Leviathans! I will build an army forged from the greatest soldiers available under my reign. With the unity of Roanfire and the Glacial Empire, our militia will grow to be the strongest the world has ever seen."

The crowd cheered.

Why couldn't I join them? Was it because of Ikane? What was wrong with me? The ugly brand on his shoulder burned behind my eyelids. He was a Leviathan.

I shook my head. I knew my loyalties. I needed to obey, to uphold the law, to honor my king.

King Sander returned to his throne, sitting stiffly beside his bride.

As soon as the music resumed and attention turned from him to the festivities, his body sagged. He had just taken the whole of Roanfire on his shoulders.

# CHAPTER 21

# DARAM'S UNFORTUNATE PREDICAMENT

*A*rchduke Goldest held a beautiful lady in a bright yellow dress in his arms. They floated across the dance floor like leaves in the wind, resting only a moment as the music paused.

He'd been avoiding me all evening.

I pushed through the throng, my fingers inches from his shoulder when he bowed to another lady, took her hand, and swept her into a dance.

I had to admit he had stamina.

"Lady Brendagger."

I turned, scanning the crowd for the source of the voice. A tall, handsome figure moved toward me. His deep-brown hair was pulled back into a warrior's tail, combed and clean. So different from the night before.

How dare he show his face!

He wasn't here to . . . where was King Sander? I scanned the room, unable to find him.

Ikane extended a hand. "Dance with me."

I couldn't refuse. I would make a scene and embarrass Daram.

Setting my jaw, I took his hand, the hand that had helped me through nights tormented by fire. He slipped an arm around my waist, pulling me close. Heat soared through his touch, my heart bursting into a thousand butterflies. What should I do? Fight? Blend in? Enjoy the moment in his arms? It felt like treason.

He moved as gracefully as he fought, making my clumsy steps appear elegant and deliberate.

"That dress does something for your eyes," he said. "Like the sea after a storm."

Was he really trying to flatter me? "What are you doing here?"

"Monitoring you." He guided my body into a spin, the dress swirling. Pulling me back, his arms wrapped around me.

He was so close with his eyes of meadow and sky locking onto mine. He smelled of mint and sage with a hint of steel.

I had to stop letting him do this to me. I squirmed from his embrace. "You—"

"Might I steal your lovely partner for a moment?"

King Sander! He held his hand out for me to take. The King of Roanfire. My father. The butterflies in my stomach solidified, turning into thundering hoofbeats.

"Certainly, Your Majesty." Ikane bowed, stepping back. His eyes shot to mine, warning me. How I hated him.

Swallowing, I turned my attention to King Sander. His hand was warm and calloused, no stranger to demanding work. Something black smudged his fingers. Ink, perhaps? Unlike Archduke Goldest, he wore a single ring with the sigil of the firebird. His arms were firm, and his steps were as graceful as Ikane's, though rougher.

"You look very much like your mother," he whispered.

I stumbled. "You . . . you know who I am?"

His eyes burned blue, like the sky over the sea after a storm. Just what Ikane had said about mine. Lines creased the corners of his eyes.

"I've always known." He stopped our dance, pulling me close. He whispered in my ear. "You must leave. Now. It is not safe for you here."

Me? In danger? It was the king who was at risk.

He stepped back, tipping his head formally. "Thank you for the dance, Lady Brendagger. I hope we meet again." He dropped my hand. Dancers paused and parted, making way as he returned to the dais.

I wasn't safe? Why? Ikane's brother? What good would that do now? I had done what I came for. Daram was represented. We would stay in the king's favor. Whatever the Leviathans had planned, I had done my part in thwarting them.

Laughter rose from the side of the room, booming and raucous. Ropert? A gaggle of impeccably dressed ladies surrounded him, and his cheeks were rosy. Was he drunk?

"Ropert?"

"Lady Bren'agger." He grinned as I approached.

"Have you been drinking?"

"Nah. I don' touch the stuff." He shook his head, stumbling as his tall frame careened to the side. The surrounding ladies screamed and giggled, holding him upright.

He was going to ruin everything.

I grabbed his arm. "We should get you to your room."

"No, no." He planted his feet. "I want you to meet . . . Nana? Nena? Nomea?"

"It's Niveah," one lady giggled.

"Ah, yes. Nela."

I scanned the crowd. *Please let everyone ignore this.*

I felt eyes on me. King Sander. He watched me from his throne, irises burning, pleading for me to go.

"Come on, Ropert." I pulled his arm around my shoulders. My legs strained to hold him up. "You've had too much to drink. Let's get you to bed."

"I'm not drunk," he said. "I never drink. I may be a lil'—" He hiccuped. "Oh, look! There's Ikane!"

Ikane leaned by the doors at the top of the stairs, his arms folded across his chest. He pushed off the wall as we approached.

"Ikane!" Ropert's animated voice drew the attention of several people. "Dagger told me you left, but I knew you'd be back. You promised me a spar. How 'bout we do it tomorrow morning? I think we 'ave some time before returning to Daram, don't we, Dagger?"

I wrinkled my nose at his breath.

Ikane patted Ropert's shoulder. "I think you had best get some sleep and see how your head feels in the morning." He leaned close to me, whispering. "Let me help him. It doesn't look good when a lady is escorting her drunk bodyguard from the room."

I gripped Ropert's wrist firmly. "You've done enough." I pushed past him.

We staggered through the hallway, coming upon the small door of Ropert's servant's quarters. What had gotten into him? He knew better. He never drank, even on rare occasions when it was permitted in Daram. Why did he choose tonight, of all nights, when Duchess Caitelyn was counting on us?

The cot groaned under his weight. Tugging his boots from his feet, I dropped them on the floor with two solid thumps.

"Dagger?"

"What were you thinking?"

"I . . . I didn't get to dance with you." His eyes closed, head lulling on his pillow, as his breath deepened.

"Idiot." I brushed his hair from his face. He was going to regret this tomorrow.

Slipping out of his room, I pulled the door shut. Festive noises echoed down the hallway. There was no point in returning to the celebration; I had accomplished my task. After tonight, I would no longer be Lady Brendagger. I would be a corporal again—if Duchess Caitelyn didn't strip me of that rank, too.

All I wanted was to go home, and Ikane had robbed me of that. How would I tell Ropert? *What* would I tell him? Flaming feathers, why did Ikane do this to me? Daram needed help, and all I could do was chase the overdressed archduke who was as slippery as a bar of soap.

How long would I need to stay here for Ikane to honor his agreement? A week? A month? Sitting idle would drive me mad. Maybe I could find a room somewhere in the city and keep working at the library. There were so many more scrolls left unread, so much more to discover . . .

A figure stood outside my door, yards of rich fabric draping over his arm.

"Archduke Goldest." I bowed. What was he doing here, at my door? I'd been trying to speak with him all evening.

"I have news concerning Daram."

My heart jumped into my throat.

"Rise. We need to speak in private." He gestured to my door.

Pulling the key from my pocket, I stuffed it in the lock. It clicked, and I pushed against it. It didn't move. Wasn't it locked? Adalyah must have forgotten when she left.

I turned the key again, opening the door.

A fire glowed in the fireplace, the only source of light in the dark room. I held the door open for the archduke who sauntered inside, twisting a ring on his finger.

Sitting in the armchair, he motioned for me to close the door. "I have made arrangements for two hundred soldiers to assist in Daram's unfortunate predicament."

"I do not know how to express my gratitude." I sank to the armchair across from him, weight lifting off my shoulders like shedding a suit of armor.

He laced his hands together, leaning forward in his chair. "I do." His voice was low and calculated, dangerous.

Cold raced up my spine. Something wasn't right. My eyes shifted to the desk behind him. Where was my sword? I'd left it there.

"I have a proposition for you, Lady Brendagger." Archduke Goldest stretched one of his ring-adorned hands to the fire, wriggling his fingers. The various stones glimmered in the firelight. "You are no stranger to Prince—I beg your pardon—*King* Sander's greatness as a military leader. His skill is unmatched. He has driven the Leviathan pirates farther from us than any other monarch."

"He has." Where was my sword? Where were my knives? Even my cloak and boots were missing. Why would Adalyah move them now?

"However," the archduke continued, "our economy is failing. We've been forced to retire some of our best soldiers for lack of funds. The new king may be a god of warfare, but he is in no way suited to bring Roanfire wealth and power."

I frowned, rising from my seat. "I don't like what you are insinuating, Archduke Goldest."

He leaned back in his chair with a heavy sigh. "I thought you might become defensive. That is why I have not as yet sent the troops to Daram."

"What? Daram is vital to protecting Roanfire from the Leviathans. You must send them immediately. This is not something to—"

"You dare to counsel me?" He leapt to his feet.

I was going to ruin everything. I fell to one knee in a typical soldier's bow. "Forgive me, Your Grace."

He straightened, adjusting the sleeves of his embellished coat. "This is my proposition, Lady Brendagger. Pledge your allegiance, and the allegiance of Daram, to me. Then shall I defend your province from the Leviathan pirates."

"You are asking me to commit treason."

"No, Lady Brendagger. I am asking you to think of Roanfire's future. My patience is wearing thin. What is your decision? Will you spare Daram? Or will you let it fall?"

I stood. This man did not deserve my respect. "If Daram falls, it will be on your head. And even if it were within my capabilities, I would never pledge my allegiance, or the allegiance of Daram, to a man so wrapped up in gaining power and wealth. I am loyal to King Sander alone."

"So be it." He moved for the door. "It was most unfortunate that Lady Serah was assassinated."

My fists clenched, watching his back. How could a snake like this be so close to the king?

He stopped, glancing over his shoulder. A treacherous glint sparked behind his dark irises. "It should come as no surprise that you, too, were murdered." He snapped his fingers.

Movement pulled at the corners of my eyes. Two black figures emerged from the shadows, firelight glinting on their polished weapons. One on the right held a sword. The other held a battle-axe. Ikane's brother? No, he was too short.

"Make it quick, gentlemen." Archduke Goldest slipped out the door.

The swordsman lunged. I arched back, stumbling to the fireplace. The fire poker. I grabbed it, bringing it up as his sword whipped at my torso. A harsh clang rang out. The impact drove the thin metal into my hands. I twisted, sparks flying as the sword's edge ground down the rod.

He was slow compared to Ikane, but I wanted my sword. He struck again, the blade catching on the fire poker's hook. He pulled, the thin metal slicing my palms.

Silver flashed between us. The axe came down. Dropping the fire poker, I stumbled back. The swordsman sent a fist at my face. I dropped into a crouch, his fist hitting air. Lunging past his legs, I scrambled behind the armchair. My ribs screamed.

A dull *thwack* rang beside my ear, the sword cutting deep into the wooden frame of the armchair. I had to get out of here. I was outmatched. I could not fend off a sword and an axe, not without a weapon. Not in the state my body was in. Where was Ropert when I needed him?

Pieces fell into place. That was it. That woman. Nomea, Nivea . . . whomever she was, she had been collaborating with Archduke Goldest. She had to be. She'd gotten Ropert drunk.

Something glinted under the bed frame. Adrenaline soared as I recognized the shape. My sword.

I scrambled for it.

The sound of rending fabric and flesh rushed through my ears. A man groaned behind me. What was going on? The vibration of a body crumbling to the floor begged me to look back. Was it worth the risk? The thud of boots moved toward me.

I reached my sword, dragging the weapon out from under the bed. Rolling onto my back, I whipped the blade up. The tip ripped across the axe-wielder's torso, tearing through his black tunic.

He clutched his chest, red leaking between his fingers.

Wait. His axe wasn't raised. My back had been to him. It would've been so easy for him to slam his weapon into my spine.

Where was the swordsman? A body sprawled before the fire, the sword lying beside his limp hand. Had he killed his comrade? Why?

Shouts echoed down the hallway outside, coming closer.

The axe-wielder staggered to the corner, dropping his axe. "You need to go." His voice was muffled by the black mask covering his face. He pulled my satchel from the darkened corner and tossed it at my feet. It was bulging with supplies.

Keeping my sword pointed at him, I stood. "Who are you?"

"Go," he said.

I grabbed my satchel, finding it heavy with gear as if he had anticipated this. Why would he help me?

Pounding fists rattled the door.

"The window," he said. "Hurry." Blood dripped onto the floor from the wound on his chest.

"Who are you?" I asked again.

"Damn you, go!"

The pounding on the door intensified.

Darting to the window, I threw it wide. Cold air hit my face. What was I doing? I hadn't done anything wrong. I'd defended my king. I paused, looking down.

The ground spun, shifting distance. I couldn't jump that far. Not the way Ikane had.

"What are you waiting for? Go," the man urged.

I dropped my bag. It flipped twice, sinking into the shadowy snowbank. I'd never survive this. Ikane had done it, but he was a Leviathan with bones of steel.

The door burst wide, and soldiers bled into the room. "Get her!"

"Traitor!"

"Murderer!"

All I did was defend myself. The archduke had done this. He wouldn't let me live, not after revealing his true intentions. It was my word against his. I'd rather take my chances falling three stories.

I jumped. My stomach heaved into my throat. Wind rushed under the skirt as I plummeted to the ground. My feet sank into the snowbank, a sharp stab wrenching through my leg. I rolled forward, distributing the impact of the landing.

The world stopped spinning. I laid on my back, heart thundering, looking up at the solid stone wall. I'd made it. Somehow, by the flaming feathers of the Phoenix, I'd survived with a minor ache in my ankle.

A soldier leaned out the window. "She's in the gardens!"

I staggered to my feet, fire spreading up my leg. This was going to slow me down.

Grabbing my bag and sword, I sprinted for the stables.

Gossamer's ears twitched as I burst into his stall. There was no time to saddle him. Throwing my bag over my shoulder, I mounted bareback, spurring him from the stable. He bolted toward the castle gates. Guards jumped up from their half slumber as Gossamer galloped past them into the deserted market square.

Shouts erupted in my wake. A loud horn blew, an alarm reserved for only the most heinous of events. Curious people emerged from their houses, crying out and ducking back as Gossamer thundered by.

All this for the death of Archduke Goldest's assassin? I was missing something. There had to be something more.

At the outer wall, soldiers dug their heels in, pushing the solid wooden gates shut. I sank low to Gossamer's neck, kicking his sides. We could make it. We had to.

Gossamer barreled through the closing gap, my skirt brushing the wooden doors.

Soldiers roared as we tore blindly into the moonlit fields.

# CHAPTER 22

# KING-SLAYER

*M*oonlight darted in and out of the trees as Gossamer's hooves kicked up snow and mud. My ribs screamed for me to slow down—my adrenaline must have been waning. My ankle throbbed, and a sting burrowed through my left bicep, inches below the healing arrow wound. Blood saturated the sleeve of my gown. It'd probably happened when the swordsman struck the armchair as I hid behind it. Why was it always that arm?

I slowed, tearing the decorative length of my ruined sleeve. Using my teeth, I tied off the bleeding. How was I going to make this right? A mere soldier accusing the archduke of treason? Who would listen?

Gossamer's tracks sank deep into the snow behind us, leaving an obvious trail for the soldiers to follow. I couldn't keep to the road.

Pain shot through my ankle as I dismounted. These shoes were not meant for traipsing through ankle-deep snow. Limping, I guided Gossamer into the dense trees flanking the road. The thick canopy of pines held most of the snow aloft, making it easier to hide our tracks.

Maybe I could go to King Sander directly? He knew who I was. Surely, he'd listen.

He warned me. I saw the worry in his eyes. But if he knew of the archduke's treachery, why would he permit him to stay? Maybe he couldn't?

I didn't understand politics. Being a soldier was simple. Someone wronged you, you fought back. Simple.

My foot slipped on a stone, ankle screaming as I went down on a bed of river rocks. A little stream trickled through the extensive remains of smooth boulders, evidence that this used to be a wide river.

Dusting myself off, I guided Gossamer through the stones to the stream. He dipped his snout into the icy water, drinking giant gulps. I stroked his neck. His coat steamed in the crisp light of morning.

I shivered. We both needed shelter and sleep.

A promising cluster of bulky pine trees lay ahead. Cupping a handful of water, I wet my parched mouth.

"Come on, Gossamer." I slipped a hand under his neck, urging him to follow.

We pushed through the heavy pine branches, stepping into a shelter of silent green. The earth scrunched under my feet, layer upon layer of lost pine needles softening the ground.

I dropped my bag and sword. This would have to do.

Gossamer nibbled at dry tufts of grass sprouting between the pine needles as I rubbed him down, checking his legs and hooves for swelling. He didn't look good. I'd pushed him too hard.

He curled his front legs under himself, lowering his body to the ground. Snorting once, he eased his head down.

I sank beside him, stroking his neck. "That's my boy."

His ears flicked at the sound of my voice.

Pulling my bag close, I opened it and instantly spotted my cloak. Thank the Phoenix. I draped it over my shoulders, tugging it around my legs. The mysterious axe-wielder had thought of everything. Bread and dried meat, my knife, a small waterskin, flint and steel, and thickly woven knee-high socks.

I'd never been so grateful to see socks.

I removed the delicate slippers from my feet. My ankle was swollen and three different shades of blue. I barely pulled the stocking over it.

What I wouldn't give for a pair of sturdy boots. But there was nothing more in the bag.

I stuck a piece of dried meat between my teeth, sinking against Gossamer's warm belly. What had I gotten him into?

*My skin blistered. Bones turned brittle and cracked. Hot oil coursed through my blood, filling my lungs.*

*"We will meet soon."*

My body spasmed, curling over my knees. Hot bile seared up my throat. The precious meal I'd eaten splattered on the ground beside me. Tears burned my eyes. I couldn't endure this nightmare anymore. It had to end. But all my answers were locked in Meldron's library, a place I could not go.

Trembling, I wiped my lips with the back of my sleeve. My nose was bleeding again.

Gossamer sighed, his breath blasting pine needles from his nose as he lay on the ground. His black coat glistened in the noonday sun. He made no move to rise.

"Gossamer?" I rubbed his neck. He was hot, his skin clammy. I checked his legs. His left hind leg was swollen. I'd done this to him. He needed herbs and medicine, a warm place to rest, water, and food. I couldn't give that to him, not here.

I rubbed my temples. Why was everything being torn from me? Lady Serah, Valine, Illorce, Fortin, Ikane, Ropert, and now Gossamer. This was the last part of Eamon I had. The last piece of Daram.

Gossamer's ears twitched. He'd heard something.

I crawled to the edge of the canopy, pushing a thick branch aside, listening. Birds lifted from the trees, the sound of their flapping wings carrying across the wide riverbank. Dogs barked in the distance, at least half a dozen.

Bloodhounds? Was the archduke that desperate? The houndmasters of Daram had never once returned from a hunt without catching their prey.

I ducked back into the canopy, eyeing Gossamer.

He picked up his head.

"No." I crouched beside him, stroking his neck. "The soldiers will care for you. Rest. You've earned it."

Grabbing the bag, I swung it over my head. I pushed from the pine shelter, moving away from the river and deeper into the woods.

The howl of a dog soared through the trees, causing a surge of birds to take flight. Men shouted, excitement filling their voices. They'd either found Gossamer or my trail—or both.

My ankle screamed as I wove between the trees. If only I could blend into them, merge into their bark. Snow hugged their bases where shadows refused to let the sun shine.

The barking grew louder. Distinct voices of a dozen soldiers called out to each other.

"This way!"

"She's close!"

I had to keep moving. My lungs burned, ribs aching more with each huff of breath.

"There she is!"

My legs surged, driving me through the trees. Needles dove into my lungs, dust coated my mouth. My toes slammed against a protruding root. I crashed to the earth, dry soil swirling over my hands.

What . . . ? Where were the pine needles? The snow? The muddied earth, leaves, and underbrush?

I staggered to my feet, lifeless dust swirling around the shredded hem of my dress. Not a single blade of grass pushed from the ground. No birds dared to rest on the broken, skeletal fingers of the barren trees reaching into the gray winter air. Not even the wind dared to howl. A clean line cut through the woods, one half living, the other half parched and dead.

My mouth went dry.

*The Dead Forest.*

The nightmare slithered ugly tendrils around my chest, wringing the stale air from my lungs. I had to get out of here. I had to go back.

But feathers, I couldn't.

Crimson tunics wove through the trees in my direction, the heads of barking dogs appearing over the foliage.

"I see her!"

"Shoot her!"

Archers? They had archers!

I ducked behind a tree, feeling the dusty bark crumble down my back. Swallowing and licking my lips did nothing for the dryness in my throat.

I could run deeper. There was a reason no one entered the Dead Forest. Would it be enough to keep the soldiers from following?

I risked a glance back. Trails of dust swirled behind two dogs racing for me.

I pushed off the tree, running.

A soft whistle came up behind me. Fire tore through my lower back, spreading down my leg. It seized. My body pitched forward, landing hard on the barren earth. Dust curled into my lungs.

"She's hit!"

It was an arrow. It had to be. Sucking air through my teeth, I twisted. Feathered fletching protruded from my lower back. My leg couldn't move—I had to get it out.

I reached back, fist wrapping around the arrow shaft. I yanked. Pain exploded as the arrowhead pulled against flesh. Red sparks flashed across my vision. I couldn't do it.

The dogs skidded to a halt beside me, teeth bared, drool hanging from their curled lips.

I ducked under my arms.

*Phoenix, please. Why was this happening to me?*

"King-slayer." A soldier crouched beside me.

I blinked at him. What did he just call me?

His hand shot out, grabbing the shaft of the arrow. He jerked. Rending flesh and fabric vibrated through my body. My teeth ground together, stifling my scream.

He pitched the bloody arrow away. "May the Phoenix feed you to the Leviathan. May your soul rot in the sea."

Two dozen soldiers surrounded me. Three gripped leashes to barking bloodhounds. A handful of archers pointed tautly strung arrows at me.

*King-slayer?*

The king was dead?

They thought I did it!

"I didn't—"

The soldier's fist slammed into my jaw. My head whirled,

rebounding off the dirt. Darkness swarmed across my vision. Blood pooled in my mouth.

"King-slayer!"

Ikane promised. He wouldn't do it if I didn't go back to Daram. I'd abandoned my home for this?

I spat the blood from my mouth. "I didn't kill him."

"Liar!" His boot slammed into my ribs. A crack tore through my body, fire shooting through my chest. I pulled into a ball, the trees and red uniforms blurring. Something hit my back, shooting the air from my lungs. I rolled from the blow of a boot only to be struck from behind by a fist.

I curled, shielding my face against the flood of kicks and punches.

*I have not waited this long to have mere mortals destroy my only hope of rebirth.* The voices carried across the barren landscape like a harsh whisper.

The beating stopped.

My brain screamed at me to move, to get away, but my body wouldn't budge. My heart banged through my skull. The sharp smell of blood filled my nose. I could taste it, feel it leaking from me.

Something moved across the dusty earth, rolling toward us. Soldiers staggered back as the ashen haze moved between their legs. It settled over my body like a blanket of cinders.

Hot red energy leeched into my muscles, pushing through my bones. It burrowed into my chest, expanding like something trapped and raging.

No. Not this. I'd rather die by the hands of these soldiers than feel her fire.

Energy exploded, all heat pushing from my body. The air distorted. Throbbing silence pulsed through my ears.

The heat was gone. My body collapsed, melting into the dust of the Dead Forest. Blurred images of crimson tunics and bloodhounds scattered on the dusty earth, lifeless, met my eyes.

*This* was a nightmare I wanted to wake from.

My eyes closed.

"Hang on, Little Brendagger . . ."

# CHAPTER 23

# A THOUSAND VOICES

*R*ocks crushed every limb, weight bearing down on joint and muscle like stone armor. Everything hurt. Swelling pushed my tongue to the roof of my mouth. Dry. So dry.

Why wouldn't my eyes open? It was like something had glued them shut. Firelight flickered across them, pops and snaps sounding to my left.

If I could just rub them . . .

"Don't move." Someone scrambled to my side. The sound of boots scraping against stone echoed. Where was I? A cave?

One eye cracked open. A fuzzy shape lingered over me, firelight flickering behind him.

"Drink." He tipped something into my lips, and cool, soothing moisture coated my tongue. Swallowing ignited sparks of pain in my jaw and neck.

He moved the cup away, stroking my hair from my forehead. "Rest now. I'll watch over you."

My eyes closed, his touch as soothing as the cool water lingering on my tongue. Darkness pulled me into it, a blanket of nothingness swallowing every throb and ache.

Stale air filled my lungs. Fire crackled, and the sound of a log collapsing drew my attention to the hearth.

A spasm tore through my neck as I turned. My eyes barely opened. Hazy firelight danced across a barren gray wall where three arched windows had been plugged with mud and rock. Where was I?

A figure crouched beside the fire, broad shoulders moving as he added new logs to the flame. Pausing, he looked up. Then he turned to me.

Ikane.

How dare he show his face! How dare he come here and pretend to be my savior! He was the one who'd caused all of this.

"You . . ." My throat scratched and cut, my tongue sticking to my teeth. "You killed him." I pushed the blankets from my chest, joints aching through my shoulders. The fine work of Seamstress Shima was nothing but rags, the bodice cut to reveal my bruised midsection.

Where was my sword? I would run him through.

"Don't move," he cried, scrambling to my side, pushing me down. "The wound in your back just closed. I will not have you tearing it open again."

He didn't even try to hide his accent anymore.

"You should have let me die." My voice sounded like I'd swallowed a frog.

Ikane sat on his heels. "Spare me your self-pity, and save your wrath. King Sander lives. It was King Myron who was assassinated."

King Myron? "Why . . . why did you do it? You promised."

"I didn't do it," Ikane said. "It was not the doing of the Leviathans, either. Someone else wanted the king gone."

Archduke Goldest? But why? Just to frame me? Just to keep me from revealing his treachery?

I shut my eyes. "I should have listened to Eamon."

"I have done *nothing* to harm you." His words dripped with quiet anger.

"You forced me to abandon Daram!"

"I saved your life," he snapped, green eye sparking.

My mouth clamped shut.

He didn't have to save me. I would have been better off dead. No one would hunt me. I wouldn't dream anymore. And I wouldn't be indebted to a Leviathan pirate.

He grabbed a chipped mug from beside the hearth. "You need to eat." He knelt beside me, slipping his hand under my head, lifting the mug to my lips.

I pressed them tight against the warm broth thick with the fragrance of carrot and meat. I didn't need his food, no matter how dry my lips were or how much my stomach ached.

He pulled the mug away. "Are you going to be that stubborn?"

"I don't trust you."

"I'm not asking you to." He moved the cup to my lips again. "Just drink."

Saliva flooded my mouth as the fragrant steam rose to my nose. Warm liquid touched my lips, coaxing them open. Rich flavor flooded around my tongue, soothing my throat, warming my belly.

"If you want to clear your name, you'll need to heal and hone your skills," he said. "This place is safe."

I swallowed. "And where are we?"

He tipped the mug back to my lips. "The ruins of Fold."

I choked, spraying the broth across my lap.

Ikane pulled the mug away, shaking the moisture from his hand. "Spines, Kea. What's wrong with you?"

Fold? Rion was here. It was the reason the woods were dead. She drained life and energy. It was her voices that had spoken in the woods. The gray mist was *her* doing.

The soldiers. The hounds. She had killed them. It wasn't a dream. They lay lifeless in the woods now, their souls devoured by the ruby.

"We can't stay here."

"You're safe here, Kea. No one will—"

"The soldiers. The bloodhounds. Did you see them?"

"Aye." He spoke slowly. Something dark and wary filled his eyes, like a storm building over a mountain range, a warning to seek shelter. Had I looked at him that way the first time I saw his green eye spark?

This was not me. I was not a monster. My heart thundered under my ribs, threatening to crack them from the inside. "I didn't do it. It was Rion."

"Who is Rion?"

I laid back on the pillow. Firelight flickered on the gray stone overhead. I wanted to tell him. I needed someone to understand. Why did he have to be a Leviathan? I didn't need him involved in my life any more than he was already.

He set the mug on the ground and stood. "Very well. Don't tell me. I will leave you in peace." He reached for his swords, effortlessly strapping them to his back.

Was he leaving me here? Flaming feathers. I hated being so helpless. I needed him.

"Will you . . . will you come back?" The question tasted sour on my lips.

"If you wish it."

How was I to respond to that? He was pushing, wanting me to admit I needed him.

He walked toward the arched doorway leading to the murky hallway. My stomach flipped as he looked back at me, a pleading in his eyes. He wanted to stay, and I needed him to. But why would he linger if I treated him like a broken weapon?

He stepped over the threshold.

Charred rachis. "Ikane, wait."

He turned back to me.

"I . . . I need you."

A smile pulled on his lips. "I thought you'd never ask."

"Don't push it."

He held his hands up. "Will you be alright for a few hours?"

"Where are you going?"

"To get supplies."

And leave me alone in the Fold Garrison, the place of my nightmares? What was I to do? Ikane couldn't protect me—no one could. The sooner I healed, the sooner we could leave this place.

"Don't be long."

He shrugged his bag higher. "I won't."

He slipped away, the sound of his soft leather boots crunching down the hallway.

The fire cracked and popped, consuming the wood. Orange light flickered across the stone ceiling that was supported by a few beams of dark wood. No cobwebs. No rodents. No insects. This was the Dead Forest. Even those creatures of nuisance couldn't be found here.

A strange purr emanated from the fireplace. My neck burned as I faced it. Why did it sound like it was roaring? Only four logs smoldered.

The humming vibrations intensified, and the orange light transformed to fervent greens, blues, and reds. The indistinct whir distorted to laughter, growing with the light of the fire. A hundred voices chuckled, male and female, old and young. It penetrated the stone walls like ghosts from the past.

*Phoenix Daughter . . .*

My breath stopped, heart leaping behind my spine.

*Long have I awaited you. At last, I will be reborn and rule Roanfire as its rightful queen.*

This was no dream. This was real. She was in my head. I had to get away. My body protested every movement as I pushed to sitting, fire searing through my back where the arrow had struck. My ribs stabbed. Stinging tore through my right leg.

I couldn't move. I couldn't hide. I was at her mercy.

"Leave me alone!" My voice echoed through the fireplace, mingling with the millions of voices emanating from it.

*You poor child. Your frame is beaten and broken. Heal, my Phoenix Daughter. Rest. Regain your strength.*

The fire shrunk to its natural character, the voices lingering in the stone like a whisper.

Something hot leaked from my back. I must have reopened the wound.

"Ikane." Oh, why did he have to leave?

Footfalls echoed beyond the door. He was back. Thank the Phoenix.

Ikane entered, laden with blankets and a bulging sack.

"Ikane." Why did my voice sound so relieved?

He dropped the bundle. "Kea? What in the . . . ?" He hurried to my side, lifting the blankets. "You tore it. Spines, Kea. I told you not to move."

He could reprimand me all he wanted. At least he was back.

"It's a good thing I found more bandages and ointment." He crouched beside the bundle, pulling items from it.

"Where did you go?"

"There are folk who live in the ruins of Fold City."

"So the rumors are true, then? Bandits, traitors, and criminals dwell here?"

"Call them what you will." He pulled a large cotton shirt from the pack, shaking it out. "Like me, they are simply misunderstood."

I pursed my lips.

"I found some clothing for you." He set the cotton shirt aside, pulling out a pair of trousers about my size. "The shirt is large, but it'll do."

Why was I so cruel to him? Was it the inbred hatred for the Leviathan pirates? Eamon's reaction to Ikane when he showed up in Daram? Was I simply following the prejudice of others?

Everything he did, he did with kindness. Even while monitoring my injuries, he respected me, taking extra care not to expose my body more than needed. He could have removed the dress completely. It would have made dealing with my injuries much easier.

"Did you find any boots?"

He smiled. "None that would fit. Besides, it'll be a while before you are walking again." He pulled a clay pot from the sack. "The dogs mauled your leg pretty bad." He moved the blanket from my feet, pulling the hem of my tattered gown over my knee.

Shredded skin, red and yellow with infection, wrapped around my calf and shin. My stomach rolled. I lay back, staring at the ceiling.

"Does it hurt?"

Feathers, it did. "A bit," I said.

He opened the clay pot, dipping his fingers into the ointment. "There is an exceptional healer living among these folks. She has been coaching me through your recovery." He moved his fingers to my leg, the orange-green ointment glistening.

Was that firedust? Faslight's warning raced through my head. I retracted my leg, the movement sending stabbing pain through my back. Redness blurred my vision.

Ikane paused.

"I don't trust healers."

"You don't trust anyone." He lowered the back of his hands to his legs, keeping the container of liniment and his slathered fingers away from his trousers.

"It's because of Illorce, isn't it?"

How did he . . . ? Then it struck. It was him. He had been Cheraric's guest the night I sought out a healer. He was the one who argued with the healer behind the curtain. He was the one who made the charms sway in the window when we returned.

I groaned, throwing my head against the makeshift pillows. Clenching the rough blanket, I slammed my eyes shut against my stupidity. "You were there. You knew what he was going to do."

"I tried to stop him."

"Why, Ikane? Why did he do that to Illorce? He was a harmless old man!"

Ikane brought his knee up, resting his arm on it. He rubbed his fingers together, moving the ointment. "There are Leviathans all over Roanfire posing as healers. Firedust successfully burns out infections."

"But it turns bones brittle."

Ikane's gaze fell.

My blood roiled. "How long?"

"About a year."

An entire year? People of Roanfire had been "cured" by this Firebalm for an entire year? How many were infected? The Leviathans had bones of steel while the skeletons of Roanfiriens were slowly being turned brittle. If there was an attack, we wouldn't stand a chance.

"Was this part of the plan to overthrow Roanfire?"

Ikane nodded. "Like I told Eamon, my brothers have been preparing for years, laying the groundwork, setting everything in motion."

A growl tore through my throat. "And you expect me to trust you with that?" I gestured to the ointment on his fingers.

He set the pot of salve beside him. "Look, Kea. I am not your enemy. I wish you saw that."

I wished I did, too. "Are you sure there is no firedust in there?"

He held up his fingers. "No red flecks."

What more did I have to lose? "Alright."

He bent over my leg, dabbing the thick ointment with a featherlight touch. "It's going to scar."

I looked away, watching the fire. Ikane was here. The voices wouldn't come, would they? Even if they did, would he be able to hear them? Was it all in my head?

"I've been thinking about what you said." Ikane worked the ointment around my calf.

"About what?"

"About the name Rion. It sounded familiar. I just couldn't place it."

I caught his eye. "What are you talking about?"

"The first pirate-king of the Leviathans was Simian Ormand. Stories say he was one of three advisors to the original Queen of Roanfire, Rion Noirfonika. They say she was touched by the Phoenix, blessed with power and beauty. The thought of losing either drove her mad."

I lifted my head.

"Simian tried to reason with her, but her head was turned with the need to become equal to the Phoenix who blessed her. She swore she would rise from her ashes. A jewel was forged, one that would grant eternal life to the one who wore it." Ikane wrapped my leg with a roll of white linen.

"And?" My mouth was dry.

"She banished him. He knew she had been led astray by her own greed. Simian and his men settled the Leviathan Isles, intending to build an army strong enough to overpower her and destroy the jewel." He tied off the bandaging, pulling the blankets over it.

"But every time he tried, he was driven back. And the jewel was never found." He sat back on his heels, looking at me. "Was our tradition of raiding Roanfire's shores built on that?"

"It could be." What was wrong with me? I was agreeing with him, seeing his side of things.

"I need to look at your back." He removed his cloak, rolling it up and tucking it into my arms. "It'll help ease the pressure on your ribs."

I hugged his cloak, still warm, rolling onto my side. It smelled of steel, dust, and mint.

"Spines, Kea." Ikane sucked air through his teeth. "It's bleeding again."

"Sorry," I mumbled into his cloak.

"Hopefully, the salve will help." Something cold pressed against my back.

"Have you heard anything of Daram?" I asked.

His silence was answer enough.

"And Ropert?"

Ikane slipped a hand under my waist, winding a bandage around it. "He's been sent to Pedre."

My eyes burned. Pedre. A penal colony. A marble quarry worked by traitors and criminals. My poor Ropert was even more innocent than I was. I should be the one there, not him.

"You care for him very much, don't you?"

I sniffed. "He's my brother."

Ikane spread his bedroll beside me. "You are one of Roanfire's finest warriors. You will make this right."

Rolling to my back, I relinquished his cloak.

If only he was right.

# CHAPTER 24

# FLESH AND BONE

*A* chill touched my cheeks, soaking into my skin. Pulling the blankets to my neck, I rolled over, sucking air through my teeth as the skin on my back pulled.

How long would it take to heal? I'd been lying here for days. The only movement Ikane allowed was when he escorted me to a small room resembling a water closet where I could relieve myself. My bladder ached.

I blinked at the bedroll beside me. Empty.

Where was he?

The fire had burned down to embers in a pile of black ash, a taunting smolder, a rancorous reminder of my nightmares.

"Ikane?" My voice echoed through the lonely chamber. His cloak was gone. And his swords. "Ikane!"

*Why do you tremble? You are not alone. I am here,* the voices crooned through the ruins.

When had waking become the nightmare? Where were her voices coming from? The fire? It flickered, quietly mocking, pulling on every memory of her inferno searing through my bones.

*You should consider yourself honored to be my host.* Her voices paused. Something pushed into my mind, hot and slithering like a string of flames leading to a vat of pitch.

Her host? Feathers, no. She would not take me the way she had

Queen Damita. I had to find the White Wardent. He said there was a way.

*You seek that arrogant fool? I am no curse. I am the life and future of Roanfire. The phoenix shall rise in glorious flames of power and light. I shall be a goddess among men, feared, loved, and cherished.*

I shut my eyes. Sleep. Please, just sleep. Slip into darkness. Escape.

She was no goddess of mine. She was a nightmare, a plague, a scourge.

*I saved your life.* The heat in my mind snapped, sparking like an ember, sizzling against my thoughts. How did she get there? Inside, deep, knowing, pushing into every thought I held sacred.

"Ikane!" Tears blurred my vision, streaking down my cheeks. "Ikane, where are you?"

Her heat recoiled from my mind like fire reaching grass too wet to burn. *I am disappointed in you, Phoenix Daughter. I have chosen you. You should consider yourself honored.*

"Ikane!"

"Kea?" His voice was distant, echoing through the hallway beyond the arched door. Rhythmic pounding of his boots reverberated against stone, growing louder.

I needed him here now. He was fast, faster than a horse. Why did it feel like hours before he burst through the makeshift curtain door?

"Kea? What's wrong?" He held a sword in his hand, eyes scanning the room for an enemy, an enemy he could not see. An enemy he could not fight. An enemy who could burrow into my mind as easily as his sword could plunge into flesh.

I couldn't do this. Tears burned down my cheeks, searing into my skin. I'd never felt so helpless. Even if I could wield my sword, there was nothing I could do.

"Kea . . ." He dropped his sword, kneeling beside me. His hands hovered as if he feared his touch would make me scream.

"Where were you?" I croaked.

"Getting firewood." His eyes jumped from my face to my body, searching for something wrong enough to warrant my outburst.

He must have thought I'd gone mad.

"Are you alright?" The accent he so often hid was laced with raw emotion.

I grabbed his hand, his skin warm and soothing, his muscles strong. I squeezed. "Don't leave me again."

"I'd never leave you." He leaned forward, wrapping his arms around me. My fingers dug into his shirt, wishing I could crush him to me, feel his strength, draw on whatever energy he held that kept Rion at bay. Curse these injuries. They prevented me from something as simple as an embrace.

He pulled away, brushing my hair from my forehead. "It's cold in here. Will you be alright if I go fetch the firewood I dropped downstairs?"

I half-sobbed, half-laughed, brushing tears from my cheeks. I was pathetic. "Hurry back."

"Our rations are low again," Ikane said as he ran a whetstone across the sharp edge of his sword in a rhythmic gliding motion, firelight flickering against the black steel. "If I leave now, we'll have fresh meat tonight."

I dropped the log on the fire. The burning wood rolled, smothering the flame. "Let me come."

"You can barely walk ten minutes let alone ride a horse."

"It's been three weeks. I won't get any stronger sitting here."

Ikane sighed, gliding the stone across his blade. "It is not safe for you out there, Kea. You can come once you are strong enough to wield your sword again."

"But that could be another month!" I rubbed my face. "Please, Ikane. I can't stay here anymore. The voices are driving me mad."

He arched an eyebrow. "Voices?"

I clamped my mouth shut.

He set his swords aside, shifting to face me, his knee almost touching mine. His meadow-green and sea-blue eyes burned with undivided attention. "Kea, what voices are you hearing?"

I stared down at the pair of oversized woolen socks Ikane had found for me on his last excursion. Rion's voices visited me every time he left.

His hand found my knee. "You can tell me. It's alright." His voice was smooth, his Leviathan accent so true. He didn't hide it anymore, not with me. He trusted me.

I wanted to trust him, too. "I . . . I didn't want you to think I was going mad."

"I couldn't think that, Kea."

What did I have to lose? He would either believe me, or he wouldn't. "Do you remember sitting with me on the deck of the *Otaridae*? The night you showed me the stars?"

"Aye."

I tugged on my ear, nearly feeling the hot stickiness of blood.

His hand followed mine, touching my cheek. It was warm and gentle, filled with something pure. "You were bleeding. I was worried for you."

Why did he have to be so kindhearted? His touch sent a wave of warmth through my body, distracting and perfect.

This was not the time. I pulled his hand down, squeezing it. "The nightmares began in Daram. The Leviathan pirates attacked Fold. Fire consumed the wharf, smoke blackened the sky, people ran for the safety of the garrison, and all Queen Damita could do was watch from the windows of a tower."

"Is that why you were so terrified when I told you where we were?"

I crushed his hand. "Please. Let me finish."

His mouth clamped shut.

"There is a ruby in my dream. It burns with heat and fire, it speaks of being born again, it consumes the entire forest. When you shared your tale of Simian Ormand, Rion, and the jewel, I knew it was the same thing." I swallowed, something catching in my throat. "She speaks to me."

His brows furrowed. "I don't understand."

"From what I could gather in Meldron's Library, the stone was designed as a vessel, something to store energy for Rion's rebirth. It was handed down from mother to daughter for centuries. Damita was the last Queen of Roanfire to inherit this 'curse,' and the ruby killed her. The Noirfonika family line has been barren of female heirs for the past four hundred years."

Ikane blinked at me.

"I knew it. You think I'm mad." I pulled away.

"No." He snatched my hand again. "I don't think you are." He stood, dragging me with him. Grabbing two candles from the crumbling mantlepiece, he lit them with the dying fire. "I wasn't going to show you this, but there is something you need to see." He handed a candle to me, the light flickering across our faces.

I followed him through the blanket hanging over the door, and we emerged into the crumbling hallway of timeworn neglect. Our footfalls echoed, the quivering light of our candles revealing dilapidated wooden arches that supported the vaulted ceiling of the long corridor. The paint, now cracked and peeled, displayed once-vibrant depictions of trees, birds, flowers, and elemental sprites.

The murals gradually altered to illustrate the four beasts of ancient folklore: a phoenix, a griffin, a sea serpent, and a black unicorn. He'd never taken me this far before.

Ikane paused at the base of a wide, spiraling staircase. A disturbing odor trailed from it.

He held out his hand. "It's a long way up."

I'd never felt his hand so sweaty. And why did he keep glancing around the bend as if some monster would appear? Did I really want to see whatever he had to show me?

My thighs burned after ten steps, the muscles from my lower back aching all the way down my buttocks and hamstrings. The stairs wound higher and higher, a never-ending spiral of crumbling gray stone. I was in poor shape. I huffed like an old woman.

I reached the landing where a wide doorway opened to a chamber. Ikane stopped, his hand crushing mine. His eyes bored through the opening, and I watched his throat bob as he swallowed hard.

"Ikane?" What had him so terrified? My Leviathan prince, the Terror of the Sea, the Bane of Roanfire, was trembling.

"I . . . I will accompany you if you'd like." His voice was tight, and his body was stiff, prepared to flee. What about this place scared him so much?

I wouldn't force him.

My hand trembled as I handed him my candle. "Wait here."

I stepped over the threshold.

I knew this place—the massive circular room, the expanse of arched windows open to the hint of dawn. The sea stretched to the horizon, a sheet of black reflecting the stars. Queen Damita had stood here, looking down at her city as it burned.

*You came.*

Her voices pushed through the lifeless air reeking of withered flesh and dust, and heat slithered into my mind. A red glow flickered in the center of the chamber, the light revealing the outline of shriveled gray fingers.

Bodies. Hundreds of them. Mummified corpse upon mummified corpse with wilted, outstretched hands reaching for the glowing ruby in the center.

My stomach rolled into my throat. She had devoured a forest, a city, an entire civilization, and yet she thirsted for more blood, more souls, more lives. Her posterity wasn't enough. Now she drained the lives of innocent people for her personal agenda?

*Don't you see? Flesh and bone are weak. They age, they wither, they break. These are chosen ones. I have saved them. Their souls shall live forever through me.*

How twisted had her mind become? This would be what was left of Roanfire if she were reborn. Ruins, corpses, parched earth.

*And you, my Phoenix Daughter—you will help me rise.*

Did she honestly believe I would submit like a spineless coward? She had plagued Roanfire long enough. Queen Damita resisted; I could, too. "I am a soldier."

*You are nothing but a mortal of flesh and bone, easily eliminated.* She laughed. *Even now, I feel the way you tremble, the way your heart thunders, the weakness of your limbs. When I am reborn, your body will become perfect. We must work together. You, my daughter, must heal. And I must replenish the energy I expended to spare your life.*

I didn't ask her to, and I wished she hadn't. "Get out of my head." My teeth ground together.

"Kea?" Ikane peered inside the tower, not daring to cross the threshold.

Heat spun through my mind, weaving through every moment Ikane and I shared. Our first meeting in Daram, the night under the stars, the way he fought to defend me, the touch of his hand. What did she think she was doing? This was *my* mind, *my* life. She had no right to infiltrate.

*What a feast he would be.* Her energy surged like a collector stumbling upon the missing piece to a set. *Do you feel it? Strength. Valor. Honor. Integrity. Delicacies I have not tasted for centuries. Oh, the power he will provide.*

"Stay back, Ikane!" I snapped. If only I could shatter her mocking beauty, turn her into dust, scatter her remains into the depths of the sea.

My nightmare had become real.

"Kea. Come away." The urgency in Ikane's tone sent a shiver up my spine.

*What is this?* Her thread snaked for him, reaching. *Love? Yes ... pure love! Unpolluted by lust or desire. Unwavering. He cares for you, Phoenix Daughter. Such a feast is rare.*

"You will not have him." My heart crashed against my ribs as my feet moved faster, carrying me from the room.

She sighed. *I shall give you respite for a time.*

What did she mean by that? Was she going to let him be? Was she waiting for another moment? Her crimson light dimmed, plunging the corpse-filled room into violet darkness.

My knees buckled as I cleared the door. Ikane dropped the candles, arms flashing out, pulling me against him. Darkness engulfed us.

The nightmare had come to life. Rion would overpower me or drive me mad if I didn't do something. The White Wardent's journal said every Princess of Roanfire was endowed with the ability to overcome this curse—I had to try.

But how? And where would I begin? I couldn't go back to Meldron. Faslight, perhaps?

"Ikane?" My cheek pressed against his chest, fingers digging into his back. Was his heart thundering, or was it mine? How had he gotten mixed up in this? "Will you help me?"

He stroked my hair. "Anything."

"I need to find the White Wardent."

"Do you believe he exists?"

"I have to."

"Then we must make you strong again."

My legs trembled as I knelt on the cold stone, my body drained from the excursion up the tower. How long before Rion made a move? She had reached the soldiers at the edge of the Dead Forest, devoured them along with the bloodhounds. Yes, she was weak and needed to replenish her strength, but was that enough to stop her from stretching out and taking Ikane, too?

"We need to get out of here." I grabbed the blankets from our beds, rolling them up.

"Kea, stop." Ikane grabbed my wrist. "You're not strong enough yet."

I jerked my arm free. "That abomination up there wants you. Do you understand? You remember those corpses? She drained them, sucked their souls into her. She tasted something in you. I don't care where we go, but we can't stay here."

Ikane bit his lip, eyes lifting to the curtained door. "I may know a place."

"Then let's go."

"We can't rush this, Kea." He grabbed his swords, strapping them to his back. "Before we go anywhere, we need provisions."

My heart hit my chest. He was going to leave me here. After

what we'd just seen?

I leapt to my feet, the arrow wound biting at the sudden movement. "Take me with you. Please."

He pressed his palm against my cheek, warmth soaking into my skin. "You need to stay hidden, Little Brendagger. The bounty on your head is too tempting, even for the most compassionate heart. Pack what you can. We'll leave this place as soon as I return."

The tattered blanket hanging over the doorway swayed closed.

Swallowing the dusty air, I turned to the fireplace. Pops and cracks rolled through the hearth. Embers smoldered, giving off insufficient light in the windowless room.

What was I doing? Waiting for Rion to torment me now that Ikane was gone? Was I that accustomed to her voices?

Turning away, I pushed my sleeves to my elbows. Over the past three weeks, Ikane had furnished our secluded hideout with layers of thick blankets. Chipped dishes sat on a small trunk under one of the plugged windows. Half-spent candles lay on the mantle beside the pot of ointment. A sword and scabbard sat in the corner, leaning against the wall, awaiting the time I could wield it.

And I would.

I pulled a large, worn tunic over my head, the green sleeves hanging over my knuckles. Instead of boots, Ikane had found soft leather shoes that laced at the ankle.

Buckling the sword to my waist, I set my teeth against the weight biting at the healing wound in my back. What had become of me? I'd gone from a respectable soldier to a lady to a fugitive with a bounty on her head.

I couldn't step back into the world looking like Keatep Brendagger. Not until I cleared my name.

Unraveling my braid over my shoulder, I ran my fingers through the chestnut tresses reaching my belt. It would be the easiest and quickest change.

I clutched the locks in a fist, heart pounding. This was my hair, the one thing I took pride in besides my skill as a soldier.

I drew my knife, bringing the blade to my neck. Shutting my eyes, I sliced.

The last of who I was fell away, curling onto the stone at my feet.

# CHAPTER 25

# FOLD CITY

*T*he bags thumped down the stone steps as I dragged them behind me. Where was Ikane? What was taking him so long?

The air outside was just as thick and suffocating as the air inside the garrison. The warmth of the sun sitting smothered in a cloudless sky infused with brown haze was stifling.

Walls of the Fold Garrison lay in crumbling heaps around what would have been the courtyard, crippled trees soaring behind it. How desperate had Ikane been to bring me here? The curse strangled everything, even the sun.

I dropped the bags into a heap at the bottom of the stairs leading into the garrison. Gray stone rose to the sky, a crumbling outline of what infested my nightmares. The tallest tower loomed like something ready to collapse and bury me.

The distinct snort of a horse carried from a gap in the wall. Ikane turned the corner, leading two saddled horses into the dilapidated courtyard. Hazy light lanced across the black coat of the larger horse. My stomach clenched for Gossamer.

"Kea? What are you doing?" Ikane dropped the reins, jogging to me. Was he wearing new armor? Black steel of a quality I could only dream of covered his shoulders and forearms. "You shouldn't have moved all this by yourself."

"You took too long."

He hefted two bags. "You didn't strain your back again, did you? It's going to take you that much longer to—your hair." His eyes froze at my neck where wisps tickled my skin.

I ran a hand through it, the strands falling free much sooner than I was accustomed to. "Is it different enough?"

He cleared his throat. "It suits you."

"That's not what I asked. I can't look like Keatep Brendagger anymore."

"I don't think I'm the right person to ask. No matter what you do, I'll always recognize my Little Brendagger." He secured both bags to the back of the brown horse.

A burly-looking figure limped into the courtyard, his cane stirring up dust as he approached.

"Ikane?" I whispered.

He followed my gaze.

"Pull your hood up." He grabbed my arm, pushing me behind him as he faced the man. "Ardon."

"I knew you were up to something when you took those horses and so much food." One of the man's eyes focused while the other strayed to the side. His graying hair stood wild, and his beard was thick and tangled, reaching clear to his navel. "We can't raid without you. Do you intend to abandon us now?"

Raid? What was he talking about?

"It's time for us to move on." Ikane guarded his accent again. He turned back to the horses, checking straps and ties, worry burning behind his eyes.

"You must be Ikane's sister, the one he's been nursing back to health." Ardon hobbled forward, reaching for my hand.

I stepped back, trying to find Ikane under the deep folds of my hood.

"You are looking fine." A lecherous smile crossed his crooked teeth. "I can't imagine you getting much rest in a place like this. My home is much warmer, more suited to the needs of a delicate creature like yourself. You would be more than welcome."

"We are moving on, Ardon." Ikane stepped between us. "Thank you for the offer."

"You can't leave us now." Ardon's eyes widened. "We need you. We need your skills. You wouldn't leave Malese to fend for herself now, would you?"

Ikane's green eye flashed.

"His skills?" I asked.

Ikane's throat moved, eyes locking on mine, pleading with me to let it go.

"Oh, yes," Ardon said. "I'm sure you already know how skilled your brother is in combat. Why, those caravans never stood a chance."

Caravans? I tried to keep my expression calm. Everything in the room, everything in the bags, everything I was wearing was stolen? Ikane had been raiding this whole time? My skin crawled, the tunic suddenly itching as if it were infested with ants.

"Give us a moment to think about this, Ardon." Ikane took my arm, steering me out of earshot.

"You've been raiding?" I hissed.

"What else was I supposed to do?"

"I don't know. Honest work?"

"It was."

Only a Leviathan would say that. It all made sense. He didn't want me to come with him because he didn't want me to know. Not because I wasn't strong enough.

"Don't look at me that way." He pinched the bridge of his nose. "Fine. Let me show you." He turned to Ardon. "We'll stay a little longer, but on two conditions. We need a place of complete solitude where no one will disturb us. Even you."

"Excellent." Ardon grinned. "There are homesteads built into the cliffs. Perfect for your needs."

"And we get first choice on pillage."

"Ikane." I grabbed his arm. How could he agree to this?

"Done." Ardon extended his hand.

Ikane clasped it. "When is the next raid?"

Was he really planning to raid a caravan right under my nose? I was a soldier of Roanfire . . .

Something coiled around my chest. I *had* been a soldier of Roanfire. I was a fugitive now. I wouldn't be able to work for honest wages without being arrested. Was this what I'd have to resort to? Plundering? Thieving? Becoming just like the Leviathans?

"A large caravan has been spotted heading north." Ardon limped to the disintegrating wall. "If we time it right, we should cross paths at noon tomorrow. Torquin has called for all able-bodied men and women to meet in the square at dawn."

"I'll be there." Ikane pulled the brown horse around.

I grabbed the reins to the black horse, following them from the garrison walls. The dusty road wound down the hillside, sloping into a sea of buildings sitting beside the ocean. Just like my dream.

Everything was in place. Every little detail, save for the ships docked in the marina. I could almost see the trail of torches heading our way, thick smoke billowing, firelight reflecting on the black water.

"The homesteads are on the northeast side of the cliffs." Ardon pointed to an area overlooking the sea. "It's a treacherous path."

"It'll do." Ikane took position beside me as the buildings engulfed us in shadow.

"I will take my leave then." Ardon turned down an alleyway, pausing. "And Ikane? Thank you. Sincerely, from the bottom of our hearts, the Phoenix has blessed us with your presence."

"Get some rest," Ikane said.

How could he show such gratitude to someone who plundered so ruthlessly? It was never right to steal from those who worked hard to earn a living.

Dust swirled around my shoes, the place dryer than the Tolean desert and colder than the Glacial Empire. Tattered blankets hung in the doorways and windows. Muffled sounds of sickness came from the broken, crumbling walls.

"Ikane?" A woman emerged from a building, a teary-eyed baby on her hip. How could she stand? Her legs were as thin as Ardon's cane, and her bones poked through the blanket around her shoulders. Her cheeks sunk into her mouth, her skin almost as gray as the sky. Her hollow eyes tried to sparkle at me but barely managed a faint glimmer. "Is that her? Oh, Ikane. She looks well."

Ikane stopped. "Malese, meet . . . Paige. Paige, this is Malese, the healer who has coached me through your recovery."

The baby whimpered, burying his face into her flat chest. She cradled him, her own face looking pained.

These people were starving. We had been eating like kings in the garrison while the woman who saved my life withered to nothing.

"Are you out of food again?" Ikane asked.

She nodded, her eyes brimming with moisture. "Torquin went hunting last night. He hasn't come home. I'm worried."

Ikane reached into our bags, retrieving a bundle of dried meat.

"Give her the bread, too," I said. We had enough meat on our bones. We could go hungry for a few days.

Tears streaked down her cheeks as she hugged the provisions. "Thank you."

Ikane placed a hand on her shoulder. "Torquin will come home. He's strong."

A fresh wave of tears trailed down her hollow cheeks. "Phoenix bless you."

Ikane stroked the baby's wispy-thin hair, grabbed his horse's reins, and continued down the street. I tugged hard, urging my horse to catch up to him.

"What is this place? Why are there women and children here?"

"These women and children have followed their deformed husbands, fathers, and brothers into exile," Ikane said.

"Exile? Just because of their deformities?"

"Aye. You saw Ardon's leg and wandering eye. Torquin has a bad arm, stunted from birth. You'll see many here like that." His accent returned. "The Dead Forest has no game, so they must travel half a day just to hunt the living woods. Even the sea holds no bounty here. No fish, no kelp, nothing. Food and water are scarce."

His raiding had kept them alive. Like me, they were forced to survive by living like pirates. He couldn't leave them. Especially not while Malese was skin and bones. But was it safe to stay so close to the ruby?

I looked back at the garrison looming over the city. I could spare a day or two, couldn't I? Ardon said the next caravan was large. There would be plenty to go around.

What was I thinking? This was wrong. We couldn't thieve like this. Even if we did, the people would be hungry again by week's end. It would start all over again.

Stone crunched under Ikane's boots as he stepped onto the wide pathway clinging to the side of the cliff. The ashen sea moved below as if carrying a weight too much to bear, sluggishly rolling against stone.

How far was Rion's reach? Even the wind stood still, the salty brine stifled under her leeching power.

"Are you steady?" Ikane asked over his shoulder.

Something sparked in my chest. "I'm not weak." I hugged the cliffs as the pathway narrowed, coaxing my new horse to follow.

"That's not what I meant."

"I know what you meant, and I'm not weak. I can ride. I could have come with you. You just didn't want me to see what you were doing."

"Can you blame me?"

My mouth clamped shut.

The road grew too narrow to walk beside my horse. Her eyes grew wide as the sea opened below. She jerked back, tugging me with her. A corner of the road broke free under her hoof. Stone plummeted, slamming into the cliffside, a brittle shattering swallowed by the sea.

I drew her close, stroking her nose. "Settle."

Ikane peered around the body of his horse, eyes wild. "Are you alright?"

"How much farther? She's going to bolt."

"The homesteads should be here." He stared ahead. The road continued around the ragged turn, an endless snake hugging the vertical stone.

He pressed on, coming to a wide section. "There." He guided his horse into a carved-out crevice leading into the cliffside. Dull stone swallowed the hazy sunlight, the thick air plummeting in temperature. How could it be so cold and stifling at the same time? Should I hug my cloak tighter or loosen my collar to breathe?

The narrow passage opened to a place frozen in time. Sunlight streamed into the hollow center. One side of the crags held two tiers of windows carved into the cliff's rocky face. Two stained glass windows remained intact on the bottom corner, the blue-and-green glass boasting color in a dusty world drained of life.

"This will do nicely." Ikane led his horse toward a single-story building protruding on our right. The doors to the small stable were warped and splintered but somehow remained whole after decades of abandonment.

I guided my horse into one stall. "Do you really think raiding is going to help these people?"

Ikane shouldered our bags. "What do you mean?"

"We can give them food, but they will be hungry again in a day."

"It's all I know." He closed the gate, falling into step as we moved to the larger building with the green-and-blue windows.

I must be going mad. "We need to teach them to fend for themselves."

"You mean teach them to raid?"

My stomach churned as he said the words I couldn't. "Do you think they can?"

"They may have deformed bodies, but I've seen them do things I didn't think possible." He pushed the parched door open, hinges squealing. An enormous baking oven cut deep into the rock at the far end. Blue-and-green sunrays filtered through the windows, casting cool light on a wooden table, overturned stools, and broken pottery. A hutch carved into the cliffside held treasures of the past in sheltered cubbies.

Ikane dropped our bags, a cloud of dust bursting from the floor. "I'll get a fire going." He grabbed the leg of a broken chair. With the stomp of his boot, the leg broke free. He pitched it into the fireplace.

I closed the doors branching from the kitchen and leading to various rooms, trapping the fire's heat. As I unrolled our bedrolls, I saw they fit snugly in a corner under the windows.

Ikane leaned against the wall, bringing his knees up as he sat down. He loosened the buckles of his new armor, stripping the black steel away. "This wood won't last long."

Firelight danced as it consumed the dry lumber. It was already black, already hungry for more. Just like Rion.

I lowered myself to my bedroll. The muscles down my back and leg pulled and stretched. Would I ever regain my mobility? "Will you take me with you tomorrow?"

He glanced up. "On the raid?"

I nodded. "And don't say I'm not strong enough."

A smile tugged on his lips. "I never thought I'd see the day when the most dedicated soldier of Roanfire would go rogue."

"Well?"

"Not yet. You still limp, and the way you cringed just now tells me you're still in a great deal of pain. I can't watch your back and mine. It's better you stay."

I groaned. "When? My body may never fully heal."

"You will." He dragged his black pauldrons over his head, letting them crash on the floor beside him. "Be prepared, Little Brendagger. When I return from the raid, your training will begin."

# CHAPTER 26

# ROGUE SOLDIER

*H*azy sunlight flashed on the polished black steel of Ikane's swords. His feet were poised for battle— legs bent, dust curling around his boots.

This was my chance. Sweat coated my palms as I crushed the hilt of the sword, muscles ready.

He charged, and I brought the sword up. His strike was fast and calculated. Metal rang . . . and the weapon spun from my grip. It was like I wasn't even trying.

Ikane dragged back, a flicker of worry crossing his face.

"Again." I grabbed my sword from the dirt.

"Kea . . ."

I didn't need his pity. I charged, whipping my sword at his legs. He danced back as the weight of my sword twisted my torso. Lightning tore from the arrow wound down my leg, seizing the muscles.

"Charred rachis." My teeth ground together, trying to keep my growl from turning into a cry. The tip of my sword plunged into the earth as I leaned against it.

I'd worked tirelessly over the last few weeks strengthening my body, stretching my muscles, learning to use my leg despite the sharp pricks lancing through it. I wanted to leave this place. I wanted to help Ikane with the raids and training.

Ikane lowered his swords. "You've done enough today."

Heat burned my eyes, pressure building behind them as my

vision blurred. What more could I do? It had been six weeks since the attack.

"It's alright." Ikane's hand rested on my shoulder. "You just need more time."

"How much more? I should fly across the battlefield. I should be helping you, helping the people." I tore a hand through my hair.

"You took an arrow to your back. That is not an injury to take lightly. You've made more progress than you think."

*He's right. You've grown stronger.*

The stale air froze in my chest. She was back, her fire slithering into my mind as easily as a snake through grass.

"Kea?" Ikane's hand lifted off my shoulder as if I'd burned him.

I pinched my temples. "Get out of my head." The words pushed through my teeth.

*You will be happy to know that I, too, have regained strength. Another soul has found eternity in me.*

Another soul? Did that mean another human life? She'd added another corpse to her growing crypt in the tower?

"Kea? What's wrong? Is it the ruby?" Ikane sheathed his swords, taking my shoulders in both hands.

"Witch." My eyes scrunched shut. If only I could see her in my mind's eye, find her weakness. *Forging the Phoenix Stone was a mistake, one I will rectify.*

Heat flowed through my mind, burning behind my eyelids. It seared down my throat. *The phoenix cannot die. It rises from its ashes. You are of my ashes. Why do you resist this great honor?*

*Because I deserve to live a full life!*

*How full can your life be? You cower here in the ruins of Fold, hunted by your own kingdom for a crime you didn't commit. Help me, and you will see them kneel in humiliation for what they have done.*

"Kea, please." Ikane's hands pinched my arms. "What can I do?"

*Oh, to taste love again.* Her heat reached through my body, tendrils stretching for him.

Not Ikane. Never. He had nursed me back to health despite my prejudice. His heart was bigger than Roanfire, deeper than the Rethreal Sea.

Her smoldering vines brushed against his essence, shuddering and flaring as if they'd just touched oil.

I twisted out of his grip, stumbling away. My knees buckled, hitting the dirt.

"Kea!" He dove for me.

"Stay back!" I scrambled backward.

"What did I do?" The pain on his face sank into my chest like a dagger.

*You think you can keep him? The only way to have him forever is to relent. Come to me. Live in me. Become the vessel for the Phoenix Goddess.*

She would never be reborn, not through me. Something flickered in my mind, a white light flashing like an elusive firefly in tall grass. Soothing warmth, so different from her scorching heat, flowed from it, a promise of shelter and strength.

*What are you doing?* Her voice shook.

Another white light flashed, and her fiery tendrils shied away from its brilliance.

The roar of a thousand voices cut through the light, stomping it out like boots on glowing embers. Fire rolled down my throat into my lungs. A furnace of violence exploded, tearing through bone and muscle, flowing through my blood. Hammers cracked against my skull.

*This is only a taste of what will be yours if you dare challenge me again.*

Her fire recoiled, sucking into itself, pulling from my mind like a whip. Cold rushed in, coating my bones in ice. My stomach heaved. I rolled to my hands and knees, my last meal hitting the dust. I'd never trembled this badly.

Ikane crouched before me, hands up as if too afraid to touch me. Redness blurred his image, and something thick and hot streaked down my cheeks, nose, and ears.

She'd cowered. It was brief, but she'd recoiled at the tiny white lights.

I pushed to my knees.

Ikane's face contorted. "Why are you smiling like that?"

"I fought back." I wiped the blood from my nose with the back of my sleeve. "I resisted her fire."

Ikane swallowed hard. "We should go." He stood. "I shouldn't have kept you here. I should have never agreed to raid for these people."

"They needed you."

"You are bleeding tears, Kea."

I tasted blood in the back of my throat, but I ignored it. How did those lights flicker to life? How had I resisted?

"Come." He held his hand out to me. "I'll prepare the horses. We'll find the White Wardent like you asked."

I grabbed my sword, using it as a cane to pull myself from the dirt. Ikane took my arm.

I shoved him back. "Don't touch me!"

"I'm sorry. I didn't mean to—" His brows furrowed. "But why?"

"Didn't you feel Rion leaching life from you before?"

"I'm not sure what I felt. I was worried for you, Kea."

"That was Rion, trying to take you. She reached through me."

He rubbed his face, pushing his hair back. "Kea . . ." His tone said he didn't quite believe me.

"Trust me, Ikane. For your own safety, you mustn't touch me. At least not until I figure out how to stop her." Was she hearing this now? I defied her, even after her furnace nearly tore me apart.

"As you wish." He looked away.

"And you cannot abandon these people. Not yet."

He tugged on his bracer. "I think you're ready."

"We barely crossed blades."

His sea-blue and meadow-green eyes locked on mine. "That is not the only thing that determines strength."

Ikane pulled a scrap of cloth from beneath his cloak and handed it to me. It was soft and thin, holding the familiar dusty-blue color of the gown I had worn at the coronation. Four tattered ribbons hung from the corners. A mask? Made from my gown? I'd left it in the—

"You went back?"

"There's no fabric like that out here," he said. "It's lighter and breathes easier, and we have to protect your identity. So if you're going to join the raid, I thought—"

"Do you know what could have happened? You don't

understand how far she can reach, how much she wants you!" I crushed the mask in my fist. "I would have worn a mask made of wood rather than have you go back there."

"I was careful."

"She reached the soldiers at the edge of the forest! Half a day's ride away. What makes you think you can go to the garrison and be safe?"

"Kea, I . . ." His hand stopped midair before touching my arm, curling into a fist. He bit his lip. "I'm sorry. I won't go back there again."

I missed his touch, the warmth and strength that flowed from his fingers. "Promise?"

"I promise." He opened the door to the pale light of dusk. "Now put it on so we can go."

Torches flickered around a crumbling well in the center of the marketplace. A dozen shapes of men and women faced a man on horseback. Long hair rippled down his back, his bear-like build reminding me of Ropert. Broad shoulders, narrow hips, firm jaw.

His eyes flicked up. "Ikane. You've brought a friend?"

What was wrong with his arm? Instead of a hand, a twisted stump was attached to his wrist, a single finger so crumpled it was hardly recognizable. His other arm boasted its size.

Ikane rode up beside him, clasping the man's good hand. "Torquin. This is my sister, Paige. She's going to help us today."

"Ah." Torquin smiled at me. "Malese was wondering what happened to you."

"Malese? Your wife?"

"The love of my life." Torquin pulled his shoulders back, turning his attention to the gathered crowd and raising his voice. "Alright. Our target camps just beyond the stream by the borders of the Dead Forest. We should reach them by late morning."

Did no one here have horses besides Torquin and two others? How would we bring the loot back? This was really happening. I was going to raid just like a Leviathan pirate.

Torquin called out five names. "You are with Ikane. Follow his orders."

Five individuals shifted to Ikane's side.

"Let's go."

With Torquin in the lead, we left the crumbling buildings of the city behind, coming to the river that cut through dead stumps of trees stripped bare for firewood. The river gradually reduced to a stream, leaving a wide riverbank of rock and dust.

The group moved forward at an irritating pace. We'd miss the caravan entirely at this rate. Only five seemed to have energy enough for this raid. The rest trudged onward with brave faces and hunched shoulders as dust swirled about their tattered boots.

"Slow down." Ikane leaned over, grabbing my horse's bridle. "We have at least two hours of riding ahead. They may be slow, but they are wise. They know where to spend their energy."

I tucked my hair behind my ears. "How many have fallen in these raids?"

"None," Ikane said. "They are full of surprises."

"How many live in Fold?"

"About fifty."

Fifty? We only had five horses. How would we come back with enough food for fifty? We'd have to raid more than a caravan—we'd have to raid a marketplace. Was this attempt at robbing a little caravan worth so much energy?

"No more talk. Our voices carry with the lack of shrubbery and leaves." Ikane straightened in his saddle. "Follow my lead, and you'll do fine."

I bit my lip. Me. A soldier of Roanfire. Raiding. Ugh, I had to stop thinking of myself that way. I was a fugitive now. This was the only way to survive.

When was the last time I'd heard a song as sweet as this? Birdsong taunted the Dead Forest with the promise of life.

Dead trees striped across the living woods like iron bars, and sunlight lanced behind them, breaking through snow-laden branches of evergreen trees.

Torquin, Ikane, and the others slipped from their mounts, dust bursting beneath their boots as they landed. I followed, guiding my horse to the unnatural line in the trees. Snow piled high like it leaned against an invisible wall, and tracks of wildlife meandered in the glistening white powder.

My boot sank deep, a soft crunch rippling up my leg. Pressure lifted from my chest, my lungs inhaling sunshine and snow. The sharp, earthy fragrance of pine expanded around me, a scent I'd nearly forgotten.

Ikane and the others released their horses' reins, allowing the animals to bury their noses in search of grass.

I slinked after them, careful to keep my feet light, pressing against every shadow and trunk willing to hide me.

Torquin stopped, holding his fist up.

I froze.

A figure moved ahead, and a brief flash of a gray-blue tunic appeared between the trees. Voices carried.

This was it. The caravan.

Torquin slinked closer, arching around a tree, surveying what I could not see.

My heart thundered through my ears, body shaking. My underarms grew damp. I'd fought before. I'd crossed blades with Ikane. Why did this terrify me more than facing the Leviathans?

Torquin looked over his shoulder, making eye contact with Ikane. He gave one nod.

Ikane pulled his swords from his back in a slow, calculated motion. Jerking his head, five impaired bandits followed, moving through the trees like vipers, seamless and silent.

Crushing the hilt of my sword, I followed, catching sight of a family loading their wagon through the trees. Another wagon stood in the clearing beside it. A wheel protruded from behind a trunk, slipping out of sight.

Three wagons. That was promising.

Ikane stopped, the disabled bandits taking position around him. Cupping a hand beside his lips, a soft whir escaped like a purring bird.

A silent storm of bandits barreled through the trees. I moved after them, their energy pulling me forward.

Screams tore from the merchants. Some bolted. Some cowered under wagon wheels. Others barked at hired swordsmen, urging them to brandish their weapons. A driver slapped his horses' reins—one wagon was slipping away.

Deep-brown eyes bulged up at me, a boy's face chubby with youth. He trembled, mouth open, the scream frozen in his throat.

Ice crystalized in my veins. He was looking at me. No one had ever looked at me that way before. I was a protector and guardian. I was supposed to defend Roanfire and its people.

"Fin!" a woman in a gray skirt screamed at him.

He bolted. She grabbed his tiny hand, dragging him into the trees.

"Kea! What are you doing?" Ikane held the reins of two giant horses freshly harnessed to a covered wagon. They stamped their feet at the pandemonium, the wagon rocking back and forth.

The feeble group of bandits converged on the wagon, armfuls of items crashing inside.

I couldn't do this. I couldn't plunder and steal from these hardworking people.

"Kea." Ikane's fingers dug into my arm, pulling me forward.

When had he come to my side? Torquin sat in the driver's perch of the wagon, barking at the team of horses to move. The wagon rumbled through the trees, wheels crunching over snow.

"Come on, Kea. Move."

My feet stumbled after Ikane, flying from the destroyed campsite. The mask pulled into my mouth as I huffed.

Lifeless trees and brown dust opened through the foliage. I deserved to go back. To feel the air crushing my body, the moisture leeching from my skin, the silence. I deserved to rot in Meldron's dungeons.

"It'll get easier." Ikane stepped over a fallen tree, his horse trailing. "You'll learn to ignore the faces."

Easier? I never wanted to do this again.

"Ikane!" Torquin called after us. He pulled the horses to a stop, jumping from the wagon.

Dust curled around the unconscious form of a willowy man lying on the ground.

Ikane sprinted, boots skidding to a halt as Torquin lifted the man. "Help me get him in the wagon."

He'd given all he could on this raid. For what? Just to try again another day? This was no life. How could Roanfire simply banish them because of their appearance?

Ikane returned, taking his horse's reins from me.

"Is he going to be alright?"

"He's weak, but he'll survive. This happens often after the raids."

"They need more."

"They do."

Fold City appeared through the trees, a gray-brown sprawl of buildings along the seaside. The wagon jolted and rumbled into the market square. People emerged from tattered curtain doors, hungry eyes piercing the wagon's exterior. Their thin bodies pressed together, pushing and shoving.

Ikane reached over his shoulder, a hand curling around the hilt of one sword.

The need for survival pulsed through them, like a rapidly growing fire. In a moment, it would strike like dry tinder and flare.

I pressed my back against the wagon as it stopped.

The crowd drove forward, hands clawing at the sideboards, wheels, and canvas. The horses shifted, and the wagon rolled back, knocking into the crowd behind them.

They were going to kill each other. Men and women had risked their lives, sacrificed every morsel of energy, pushed beyond their physical abilities to bring life to these people.

I had not challenged my virtues for this.

The noise of my sword hissing from its leather scabbard caused them to fall back. "Where is your dignity?" I swung the blade, driving them further. "Where is your respect?"

The crowd surged behind me. Ikane and Torquin brandished weapons. Several weary bandits pushed through their exhaustion and surrounded the wagon, pointing weapons at the throng.

"These men have risked everything to bring this back." The mask covering my mouth muffled my voice. I roared. "Don't make them fight you, too."

The raging greed ebbed, silence sweeping through the market square. Sunken eyes and gaunt faces stared at me like I was the answer they had been waiting for. They needed guidance and direction, hope and validation.

I climbed onto the driver's bench. "There is more than enough. Form a line. One person, one item. Return to the end of the line. You will receive seconds and thirds as long as we continue to have goods."

People shuffled, a winding row taking shape through the expanse of the market square. I sheathed my sword, looking at the first person in line.

A young girl no older than ten twisted her bony fingers about the folds of her filthy skirt. Her eyes brimmed with hope. Her mother stood behind her, hands resting on the girl's shoulders.

They needed food. More than anything, these people needed nourishment. Did we even have food? What had been tossed into the wagon in our frenzy?

Ikane sheathed his swords, leaping into the wagon bed. It pitched and wobbled as he scrounged through the carelessly tossed plunder inside. He held a morsel of bread out to me.

I leaned in, taking it. "How much food do we have?" I whispered.

"There is a lot of clothing and fabric in here. I think we stole the wagon of a tailor."

This was going to be harder than I thought.

I handed the girl the wedge of bread.

"Please. My son is ill at home," the mother said. "He needs food."

My heart dropped into my stomach. The line behind her stretched on. How many needed bread? If I could, I would load her apron full. But I had to make it stretch.

"Kea." Ikane pushed something rough and long into my hand. Jerky. "I found a sack in here. There is enough for all."

One meal. That was it. At least they wouldn't go to bed hungry tonight.

The woman clutched the jerky to her bony chest, her eyes shining as she steered her daughter to the back of the line.

A gaunt middle-aged man hobbled up, leaning on a cane. He

was missing a leg and I found myself wondering about Fortin.

"Do you have any shoes?" he asked.

Shoes? He only had one foot.

"My son." He motioned to a lean figure behind him. A threadbare blanket hugged the boy's shoulders, his trousers hanging in rags just below the knees. Scraps of cloth swathed his feet.

Ikane showed us two pairs of soft leather shoes, but both were too small.

"We will try again next time." I lowered a blanket and a thick wedge of jerky to them.

"Thank you," the man said. The boy smiled, his mouth moving, but no sound came out. He was mute.

Hands reached up, and eyes shimmered with tears as the people hugged items to their chests. The horses and wagon found a home. The crowd dispersed as daylight shifted to evening violet gray in the sky. Cold settled on my hands and face, and the arrow wound in my back screamed for me to lie down. My stomach rumbled and pinched.

In the chaos, I'd forgotten to save any food for Ikane and me.

Torquin held his hand out to me. "Thank you for your help. There is something about you . . . something we needed today."

His grip held hidden strength beneath his lack of nourishment.

"I did nothing."

"You did more than you know." Torquin turned to Ikane. "We make an excellent team."

"That we do," Ikane said.

Torquin shifted the bundle under his withered arm. "I had best get back to Malese."

"Did you get some food?" Ikane asked.

Torquin's shoulders sagged. He shook his head. "I took a blanket and a new dress for her."

Ikane pulled a wedge of bread from his pocket. He broke it in half, handing Torquin the larger portion. "Let me know when the next raid is."

Torquin blinked, his eyes shining like so many I had seen today. "Phoenix bless you."

Ikane broke the bread again, handing me half. "Let's go home."

Dust swirled from the horse's russet coat under Ikane's brush strokes. Ikane had come a long way with horses since leaving Daram.

He set the brush aside, offering the horse water from the rain barrel. We'd have to refill it tomorrow, a laborious task. It didn't rain in Fold. The only water came from the small river cutting through the heart of the Dead Forest.

"Perhaps we should let the horses go free." I stroked the nose of the black mare. "This isn't a life for them. They need to run. They need grass and water."

"I've named him Rudder," Ikane said, brushing his horse's forehead. "You should name yours, too."

"Ikane."

"Have you noticed the saddlebags?" he asked.

"What about them?"

He closed the pen, walking to the exit. "They are packed with the essentials should we need to leave at a moment's notice. We need the horses."

He still worried I would be recognized. "We can't leave until the people can fend for themselves."

"Then will you help me?" He stopped outside the door. "A few have promising skill, but they've made little progress. I'm not as skilled a teacher as Eamon was."

I bit my lip. Teach? If I taught the people tactics and how to wield weapons, was that as disgraceful as if I raided the caravans myself?

I hugged my shoulders, looking to the sky. Stars flickered overhead, flashes of eternal lights beyond Rion's scope of influence. If only I could sprout wings and soar into their embrace.

"I think I'll name her Halfpace."

Ikane smiled.

# CHAPTER 27

# BOUNTY

ome on, Paige." Malese slipped her arm through mine, pulling me through the torchlit street. Color met her cheeks. Her body filled out her dress. Her touch was vibrant, burning my skin.

How long had it been since I'd felt contact with another human? I didn't dare brush elbows with Ikane. What if Rion felt her, too?

"They've prepared everything," she said. "Venison and flatbread, even the mead from the last raid." She skipped a step, beaming at Torquin who carried their son, Pan, in his good arm.

"I can smell it," Ikane said.

Multicolored banners stretched from building to building over the market square. Torchlight flickered across tables and benches bursting with people and food. Twin fires burned, roasting juicy sides of venison. Fat dripped. The fire sizzled, rich flavor infusing the air.

"Here they are!" Ardon bellowed from a table, arms outstretched, his cane in one hand.

The crowd erupted in applause and cheers. Was this for us?

Malese squeezed my arm. "You deserve this." She slipped her other arm through Ikane's. "You both do."

"Tonight we celebrate new beginnings!" Ardon raised a mug. "Ikane and Paige, we will miss you. We are forever in your debt."

Everyone cheered again, raising drinks.

How did they know we were leaving? Ikane and I had only decided last night that it was time. After a month of training, our twenty-three students had completed two successful raids without us. Torquin had grown most of all, his body transforming into muscle and power.

Two flutes and a drum played.

Ardon's daughter, a young woman with midnight curls, took Ikane's hand, leading him into a dance. She moved like water, her curves alluring and sweet, her hand slipping around his neck. He stiffened. Something in me tensed, too, a green finger scraping on the bottom of my stomach. He was mine . . . wasn't he?

"Sit with an old man for a moment?" Ardon limped past me, sighing heavily as he sank onto a vacant bench behind the tables. He stretched his disabled leg awkwardly, patting the space beside him. "Tell me, where will you go once you leave our little sanctuary?"

I slipped onto the bench beside him. The raven-haired beauty pressed against Ikane, whispering something into his ear. His feet froze.

"Paige?"

I looked at Ardon. "Uh, what?"

"Are you and your brother not happy here?"

"We are."

"But?"

"But there is something we need to do."

He shifted his cane to one hand. "You have been such a blessing to us. We shall be eternally grateful for what you have given—and what you have yet to give."

What did he mean by "yet to give"?

A coiled rope flew over my head. It pulled into my mouth, shoving the mask I always wore through my lips. Iron grips locked on my arms. I kicked the table, the bench rocking as my body was dragged back.

Ardon knew. Somehow, he knew who I was. Ikane was right. Where was he? Did Malese and Torquin know? Was this all part of the plan?

The shadow of two buildings engulfed me, the sounds of the celebration growing faint.

I dug my heels into the dirt. All I needed was enough leverage to knock one of my captors off-balance. The man on my right stumbled, losing hold of my arm. I twisted, my fist slamming into his jaw.

I knew him. I knew them both. They were students of mine, Detron and Perchek. Heat rushed through my chest, pushing into my head. How could they do this to me?

My neck jerked back, the rope digging into the sides of my mouth as Perchek pulled me against his chest.

"Now, now." Ardon limped through the alleyway, sounds of laughter and music echoing after him. He stopped before me.

Traitor. The mask stuck to my tongue, pushing against my nose as it flared with each gasp.

He leaned in, his breath smelling of mead. "I knew who you were from the first day I met you. King-slayer, Keatep Brendagger." He straightened. "Take her to my house and bind her."

I screamed for Ikane, my cry muffled by the mask and overpowered by the celebration. Perchek and Detron pushed the door to a building open. I braced a leg against the frame, arching back. If they got me inside, Ikane would never find me.

An elbow slammed into my thigh. Numbness raced down to my foot. I stumbled inside. Detron's boot plowed into the back of my knee, making it buckle. Driving my belly to the floor, he dug his knee into my back.

The mask muffled my scream.

Rope bit into my wrists and ankles. Then the door pulled shut, plunging the cold room into silent darkness.

I rolled to my side, my leg seizing again. Was this permanent? I couldn't rely on my body anymore.

There had to be a way to escape. If I could get ahold of something sharp enough to cut the ropes . . . The fire iron, perhaps, or the dented shovel by the ash pail? Or the dishes displayed on the freestanding shelf. If I could just roll over and knock—

Lightning surged through my back, forcing me to lie still.

I should have listened to Ikane. I should have stayed hidden.

The door creaked open. Ardon's heavy *thump*, shuffle, *thump*, shuffle came near. He lowered himself to the hearth, back facing me as he set his cane beside him.

"I hope you understand. We do what we must to survive." He stacked logs in the fireplace. A flicker of orange illuminated the room.

Feeble lout. Ikane and I had given them tools to thrive. They had everything they needed. Their bellies were full. Children laughed and played. Men and women had filled out.

He twisted to face me, his bad eye wandering to the corner. "Let's get that off you, shall we?"

The rope dug and pinched the corners of my mouth as he loosened it. He pulled the mask down. "Lovely." His fingers brushed my cheek.

I jerked back. "Don't touch me."

"Now, now. I want to make your last days as pleasant as possible. The more you resist, the more I will have to hurt you." He rubbed his hands together. "Though the bounty won't change no matter what condition you are in."

"Ikane will find me."

He laughed. "My daughter is a sage in the art of seduction. He won't even think of you 'til tomorrow when the sun is high. You will be halfway to Meldron by then."

"Are you willing to risk his wrath? You've seen him fight."

"He's not your brother, is he?"

I clamped my mouth shut.

"Ah, a lover. Oh, that must cut deep, knowing he is in the arms of another." He grabbed his cane, pulling himself to his feet. "I hope you ate something. We have a long journey—"

The door banged open, dust bursting from the dry wood as it cracked. Ikane's green eye smoldered. He jerked Ardon's daughter into the room by her wrist, her eyes wide, body trembling.

He'd come.

Ardon took a step back. "Now, now, Ikane. Don't be rash."

A growl tore from Ikane's throat, more animal than human. "We gave you a new life!" He shoved the girl into Ardon. They stumbled back, hitting the shelves. Dishes crashed to the floor, shattering.

"You can't honestly tell me you haven't thought of turning her in yourself." Ardon steadied himself. "We could live like noblemen, you and I, with the amount they have—"

"You greedy maggot!" Ikane turned into a blur. His hand crushed Ardon's throat, driving the old man against the shelf. More dishes crashed. Black steel touched Ardon's rounded belly.

"Don't hurt him." The girl sank to her knees, hands clasped, her cheeks glistening with tears. "Please."

"Untie her." Ikane's words pushed through his teeth.

The girl shuffled to my side, her fingers shaking as she worked the knots. Blood raced to my fingertips, stinging like the bite of fire ants. She offered me her hand, helping me to my feet.

Ikane's shoulders heaved with enraged breath, his hand shaking as he resisted the urge to drive his sword into the man's stomach.

"Ikane." I rubbed the ache from my wrists. "He's not worth it."

Ikane fell back. Ardon sank to the floor.

"Papa." His daughter flew to his side.

Ikane turned to me, his eye like green fire. "Are you hurt?"

"I'm alright." He was here. As long as Ikane was by my side, it didn't matter what happened.

Ikane sheathed his sword, glowering at Ardon and his terrified daughter. "We've outstayed our welcome."

The clopping of Halfpace's hooves were absorbed in the thick air. Dust churned in her wake. Ashen tree trunks slipped by, their long shadows striping across us as the sun rose. Bud-encrusted trees sprung through the brown, the distinct barrier cutting like a knife between the two forests. Birdsong lured me forward.

We were almost there. Finally, I would be on my quest to find the White Wardent. Should I dare feel Ikane's touch again? Was this the end of Rion's reach?

*Where do you think you are going?*

Her voices barreled through my mind like a fiery rockslide, suffocating and thick. The trees pushed to the side, warping as if seen behind a glass bottle.

I clawed at Halfpace's black mane. Something smooth and

leathery caught my fingers instead. The saddle. I clung to it, and Halfpace shifted to the side as my legs squeezed, giving her conflicting signals.

My body dropped.

A dull ache jarred up my shoulder as I hit the ground, dust coating my mouth as I rolled.

"Kea!" Ikane cried, yanking Rudder around.

I pushed myself from the dirt, trees whirring. Fire snaked between memories.

*Come back to the tower,* Rion demanded.

I would never set foot in that tomb again. If she wanted a host, she would have to come to me.

Ikane slipped from his saddle, hurrying to my side. "Kea, are you hurt?"

I held up a hand. "Stay back."

He went rigid.

*Come back to the tower. Claim your birthright.*

*When I die,* I said, *it will be on my terms. Not yours.*

She laughed. *Don't you see? You will never taste death.*

*Then stop talking, and just do it!*

Her voices sighed like a staggered moan across a battlefield. *Do you intend to make me expend that much power again? Come to me. Now.*

Fire surged behind my eyes, the dust, the dirt, the dead trees igniting in flame. It had been two months since my last dream and five weeks since I last heard her voices.

How could I have forgotten this fire? We had to get away, out of reach.

A heatwave surged through my blood, spreading to my bones.

*Every time you run, every time you force my hand, I spend more energy. Come to me. Now.*

"Kea." Ikane's hands hovered by my shoulders. "Please, tell me. What can I do?"

She reached for him, tendrils of fire searching and groping a hair's breadth away from his skin.

"Stay back," I warned him through clenched teeth. I clutched my head, staggering away.

"Kea." His voice held a pitch of pure terror. "What is that?"

I glanced up, his eyes drawn to something behind us. I squinted through the fire behind my eyes.

Feathers, no.

Gray mist rolled forward, coursing around the base of the trees like rushing water. She was going to take us both.

"Run, Ikane. Run!"

Hot coal ignited under my feet as I sprinted for the line in the trees, fire licking up my legs. Smoke filled my lungs. I would never reach the edge in time.

At least Ikane could make it. He was fast.

He glanced over his shoulder, turned, and ran back toward me. What a fool. He couldn't help me—I'd slow us both down.

A white spark flared inside, a solitary star pushing through fire.

The shield.

The magic.

I didn't care what it was.

It repulsed her.

I leapt for it, holding it close, wrapping everything I was around the tiny flicker. A soothing breath gusted against Rion's fire. My lungs opened, my legs moving faster.

Ikane's hand crushed mine, his boots skidding in the dirt as he shifted direction.

He was touching me. His hand was firm . . . and Rion wasn't consuming him. Her fire hit a wall, the shield of white lights flickering to life across every corner of my mind like stars waking in the night sky.

*You are just as foolish as Queen Damita. Your fate could have been different,* she roared.

Terrible screams split the stale air.

Behind us, Halfpace and Rudder thrashed in the dust as the mist overtook them.

*Leave these woods, and I shall haunt your dreams. I shall invade your mind. I will curse those around you. Do not think you will be safe. I will have the soul of the man you call Ikane. He will be mine.*

My boots struck the moist earth of the living forest. Her essence floundered, the gray mist deteriorating before reaching the edge of the Dead Forest.

She could reach no further.

Ikane stopped, his hand crushing mine as he looked back, breathing hard.

Splinters tore through my lungs—my mouth had been leeched of all moisture. I licked my lips.

She had almost destroyed us. We could have been trapped in her ruby prison for another four hundred years.

Trembling, my muscles turned to sludge. My knees hit the ground, moisture soaking through my trousers. Blades of spring grass pushed beneath rotting leaves. We'd made it.

Ikane sank beside me. He reached up, hesitated a moment, then brushed my hair from my cheeks. "Are you alright?"

His skin was like the breath of life, warm and tender.

*I will have you. Both of you.* Rion's voices pushed through my mind, distant and weak, as if shouted through a stone wall.

I pressed Ikane's calloused palm against my cheek. "We're safe . . . for now."

# CHAPTER 28

# LEATHER BOOTS

Spring rain drizzled across my shoulders as I sank to the grassy hillside. Below, ships sagged at the docks, masts and sails sporting black stains from fire damage. Another limped in from the sea, a thin trail of smoke rising to the gray sky behind it.

Red tunics dotted the streets between the timber-framed buildings. This was Dragontooth Harbor, wasn't it? The city of the sea? The central port for Roanfire's warships?

Ikane dropped his makeshift pack beside me, his eyes narrowing at the scene. "That doesn't look good."

"The Leviathans?"

He brushed his damp hair from his face, crouching. "It must be."

If the Leviathans overtook Dragontooth Harbor, Roanfire's first line of defense would be obliterated.

Ikane unbuckled his swords, revealing dry patches on his shoulders where the leather belts had protected his tunic. He set his swords on the pack.

"What are you doing?"

"I'm going to the market. With so many Phoenix soldiers reinforcing the place, we can't risk staying at an inn. I'll get some food."

"Do we have money for a horse? My feet are killing me."

He chuckled. "I'll see what I can do."

Taking calculated steps, he surfed down the slick incline, growing smaller and smaller.

I brought my knees up, resting my chin on my arms. No inn again. We'd lost everything when Rion took our horses. Our rations, our water, our clothes, our bedding. We'd slept on nothing but the ground, huddled in our cloaks, for the past five days. My stomach pinched, wanting more than baby dandelion leaves and clover. I had been looking forward to a hot bath and a warm meal.

Something bit behind my eyes. A red spark danced across my vision.

Was it her?

I dug my fingers into the rain-soaked grass. The scorching heat would begin any moment.

*Did you think my promise was empty?* Her tone burned with venom, but it was weak and distant as if shouted across a vast body of water. *I am wasting lives, vital energy that could have endured forever. Squandered because of you.*

Why wasn't she burning me?

Maybe she couldn't. Maybe the distance was too much.

*Five souls have met their end in order to reach you. Their lives are on you. Know this: Every time you hear me, every time you feel me, you have spoiled more lives. Claim your birthright!*

The stinging redness in my vision dissolved.

Rain struck my cheeks, dripping down my chin. I pried my fingers from the grass. This was only the beginning. I needed to find answers now. Faslight must know something.

Ikane climbed the slope. A bulging leather bag slung across his shoulder. His boots slipped, forcing him to brace himself with a hand to the ground. "No horses," he huffed, rain dripping from his lips. "Everything has been seized by the soldiers."

I stood.

"You're shivering."

"I'm alright." I didn't need to worry him.

He pulled me close, rubbing my shoulders. "We need to get out of this rain. I think I saw a rock formation at the bottom of the hill, just outside the city."

"Promise me we'll sleep at an inn when we reach Wetmond."

"Inn or no, I promise you'll sleep dry and warm."

Soft leather shoes were not meant for traipsing through the woods. Cold wetness leeched through the seams. Mud squished, suctioning my feet to the ground. Burning tore at my heels.

We couldn't risk traveling on the main road. There were too many soldiers making their way to Dragontooth Harbor. And the ships that used to sail up the Karn River delivering passengers and supplies had been commissioned to battle the Leviathan pirates.

If only I had my boots. They would hold up to this terrain.

"We're getting close. Pull your hood up." Ikane veered off our shrubbery-filled path, merging onto the main road leading to Wetmond. Two-story buildings lined the street. Horses and carts rattled down the cobblestone road. A group of Phoenix soldiers marched after it.

Ikane pulled me behind him as they passed. The sooner we could get indoors, the better.

"We shouldn't be here," he whispered.

"I'm not spending another night in soggy clothes." An inn stood across the way, warm light spilling from the windows, drawing me like a moth to a candle.

Ikane didn't move. "The rain is tapering off."

"We're as wet as storm-tossed ships, and your lips are blue. If we don't get warm soon, we'll both be fighting fevers."

Ikane pursed his lips. "Alright, but not that one." He headed down a side street. "The inns along the main road are monitored more closely."

I tore my eyes from the warm glow, following Ikane down the puddle-filled street. Homes grew smaller as we neared the edge of the city, strangling the street in tightly packed rows of shadow.

Ikane turned to a building slightly larger than the rest. The wooden sign was faded. The roof sagged on one end, and light glowed between gaps in the wooden planks. At least we would have a roof over our heads.

Smoke billowed from the chimney. Where there was smoke, there was fire. And where there was fire, there was warmth.

Ikane pushed the door open.

"If you're looking for a room, we have none." A plump man

wiped his hands on a rag, dropping it on the splintered counter. He scratched his rounded belly. "Those vile Leviathan pirates have driven everyone from the coast. Every soul is hunkering down at inns from here to Bakka."

I didn't need a room. I'd sleep on the floor right here as long as I could get dry.

"Will this change your mind?" Ikane dropped a small purse in the innkeeper's hand.

He pried it open with meaty fingers, peering inside with one eye. He looked up. "I suppose I can find space for you." He sniffed, wiping his nose on his sleeve, and tucked the purse into his apron. "I have a room on the top floor at the very end. It's drafty, and the roof leaks."

"It'll do. We'll need our clothing washed and mended as well."

"That'll cost extra."

Ikane placed two more coins in the innkeeper's hand.

"Welcome to the Willowbark Inn," the man said.

Ikane shouldered his bag, climbing the warped staircase to the second floor. The hallway grew narrower as we reached the door at the end. He pushed. The door groaned as wood ground against wood, barely opening. He set his stance, driving his shoulder against it. The door swung out.

I ducked inside, keeping my shoulders hunched under the sagging timbers of the roof. An earthy, mildewy scent seeped from the wood. The steady *drip, drip, drip* of water hitting the pail in the center of the room echoed the pattering rain outside.

Ikane dropped his bag, shaking the rain from his hair like a hound. "I thought there would at least be a fireplace."

I moved to the single bed standing against the slanted ceiling. The quilt was moth-eaten and thin, and straw filling spilled from the pillow onto the floorboards. Little black slivers of mouse droppings filled the hay.

Ikane shivered. "I'm going back downstairs. With how much I paid that innkeeper, he should at least provide us with clean blankets and something dry to wear while our clothes are mended."

"Try to squeeze a hot meal out of him, too," I said.

He smiled. "I'll be back in a moment."

I sat against the wall opposite the mouse-infested bed and pried the mud-caked shoes from my feet. Redness blended into the heel of my stocking as I peeled them off. Angry blisters bubbled against my skin, stinging where they had burst.

Ikane returned, carrying four blankets and two nightshirts. He crouched beside me, his eyes falling on my bare feet. "Spines, Kea. We should get some ointment for those."

"They don't hurt anymore."

"They will tomorrow." He handed me the stack of blankets, taking one and spreading it on the filthy floor. "I'll step outside while you change."

I peeled the sticky layers of clothing from my skin, gooseflesh stinging like a thousand lashes. The nightshirt was three times too large and smelled of herbs and a hint of body odor. It probably belonged to the innkeeper.

I swallowed the sickening bile rolling up my throat. I'd have my clothes back by morning, washed, mended, and dry. I could endure the smell until then.

"I'm done, Ikane." I gathered my drenched clothing.

He drove his shoulder into the door. "My turn. Then we'll go downstairs for supper."

Hot energy slammed into my skull. My feet stumbled, body careening into the doorframe. Rion. Her fire dripped like hot oil over my head. Smoldering coals seared down my throat, my lungs freezing.

*Ten.* Her voices said the number like a curse. *Ten souls. Ten lives. Ten. That is how many have lost their eternal existence this time.*

"Kea?"

Why was Ikane standing so close? His hand fell on my shoulder, the weight like a mountain, the touch like a brand. My knees buckled. He shouldn't touch me. Didn't he know that? Rion would—

Her threads shot through me, wrapping around his energy like a net around a fish.

*No!*

His eyes flew wide, his body stiffening into ice. She drew on him, pulling him across the expanse of Roanfire, toward Fold. He groaned, falling to his knees.

The white spark ignited like fire to dry reeds. Flickering stars winked across my mind, whirring to Ikane like soldiers storming castle walls. They tore at her threads, slashing and biting, reaching for Ikane's energy.

She let go. His soul flew back into his body like a whip.

My lungs opened.

*You tamper with magic you do not understand!* Her voices were growing softer, the distance diminishing her hold. The fire searing through my bones fizzled as if touched by the rain.

*At least I don't rely on the strength of others.*

*Oh, foolish child,* her choir of voices cackled. *If only you knew what you condemn me of.*

She vanished.

Cold rushed in like the waves of the winter sea. I blinked through the dull pounding behind my temples. Fear spoiled the sea and meadow hues of Ikane's eyes as if a storm had blasted through, destroying everything. Was that blood dripping from his nose? Feathers, no. Not Ikane. He didn't deserve this.

His hand shook as he wiped it with the back of his wrist. His eyes widened at the crimson streak left on his skin. "What . . . ?"

Tears blurred everything. It wasn't safe for him to stay with me. "She's not going to stop."

He glanced up. "She . . . I . . . I can't explain . . . Kea, is that what it always feels like?"

"She nearly took you." My fists clenched, wishing I could drive them into the White Wardent's gut. He should have never created that abomination. "You need to go." The words stung my lips. "You need to protect yourself."

"What? No."

"I can't lose you. Not to her."

"I'm sorry. I didn't mean to touch you. I promise I won't do it again."

"How long before she reaches you without touch?" I braced against the doorframe, standing. "I have to fight back. I can't have you caught in the middle."

Something broke in his eyes.

"I'll find another inn—"

"No." He steeled his jaw, a pearl of moisture running down his cheek. "I'll go. You're safe here. I'll have the innkeeper leave food at the door."

His hands continued to shake as he strapped his swords to his wet torso. He replaced his drenched cloak. He stepped near me, so close his warm breath brushed my forehead. Every part of me needed to reach out and hold him, if only for a moment to say goodbye.

But I didn't dare. I *couldn't* dare. I held him with my heart instead, crushing him with an embrace as real as any touch could be.

He pried the door open like it was the last barrier keeping him from leaving, slowly and reluctantly.

"Be careful, Little Brendagger."

My lip trembled. I'd fallen in love with a Leviathan pirate. My heart cracked as he stepped into the hallway. This wasn't a true goodbye. I would destroy Rion and her accursed ruby prison. I would see him again.

Something moved across my blankets. I squinted. Morning light pierced the cracks in the wall, illuminating the little body of a gray mouse with beady black eyes standing on my blanket. Its tiny nose wriggled as it sniffed the air.

They were all over me.

I bolted upright, sending six brown-eared furballs scurrying toward the bed frame.

I had to get out of this place.

At least the rain had stopped. I could make good time traveling today.

Checking the door, I found my clean clothes neatly folded on the floor. A pair of strong leather boots stood beside them along with a small pot of ointment for my feet. Ikane. How could I miss him so much when we'd only been apart for one night? It was like I'd lost a limb.

But he was safe. That was all that mattered.

The sooner I could destroy Rion, the sooner we could be reunited.

I purchased a loaf of bread and a sack of dried meat from the innkeeper and resumed trekking beside the river, off the main road. Earthy smells filled the air as warm sunlight dried the rain-soaked woods. Rabbits darted between bushes. Birds danced overhead, sweet songs of spring mingling with the breath of the trees.

*I should thank you.*

My heart slammed into my ribs. How did she . . . ? I felt nothing slither through my mind. No burning. No redness.

*I thought summoning souls into my tower was the only way,* she said, *but war has reached the shores of Roanfire. The Leviathans cut down life after life, priceless energy wasted.*

I swallowed the dryness in my throat.

*In our last encounter, when I returned to the tower, my arms were still outstretched, reaching for life. I hungered for the man you call Ikane, but I found a trove of power in the lives destroyed by the Leviathans.*

*Like I said before, you have no power without others.*

*The more destruction, the further I can follow you and the less you can resist. Spare yourself, and return to me. Claim your birthright. I will end the war with the Leviathan pirates. I will bring peace.*

She promised the same to Queen Damita. *I've seen enough of the Dead City to know what sort of queen you are.*

*You leave me no choice.*

I knew the tone. The pain was coming. I needed the lights now.

Every time Ikane was in danger, the stars flickered to life. Would they come now that he was out of harm's way? Would they defend me, too? Feathers, please. Where were they?

A red-hot dagger of energy spun for me.

*Please.*

White flashed like the glint of sunlight on steel. Her fire recoiled, dissolving into the void of time.

*Impossible,* she breathed.

I'd done it. Somehow, I'd summoned the light. It surged with energy. Not like a flame, but a glow. A pure glow of endless stars swarming around me as if I were the queen bee.

Her energy surged, violent heat designed to incinerate, roiling like a river of fire into my mind. She was going to kill me. Just like Queen Damita, I was going to die out here in the woods, burned from within.

I couldn't think that way. I was stronger than this. She drove Ikane away. She would not win.

The lights hummed together, blending with my body and soul as if a part of my beating heart. They knitted around my mind like chain mail, then the links shrunk, turning into a solid orb of steel.

She roared, clawing at my mind like a crazed animal. I deflected every stroke and assault.

Her voices faded. The prickling heat that accompanied her presence was gone.

I opened my eyes, sunlight lancing through the trees like spears. A hammer thundered against my head, wild and furious. It was Rion. It had to be. She was striking out in any way she could.

My legs shook, knees giving out. Phoenix help me. Rion had an endless source of energy. I was limited to what my body held. It wouldn't be enough.

Bracing against my knees, I stood, staggering on. I needed to find Faslight.

# CHAPTER 29

# FASLIGHT

ed danced across my vision with every crack in my skull, the midnight-blue shadows of trees momentarily flashing maroon. Rion was relentless. Gummy sap coated my hands as I braced against their trunks. I had to be close. I'd passed Shard hours ago. Her cabin should be here.

A square patch of yellow light gleamed ahead. That had to be it. My feet moved faster.

White smoke billowed from the chimney on the thatched roof, and budding rosebushes hugged the cabin walls. The door opened, the silhouette of a strange figure filling it.

I stopped, cheek pressed against the rough bark of the tree holding me up.

That wasn't Faslight.

The contorted figure hobbled across the clearing to the small barn beside the cabin. His right leg trailed behind him like a long stocking tucked into his belt. One shoulder sank lower than the other, the use of a cane making it worse. Silver moonlight struck his white hair. Illorce?

He struggled to open the barn door, mumbling a curse. His twisted fingers managed to crack it open. He slipped inside.

Cardinal light flickered across the scene. I scrunched my eyes shut, swallowing the tightness in my chest. Firedust. His body had been destroyed by the Leviathan pirates.

I pushed off the tree, staggering to the cabin door. The smell of herbs leaked from the gaps, wafting through the night. What if she turned me in? What if she thought I killed King Myron?

My hand curled into a fist and pounded against the wooden door.

"You know you don't need to knock, Illorce." Her rattling voice was filled with annoyance.

I lifted the lever, pushing the door open. Warmth caressed my cheeks, the dusty scent of herbs filling my lungs. "Faslight?" I whispered, legs braced, ready to bolt.

She looked up from her seat at the table, steam rising from the mug in her trembling hands. "Flaming feathers." She set the mug down. "Hurry. Come in. Close the door."

Weight lifted from my chest, my heart mending a little. She didn't condemn me.

I shut the door. "I need your help."

"Who is it, Faslight?" A muffled voice called from the adjoining room.

Someone else was here? Could they be trusted?

A plump woman emerged. Her dark eyes squinted up at me.

"Mayama!" My bag crashed to the floor. Tears flooded my vision as I ran into her pudgy arms. She wasn't dead. She hadn't been destroyed along with Daram. "You're alive."

"Oh, my Sweet Pea." Her hand was gentle, like the touch of a mother stroking my hair. "Hush, now. It's alright. I am safe." She held me at arm's length. "But what happened to you? You are no king-slayer. Why are they calling you this?"

"Archduke Goldest is behind it." I wiped furiously at my tears. Hot anger completely my own bubbled through my veins, boiling through my head, igniting red with every heartbeat. "I refused to betray Prince . . . I mean, King Sander, and Goldest tried to have me assassinated."

Mayama patted my hand. "Hush, Sweet Pea. You are trembling. Come, have a cup of tea."

I sat in the vacant chair beside Faslight. Mayama pushed a steaming mug toward me. My fingers wrapped around the warmth, the tea trembling from my shivering.

Faslight pushed a piece of buttered bread in my direction. "You can't stay. Illorce will not take kindly to you being here."

I stared at the bread, watching the butter melt into the pores. "The firedust did that to him, didn't it? The Leviathans are behind it. There are imposters all over Roanfire infecting people with firedust."

"How do you know this?" Faslight asked.

"I have a source."

Mayama draped a quilt around my shoulders. "Enough about Illorce. Why are you here?" She took a seat across from me.

The tips of my fingers turned white, crushing the mug. "I've been to Fold."

"The dream," Mayama breathed.

I swallowed, searching Mayama's dark eyes and Faslight's green ones. "The curse is going to kill me, just like it did the queens of the past, if I don't find the White Wardent."

Faslight looked at Mayama.

"Please. Tell me anything. A hint. An absurd children's tale. I don't know where else to turn. I've searched Meldron's library. I was getting close, but I can't go back."

"What did you find there?" Faslight asked.

"Letters. And I transcribed two journal entries from the White Wardent himself. He said something about uniting with the four kingdoms. Keys of some sort. He mentioned Emperor Skar—"

"Skarand? Of the Glacial Empire?" Faslight tilted her head.

"I believe so."

"Then you must go there." Mayama reached across the table, taking my hand. Red sparked behind my eyes, pain slamming against my forehead. Curse Rion and her relentless hammering.

"What pains you, child?" Faslight asked.

How was I to explain a magical pounding in my head? I rubbed my temples, wishing I could squeeze Rion out. "I've had a headache for the past week. Nothing helps."

"Is it . . . magical?" Her green eyes bored into mine, as if she could see the redness burning in them.

I nodded once.

"There's never been a headache the great Faslight couldn't conquer." Mayama leaned back in her chair.

Faslight flashed a toothless smile. "You make me sound like one of your spoiled soldiers." She stood with the help of her cane, turning to her kitchen shelves littered with sacks, jars, and vials of spices and herbs.

"A soldier can't fight on an empty stomach," Mayama said.

Faslight pulled item after item from the shelf, measuring them into a small pouch. "True, but gruel and pith are just as filling as herb roasts and salted vegetables."

Mayama chuckled, turning to me. "Did you find my food too luxurious back in Daram?"

Her food was amazing. What I wouldn't give for another meal in the mess hall, surrounded by soldiers and friends. "Is Eamon . . . is he . . . ?"

"Oh, dear me. Yes. He is alive and sober as a church mouse. Whatever your terms were before you left worked. He's never been more formidable."

I forced a smile. I hadn't kept my end of the bargain. I'd fallen in love with the very man he told me to stay away from. "And Daram?"

Mayama's face turned solemn, her dark eyes staring at the wall for a moment. "It is lost, Sweet Pea. Daram is no more."

Faslight returned to the table. She opened the pouch, withdrawing a large pinch of the mixture, dropping it into my mug. "A magical headache requires a magical antidote."

Large chunks of dried herbs caught in a whirlwind. The spinning didn't ease. It was like an invisible spoon kept stirring.

"Drink," she urged me. "It won't last forever."

I lifted the whirling tea to my lips. The bitter taste was earthy and dry. The water felt strange to my tongue, like I was drinking air. A light breeze surged through my body. Rion's relentless hammering transformed into the harmless, annoying tap of a gnat.

"Winddust is what you feel now," Faslight said. "Its effects only last a few minutes, but the herbs will take over in time. Drink one cup every morning and evening for as long as you need. Too much may dull your senses, so do not take more than is absolutely necessary."

I nodded. "Thank you, Faslight. How may I repay you?"

She gave me a sympathetic frown. "Leave," she said. "If Illorce finds you here, then we are all in danger."

I grabbed the pouch of herbs and stood, handing the blanket back to Mayama. "I am happy that you are both safe." I tucked the herbs in my bag.

The sisters escorted me to the door. I embraced Mayama, wishing I didn't have to leave. "Please, be safe."

"And you," she whispered. "I pray you will find the White Wardent."

The sun broke over the trees, the orange glow diffused by morning fog. Soft gurgles drew me to the lush edge of a riverbank. My satchel dropped to the ground, then I fell to my knees. Four startled bullfrogs leapt into the water, ripples expanding in their wake.

I dipped my hands into the freezing water. The pounding in my head was getting worse. Faslight's tea would help, but it would be a month before I reached the Glacial Empire on foot. I had to ration the herbs.

*Where is he?*

I pulled my face from my hands, water dripping down my chin. Red swarmed my vision as if I were looking through the tint of a stained glass window.

*Where is the man you call Ikane?*

Ikane was not here. She could not hurt him.

*You sent him away.* Her voices held an edge of surprise. *Don't you love him?*

She knew I did. *You drove him away.*

*I was giving him eternal life!*

A fist of fiery anger hammered against my skull. The vibration twisted in my head. She was growing stronger.

I scrunched my eyes, shutting out the world, searching for the warm light somewhere inside.

Something coiled around my torso, squeezing. My ribs strained.

Where was the light?

I dug my fingers into the ground, curling them around the clusters of damp grass lining the riverbank. She was breaking through. Phoenix help me, I needed the light. I needed to protect myself the same way I did Ikane.

There. A white flicker, a candle struggling against the wind, hugging a memory like a shield. Ikane's touch. His warm, calloused hand holding mine. I reached for it.

*Don't!* Her voices pierced the solid sphere protecting my mind. Dents and scrapes warped the surface like armor after a battle. Heat soared through my body.

I brushed against the star. It flickered. More lights winked awake, knitting together, swarming around the sphere. All I needed was to reinforce it.

Her voices growled, like animals frustrated to have lost prey. *Soon there will be no land distant enough to protect you!*

Her crushing power evaporated.

My lungs expanded, gulping air as I caught myself on my hands. Brittle grass crumbled under my weight.

My eyes flew open.

The riverbank beneath me had turned brown, grass hanging like it hadn't received rain in years. A section of river, which had been clear and tranquil moments ago, flowed gray. Dead fish, frogs, and insects flowed downstream.

Like the Dead Forest.

I scrambled from the patch of death.

This had to stop. I needed to get as far away from Fold as possible.

And fast.

# CHAPTER 30

# SHEEP AND SHEPHERDESS

The bread smelled old, and the crust was like rock, but it was all I could afford. The ferryman's price to cross the river to the city of Karn bordered on thievery. The man was taking advantage of the displaced souls fleeing deeper into Roanfire.

I shoved the bread into my satchel, eyeing the next stall that displayed thick wedges of cured meat. I didn't have enough. I needed to save what coin I had left for the crossing of Glacier Lake.

"We cannot travel with only two swordsmen." A young female voice carried down an alleyway. "The sheep pups aren't old enough to protect them. The new lambs will be fodder. Oh, why can't we wait another month?"

"My love, you know we can't stay. There is no land for us here." A tall man dragged a hand down his face. "I am doing everything I can to keep our flock safe. Warriors are impossible to come by. They've been called to the coast to help fight off the Leviathan—"

"Don't say it! Don't say their name." Her knuckles turned white around the shepherd's staff in her grip.

He put his arm around her shoulders. "I'm sure we'll find a dozen swordsmen eager to earn a good sum in Osdak. We just need to hold out until then."

Osdak? That was halfway to Advent. They needed a hired sword, and I needed food to reach my destination. Phoenix help me—I'd have to risk it.

"Pardon me." I slid my hood from my head. "I couldn't help but overhear. I would like to offer my sword to you. At least until Osdak."

The woman's eyes sparked, scanning me from head to toe. "Yes. Oh, yes." She grabbed the man by his arm, shaking it like a child. "Please, dear. She looks strong."

The man's thin brows narrowed over his long nose. "What price do you ask?"

"A full stomach at the end of each day and five silver."

The man arched an eyebrow at me. "Is that all?"

I shrugged.

He extended his hand. "Borwick Followhide."

The woman squeaked, leaping to my side, slipping her arm through mine as if we were the best of friends.

The man chuckled. "That adorable creature clinging to your arm is Cherry, my wife."

"Natlee. Natlee Larbright." The false name slipped from my tongue, stinging with the lie that it was. Would I ever be able to use my actual name again?

Cherry dragged me down the road. "It will be your sole responsibility to protect my children. I'm sure you have everything you need. Even if you don't, we will provide for you. We have a wagon filled with provisions and an extra bedroll if you need it. Oh, I am so grateful that you have come. Phoenix bless you, Natlee. I have been dreading this journey for days, but it is time that we move. The Leviathans have gotten much too close to our land. My brother lives in Pedre and offered to let us stay with him until the war is over. Oh, you should see the crops and grasslands there. So lush and green. There is want for nothing . . ."

Flaming feathers. How could anyone talk so much without breathing?

"Our pups will eventually guard the sheep from predators, but they are too young and small. Our old dog, Shep, died a few weeks ago. She was such a loyal thing. Without her, I'm afraid for my lambs. They are so helpless." Cherry escorted me to the edge of the village and over a small bridge. The brook bubbled beneath our feet, vibrant and fresh as spring itself. Painted wildflowers bloomed across a lush field dotted with dozens of grazing sheep. New lambs played on lanky limbs, stumbling and flopping onto their sides. A pair of fluffy white sheepdog pups romped with them.

"Oh." Cherry released my arm, hurrying across the field. She dropped to her knees beside a sheep lying in the grass. Insects and pollen burst from the surrounding flowers.

She wrapped something in her apron. Standing, she turned to me, beaming proudly. A tiny white lamb, still moist from birth, sat in her arms. Its mother got to her feet, trailing behind the shepherdess.

This was what I was protecting. Several dozen white furballs ready to deliver in a time when wolves, bears, and cougars were waking from winter's sleep. They would need a dozen swordsmen to cover the loss of their sheepdog.

A wagon rattled onto the field with Borwick driving. Two men followed with thumbs tucked into belts straining against rounded bellies. Those were the mercenaries? Their armor sagged off their shoulders, and their armguards were twisted, held secure with shredded scraps of fabric rather than leather belts. True warriors wouldn't carry half a dozen knives in such a vivid display. This was going to be harder than I anticipated.

Borwick pulled the team of horses to a halt.

"Where is Lodar?" Cherry asked.

"I'm here." A young man sprinted over the bridge with something long strapped to his back. It was wrapped tightly, showing the outline of a sword. His shoulders were broad, and his forearms thick. He had the body of a fighter, but something about him didn't fit the mold. His attire was too simple.

I turned to Cherry. "Is he one of the hired swords?"

"Lodar? If only." She sighed. "He's an apprentice blacksmith on his first assignment as a journeyman. He's helping us guard the flock to spare some cost of his journey."

A blacksmith. That explained his physique. Was it too much to hope for someone with a morsel of skill?

Borwick stood on the driver's perch, claiming the attention of our little party. "The smallest lambs do not have the stamina to walk far. If you see one lagging, carry it. Keep a close eye out. They curl up in shady areas. As of right now, we have forty-six—"

"Forty-seven, dear." Cherry held the lamb for him to see.

"—forty-seven sheep in our flock. I expect you to count them at every stop and report back to me and Cherry."

"Yes, sir!" My voice rang alone.

Heat spread up my neck into my cheeks as Lodar and the others turned to me. I'd need to rein in my soldier's instincts.

An approving smile tugged on Borwick's lips. "At least someone knows how to answer. Many of our ewes are due to deliver at any moment. Alert us the moment they stop or break from the flock."

"Yes, sir." This time, Lodar and the others chimed in as well.

"Alright then." Borwick took a seat, twisting the reins through his fingers. "Let's move."

I squinted through the red pain pounding through my head. Every flash jarred the black silhouettes of trees reaching to the starlit sky. If I didn't get Faslight's herbs soon, I'd miss the signs of moving grass or yellow eyes slinking closer to the bleating sheep. Every predator within half a mile would hear it. Cherry was somewhere in her flock, comforting the two ewes that had gone into labor just before sunset.

"The water is hot." Lodar pulled the pot from the fire, the light enhancing the pale scars on his hands and forearms. He handed me a steaming mug.

I slipped a pinch of Faslight's powder into it.

Air touched my tongue, breathing down my throat, blowing the flashes of red to the back of my mind. The night suddenly seemed brighter. The stars winked overhead, as close as the night Ikane and I had slept on the deck of the *Otaridae*. Oh, how I missed him.

Borwick crouched by the fire, stretching his hands to the warmth. "Where are Sam and Collen?"

"Natlee sent them on perimeter watch," Lodar said.

Borwick appraised me, brows raised. "You have some military training?"

There was no point in denying it now. I shrugged. "A little."

"Are you sure you won't consider escorting us to Pedre? I promise to make it worth your while."

Pedre? That was where Ropert had been sent. Was he still there, starving and sweating, with dirt and dust from the quarry coating his skin? Were his hands blistered and raw? Did they beat him? Maybe I should consider his offer. Ropert didn't deserve to be there. I could . . . could what? Break him out? He would end up running, just like me.

I set the empty mug by the firepit, keeping my eyes on the lazy shadows of sheep. I couldn't deviate. How long before Rion had enough power to break through again?

"I am headed to Advent."

"Ten gold coins?" Borwick pressed.

I shook my head.

"Twenty?"

He was determined. "I'm sorry."

He sighed. "I suppose I'll just have to chase my luck and find a replacement in Osdak."

Grass rustled. My attention snapped back to the sheep.

Cherry dragged into the circle, sinking down by her husband. She wore a tired smile. "The latest lambs are perfect. We have three new additions."

"Three?" Lodar asked.

She grinned. "Twins."

I made a mental note. That put us at fifty sheep. "Are twins this common in sheep?"

"In a healthy flock, yes," Cherry said.

Borwick slapped his knees. "And ours is one of the best." He stood, drawing Cherry with him. "Wake us if there's trouble." They slipped into the wagon, pulling the pale canvas closed.

"Do you prefer first or second shift?" Lodar asked.

"I prefer first."

"So do I. Shall we draw for it?" He plucked a couple blades of grass from the ground.

I never had luck with games of chance. My odds were better in a spar, but it was probably safer not to resort to things from my past. I couldn't count on a dirt-smudged face and a bandana-wrapped brow to hide my identity forever.

I moved around the fire as he situated the blades of grass between his fingers. "Short one gets second watch," he said.

Pinching one of the thin green blades, I drew it.

"Hah!" He held up the longer one.

"Feathers." I tossed the blade over my shoulder. "Go relieve Collen and Sam."

"Are you really leaving once we reach Osdak? I don't know how to protect sheep. I'm not a shepherd."

"Neither am I." I unraveled my bedroll beside the fire, curling onto it. "Just watch for predators."

"This is my first assignment as Journeyman."

"So I've heard." I tucked my arm under my head, closing my eyes to the firelight.

"I've been working under the tutelage of Master Juston for five years. If I complete three more of these runs, I'll become Senior Journeyman."

"Impressive," I mumbled. If I wasn't going to get first watch, the least he could do was let me sleep.

"What about you?"

I opened one eye.

"You stand like a soldier yet cower as if afraid to be seen. And you have an air of nobility about you, but you're as coarse as a commoner."

He saw through me. The way I walked, the way I spoke, and the way I hid in the shadows betrayed me. What should I tell him? More lies? Half-truths? I didn't need to tell him anything. But would that raise suspicion?

"My father is a soldier. He trained me."

Lodar smiled. "I'd like to see you in action sometime."

"If you don't let me sleep, you'll see it sooner than you'd like." I rolled my back to him. "Wake me at midnight."

He laughed, the sound coming from deep in his chest. "Alright. Sleep well, Natlee." The sound of his boots kicking through grass faded as he finally left.

I had to be more careful.

Bleating cut through the night, tearing me from the darkness of sleep. The sheep!

I sat up.

Sam and Collin's sleeping forms huddled by the lazy fire. Lodar lifted a glowing stick from the coals, blowing the tip to make it flare. "Another sheep is in labor. Cherry is with it."

What did he think he was doing? He should be watching her. I grabbed my sword. "I'll take over."

He dropped his stick into the fire and stretched his arms to the sky. "If you insist." He slipped onto my vacant bedroll, closing his eyes.

Heavy moisture clung to my boots as I wove through the sleeping flock. Cherry knelt beside the panting ewe, stroking her white fleece.

She looked up as I approached. A tear glistened on her cheek. Her hands were wet, her apron stained. "The lamb is stuck." The sheep let out a frantic bleat. Cherry hushed her, stroking her neck. "The first delivery is always the hardest, but I'm afraid . . ."

I knew nothing of sheep and even less of the birthing process. "Do you want me to fetch Bor—"

Movement. My head snapped to the creeping shadow at the edge of the flock. Firelight glinted against a pair of yellow eyes.

My hand gripped my sword, drawing it free in a slow, calculated movement.

Cherry twisted, her eyes wide. "What is it?"

I didn't dare take my eyes off the creature. I might lose it if I did. "Wake the others."

She darted into the camp.

Stepping over the laboring ewe, I moved toward the creature. Was it a wolf? Didn't they typically hunt in packs? I saw no more shadows.

The silhouette slinked closer, shoulders shifting, the movement fluid. A cougar.

Moisture fled my tongue, my feet turned to rock, and my heart thudded against my ribs like a war drum. I was too close to retreat and too far to strike.

But I was not prey. My fist crushed the hilt of my sword, swinging it, a whistle splitting the air.

The cat recoiled, hissing, its bone-white teeth as long as arrowheads. It batted at me, claws flashing in the starlight.

I took a step closer, a backhand stroke sweeping my blade across us. "Get out of here!"

It lunged.

I wasn't fast enough. Biting pain pierced my shoulders as claws sank into flesh. Red flashed across my vision, ears popping. I fell back.

Hot pressure pulsed, throbbing through my body like blood pumping through a heart. The cougar's muscular body collapsed, its weight shunting air from my lungs.

Why wasn't it moving? I hadn't run it through, had I? The cold hilt of my sword still sat in my fist beside us.

"Natlee!" frantic voices screamed.

Grabbing a handful of scruff, I bucked my hips, rolling the limp form off me. It wasn't breathing.

"Natlee." Cherry's skirt swayed as she halted a few paces away. Borwick held a torch aloft. Lodar and the others stopped, chests heaving, eyes wide.

"You . . . you killed it," Lodar said.

Borwick's torchlight shone clean against the polished, unblemished surface of my sword. I hadn't struck the cougar at all. Blood glistened on the cougar's chest. Something was wrong.

The grass. A patch of brown lay beneath the body. Lifeless. Brittle.

My lungs turned to ice. Rion had done this.

I scrambled to my feet.

"You're bleeding," Cherry said. "Borwick, my love. We have a healer's kit in the wagon. Fetch it, will you?"

What was she talking about? I didn't feel any . . . redness pulled my eyes down to my shoulders. Blood drenched both sleeves, clinging to my biceps.

Lodar took my hand, prying my sword from my fingers. "I'll take care of her. Sam, you take watch."

The mercenary nodded.

Lodar guided me through the sheep, collected the healer's kit from Borwick, and led me back to the fire. Didn't they see the brown grass, the patch of death? Didn't they see how clean my sword was?

The blood on the cougar's chest wasn't his, it was mine. Rion had reached this far to save my life. Why? Didn't she want me dead?

"Sit." Lodar urged me onto my bedroll. "Let me see." He pulled at the collar of my shirt.

I pushed his hand away. "I'll be fine."

"The bleeding isn't going to stop on its own. Look at it."

My sleeve was twice as wet as before, soaking down to my elbow. I swallowed, unlacing the collar, pulling it over my shoulder.

He squinted at it, fingers dabbing the edges. "It's not as bad as I thought. It's deep, but it should close nicely."

He threaded a needle by firelight, something I had done for Ropert a few months ago. A sting raced through my skin as Lodar pushed the needle through it.

"You remind me of my mother." He tugged the thread. "My father was a heartless, violent man. He stole, threatened, and beat anyone who stood up to him. He often came home reeking of ale." His hands turned rougher, jabbing the needle a second time with a little less tact. I set my jaw.

"I hid like a coward. When he could not find me, he would beat my mother. She did not scream. She did not cry. And she never told him where I was."

"She sounds like a brave woman."

"She is." His voice was soft, brimming with admiration. "One day, my mother said he would not be returning. He never did. After that, she was happy. She worked hard to get the money for my apprenticeship." He tied off the sutures, cutting the thread with his boot knife. "I've worked even harder so that someday I can provide for her. She deserves so much more."

I pulled my shirt over my shoulder, threads snagging against the blood-soaked fabric. "Your mother must be proud of you."

"I hope so." He returned the needle to the healer's kit in a slow, thoughtful motion. "Age has caught up with her. I don't know how much longer before she will meet the Phoenix. Her last wish is to see me marry."

"That shouldn't be hard for you. Any woman would be honored to have a hardworking and successful man by her side."

His eyes rose to mine, gray-brown irises burning.

Flaming feathers. He couldn't mean me. We'd only just met. "Have you a sweetheart back in Shard?"

He scoffed. "There are some women who are eligible for marriage in my hometown, but they have a habit of holding kerchiefs to their noses whenever I am near. I am a blacksmith. I sweat. What do they expect me to smell like? A pansy?"

A smile cracked my lips. "You'll find someone."

"You intrigue me, Natlee. You don't turn your nose up at me. Actually, at this point, you probably smell just as bad as I do. And you have skill with a sword. What better way for a blacksmith to test his work than with a wife who can wield the weapons he makes?"

"Lodar, I did not mean to give you the wrong impression. My hand has already been promised to another." The lie didn't sting as the others had. In my heart, I belonged to Ikane. I could never look at another man the way I did my Leviathan prince.

"Maybe if I were to meet your father, he would change his mind." Lodar tucked his knife into his boot. "Once I have completed my errands as Journeyman, I will be the youngest full-fledged blacksmith on this side of Roanfire." A boyish smile crossed his dirt-smudged face. "What does your betrothed do for a living? Unless he is a lord, he won't be able to provide for you as well as I can."

This was getting out of hand. "He is a warrior just like my father."

"Think on it, Natlee. We could make a perfect match."

"You'd best return the healer's kit to Borwick." I curled onto my bedroll, dragging my cloak up to my neck.

"Give me a chance."

"I'm tired, Lodar. Please, let me sleep."

He sighed, shoulders dropping. "Alright." Standing, he dusted his trousers, grabbed the healer's kit, and slipped out of sight.

This was too dangerous. I shouldn't have placed my welfare in the hands of strangers. Cherry had been so elated to have me, and I'd fed on her joy. It was only a matter of time before someone here recognized me, only a matter of time before Rion drained their lives the way she had the cougar's.

I couldn't endure that.

Tingling trailed the length of my spine, a whisper of eyes watching me. But who would watch me? I was at the rear of the party. I peered over the lanky legs of the lamb hanging over my shoulders. The canopy of trees behind us reflected hot sunlight, shading the layer of foliage beneath.

Nothing.

"Borwick, hold up," Lodar called.

Ahead, a ewe broke from the flock.

I would have been in Osdak yesterday if it weren't for these frustrating sheep.

Borwick pulled the wagon around.

I lowered the lamb from my shoulders, arching my back, loosening my collar. The wobbly little creature tittered into the flock to find its mother.

The whisper moved up and down my back again. I glanced behind me, the tree line warbling through rising heatwaves.

"What is it?" Lodar stepped beside me, following my gaze.

"I'm not sure." We had to keep moving. Oh, why did the sheep have to go into labor now? This patch of open grassland begged for an attack. The only other choice was to attack first—or at least find out what we were up against. I drew my sword, stalking to the trees. Lodar followed.

"Stay with the sheep," I said.

"You were almost killed by a cougar two days ago. Phoenix help me if anything happens to you now."

"Flaming feathers, Lodar. For once, will you do as I say?"

He stopped, hurt spreading across his face as if I'd cut his heart.

"I need you to watch the sheep. If something comes out of those woods, you are the only one I can trust."

He straightened a little. "Alright."

I stepped into the trees, the heat of the sun dissipating. Birds chirped. A squirrel soared from branch to branch. Leaves rustled in the breeze.

Nothing seemed amiss. Was I overreacting?

Lingering patches of snow hugged the base of the trunks, holding onto winter. Animal tracks wove through the damp earth, more prominent where they dug into the snow. I crouched, fingers brushing the ridge of a print as large as my hand. Wolves.

I stood, searching for more. An imprint beside a tree looked different, the muddy crater deeper and larger than the others. I leaned closer.

Boot prints? They were fresh, moving with the pack.

The tingling reached my neck, my muscles turning solid. My head jerked up, eyes scanning the shadows. "Who's there?"

Birds chirped in reply.

Swallowing, I hurried from the trees.

Lodar stood beside Borwick, watching as I wove between the sheep. Cherry sat by the panting ewe, stroking her white fleece.

"What did you find?" Lodar asked.

"Wolves," I whispered.

Borwick's face drained to bone-white. "Are you sure?"

"I'm afraid so." Should I mention the boot print? It didn't make sense. Who would run with wolves? Maybe someone was tracking them. Maybe we had nothing to worry about. But it was better to be prepared.

Borwick looked at Cherry kneeling in the grass. "What do you suggest we do?"

The log crashed into the fire, sparks flying to the night sky, illuminating the pacing shadows. Moisture built on my palms, making it hard to grip my sword. They were getting closer. My neck prickled as howls echoed from one end of the camp to the other.

"Keep those fires strong!" Borwick shouted from his edge of camp.

Mine roared, heat penetrating my shirt in the warm night. Five fires burned around the flock, the wagon standing as a wall on one end. White fleece huddled in the center, bleating and jerking as the shadows drew near.

We were going to lose sheep tonight. The flock was too large, the fires too spaced out.

Low growling drew me back to my corner. A wolf. Its lips pulled back, eyeteeth glinting, white strings of saliva dangling from the corners of its mouth. It skirted to the other side of my fire.

It was going to slip through.

My feet moved, sword whipping across the gap. The wolf's gray-black coat blurred by, shooting for the flock.

"Cherry!" My throat ached as the warning tore through it.

Bleats and snarls exploded, the sea of white fleece rippling and parting as the black form cut through. A sheep broke away. The wolf snapped at her hindquarters. Her legs pumped wildly, bringing her to the edge of Lodar's fire.

I shifted my run. I was close. I could—

Another wolf slammed into the sheep, jaw locking around her throat.

"No!" Cherry's voice was shrill, the cry of a mother for her child.

The wolf jerked, twisting the sheep's neck. Her body collapsed. Red leaked onto her white fleece. Three more wolves appeared, dragging the limp animal to the edge of the trees.

I lowered my sword, breath coming in dry gasps.

"Back to your fires!" Borwick shouted. "They have what they came for. Don't let them get any more."

I hurried back to my bonfire, dumping more logs onto it. That wouldn't happen again.

Sap stuck to my skin, tree bark staining my fingers. I dropped the bundle of firewood into the growing pile beside the newly constructed pit. Logs tumbled and shifted.

A gentle breeze whispered across my cheeks, blowing the heat of the day into the violet hues of sunset. I tucked a strand of hair behind my ear. Borwick and the others emerged from the trees, dropping firewood beside their own pits arranged around Cherry's flock. The young woman sat in the grass, a lamb sitting in her lap and another curled at her hip. Her smile was gone. Her endless string of jubilant words silenced.

I'd failed her. Not only had we lost a pregnant ewe, but we'd also lost a lamb who had been trampled under the terrified sheep. And a sheep-pup had somehow gotten injured. The pitiful thing had limped as far as it could before lying in the grass. I'd carried it the rest of the way.

"There's nothing more you could have done." Lodar dropped an armload of firewood onto my stack.

"What are you doing here? You should be preparing your own fire."

"I'll have it done in time." He crouched, fiddling with my arrangement already in the firepit. "We arrive in Osdak tomorrow."

"I know." Why did this man refuse to do everything I told him to? My head was already throbbing. I didn't need him adding to it.

"I've been thinking about us. About how perfect we would be together." He stood, stepping closer. "Have you?"

"You are a good man, Lodar." I filled my water tin in preparation for Faslight's tea, setting it beside the firepit. "You are hardworking, kind, strong, dependable, and would certainly make a fine husband for a wife deserving of that. But not for me."

"Why?" His face looked pained. "I don't understand."

Didn't he want to find genuine love? Something deep and real that would reach beyond the borders of any kingdom? Something that defied all logic and reason? Something like what I felt for Ikane?

"It's time to start the fires," I said. "You'd best go."

"Not until you tell me why. I'd do anything for you, Natlee."

The red pangs behind my eyes were growing more intense. "Because I don't love you. You are thinking with your head and not your heart."

"But I am. Don't you see? From the first moment I saw you standing beside Cherry, my heart wasn't mine anymore. You are everything I've ever wanted in a wife. You are perfect."

I rubbed my temples. "Go tend to your fire, Lodar."

"Let me prove it." His thick blacksmith's hands grabbed my head, pulling me forward. His eyes closed, pushing my face against his. A sour sensation rolled through my chest, flaring up my throat.

How dare he!

My fists hardened, driving into his sternum. The air drove from his lungs, blasting my face as he pulled away. He curled over his stomach.

Why was he smiling? Did he think this was a game?

"Never touch me again, you hear?"

He laughed. "You enjoyed it. Admit it. Can't you feel the heat between us? It's like a forge. The metal is cold and hard at first, but heat it up, and it will bend and mold to whatever we choose."

"Love cannot be forged," I snapped.

"With the right leverage, anything can." He took a step forward, something dangerous flaring in his eyes.

Hiding my skills wasn't worth this. My sword hissed from its scabbard, slashing the air between us.

He stepped back, smile widening. "Finally, I get to see you in—" His smile vanished, eyes widening, the rosiness of his cheeks fading like he saw something in me, something treacherous and deadly. Phoenix help me. Did he finally see it? Did he know who I was?

A growl rumbled behind me.

I whirled.

The wolf's deep-brown coat bristled in the silver moonlight. Its muzzle drew back, nose contorting in a series of folds and creases. Dagger-like teeth were exposed as it snarled.

It was huge, twice the size of the wolves we'd encountered the night before. Its eyes fixed on the young blacksmith standing behind me, burning blue and green. Just like Ikane's.

I blinked through the pounding in my head. It couldn't be.

*He's come back.* Rion's voices pushed through the heavy barrier in my head, a pang of red hammering behind my eyes.

This was Ikane? A wolf? What did he think he was doing? Rion had reached the cougar. She could reach him, too.

Something coiled around my throat, threatening to cut off my air. I'd die before I'd let her take him.

"Get out of here." My shoulders ached at the speed of my strike, the metal tip of my sword whistling. "Go. Now. Go!"

The wolf sank back, ears flattening.

Didn't he sense the danger? I charged, slicing the air again. "Leave."

Hot sparks shot through my skull.

*I will have him.*

The dented surface of my shield cracked. Flaming tendrils licked through the fissure. I clutched my head, biting heat searing bone and muscle as if I'd been buried in a pit of smoldering coal.

*Your life is in my hands.* Rion's heat restricted like a vice, suffocating the air in my lungs, freezing my muscles. *One breath, and you could be here with me, existing eternally as an essence of my power. Is that what you want? Just to exist? Or to become?*

Become what? What was she talking about?

*I need you. I need the blood in your veins. The rightful heir to the throne of Roanfire.*

*Then do it,* I cried. Anything to make this pain stop. My knees struck the earth, fire roiling up my thighs and spreading up my chest as smoke permeated my lungs.

*I need you here.* Her voices grew soft, solemn, like she regretted admitting this weakness. *Come back. Claim your birthright.*

I would never go back.

Orange-red energy smashed into my mind like a flaming harpoon. The world turned to flame and smoke.

Black.

# CHAPTER 31

# JOURNEYMAN'S VICTORY

hrobbing lances of heated iron slammed under my skull. My eyes ached as I blinked at the sunlight flashing across the pale canvas overhead. The earth jolted and pitched beneath me. Something cool and damp pressed against my forehead.

"Thank the Phoenix, you're awake." Cherry leaned over me, one hand gripping the wagon frame as it rattled and swayed. "I was so worried. Lodar said you just collapsed. You were bleeding from your nose and ears. Oh, Natlee. Your eyes."

Something wiggled against my side. I pushed myself up, finding a lamb snuggled beside me. Little fluff-balls were all around us.

"Just lay still. You're safe." Cherry's gentle touch sent a chill through my body.

Rion. She was here, sitting in my mind, waiting. She could take them, all of them. Why hadn't she already?

I scrambled to the back of the wagon, leaping over the frame. My boots hit the dirt, knees buckling. Splinters tore into my hand as I grabbed the wagon frame for balance.

"Borwick, stop!" Cherry called.

Borwick pulled the caravan to a halt, turning in his seat.

The flock stopped. Sam and Collin prodded the stray sheep into the center. Another swordsman accompanied them. Where was Lodar?

Borwick climbed from the wagon. "Natlee? Are you alright?"

I stepped back. I shouldn't be here. Everyone was in danger.

Borwick held up his hands. "Natlee. It's alright. We're your friends. Lodar has gone ahead to find a healer." He helped Cherry from the wagon.

I rubbed my forehead. Where was the headscarf? They were going to recognize me. "I . . . I need to go. Where are my things?"

"Go? You are ill, Natlee." Cherry held my headscarf in her hand, the rag she'd used to wipe my face. "It's just another hour to Pedre."

"Pedre?" I was going to Advent. I was supposed to leave this caravan in Osdak. I had to get to the Glacial Empire. Pedre was in the wrong direction.

"We couldn't leave you," Borwick said. "And Lodar insisted we take care of you."

"He's worried," Cherry added. "We all are."

I swallowed, looking over the flock. How long had I been asleep? Pedre was at least five days from Osdak, more at the pace the sheep were going. I was no closer to the Glacial Empire than I had been before. I'd have to backtrack for days.

"May I have my headscarf back?"

"Are you upset?" Cherry offered me the damp fabric.

I tugged it from her hand, careful to avoid physical contact. "I'm . . . I'm thankful you took care of me. But I wish you had left me in Osdak."

"Lodar wouldn't have it." Cherry smiled. "He has eyes for you."

I ached to shove hot coals in his face.

Had I really seen a wolf with blue and green eyes? Was it really Ikane, or had it been a dream? I couldn't tell anymore.

I wrapped the scarf around my head, tying the knot at the base of my neck. I might as well gather supplies in Pedre.

"Now back in the wagon with you." Borwick stepped around a sheep, heading back to the driver's bench.

"I'll walk."

Cherry set her hands on her hips.

"I promise. I'll be alright."

"Very well."

The landscape changed to rocky terrain as we drew closer to the white-capped mountains. Clouds drifted across the sky, moving just as slow as the flock of sheep. Red and green flashed across my vision. Would she ever tire? Just for a moment?

We crested a lush hill. Sunlight danced on the blue ribbon of the Karn River snaking by the cluster of buildings in the valley below. A tower soared above the shingled rooftops, overlooking the thick stone wall surrounding the city of Pedre.

Ropert was here somewhere, but not in a home with white trails of smoke puffing from the chimney stack. He would be somewhere deep in the mountain quarry, housed in a drafty hut, tethered to other convicts.

Was it worth the risk to see him again?

"We're here." Cherry's shoulders eased, her sigh tangible.

Borwick steered the wagon through the gates, the soft thud of the horses' hooves shifting to sharp clops against the cobbled road. He turned the corner where a long stretch of grass followed the length of the moss-covered wall. Cherry called to her flock. A smile returned to her lips as she pulled lamb after lamb from the wagon bed.

They were safe.

And it was time for me to go.

But how far would I get without the five silver we agreed upon? Cherry and Borwick would make me see a healer before they let me leave. I couldn't do that. I couldn't see anyone. I shouldn't even have entered the city. I would just need to earn some coin after I arrived in Advent.

Slipping beside the wagon, I lifted the canvas edge, slid my sword and satchel from the hay, and shrank into the shadow between two buildings, hurrying to the main road on the other side.

Before I stepped out, I stopped, my heart skipping.

A dozen gold-trimmed tunics lined the street. Those weren't Pedre's uniforms.

Retreating into the shadow, I pressed my back against the wall. What were the Phoenix soldiers doing here? And why so many?

Gathering supplies from the market was out of the question. I'd have to continue with what I had in my bag.

Clopping hoofbeats filled the street. I peered around the corner, finding six soldiers approaching the gate on horseback, hailing Cherry and Borwick.

They knew.

Somehow, they knew I was here.

I shut my eyes, turning my face to the sky.

Lodar. He did this. He'd set up an ambush. How was I going to get—

Something sharp bit my back.

"Keatep Brendagger." Lodar's voice was stiff, as if it burned his tongue to say my name.

I raised my hands. "Lodar."

He spun me around, shoving me against the wall, pushing his knife against my throat. His eyes shimmered. "Tell me it's not true."

"Would it matter if I did?" My fingers brushed the hilt of my sword.

His eyes flicked down, catching the motion. "Not today, king-slayer." With one fluid motion, he pulled my sword from its sheath and flung it across the way. Metal crashed against stone.

"Lodar—"

"She's here!" His fist crushed the collar of my shirt, jerking me from the wall.

My neck snapped back. "I didn't do it, Lodar."

He pressed the tip of the knife against my side, herding me into the main street while tearing the scarf from my head. "The king-slayer is here!"

Soldiers whirled from the gate ahead, and a platoon marched from the market behind. This wasn't good.

*I am here.* Heat pushed through my skull, turning everything a shade of red. Rion's eagerness was tangible.

*I will get out of this without your help.* I hissed the thought to her.

*As you wish.*

A bitter taste rushed through my mouth as her heat retreated, and the red pounding behind my eyes faded like a single drop of blood dissolving in a basin of water.

Lodar shunted me forward.

Cherry stepped back, her eyes wide, watching me as if I had transformed into one of the wolves who'd attacked her sheep. When would anyone see me for who I really was? What I was about to do wouldn't help my case, either.

My feet planted on the cobblestone road. Lodar's knife pricked my skin.

"Keep moving," he growled.

Keeping my hands raised, I turned to him.

"What are—"

I grabbed his wrist, striking the nerves at the back of his arm with my knuckles. Jerking the knife from his limp fingers, my elbow cracked against his nose, sending him rocking. I spun behind him and slid the blade to his throat. Warm blood dripped from his nose onto my hand.

"Stay back," I warned the soldiers.

They stopped, eyes darting to a woman among them who dared to take one more step.

"Release him," she said.

I pulled Lodar around, trying to keep an eye on the surrounding soldiers. "I didn't kill King Myron."

"I didn't say you did." The uniformed woman took another step. "Release the blacksmith. You don't want his blood on your hands."

She was pushing me.

Lodar stiffened as I pressed the knife a little deeper into his skin.

The commander stopped, eyes hardening. "King Sander wants you alive. You don't need to do this. You will have a fair trial."

A warning blared through my skull. A fair trial? Ropert hadn't received a fair trial, and he was more innocent than I. Now he worked Pedre's mines like a common criminal.

I searched the buildings standing like walls on either side of the street. I could try to slip through an alley, but that would result in a wild chase through the city, a hunt I would not survive. I didn't know these streets.

I stood a better chance if I could escape into the woods.

"I am trying to help you," the woman, likely their commander, said through her teeth, her patience falling away like a curtain, revealing her true intentions. Murder shone in her eyes. All the soldiers held it. A burning that would leave me maimed and dead if they caught me now.

A soldier from the street took a step closer.

My eyes flashed to him, my grip on Lodar tightening. The blacksmith inhaled sharply through his nose, forcing the soldier to rethink his movement. He slunk back.

"You don't want the truth. No matter how many times I say it, you won't believe me." I dragged Lodar with me as a shield, inching my way to the unattended horses by the gate.

"If you didn't kill King Myron, then tell me who did."

"Ask Archduke Goldest."

The commander bristled. "That is a serious accusation."

"For a serious crime. I am loyal to King Sander. I am loyal to Roanfire. I'd never do anything to put our kingdom in jeopardy."

I was close now. Five more steps, and I could jump onto the nearest warhorse's back.

"Then come with us, and you can present your case to the king," she said.

What a lie. These soldiers didn't care for the bounty on my head. They would sooner see me face down in the mud with a knife in my back than take me to Meldron.

"I'm not the killer." Driving my boot into Lodar's back, I shunted him into the commander.

Five strides, and my foot slipped into the stirrup. I swung over the horse's back, heels digging into his sides. The horse's muscles tightened, launching for the exit.

"Stop her! No! Don't let her—"

The horse barreled past soldiers, flying through the arched gateway, the sharp clop of hooves on cobblestone shifting to a dull thump as we hit the dirt road. I steered the stolen warhorse to the river cutting through the valley. It was my only chance to slow their pursuit.

We plunged into the water. I held my breath as biting cold stung my skin, filling my boots, soaking my trousers. The horse's body sank into the rapids, and water rose to my neck, lifting me from the saddle.

"Don't let her get away!"

I didn't dare look back. I kicked, frozen fingers gripping the warhorse's mane, the current threatening to tear me away. Water filled my mouth, rushing against my ears.

A sharp click slapped the water by my shoulder.

I jumped, watching the long, slender shaft of an arrow burrow under the surface. It was the Dead Forest all over again.

Glancing back, I found three soldiers on the riverbank with raised bows, sighting down arrows. An archer's hand flew back, her arrow racing for my skull.

I spun in the water, the arrow hissing past my ear, slapping the water hard.

Feathers, that was too close. I whirled, my arm pushing through the water, the other clutching the horse's mane, trying to swim out of range.

A hollow thump jarred up my back.

My heart slammed into my chest, my body bracing for the bite. Nothing?

The warhorse's hooves struck earth. I pulled my legs over his back as he lunged from the river, water weight dragging against my cloak. Cold pinned my muscles to the saddle.

My breath came hard as I glanced back. The archers lowered their bows, exercising caution as two riders ventured into the river after me. A dozen soldiers stood on the riverbank, raising fists and shouting.

Except for the commander. She stood silent, seething, knowing her quarry had escaped.

Turning the warhorse about, I spurred it into the woods beyond.

*I could have helped you.* Rion's voices were soft and reprimanding.

*I made it, didn't I?*

*They are following.*

*I can outrun them,* I said.

*They won't give up.* Her tone bordered on annoyance. *Let me.*

Piercing screams tore through the trees.

Everything in me froze. I'd heard the sound before in the Dead Forest, when Ikane and I had fled from Rion's mist. A painful lump slammed into my throat as I pulled the stolen horse to a halt and looked back.

"Rion, stop." I wanted to shout, to scream at the top of my lungs, to overpower her with the sound of my voice, but it came out as a strangled whisper. How strong had she become to reach clear across Roanfire?

The pursuing riders clung to their horses as the animals reared, spun, and tossed in pain, red dripping from their flaring nostrils. A soldier cried out as his horse flung itself against a tree, smashing his leg.

The other jerked on her horse's reins as the animal collapsed onto its side. She scrambled away, taking shelter behind a tree as her horse kicked and screamed.

Her wide eyes found mine, her face drained of color.

She thought *I* was doing this.

*Rion, stop. Stop now.* My thoughts raced. *Do you have any idea what you've done?*

*I made them fear and respect what they should,* she said. *One day soon, you will be their goddess and queen.*

I would never . . . especially not like this.

The man's horse collapsed against the tree, the leaves shuddering. He cried out, pinned beneath the writhing animal. He needed help.

*Do not worry about him,* Rion said. *Go.*

The man's face contorted with pain, cries hissing through clenched teeth as his horse's body rolled and thrashed on his leg.

*If it pains you so much, I can end his suffering.*

*No.* I turned away, tightness welling in my throat. *I'll go. Just . . . just make it stop.*

My muscles spasmed, cold piercing my bones as the stolen warhorse eased through the trees, carrying me away from the screams.

I wouldn't just be known as a king-slayer now. I would be known as a witch.

My trousers squeaked against the wet saddle as I dismounted. I was cold. The gray clouds building over the rocky hillside, sharp with the scent of rain, weren't helping. I glanced at the boulders towering like small fortresses on the steep incline. Perhaps I could find shelter up there.

But the horse . . . the climb would not be easy for him, and I couldn't leave him here. It would be like waving a banner at the hunting soldiers, telling them exactly where I was. Either way, he would develop sores from the moisture trapped under the tack if I didn't tend to him soon.

I stroked his powerful neck. Something about his black coat was familiar. His ears shifted forward.

"Gossamer?" I pulled his head up, checking his dark eyes and the bushy cowlick swirling on his forehead. "Gossamer!" I threw my arms around his neck, clutching him as though I were embracing Eamon. I shut my eyes, moisture squeezing between my lashes.

If only I hadn't left Daram. If only I had stayed where I was safe. If only I had listened.

A single raindrop pelted my forehead, then another. Thunder rumbled in the distance. We had to move. "Come on, boy."

I scanned the steep incline, leading him up the clearest path for his hooves. My heart soared. Something was finally going my way. With Gossamer by my side, I could reach the Glacial Empire within the month. I could find the letter and—

Fire slammed into my skull, red blossoming behind my eyes.

*Come to me.*

My feet slipped, fire soaring through my knee as it struck the edge of a rock.

*There is nothing for you in the Glacial Empire.*

Each word barreling through my mind came with a lancing throb in my temples. I shook my head. I needed Faslight's herbs. I'd take them raw if I had to.

Sinking to the rocky hillside, I pulled my satchel into my lap, my heart plummeting into my stomach. An arrow protruded from the leather bag, lancing right through Faslight's herb sack inside. Nothing but a soggy green mass of wasted herbs remained, drained of their potency.

*You think you can stay my wrath with herbs and tonics?* she mocked.

Searing energy burrowed into the dented sphere in my mind, cracking. She was breaking through.

I dropped the torn herb sack at my feet, clutching my head as her rage burst from the fissure like fire erupting from a blacksmith's furnace. The sphere trapping her split.

Phoenix help me.

Her fire coursed through my blood, ate my bones, curled around muscle. Every drop of rain turned to hot iron beads on my skin.

*Come. To. Fold.* Her words slammed against me with the force of a hammer, each one more damaging than the last.

I couldn't . . . I couldn't breathe. I couldn't scream. Everything was turning black as a thick smoke churned through my mind interrupted by flashes of raging red lightning.

She was too strong, too powerful. How on earth had I managed to fight her before? How had I trapped her in the first place?

Ikane. Always Ikane. I had to protect him. If she could reach me this easily, if she could stretch across Roanfire, drain a mountain lion and torture horses, what would keep her from finding Ikane?

A single white star flickered awake in the darkness. Like candlelight, it pushed against the smoke, making way for another and then another.

*You ignorant fool,* Rion hissed. *I warned you to never touch—*

An explosion of stars flooded my mind, catching the broken fragments of the destroyed prison and pulling them together, mending the pieces like a forge weld to a broken piece of armor. Her red light began to disappear as each crack sealed shut.

The rain no longer sizzled against my skin but turned cool and soothing as it pelted my face. My lungs expanded, filling with the crisp air infused with the storm.

*I warned you!* A thousand voices roared with frustrated rage, overpowering the thundercrack in the sky. *You brought this on yourself.* A desperate burst of flame shot through a gap in her prison.

Gossamer reared back with a scream, throwing his head. His hooves slipped on loose rock, his powerful body collapsing on the steep slope. He thrashed, blood flinging from his nose and mouth.

"No!" My body surged from the ground, scrambling around his powerful kicks. "Stop, Rion. Stop." Jagged rock cut my knees as I fell beside him, gripping his neck.

*Everything you love will be mine,* she vowed.

"Please, don't . . . don't do this." My voice cracked as I stroked Gossamer's elegant neck. He eased his head down, blood dripping with the rain from his flaring nostrils. Then his body sagged as he expelled his final breath.

Blue light flashed across Gossamer's glossy black coat.

Thunder cracked the sky.

He was gone.

Just like everyone else in my life, he was gone.

I couldn't contain the scream building in my chest. *When will it be enough for you? When will you stop all this death and suffering?*

*You don't understand, do you? Your beloved steed is here with me, and his power will live on. I have done you a great favor. When you give yourself to me, you shall have your beloved horse once again. You could have the same with Ikane.*

*Don't you dare say his name!* My stars swarmed around her prison, sealing gaps, pushing against her black fire. *You will never have him. And you will never have me!*

Her cry was cut short as the prison sealed itself around her, the polished sphere in my mind mottled with raised patches and dents like a crumpled piece of armor.

It was all I could do. All I could give.

I wanted nothing more than to crush her.

Gossamer was still warm, but no heartbeat thumped against my ear as my head rested on his neck. My tears blended with the rain.

# CHAPTER 32

# THE WHITE FOX

*M*y feet carried me on. Birdsong fell flat. Sunlight didn't warm. Soggy provisions spoiled. Berries and bitter dandelion greens did not satisfy the gnawing pain in my stomach.

Light from the midday sun filtered through the green hearts of aspens. Even the trees had more companionship than I.

Rion had chased Ikane away, stolen Gossamer. She destroyed any chance I had at returning to civilization as a normal citizen of Roanfire.

Maybe I should have let her take those soldiers. At least they wouldn't spread rumors about me.

How could I think that way? I was not a killer. I shouldn't have to defend myself for something I didn't do.

I sagged against a tree, bark biting into my shoulder as I slid to its base. Hugging my legs, I burrowed my face into my knees.

Maybe I should let her take me, let her end this loneliness, this hunger, this longing for what could never be. Would I ever feel the warm skin of another human being or run my fingers through the soft fur of an animal?

The White Wardent was wrong; I did not have the power to defeat her. I didn't even have the strength to weep. If only I could fade away, drift into nothingness, let the wind carry me where it would . . .

My eyes opened, heavy lids keeping the world small. The sun had run its course, casting the woods in the gray shadows of evening, the cool air awakening the smells of moss, decaying leaves, and flowers.

My stomach pinched. How long had it been since I'd eaten? Two, three days? Maybe more.

I should find something to eat. Berries, perhaps. I saw a patch of bitter greens blanketing the forest floor. I just needed to take three steps.

My body didn't move.

I should at least relocate, find suitable shelter for the night.

A sting flared through the arrow wound in my back. Spasms shot down my leg. My hands dug into the damp earth beside me.

Something soft brushed against my hand. A rabbit. It lay motionless, brown eyes glazed over. The brown fur around its neck lay matted with blood.

Someone had brought it here. Who would . . . ?

"Ikane?" I whispered, looking up, scanning the trees for his blue-green eyes, his dark hair, a flash of his swords. Was he really here, watching over me? Tightness coiled around my chest. I couldn't hope. If Rion caught his scent, she would devour him.

"If it is you, Ikane, thank you." I lifted the limp creature. My vision blurred, a sharp taste filling my mouth. I thought I had no more tears left. I wanted to feel his arms around me. Their warmth and strength, his heart beating against my ear. "You need to stay away." My voice broke. "She's stronger than ever. She will take you."

Crickets chirped. The soft hoot of an owl carried through the trees.

"She's already taken so much from me . . ."

The woods sang their lullaby, keeping Ikane's secret.

A man approached, his visage warped and blurry under the red dome. He was ripe and fresh, life's energy burning blue and violet around him. Come closer.

"What is it?" The voice belonged to a woman. A torch burned in *her hand, but the green-gold energy pulsing around her shone brighter. She was rich with love for the man, and—*

*What was this? A child. His innocence burned white and orange.*

*A meal with so many flavors had been brought to my chamber. It had been too long. Death tasted sour, the aftermath bitter and strong.*

*"It's beautiful." The man's fingers reached for me. His warm flesh touched my crimson surface. He tasted of excitement and longing, his violet-blue essence savory and rich, fueling my depleted fire. He collapsed, hollow eyes staring at nothing.*

*"John?" The woman knelt beside him, shaking his empty shell. "John!"*

*These mortals didn't understand. He was safe with me. All she needed to do was reach out, and her love for him would be eternal. I would show her. Expand the warmth, the heat, the light. Just touch me. I am the Phoenix. I am life.*

*My red glow reflected in her irises.*

*She reached out.*

*Her taste was sweet with love, but bitterness soon followed. Oh, why did sorrow spoil them so quickly? Her energy flowed within me.*

*She and "John" were together now.*

*"Pa? Ma?"*

*The boy's voice echoed the delightful sound of youth. No taste compared to the delicate innocence of children. They were honey and syrup, berries and cream, their energy more vibrant than any other.*

*"Do not be afraid. Your parents are with me. They are safe."*

*His round eyes stared at me.*

*"Come. Be with them."*

*He turned, short legs carrying him from my castle.*

Something hard pressed against my chest. The dream shattered into a thousand red fragments.

I squinted at the sky. Warm rays of sunlight lanced through the trees, falling across a woman's flaxen untamed curls bound in a myriad of colorful beads and elaborate braids. A white foxtail hung from a thick braid by her left ear.

Her boot pressed into my ribcage.

My hands flew to her ankle, body tensing in preparation to twist.

"Is this her?" The woman glanced over her shoulder.

I was surrounded. A dozen robust men and women, all clearly capable of wielding the weapons in their hands, formed a circle around me. Two of them nodded.

The tall woman smiled at me. She stepped back, releasing my chest. I pushed myself up. The trees spun, and throbbing pulsed through my head. Not the blistering red flares from Rion, but an ache that could only come from a fever.

The woman stepped up to a giant man with an extensive array of colorful tattoos decorating his muscular arms. *A Tolean? Here in Roanfire?* She took a staff from his hand, thrusting it at me. "Fight me. Show your skill."

She stepped back, drawing a sword from the foxtails strung to her waist. The crowd stepped back, widening the battlefield. She crouched into a practiced stance.

A sword against a brittle staff? How fair did she think this battle was? The soldier in me wanted to fight, to seek higher ground, to strike first and strike hard. But I wasn't a soldier anymore. I was nobody.

I set the end of the staff on the ground and released. It tipped, landing softly on a layer of decaying leaves. "I have nothing to show you."

She lowered her sword and smirked, shaking her head. Then she slipped it into the scabbard at her hip. "Bravery comes in two forms: stupidity and brashness. I suppose we have yet to see what sort of courage you have shown."

"Where is my satchel?"

She folded her arms across her chest. "Trying to defy the simple needs of your body won't get you far. Perhaps your refusal to spar with me is merely a lapse in judgment acquired by your obvious signs of malnourishment."

The Tolean man placed his meaty hand on the woman's shoulder. He smiled, the skin around his amber eyes wrinkling. "Hala mean well." He spoke with a thick accent. "We have food, shelter, and fresh clothing."

"Don't pretend I'm benign, Brent." The woman pushed the man's hand from her shoulder.

Brent's smile broadened.

"Why would you help me?" I asked.

"For selfish reasons." She shrugged. "I'm in need of your skills. Let's get you warmed up, and I'll explain."

The moment I pushed to my feet, the trees spun, the ground shifting. I blinked. All I wanted was to sleep.

"Come on." Hala waved at me impatiently. "Or shall I have Brent carry you? I'll not let you leave before you receive a decent meal and hear my proposal."

I bit my lip. What harm could a meal and simple conversation do?

Brent fell into step beside me. He was as tall as Hala with shoulders that put Ropert's physique to shame. A braided mohawk hung down his back, entwined with colored beads. Geometric tattoos blossomed from his back to his ears. Was he completely covered in those designs under his tunic?

"You not see my kind before?" He smiled.

I'd been staring. Heat scorched my ears. I focused on my feet, the loose sole of my boot slapping with each step. "I have. But I haven't seen tattoos like yours."

He held out his hand, studying the designs flowing up the back of it. "Someday I tell you what they mean."

"Am I a prisoner?"

He laughed, the sound exploding from his chest. "Hala put on brave face. She mean well. She kind. You not in danger here with us."

"You could have fooled me."

He chuckled . . . just like Ropert. Everything about Brent reminded me of Ropert. His smile, his shoulders, his laugh. Even the way he walked.

Hala emerged from the dense trees, leading us into a well-hidden campsite. Tents surrounded a roaring fire. How did they eliminate the smoke?

People glanced up from projects. Why were so many Toleans here? This directly violated the treaty. They should be sent back to their own kingdom.

Hala guided me into the largest tent sitting in the center of the camp. She pulled the flap aside. "In."

I ducked inside. Layers of pillows and furs surrounded a low-set table. A loaf of bread and a container of honey sat beside a steaming pot.

How did she do it? It smelled like Daram, the air thick with sage, thyme, and onion, just like Mayama's soups. A lump grew in my throat, my legs losing strength. I wanted to go home.

"Sit." Hala gestured to the table. "Eat."

I sank to the pillows, shoving a slice of bread in my mouth.

"Slow down." Hala sat across from me, ladling the soup into a bowl. She slid the bowl across the table—chunks of meat, carrots, and something green were floating in the broth. "Your stomach is not accustomed to so much food."

I blinked at her. How did she know? How long had she been watching me?

She produced a small wooden chest, setting it on the table. Cracking the lid, she exposed leather sacks and vials of dried herbs. "It's going to take some time to rebuild your strength. And we need to break that fever." She selected an herb here and there, dropping them into a mug of boiling water. She set it before me. "It won't taste like honeyed tea, but it has healed many overnight. My secret."

The last time someone claimed to own a "miracle" healing substance, it nearly killed Illorce.

She set her elbow on the table, resting her chin in her palm. "You don't trust easy, do you?"

I lowered the bowl. "You should be just as wary of me as I am of you."

She tilted her head, the foxtail attached to her hair swaying. "Why is that? Because you are a king-slayer?"

Bread stuck in my throat.

"Don't look so dumbfounded." She dropped her hand. "I knew it was you the moment my men reported a skilled warrior wandering the woods alone."

"I did not kill King Myron."

"That doesn't matter to us."

What was she saying? "Does the thought of one thousand, two hundred gold pieces mean nothing to you?"

She threw her head back, her laugh like deep bells. "You are so modest. The price on your head has been raised to one thousand and *nine* hundred gold pieces. But that means nothing to me. Your skill is worth far more than that."

My skill?

"We fight against tyranny. We need not money or wealth. All we need is heart and conviction. Most of our resistance includes those who have fled from villages plundered by Leviathans. We are striving to build an army strong enough to defeat those accursed pirates."

"Why not simply join with King Sander's militia?"

"Have you seen my men? You know of the treaty with Toleah."

She knew exactly what she was doing. She could bring down Toleah's wrath. Roanfire couldn't fight the Leviathans *and* Toleah.

"Yes, we harbor fugitives from Toleah. King Sander would not accept our aid. In fact, he would be forced to eradicate the White Fox Resistance all together. It is best that we keep this quiet."

"If Toleah discovers this—"

"I know." Her voice was sharp. "And that is why discretion is needed. Are you not a fugitive yourself, Keatep Brendagger?"

Hearing my name sent a chill down my spine, like the name belonged to some vile creature to spurn.

"I am offering you a home," Hala said. "All I ask is that you train my men."

My jaw clenched. Ardon's betrayal still lay as an open wound, a reminder. Why would Hala be any different? Betrayal was an easy act, especially toward a stranger.

"Make your decision quickly." She stood. "I'll not hold it against you if you choose to leave. But as I said, discretion is imperative—I must administer a tonic that will cause you to forget we ever met if you decide to go. And if you wait too long to make your decision . . ." She made a cutting motion across her throat. I swallowed. Her meaning was clear. "Now drink your tea. It will help you recover, I promise."

My hands curled around the warm mug, bitter smells wafting to my nose. What more did I have to lose? Hala was right. I was a fugitive, just like the Toleans. If I deserved more, how much more did they?

I grabbed the mug, opened my lips, and tipped my head back. The earthy bitterness slid down my throat, warmth spreading through my belly. Wiping my lips, I set the mug down.

I lay back on the bed of pillows and furs, softness I hadn't felt since fleeing Meldron, and made my mind up.

No more thinking. No more wondering. Right now, I needed sleep.

Something bumped my shoulder. I rolled over, the soft furs enveloping me in a nest, cradling every point of my body that had ached for months.

"It's past noon. You're running out of time." Hala's voice tore me from sleep. "Have you made your decision?"

I blinked, rolling to face her. "When do you need an answer?"

She tossed a bundle of clean clothing at me, hitting my face. "You have a few hours. If you haven't decided by this evening, then I'll have you take my tincture."

I sat up. I didn't ache. My head didn't spin or throb.

"There's a spring near here. You can wash there."

I followed her from the tent, sunlight piercing my eyes.

"Hala," a woman called from her seat around the fire, waving to us. The child sitting on her lap stuffed a fist into its mouth.

Hala veered to her. "Lolita. How is your little one doing today?"

"Much better." The woman caressed the soft, pudgy cheek of the baby. "Her fever is gone, and she ate this morning. How can I ever thank you?"

"Hearing of her recovery is thanks enough." Hala smiled. "I'll come by this afternoon and check on her again."

Hala waved to me, leading me to the edge of camp. She pointed to a path cutting through the trees and underbrush. "The spring is half a mile that way. I'll wait for you here. Don't bother trying to run off." She winked. "I haven't provided you with a new pair of boots."

Shrewd. The fox was perfectly suited for her.

The sole of my boot flopped with each step, the brown knit of my stocking peeking through the toe. A part of me wanted to stay. I could make a difference here. Maybe this could be the new home I longed for. And her cause was good, wasn't it? We could drive the Leviathans back, maybe even reclaim Daram.

Glowing specks of pollen danced in sunbeams lancing through

a gap in the trees. Ferns and moss-covered rocks lined the banks, framing the spring that was gurgling into the pond.

I shed my clothing, dipping into the brisk water. Ripples caught sunlight, penetrating the glassy surface. How could something so beautiful exist in such a corrupt world? A world Rion would turn to ash.

Pain curled through my chest, coiling around my throat. She took Gossamer. She tortured horses. She drained a cougar. What kept her from devouring the people around me? How much danger would I put them in if I stayed?

I splashed my face, cool droplets pearling down my skin. The dream. She was feeding, growing stronger. But the pounding in my head was gone.

Closing my eyes, I shut out the world. Warbling stars floated in the midnight expanse of my mind, hovering around the ugly mass of silver-black rock suspended within.

*Rion?* I said.

Silence.

*Rion? Are you here?*

Had I built a cage strong enough? Was I safe?

She hated the light. Maybe if I called to it, pulled it to me?

I felt nothing. I opened my eyes.

Was it worth the risk? Should I use this time to head for the Glacial Empire? But I was tired. Maybe Hala would let me stay for a month, just until I felt ready to travel again.

I dressed in the clean clothing, bare feet relishing the lush soil between my toes. Gathering my old things, I headed back to the camp.

Hala looked up from cleaning her sword. "Have you decided?"

I bit my lip. "What if I chose to stay, but only for a little while?"

She sheathed her blade, brows knitting. "Why?"

I ran a hand through my damp hair, looking over the families working by their tents. "No one is safe with me."

She laughed. "We are all dangerous."

She didn't understand. And I couldn't make her. "I can't stay long. And I won't train your men . . . at least, not until I can trust you."

Hala grinned. "Welcome to the White Fox Resistance, Ashia Valhorn."

Another name, another identity. Keatep Brendagger was dead.

She reached into a pocket at her belt, withdrawing three beads. One was the color of midnight, painted with a white fox. The second resembled white marble with a black dagger etched into it. And the third was the same color as her eyes, cerulean blue with a simple brown dot in the center.

"Turn around."

I turned slightly, keeping her in my peripheral vision.

Her fingers ran through my hair. Touch. A sensation I thought I'd never feel again.

Tingles ran through my skull, soft and kind. She began braiding.

"I've heard the rumors," she said. "I've listened to every tale of Keatep Brendagger, the king-slayer and witch. But one thing always bothered me. Why? What did you have to gain from assassinating King Myron, an old man who would probably have died of natural causes within the week of his son's coronation? My thought is you were framed or forced to do it."

Nothing but sincerity flowed with her words, releasing a cord around my heart. "I did not kill King Myron."

"Your word is good enough." She pushed the beads onto the new braid and tucked my hair behind my ear. "You're safe here, Ashia."

I believed her.

# CHAPTER 33

# RESISTANCE

*B*rent's dark skin prickled in the crisp morning air as he sank beside me. I jumped as the log shifted under his weight. He flashed a boyish grin my direction, reminding me so much of Ropert. Feathers, how I missed him.

"Good sleep?" he asked.

I nodded.

He leaned on his knees, waving a wedge of dried meat at me. "Hungry?"

I slipped it from his fingers. "Where is Hala?"

"She leave with scouts early in morning. There is Leviathan squadron nearby."

This far into Roanfire? Nearly to the Tolean border? Why wasn't King Sander doing anything from keeping them driving this deep?

I tore into the dried meat with a new resolve. Hala was doing a good thing. What did it matter if she harbored Toleans against the treaty? Roanfire needed all the help it could get. With someone like Brent on our side, we could purge the Leviathans from this corner of Roanfire.

His muscles bulged, individual cords standing out under his dark skin, lean and powerful. The tattoos seemed to flow with them, enhancing every curve.

"Are you going to tell me what your tattoos mean?" I asked.

He leaned back, inhaling through his nose.

Was this a sore subject? "You don't have to tell me."

"You ask, I tell," he said. "I was once elite warrior of Toleah. I study Ridarri Art. Each marking represent a skill I master. To be completely embellished is honor."

"Then why come here?"

"You get to point quickly," he chuckled. "Yes, I come here because my master not good man." Brent's dark eyes grew distant, his face hardening. "He beat me. He beat my family. He order my brother killed and sell my sister to another bad man. Because I am slave, I can do nothing to stop him."

"I'm sorry." I frowned. It wasn't right. How could Roanfire ignore this? "How long have you been in Roanfire?"

"Three years. My sister and father still there . . . if master not kill them." His eyes burned like the fire before us. "For now, I fight pirates. Later, I help them."

"There you are." Hala came up behind us. "It's confirmed. There is a detachment of twenty-three Leviathan pirates camped two miles from here. We need to move quickly."

Brent stood, smashing his fist into his hand. "You come, Ashia?"

Hala watched me expectantly, brows raised.

I wanted the pirates gone as much as the next Roanfirien. But Ikane. What if he were among them? My chest ached.

"I'll need a sword."

Grass tickled my chin. Smudges of black paint sat on my cheeks, dulling the sun's glare. Birds sang overhead, as unaware of our presence as the Leviathan pirates moving about their camp.

A pirate squinted against the bright sunlight in our direction, hand on his sword. I held my breath, muscles freezing.

He turned away.

"We will strike him down first," Hala whispered.

I counted the crudely dressed pirates. "You reported twenty-three. I only see nineteen."

Hala squinted through the trees. "They'll appear when we strike. We'll take them down." She tucked her legs under her, hand tightening on her sword.

I grabbed her arm. "We shouldn't move until we know where they are. They could flank us."

"We strike hard and fast. They won't know." She jerked her arm away.

Crying out, she sprang from our hiding place. Her sword arched, hitting the watch guard with his sword half-drawn. She was fast, I'd give her that.

The White Fox Resistance burst from the underbrush like a tidal wave, roaring.

Barehanded, Brent charged for two pirates. He kicked the sword of one man away, simultaneously driving a fist into the other man's jaw. The force behind Brent's blow knocked the man flat on his back.

The sword-wielding pirate slashed. Brent ducked, steel slicing air above his braided mohawk. He lunged, driving his shoulder into the pirate's chest. The pirate flipped over Brent's back. With a lightning whip, Brent slapped his fingers across the pirate's neck. The Leviathan clutched his throat. His mouth opened, face turning red.

Brent had collapsed the man's windpipe.

Leviathans leapt into action, forming lines, placing themselves back-to-back.

The Resistance was skilled but unorganized and scattered. The Phoenix must be watching over them. They should have been cut down.

Two Leviathans emerged from the trees, heading for Hala.

She should have waited.

My legs sprang forward as his sword flashed up, and a harsh clang resonated through the chaos. I twisted, allowing the force of his blow to drag him aside. His body opened, giving me a clear target of ribs and muscle. My sword slashed.

He cried out, stumbling away.

More Leviathans moved in.

Hala pressed her back against mine. "Five against two." Her breath came fast.

"Are you saying you can't handle it?"

"Not at all." There was a smile in her voice.

Blades and fists whirled. A sting raced across the back of my hand. Two pirates fell. One staggered away, blood streaming down the side of his face.

"Retreat!"

The remaining pirates responded to the call. Four of them slipped into the woods.

"After them!" Hala pointed the tip of her sword in their direction. "We can't have them revealing our location! Take them out!"

A handful of White Foxes pursued.

My chest heaved. "Your tactics are sloppy."

Her eyes hardened. "How would you have done it?"

"First, I would have waited until all the Leviathans were accounted for."

Her jaw tightened, but she nodded.

"Second, we were too scattered. Keep teams together. Brent is lethal—better yet, he's silent. Send him in first, and strike with a team in each direction once he is made." I gestured toward two different points of the camp.

"You're wounded." Hala grabbed my wrist. Blood glistened on the back of my hand. She tore a strip from the hem of her shirt, wrapping it around the cut. "Thank you, Ashia, for saving my life."

"You had my back, too."

The smokeless fire roared, light flickering across Brent's dark skin as he conversed with his stealth team of Black Foxes across the way. They laughed at something he said.

It would be hard to leave. Everything had been going so well. We'd organized ourselves into three teams, each overseen by Brent, Hala, or me. We'd perfected our assaults, sending Brent's stealth team of Black Foxes in first, then my squadron of Red Foxes would follow with a brutal rush. Finally, Hala would arrive at the flank with her White Fox squadron. With this tactic, we'd driven the Leviathans all the way to Gimath and Isilmire. But the headaches . . .

"You are deep in thought." Hala stepped over the log, handing me a mug thick with bitter herbs. "You realize you've needed to take this every day for the past fortnight."

I sipped at her tea. It didn't have the same effect as Faslight's concoction, but it eased the fiery stabs for a few hours. Lowering the mug, I appraised her. "It's time for me to go."

Hala's brows furrowed. "But we're so close to driving the pirates back to the sea. We need you."

I smiled sadly. "You are stronger than you realize. All of you."

"What can I do to make you stay?"

"I don't know where I would be without you, Hala. But this is something I can't ignore anymore." Red flared behind my eyes. I rubbed my temple. "If there was anything you could do, believe me, I would ask." Tipping my head back, I gulped the rest of her tea. Then I wiped my lips with the back of my sleeve. "I want to come back. You are family."

"This will always be your home, Ashia." She slumped against her knees, the foxtail by her ear swaying over her shoulder. "I don't have your skill, your vision for tactic and strategy." She sighed. "I didn't want to involve Roanfire in another war."

"What are you talking about?"

She straightened, her gaze crossing the camp to Brent. Her face softened, her lips turning upward in a gentle smile. "That man means the world to me. He came to my little resistance with nothing save the clothing on his back. I have made him a vow to free those suffering under the bondage of slavery."

"Attack Toleah?"

"I can't do it without you."

Red sparked behind my eyes, needles sliding into both temples. The mug slipped from my hands. The herbs usually worked by now. Why did I—?

The barrier.

I needed to check the barrier. But I couldn't do it here, not with so many lives around me. I staggered to my feet.

Hala stood, taking my elbow. "Are you alright?"

She shouldn't touch me. I jerked away, redness blurring into the trees, the fire morphing into an otherworldly glow. An arrow burrowed through my skull, and an inferno erupted, melting down my body.

*At last.*

No. Not here. Not with all these people.

"Ashia?" Hala took a step closer. "It's your head, isn't it?"

"Stay back!" My fists curled against my temples, eyes scrunching shut. "Please, stay away."

I dove into my mind. The mottled stone prison was cracked. Tendrils of flame slithered from the fissures, reaching and snaring, harpoons of fire burrowing into every fiber of my body.

*You shall burn!*

Cinders filled my lungs. Hot coals burrowed into my mouth, searing my eyes, stinging my nose. Hala's cry for help disintegrated in the roar of fire.

*You will find relief when the man you call Ikane returns to your side.*

*Breathe.* I couldn't breathe. Smoke and ash filled my lungs. I'd be dead long before Ikane could be found.

The fire ebbed, all but one tendril snaking away.

I inhaled, splinters tearing through my lungs.

"What's wrong?" Hala rolled me onto my back.

The trees burned.

Brent leaned down. Was he . . . ? *Feathers, no. Don't touch me. She'll kill you!*

His arms slipped under my legs and back, branding into my skin as he lifted me from the earth. Hot oil ran down my face, blood leaking from my eyes, nose, and ears.

*Send for Ikane, and all this will stop.*

*I'd rather die than allow you to feast on his soul!*

*I vow I will not harm him.*

How could I trust her? From the first time she sensed Ikane, she wanted him. *Your words mean nothing.*

Her fire shifted, a red tether searching beyond my frame. *The man holding you is tantalizing in an unrefined way. Or the woman caressing your brow. Now she has a rare energy.*

*No. Please, no. Leave them alone. I don't know where Ikane is.*

*Then I suggest you find him.*

Brent rushed to my tent. "What wrong with her?"

Hala knelt beside me, touching my cheek. "She's burning up. Fetch some water, quickly."

I grabbed her wrist. "It . . . it won't . . . help. "Find . . . find

Ikane."

"Who?" Hala asked.

"Ikane. Twin . . . swords . . . cursed eyes . . . dark hair."

Hala pulled a glass vial from her belt, yanked the cork free with her teeth, and spit it away. "Drink." She put it to my lips.

Liquid fire ran down my throat. My stomach heaved. Whatever she tried to give me dribbled down the side of my mouth.

"Come on. Drink." She tipped it again.

I swallowed, fire erupting through my belly. The tent spun. Hala's golden curls blurred. A leaden sensation moved up my limbs like I was turning to steel. Heavy darkness swarmed through my head. The fire was buried in sleep.

Everything burned.

Fire ate my bones, curled through my lungs, filled my mouth. Something brushed across my forehead like hot oil running over my skin. The vibration of my groan ignited an inferno in my throat. My eyes stung as I cracked them open.

The tent was red. Hala's golden curls were red. The damp cloth she used to wipe my brow was red. She pressed it against my skin.

I pushed her away, fire searing through my blood. Hot bile blistered my throat. My stomach convulsed. Red splattered on the ground by Hala's knees.

A body was not meant to endure endless pain. Why didn't Rion just take me? Why did she want Ikane here if she wasn't going to consume him?

Something wasn't right. Something . . . *make it stop. Please, just make it stop.*

"Ikane?" The name croaked through my throat.

"Not yet." Hala popped the cork of her vial open. "I have men combing every nearby city and hamlet." She pushed the bottle against my lips. "Drink."

I gulped, searing heat blistering down to my stomach. The heaviness grew.

Black.

# CHAPTER 34

# BLOOD MOON

et heat gurgled in the back of my throat. I rolled, spitting blood onto the ground. I couldn't bear it any longer. If Rion didn't end this, I would.

"Little Brendagger?"

I looked up, his form obscured by a crimson veil. He was here. He'd come.

I wanted to see his eyes, those beautiful meadow and summer-sky hues. But the red blurring my vision made his eyes brown and gray.

He knelt beside me, fists opening and closing against his thighs, like he feared to touch me. But I could feel it. He wanted to hold me as much as I wanted to hold him.

"It's Rion, isn't it?" he whispered.

*He's come,* Rion purred.

*Don't hurt him.*

*I gave you my word. All I want is his kiss.*

Anything to make this pain stop. And all she wanted was for me to kiss him? Was that all?

Could it be that simple?

I grabbed the neck of his tunic. His eyes widened as I pulled him close.

There was something wrong about this. I shouldn't do it. But the fire.

I pressed my lips against his.

The burning fizzled away, like a giant swell washing over a blazing forest.

My muscles sighed.

Rion's tendrils expanded, pushing me away. What was she—? Why was my hand slipping through his hair? Why did I draw him closer?

This wasn't me. This was Rion.

Ikane grabbed my wrist, tugging it from his neck. Rion resisted, drawing him closer.

*Leave him alone!* The stars flickered awake, sparking like raindrops against her tendrils.

She recoiled, releasing Ikane.

My body collapsed onto the bed, red sparks dancing across my vision. She was going to strike again. I couldn't endure that. She would kill me.

A bolt of red lightning flew into my head, slamming into the cage of rock. It shattered. Shards tore across my mind, suffocating the white lights in a thick cloud of ash.

*You are mine!* Her voices echoed like a hundred rumbles of thunder. *Ikane lives because I let him. Challenge me again, and I will destroy him. Through the kiss, I have tethered him to me. I can steal his soul in a heartbeat. Come to me. Claim your birthright. Or he will be mine.*

Her essence retreated across the expanse of Roanfire, resting in the faraway ruins of the Fold Garrison.

I pressed the back of my hand against my mouth. What had I done? I looked at Ikane, at his brows knitting together. My blood was smeared around his lips.

I let her get to him.

I ground the back of my hand against my mouth, feeling blood drag across my skin. I had to wipe her away, get rid of her touch.

My stomach clenched, tears burning my eyes. "I'm so sorry, Ikane."

How could I have been so reckless? I felt it. I knew something was wrong, and I ignored it.

"Kea?" Ikane brushed his lips with his fingertips. "What—"

A piercing scream penetrated the tent.

I turned to the sound. That wasn't a normal cry.

Ikane's eyes hardened as he stared at the ground, listening. More screams rippled through the camp. An orange glow flashed across the canvas.

"Fire!" someone screamed.

Green flared in Ikane's eye. He reached up, hand wrapping around the hilt of one of the swords strapped to his back. "The camp. It's under attack."

Not again. Not my home.

I struggled to my knees, muscles tight and aching in the aftermath of Rion's hold. Phoenix curse her if I couldn't defend my family.

"Go, Ikane. Help them." I reached for my boots. "I'll be right behind you."

His sword slipped from its scabbard. "Are you sure you'll—"

"Go!"

He ducked from the tent.

My fingers trembled as they curled around the hilt of my sword. Adrenaline pushed the aches to the back of my mind. Good. I needed to focus. I needed to fight. My sword dragged behind me as I pushed through the flap.

Phoenix help us.

Red uniforms bled from the trees. Smoke clogged the evening air, rising from smoldering tents. Women and children ran, others stood their ground. A young boy—no older than ten—faced a soldier at least three times his size.

My body sprang into action.

The soldier raised his sword.

The boy held his club.

I wasn't going to make it.

The sword came down, smashing through the wood, slicing into the boy. His little body collapsed.

A rope coiled around my throat, heart stopping. I roared.

The soldier whirled, catching my blow, swords grinding. He shifted his stance, heel striking the leg of the boy's lifeless body, making him stumble back. I lunged, the tip of my sword sliding into his stomach.

His eyes widened.

"Only a coward kills a child." I pulled the sword back.

He collapsed.

"Kea!" Ikane slipped against my back, deflecting a blow. "This is a massacre. We need to get the people out."

Running was not an option. The soldiers would mow us down.

"Red Fox!" I roared. A fraction of my squadron drew near, bathed in the filth of battle, half of what there should have been. I pointed my bloodstained sword to the flood of Phoenix soldiers coming from the trees. "Stand with me! Hold them off!"

Shoulder against shoulder, we formed a wall.

"Black Fox!" I hollered over my shoulder.

Brent and his unit of fifteen men flocked to me. Red dripped from a gash on his tattoo-covered shoulder, and his face was pale. He scanned our wall. "You, to right!" He gestured to groups of six. "You, to left!"

"How did they find us?" I asked.

"Maybe they follow your friend?" Brent's eyes frantically searched the chaos. "Where is Hala?"

"I thought she was with you." I ducked out, Ikane taking my place with raging swords. Was Brent right? Had the Phoenix soldiers followed him?

"White Fox!" Brent said.

I echoed his call. "White Fox!"

"Over here!" Hala's voice came from the trees behind us. She appeared beside a burning tent, breathless, her white foxtail bathed in red. Four of her squadron remained.

"We'll hold the wall!" I shouted to her. "Get as many out of here as you can!"

Hala turned, and White Fox members took to the trees, aiding anyone in their path. Brent sent three of his crew to help.

A man in line fell. I replaced his position.

Why had so many soldiers been sent to vanquish our little resistance? We were an asset. We had driven Leviathans clear to Isilmire. Why would King Sander waste all this energy on us? The pirates were the threat, not our resistance.

Three Foxes fell, our wall growing shorter. Soldiers slipped past us, forcing the line to warp into a semi-circle.

A shrill cry pierced the darkening sky. I whirled to find burning tents casting a strange light on the woman as her sword dropped. She covered her face, stumbling back, blood leaking between her fingers. The white foxtail hanging by her ear swayed over her shoulder.

"Hala!"

The soldier standing over her raised his sword.

My chest tightened. It was the boy all over again.

No, no, no. I broke formation, boots slipping on the blood-soaked earth.

His sword flew forward.

Mine slipped into his back.

Three more soldiers rushed in.

Whipping around, I parried a blow and dodged another. A sword flew for my legs. I leapt back, cornered beside Hala. She crouched, lashing her knife from her boot, slicing into the shin of the nearest soldier. Lunging, I drove my sword into the man's side.

Brent appeared, catching the two soldiers off guard.

A fresh wave of soldiers burst from the trees, the full moon casting them in a deadly glow. The formation of Foxes dwindled to half of what it had been. Ikane stood at the helm, his twin swords doing more damage than all of my men combined. His left eye brightened with each stroke.

"Brent." My breath came fast and hard. "Get Hala out of here."

He pulled her to his side.

"What about you?" Hala asked.

"Don't worry about me. Go!" I shoved them into the woods.

They slipped into the trees, blending with the long shadows cast by the moon and fire.

Lightning raced through my thigh and my knee buckled. Strangling a cry, I looked down. The shaft of an arrow sat burrowed into my leg. Perfect. The last thing we needed were archers picking us off. Curling my fingers around the shaft, I set my jaw, and yanked it free.

A chorus of whistling surged from the trees. Black streaks tore through the camp, slamming into the five remaining Foxes. Only Ikane remained, his swords flashing around him like black lightning. Phoenix soldiers circled him, reminding me of a pack of starving wolves.

I took a step forward. He needed me. But something red moved beside me. Spinning, I brought my sword up at an unusual angle, barely catching the soldier's blade. Metal rang as our swords clashed, his blow rippling up my arms, jarring my shoulders. His fist followed so fast I couldn't dodge it. Lighting burst through my jaw. The smoke, fire, red uniforms, and trees spun with white sparks as my head rocked to the side. My body hit the mud.

The soldier's boot collided with my wrist and my sword flew out of reach. Planting his foot on my arm, the cold edge of his bloodstained sword touched my throat.

I froze.

He tensed, ready to thrust his sword into my neck. But he paused. Recognition flashed in his eyes. "So this is where you've been hiding, King-slayer."

"I didn't kill King Myron."

Reaching down, he grabbed the collar of my tunic and jerked me to my feet. "How deep can your lies go?" He thrust me into the grips of two soldiers who didn't care how many bruises they'd give my arms.

"I didn't kill him," I cried. "The archduke is—"

A grunt and the sound of clashing swords pulled my attention back to Ikane. His movements were growing sluggish with exhaustion. A blade flashed across his bicep, and blood spread on his sleeve. He whirled to defend his back, but the soldier behind him already jabbed the tip of his sword into his leg.

I fought against the soldiers, trying to get to Ikane. "Stop! Don't hurt him. Leave him . . . leave him alone!"

Ikane twisted again, blocking too late. Blood appeared on his forearm.

The soldiers tightened their grips as I wriggled and strained. "Please!"

They were wearing him out, flirting with his weapons, taunting the last to fall.

"Please?" a soldier asked with a chuckle. He grabbed my hair, jerking my neck back until my knees hit the earth. He leaned down, his breath hot against my ear. "Enjoy the entertainment, King-slayer."

Tears burned my eyes as I watched Ikane twist to shield his side, but new blossoms of red appeared on his skin as the swarm of soldiers jabbed and pricked at his back. His swords no longer flew like lightning but dragged him forward like unwanted weights.

"Please. Stop." My voice cracked. I shut my eyes. I couldn't watch him die. I'd just gotten him back.

But the soldiers had no mercy.

A familiar warmth spread through my veins, subtle and comforting at first, then stinging with a hint of wrath. My eyes opened.

Feathers, yes. If Rion could save him, let her do it. Let her feast on the soldiers.

*I am here.* Her voices were soft.

I didn't care what she did to me. I shouldn't have kissed him. I should have protected him from her, but now she was the only one who could save him. *Help him. Please.*

Fire soared through my body. My muscles shook as her vines of fire reached and coiled through me, slithering to the soldiers gripping my arms. The soldiers went ridged, their eyes growing wide. The shine in their pupils glazed over like ice on a windowpane. Then their grips went lax, and they slumped to the blood-stained earth around me.

I gasped through the smoke filling my lungs and the heat searing my eyes.

The third soldier stepped back. "It's . . . it's true," he stammered. "You *are* a witch."

Rion's energy surged as if her fire found dry tinder. A gray-brown mist rolled around my knees, expanding, growing denser until my boots vanished. The smoke rippled like rings in a pond, stretching for him.

He staggered back. "Retreat!" He turned, running to the trees. "Retreat!"

The soldiers taunting Ikane stopped, faces shifting from villainous smiles to wide fear. They bolted after the soldier.

*I have helped you; now it is your turn to repay the favor.* Rion's power recoiled, the mist inhaling into my body. Cold replaced the heat. My legs buckled. My hands braced against the earth, dry, brittle, brown grass crumbling under them.

"What . . . what is happening to you?"

I looked up. Ikane's breath puffed, chest heaving, his beautifully mismatched eyes searching my face. It wasn't a look I recognized. There was more in his glare, a betrayal cutting into the bond we shared. He held his swords as if he didn't trust me.

My heart surged into a painful pounding. The man I loved feared me. And I deserved it.

My eyes stung, my vision blurring. I had no more strength. Not to fight. Not to face him. Not to face myself.

"You let her do this, didn't you? You allowed her magic to win this fight for you."

"They . . . they were killing you."

"Then let them!"

I flinched at the rage in his voice.

"And what about the kiss?" He brought his sword closer to me, like a warning. "That did not feel like you, Kea." Hurt lanced his tone. "You are letting her consume you."

"I know . . ."

I wanted to take it all back. I should have let Rion kill me. I should have run myself through rather than call for Ikane. Rion infected everything I was, everything I had worked so hard to protect.

A red fox emerged from the trees, drawn by the thick, metallic odor of blood. It slinked between smoldering tents and contorted bodies. Weapons rose across the camp like gravestones.

Something bored into my stomach, turning it inside out, twisting it, wringing bile up my throat. The White Fox Resistance had been obliterated.

The fox snatched something from the ground. A finger?

My stomach heaved. Everything blurred, eyes burning. So many friends . . . I couldn't save them.

This was my fault. I'd called for Ikane. I'd put them all in danger, all because of Rion.

Ikane sheathed his swords. "Let's get out of here." He extended his hand, his eyes softening, pulling me into a world of green and blue.

I looked away. It was a world I didn't deserve. I stood on my own, hugging my shoulders. "I . . . I'm sorry."

He grabbed my sword from the mud, scanning the smoldering tents and bodies. "So am I."

A subtle *thwit* raced through the trees. The sound of rending fabric and flesh tore through the night. Ikane grunted, pitching forward, sword dropping.

I caught him. His teeth gritted, his eyes scrunched tight.

"Ikane? What's wrong?"

His weight sagged against me, revealing the long shaft of an arrow protruding from his back.

Charred rachis. I *really* hated arrows.

I scanned the trees. There. The archer knelt twenty paces away by a large oak tree, nocking another arrow.

I searched Ikane's belt, finding the cold steel of a knife at his side. Taking aim, the blade spun through the air, coming to a sudden halt in her chest. The bow and arrow fell from her hands. She slumped back.

We couldn't stay here. There would be more.

"Ikane?" I studied the arrow in his back. A small nick had cut into the leather strap holding his swords, and the arrow was stuck deep into his shoulder blade.

"It's poisoned." The words hissed through his teeth. "I smell it."

Grabbing it, I wrenched the shaft from his shoulder.

A low growl tore through his throat as he fell forward, hands clawing the earth. His muscles shook, turning to steel, veins standing out on his neck.

"Ikane?" I touched his shoulder.

"Get away." He whirled, slapping my hand. His green eye burned wildly. "Get away from me!" He clambered backward.

Was he that angry with me? I didn't blame him, but I couldn't leave him, either. Not with poison flowing through his veins. "We need to flush the—"

His mouth pulled back in an animal-like snarl. Had his eyeteeth always been that long? They were like a wolf's.

I stepped back.

A wolf.

The wolf who'd come to Cherry's flock.

He was changing shape.

His fingers clawed at the earth, body jerking. "Go," he howled, eyes scrunching tight.

"I won't leave you."

He roared, curling into a ball. His body bulged unnaturally. Cracking bones echoed against the sound of smoldering fires. His cries shifted to howling, and his olive skin grew dark with a thick layer of deep-brown fur. His hands morphed, his face grew, his legs twisted and bent.

He howled again, collapsing onto his side, chest heaving. The form of a large dark wolf lay in shredded clothing, his leather belts and swords entangling his legs.

He was beautiful. A creature as stunning as he was in human form and just as dangerous. Did Eamon know about this?

Ikane wasn't just a Leviathan prince. He was a lycanthrope. It all made sense, how he could smell the poison in my shoulder. The way he heard things I couldn't. How he shook the rain from his hair. Why he was so fast. And why he was so good at hunting rabbits.

"Ikane."

His ears shifted, head jerking up.

I stepped closer.

He whirled, dragging his belts with him, legs catching in the sleeves of his tunic. He fell to his side. Snarling, he tore at the shirt.

"Ikane." I crouched, reaching for his belts.

His teeth snapped at me.

I jerked my hand away. "I'm trying to help you."

His eyes burned, warning me to stay away.

"What? You've seen the worst in me. If you think I'm going to leave just because you've shifted into the form of a wolf, you are wrong. I love you for who you are, Ikane. Leviathan and wolf."

The bristled fur on the back of his neck softened, his head tilting.

I'd said it. After so much time, I'd finally admitted to him and myself what was really in my heart. So I said it again.

"I love you."

His eyes shimmered, blue-and-green hues dancing. A warm sensation spread through my chest, and I knew he felt the same. Rion might have infected us both, but she could never sever the love we shared, however imperfect it was.

Every step sent a throb through my thigh. My breath hung in the air. The adrenaline had worn off hours ago, and the midnight frost bit my cheeks and fingers. My teeth knocked together.

How far had we gone? Was it enough? Without the sun to guide me and the trees veiling the stars, who knew where I was going?

Ikane moved silently beside me, his deep-brown fur blurring with the shadow of the trees. He would know.

I swung my leg over a fallen log. Bark broke away as I slipped to the other side. My stumbling through the woods was leaving an obvious trail for the soldiers to follow.

Wind rushed through the treetops—the breath of autumn. Had I really been with the White Fox Resistance that long? I'd only meant to stay for a few weeks.

Ikane slipped beside me. He let out a soft whimper, nudging my hip as if telling me I had gone far enough.

I dropped the bundle of supplies I'd scavenged. How many days had I suffered under Rion's burning torture? How long had it been since I'd last eaten? My body had reached its limit.

My back slid against the log, legs curling to my chest. I pulled my tattered blanket to my neck. Ikane pressed against me, warmth radiating from his coarse fur. Closing my eyes, I laid my frozen cheek against him. His chest rose and fell, his heartbeat thumping a steady song of life.

I shouldn't have stayed. I should have taken Hala's herbs and forgotten we'd ever met. I told her it wasn't safe to have me there.

I told her.

# CHAPTER 35

# BRAIDED HAIR

ire crackled. The luxurious aroma of roasted meat touched my nose. My eyes fluttered open.

Morning sun filtered through the soiled, russet fabric of the makeshift shelter hanging over me. Where was I? I'd fallen asleep against a log pricking my back, my head resting on Ikane . . .

I sat up, dragging the blanket around my shoulders.

"Good morning, Little Brendagger." Ikane smiled from beside the fire, turning the spit holding the browned meat of a rabbit. A tattered blanket hung over his shoulders, hiding the shredded remnants of his shirt. Light snowflakes glittered through the trees behind him.

I slinked to the fire. "The poison . . ."

"Wolfsbane." He produced a knife, slicing a portion of meat from the roast. The blanket fell from his shoulder, revealing the black image of the Leviathan crest. "To a mere human, it is deadly. But for a lycanthrope, it forces an instant change in form." He handed me the rabbit meat, pulling the blanket back over his shoulder.

"You've been watching over me." I eyed the juicy meat in my hand. "You brought me those rabbits, didn't you?"

He shrugged. "You're not the most skilled hunter."

I smiled, taking a bite. It melted against my tongue, rich with fat and nourishment. "I understand the glow in your eye now. It is the curse of the seventh son, the seven Leviathan princes. It's what makes you a lycanthrope."

He looked away.

"Ikane." I touched his perfectly shaped jaw, turning his face back to me. "Look at me."

He did, self-condemnation burning behind his beautiful eyes.

"I'm not ashamed to have you as a friend. And I am not afraid of your wolf form. You are good. I knew that from the beginning. I was just too stubborn to see it."

His warm hand covered mine, pushing my palm against his skin. "Did you mean what you said? That you . . . that you love me?"

"I did."

Birds burst from trees, flying over our heads toward the budding snowstorm in the sky.

Was this what perfection was like? Was this real? He was so close, his skin so warm, his touch a soothing balm I had been denied for so long.

All because of Rion.

She wouldn't stop. Her fire always reached for more. I couldn't show any affection for him, not with her lingering between us. He was as linked to her as I was now. She would always taint whatever we had.

I withdrew my hand.

"What is it? Did I say something wrong?"

I shook my head, pulling the blanket tighter. "You were right. The kiss wasn't me." My throat tightened. "I should have let her kill me. I should have ended it myself."

"What are you saying?"

"Because of the kiss, Rion has tethered herself to you." I searched his eyes. "I betrayed you. And because of that, she can steal you away whenever she wants. I . . . I have to go back to Fold. I have to do as she says."

"What about the White Wardent?"

I shook my head. "It's too late."

"No." He took my hand. "She can't have me, and you can't give up."

"I don't have a choice, Ikane."

His eyes shimmered. "You fought her before. Do it again."

"I can't. You don't understand. She'll take you if I—"

"I should have known." The deep voice came from behind us.

Ikane and I whirled. A dozen Phoenix soldiers stood at our back, eight holding tautly strung arrows. The rest pointed swords at us.

I'd ignored the signals. The birds bursting from the trees earlier should've been my warning, but I'd been too caught up in my reunion with Ikane.

A bearded man bearing a commander's insignia stepped forward. "Drop the knife."

Ikane's knife thumped against the earth. He raised his hands.

"Kill the Leviathan," the commander said, "but do not harm the girl. King Sander wants her alive."

Archers took aim.

Not Ikane. I stepped in front of him. An arrow flew, slipping past my hip, sinking into his thigh. He grunted, curling over the injury.

"Hold." The commander held up his fist.

The archers lowered their arrows.

"Are you alright?" I glanced over my shoulder.

Ikane smiled, his eyeteeth long and white. Veins stood out on his neck and brow. "Wolfsbane." He tore the arrow from his leg, throwing the blanket from his shoulders.

I stood tall, spreading my arms, turning myself into a shield. "I'll hold them off."

"That man is a Leviathan pirate!" The commander's face grew red as his sword slipped from its scabbard. "And you think to defend him?"

"Kea." Ikane's voice was strained. He grabbed my sword from under the makeshift canopy, fighting his breaking bones and shifting muscle. Groaning, he tossed the weapon to me.

"Kill him," the commander roared. "Kill him now."

The archers raised their bows again. I stood in their path,

opening my arms.

"Get out of the way." The commander charged. Our blades ground against each other, twirling until the tips crashed into the earth. His fist came up.

I arched back, keeping myself between the archers and Ikane. I didn't need to win. I just needed to give him time.

The commander swung at me, the tip of his blade whistling past my cheek. He followed with a punch. I slipped to the side, his fist racing past my ear. Grabbing his wrist, I jerked him forward, slamming the pommel of my sword into his spine.

He roared, back arching.

Something hit the back of my knees, and pain exploded through my muscles. My legs buckled. Hands trapped my arms. A soldier pried my sword from my fingers, and another grabbed my braided hair, jerking my head back.

I blinked through the white sparks of pain.

Ikane's dark body slipped into the woods. A hailstorm of arrows slammed into tree trunks and struck the earth at his heels.

He was safe.

The commander staggered to me, one arm behind his back, holding the impact site. "The king may want you alive and unharmed"—spittle rained through his clenched teeth—"but you don't deserve it."

"I'm not scared of you."

His fist collided with my cheekbone. The soldier's grip on my hair prevented my head from rocking. A burn raced across my skin, warmth trickling down my cheek.

"You should be." The commander leaned forward, his breath smelling of meat and mead. "You're not just a king-slayer; you are a traitor. You deserve whatever King Sander has in store for you."

The soldiers wrenched my arms back. Thick leather cords dug into my wrists.

"Commander Tamian?" An archer approached with her bow slung across her shoulder. "Shall we pursue the . . . Leviathan . . . wolf . . . creature?"

Commander Tamian looked in the direction of Ikane's flight. "No." He sheathed his sword at his belt. "We have what we came for. He'll be back." His eyes burned into mine. "And when he does, we'll be ready."

Commander Tamian's horse trotted ahead, setting the pace for the rest of the troop. The first snow dusted our heads and shoulders and a thin layer flurried across the frozen road.

Rion slipped into my mind. Her frustration burned through my veins, warming my frozen hands and feet.

*I told you to come to me. Does Ikane's life mean nothing to you?*

*I am coming.* The thought tore at my heart. What choice did I have? *The soldiers are taking me to Meldron. Fold isn't far from there.*

*But you don't know what will happen once you arrive, do you? Banishment? A life in prison? Death? Let me save you.*

*I said I'm coming.*

She burned in silence. *Very well. You have until the end of the month.* Her warmth slipped away.

My body tossed into a fit of shivering.

The soldier sitting behind me tightened his grip around my waist. "Stop squirming." He jerked the horse's reins. "Or I'll drag you again."

The leather cords dug into my wrists as I gripped the saddle horn. Blood coated my cuffs from yesterday's trek. He'd tethered my hands to a lead, dragging me behind like an animal. My knees still ached. He'd purposefully yanked me off-balance every few minutes.

Today, Commander Tamian had ordered the soldier to have me ride. Not that he cared about my fever or the infected arrow wound in my thigh—he just wanted to get to Meldron before the end of the month.

Commander Tamian pulled his horse to a stop. "We camp here." He slipped from his saddle.

The soldier behind me dismounted. "Come on." He grabbed my arm, jerking me down. My bruised knees hit the cold ground. "Get up, you indolent whelp." He yanked my wrists.

My legs shook, fire blazing through my thigh.

"I'll take her." Commander Tamian snatched my arms from the soldier. He hauled me into the trees where the soldiers were setting up camp. The firepit was already stacked with kindling. At least I would get warm tonight.

Tamian veered away from the fire. He aimed for a lone tree at the edge of camp. Threading a rope between my arms, he whipped the end around the trunk, jerking the rope taut. My knuckles slammed into the bark.

Was he going to leave me here all night? I looked back at the fire, now smoldering.

He finished tying off the rope and stepped back. "This should be comfortable enough."

Was he mad? I was freezing, in pain, exhausted, sick, and hungry. I wouldn't make it to Meldron if he treated me this way. "King Sander wants me alive."

Tamian's eyes burned. He grabbed my hair, jerking my head back. My neck strained.

"He doesn't know what you are." His breath was hot. "King-slayer. Traitor. Witch. You transformed the Leviathan into that wolf, didn't you?"

"No—"

He wrenched my hair, forcing me to my knees. My arms strained as the rope pulled my hands above my head, elbows grinding against bark.

His face burned red, towering over me. "Don't lie to me."

"I'm not!" What would I need to do to prove my innocence? I wasn't a witch. I wasn't a king-slayer. I wasn't a traitor.

"I saw him. I saw the tattoo on his shoulder." Tamian flashed a knife before my eyes. "As a commander of Roanfire's militia, I have the authority to mark a traitor to the kingdom."

"Please . . ." My eyes burned, the sharp silver blade blurring.

He stepped behind me, and the knife moved to my hair. My scalp jerked and tugged as he sliced into my braids. The braids Hala had lovingly formed. The braids that made me a member of the White Fox Resistance. The braids that had made me feel at home again.

"I hope he comes for you." Tamian's breath was hot and

threatening against my ear. "I can't wait to drive my sword through his chest."

Cold tears rolled down my cheeks as my head grew lighter and lighter.

Then Tamian stepped back, slipping the knife into his belt. "Take her to my tent," he said, whirling on his heel.

Maybe I should have taken Rion up on her offer.

*"We're under attack!"*

*"Fire! Get those fires out!"*

*"Watch your back!"*

*The shouts blurred together, blending with dream and reality. Images of Phoenix soldiers swarming through the trees flooded my mind. My Foxes battled the army, only to be cut down by swords and arrows. Smoke burned my nose. The clash of swords rang.*

I rolled to my back, my bound hands pressing against my tailbone.

The noises didn't stop. Outside, firelight flickered against the tent canvas, bright and wild.

"We're under attack!" someone cried.

Commander Tamian flung his bedroll away, grabbing his sword. His eyes burned as he rounded on me. "The Leviathan has come for you, hasn't he?"

The noises outside were too wild for one man. Ikane wouldn't strike like this. This was a tactic I knew well. The White Fox Resistance. They'd come for me.

"Get up." Commander Tamian grabbed my arm, hauling me from the tent. He raised his sword to my throat, the icy edge biting into my skin. "She's here!" His voice roared across the chaos. "If you want her to live, surrender!"

Fighting shadows scattered across the camp, smoke blurring distinct shapes.

"You surrender," a voice shouted back.

I knew it. Hala was here.

"I will kill her," Tamian boomed.

A quiet whistle raced toward us. Tamian jerked back, grunting, dropping his sword and hunching over the arrow embedded in his arm.

I slipped from his grip, staggering away, scanning the smoldering tents. Where was she? Which direction should I run?

"Commander," a soldier cried, running to Tamian. She pulled Commander Tamian's arm around her shoulders. "We need to get you out of here. We don't stand a chance. We're outnumbered and—"

"Not without her." Tamian's eyes speared into me as he ripped the arrow from his bicep, firelight burning against his clenched teeth. He grabbed his sword. "She will be delivered to King Sander, or she dies."

The wound in my leg screamed as I whirled, ready to bolt. Then I stopped.

She was already here.

Hala stood tall, shoulders back, golden curls untamed, a fire raging in her eyes . . . her eye. A torn scrap of linen wrapped around her right eye, hiding the red slash peaking over her brow and on her cheek. Had she lost it permanently?

Brent stood beside her, a tower of muscle and brawn.

"You have something that belongs to us," Hala said, stepping forward, her sword glinting.

"You'll be branded traitors for freeing her," Tamian spat.

Hala raised her sword, gliding it across Tamian's with an ominous grind. "What makes you think we're here to free her?" she whispered.

What did she mean by that?

Brent grabbed me, my ribs aching as I landed on his shoulder. Everything blurred and bounced as he bolted from the burning camp.

"Retreat!" Hala's voice rose above the chaos.

Shadows followed her through the trees. How many Foxes had survived? Seven? Ten?

"Brent, hold up," Hala called, her feet skidding to a halt beside us.

He planted his boots, his breath coming hard. "They not follow?" he asked.

She shook her head, a smile curling on her lips. "I made sure of it."

Brent slipped me from his shoulder, my feet hitting the ground in an uneven stumble. He held my shoulders. "Are you hurt? You not look good." He touched my cheek with the back of his hand. "Hala, she have bad fever."

Hala's smile faded.

"I'll be alright now, thanks to you," I said.

Hala reached up, running her fingers through my cropped hair. "What is the meaning of this?"

I couldn't read her. Something churned in her eyes, something strong and stinging.

"That is the mark of a traitor. Not a king-slayer."

"It's all a misunderstanding," I said as Brent began unbinding my wrists. "Everything is."

She sheathed her sword. "I want a full explanation later."

The ropes fell from my arms. I rubbed the ache from my wrists. "Thank you. How far is your camp?"

"Not far. Can you walk?" Hala asked, eyeing the rough bandage around my thigh in the darkness.

"I can manage."

"Here. Drink this." She pulled a small vial from her belt pouch. "It will help with the pain."

Opening the bottle, I tipped the liquid into my mouth. Bitter heat spread across my tongue, flowing down my throat. I grimaced, wiping my lips with the back of my wrist. "Feathers, that's disgusting."

Hala took the vial, slipping it back into her pocket.

I ran my tongue across my mouth. Why did it feel so numb? Something about this was familiar. I'd tasted this before . . . when Rion . . .

I gaped at the woman standing before me. Why was she doing this? Heaviness flowed over my limbs, like something dragging me into the earth, ready to bury me under rock and stone. Darkness flooded my vision.

Brent's strong arms shot out. "Hala? What you do?" he demanded.

"Something isn't right." Her voice grew distant. "I'm going to get to the bottom of this."

"You build White Fox Resistance with belief that everyone get second chance." Brent's thick Tolean accent pushed through the tent walls. "No do this. She help us."

I licked my lips, my tongue thick and heavy. I swallowed. Were they arguing about me?

"She brought a Leviathan pirate into our midst," Hala growled. "Our resistance was destroyed because of him. She is a traitor."

The word cut deep into my chest, splitting something inside.

"He fight with us. He help us," Brent said.

Hala growled, and I saw her shadow on the tent wall tearing her hands through her hair. "Over half of our resistance was murdered. Women. Children. The old and frail. If she hadn't called for him, the Phoenix soldiers wouldn't have found our camp in the first place."

"It not her fault."

"No? What about the headaches? What about the rumors of her being a witch? The blood leaking from her eyes. The vomiting. She's possessed by something evil."

"Then we help her."

"My decision is final," Hala said. "We turn her in. We could use the money."

I closed my eyes, lying back on the blankets. The money. It all came back to that.

I was tired of running. Tired of fighting and dodging soldiers. Tired of suspecting every new character that came into my life. And I was tired of opening my heart to those who would crush it.

The tent fabric rustled.

I opened my eyes to find Hala crouched in the opening, her stained foxtail swinging by her shoulder.

My jaw tightened as I struggled to sit. Why did my blood feel so thick, so slow?

She pulled the blanket from my legs, folding it over her arm. "Don't fight it," she said, handing the blanket to someone outside the tent. "The wound was infected."

I looked down, locating a white bandage wrapped around my thigh. "Why heal me if you're only going to turn me in?"

"Did I say I was healing you?"

What did she mean by that?

"I've cleaned your wound and placed an herb inside. That is what you feel now. The lethargy. The weight." Her gaze hardened, shimmering as her lower lip trembled. "How could you?" Her voice was a whisper. "You fought with me. You helped us drive the Leviathans back. And now I discover you are in league with one?"

"Ikane is different—"

"Do not say his name!" She scrunched her eye shut, turning away. Moisture glistened down her cheek. "I do not want to hear it. Any of it. You've betrayed the White Fox Resistance."

"Hala. I would never do such a thing. You are my family."

"You are *not* family, Keatep Brendagger." Her eye flashed, her voice hard and cold. "Ashia died the day the Phoenix soldiers fell upon us."

She'd used my real name. She meant it, every word. I was dead to her.

Her blond curls, braids, and foxtail distorted as my eyes filled with moisture. The thickness in my blood intensified, forcing me to lie back.

She swiped the tear from her cheek, raising her chin. "Don't get all worked up. The faster your heart beats, the more the herbs will flow through your body. You'll be unconscious again in a matter of minutes."

Shadow encroached on my vision.

I wanted the herbs to knock me out. I couldn't handle the sting of betrayal in my chest.

Smooth cobblestones shimmered in the afternoon sunlight, row after row of carefully shaped rock arranged in arched patterns. My feet shouldn't stumble on such an even surface, but they did. Everything spun. The timber-framed buildings, the vibrant canopies of booths, the people.

My arms ached as I hung between Brent and another Fox.

Brent's grip was soft, his every movement and touch filled with remorse. He didn't want to do this. But still he followed Hala to Meldron's gates.

A hand gripped my jaw, lifting my head, turning it from side to side. "There is death in her eyes. She's not worth the full price in this condition." My head sagged as the soldier let go. Coins clinked. "Here's one thousand gold. Take it, and go."

She said she didn't want the money. She said all she wanted was my skill. And just like Ardon, greed overpowered her.

*I am still here,* Rion's voices said. *I can free you.*

*No.*

Hala stepped closer, something silver and sharp flashing between her fingers. She pressed it against the soldier's side. "We are not peasants nor beggars. We are hunters. We've come to collect the bounty that is rightfully ours. She is worth two thousand gold alive. We will take nothing less."

"It must have been a feat catching her," the soldier said. "Bring another thousand," he called.

Hala retracted her blade.

*You are a soldier! You've killed to save lives. You've killed to prove your innocence. Why do you turn to virtue at this hour?*

*Because I am tired,* I said. *You've won. Take me. I am yours.*

Soldiers moved forward. Brent and the Fox relinquished my arms.

What was taking Rion so long? Why didn't she consume me?

*I cannot be reborn without you. I need you to come to me.* Her words came slow.

Didn't she feel the fever? The lethargy? The sluggish pumps of my heartbeat? Even if by some miracle I was pardoned, I did not have the strength to go to Fold.

*You are of the Noirfonika line. You are stronger than this.* Her voices took on an edge, but something else touched them. A hint of something human. Worry?

My mind must have been playing tricks. She couldn't feel anything but lust and greed, could she? When had she, the Phoenix Witch who tortured me over and over again, become my ally?

The soldiers hauled me across the courtyard, my boots dragging. Darkness engulfed us as we moved through a heavy wrought iron door. Torchlight flickered across stone walls. Sharp iron and mildew filled my nose.

*I can't wait another four hundred years,* Rion said.

It didn't matter what she did. My fate was sealed. I would be forever remembered as a king-slayer, a traitor, and a witch. I would never be a soldier again. I would never know love. And I would never feel Ikane's arms around me or his warm lips against mine.

"This one," a soldier said. They stopped, kicking a cell door open, the hinges groaning.

My legs didn't respond as they shoved me inside. My arms didn't catch. My shoulder struck the ground, head cracking against stone.

# CHAPTER 36

# KING SANDER

"Keatep?"

My body shivered.

"Keatep." The voice was hushed, masculine, and unfamiliar.

Something bit my neck. Fleas. The filthy layer of hay crawled with them. My elbows groaned as I reached for the collar of my shirt. I couldn't do it. Every muscle strained. Thick weight strangled my blood, like it had turned to stone.

"Hurry. Unlock the door," the voice said.

Who would dare to visit me? Who cared?

Keys jangled. The lock clicked. Hinges creaked. Thumps of boots echoed to my side.

"Oh, Keatep," the man breathed. His hands were warm on my shoulder, rolling me onto my back.

Hala's herbs must have been extremely potent. I thought . . . I thought I was looking at King Sander. He should have been wearing a crown. He should be wearing gold and silver, furs and silks. Not crouching here on flea-infested hay, dressed as a peasant.

He lifted my head, brushing my hair from my face, taking care to avoid the bruises. His eyes shimmered. "I am so sorry." He pulled me to his chest, holding me like a child. His lips pressed against the top of my head.

Could it be? Was it really him?

"King . . . King Sander?" My voice was raspy and weak.

"This shouldn't have happened to you," he said.

"I . . . I didn't kill King Myron."

"I never thought you did." He turned my face to his, his sea-blue eyes burning into mine. "But do you know who did? Please. I need a name, anything, to spare your life. I was forced to give up your mother. I won't lose you, too."

I blinked up at him. Maybe I was speaking to a ghost. This was a dream. A twisted dream, tempting me with false hope. All because of Hala's herbs.

"Why . . . why did you hunt me?"

His grip tightened. "I am not above the laws of Roanfire, Keatep. As king, I must see them through. King Myron was assassinated. Your act of fleeing the castle made you a prime suspect."

My vision blurred. "I didn't . . ." I choked back a sob. "I didn't kill him." My heart pumped hard, each pulse pushing a new wave of Hala's herbs through my body. Darkness encroached on my vision.

"Keatep." King Sander shook my shoulders. "Stay with me."

"Your Majesty?" someone said from the door. "You're running out of time."

The king turned to me. "Tell me what you know."

My eyes closed. "Arch . . . Archduke Goldest." I'd said the name before. I'd pointed at the man behind all this, and no one listened. This would be no different. I was blaming King Sander's uncle, a man who'd been with him since birth. It was a dangerous accusation, but I was already condemned to die.

King Sander shook me, slapping my cheek. "Stay awake, Keatep. Are you sure? Are you really sure? I need to know."

I forced my eyes open, his frame blurring between narrow lashes. "Y . . . yes."

My mind folded, turning dark.

Keys jangled. Hinges groaned. The door banged against the wall. Three blurry shapes wearing bright-red uniforms stepped inside. Soldiers stripped the blood-crusted rope from my wrists, replacing them with heavy iron cuffs. The gray walls spun as the soldiers slipped their arms through mine, dragging me into the hallway.

How could Hala's herbs still be this potent? Maybe it was more than that. Maybe it was the fever. Or maybe I was giving up.

*I cannot bear it any longer.* Rion slipped into my mind. *You cannot allow yourself to be destroyed so easily. Where has your fire gone?*

*I'm done fighting.*

The soldiers paused before a pair of wrought iron doors. They creaked open, revealing a massive chamber of gray stone. Wooden pillars reached to the ceiling. Torches sat in heavy iron sconces, the only light source, leading to the throne standing on the far end.

The man sitting on the throne was not the man who visited me. Red velvet and silk swathed his frame. King Sander held his crowned head high, the gold atop it glinting in the dim light, as he perused me with impassive eyes.

The soldiers pulled my arms, the chains rattling, and my boots shuffled as they dragged me forward.

Rows of benches lined the hall, filled with hundreds of impeccably dressed nobles all glaring at me. Their eyes burned, faces mixed with anger and disgust, some with expressions of incredulity. To them, I was a traitor and king-slayer.

One man stood out. The only face among hundreds filled with concern.

Could it be? Was this the same trick my mind had played in the dungeon, when I saw King Sander? The man's salt-and-pepper hair was combed back into a warrior's tail. His beard was neatly trimmed. The last time I'd seen those amber eyes, they were bloodshot and drooping.

Eamon?

The soldiers stopped at the foot of the dais, dropping my arms. My legs folded, knees hitting the floor, chains slamming against stone. Arms shaking, I braced myself.

"Keatep Brendagger." A man's smooth voice drew my eyes up. Archduke Goldest tapped a scroll against his leg from where he stood beside King Sander's throne. The burning braziers flanking the dais reflected against the jewels embedded in his heavy chain necklace, the same necklace he wore on the night he tried to assassinate me. Did he know a gem was missing?

"The charges against you are severe," the archduke said. "Murder and treason are offenses punishable by death." He opened the scroll in a dramatic wave. "On the night of King Sander's coronation, you were seen leaving the festivities early. Do you deny it?"

I bit my tongue. No matter how thick Hala's herbs were, I knew what he was doing.

"You are required to answer."

"My bodyguard was intoxica—"

"Yes or no. Did you leave the festivities early?"

"Yes." My voice was weak, barely audible.

"In that time, you slipped into King Myron's chamber and assassinated him."

"No." I wanted to shout. How many times did I have to say it?

"Commander Tamian," the archduke said. "Share what you witnessed upon finding Keatep Brendagger in the woods."

I craned my neck, locating Commander Tamian among the crowds filling the benches. His arm hung in a sling. "We found Keatep Brendagger camping in the company of a Leviathan pirate."

The room burst into murmurs. King Sander stiffened in his seat.

"Are you sure?" Goldest said.

"I saw the tattoo with my own eyes. On his bare shoulder. All of my soldiers did. They will testify."

"And was this same Leviathan pirate present at King Sander's coronation?"

"Yes," Tamian said.

"One more question, Commander." Archduke Goldest raised his voice. "How did this Leviathan pirate escape capture?"

My head jerked up. Murder and treason weren't enough for him? He wanted to convict me of witchcraft, too?

"When I ordered my men to kill the Leviathan, Keatep shielded him. She said something, and he turned into a wolf. We could not pursue."

King Sander leaned forward, something flashing in his eyes. Worry?

"Thank you, Commander. That is all. Sergeant Fortin Gray?"

Fortin? I searched the benches. He rose with the help of a wooden crutch, balancing on one leg. His face had always been hard, but today, it was stone.

"It has come to my attention that this same Leviathan pirate wormed his way into your company with the help of Keatep Brendagger. Is that true?"

"Yes, Your Highness."

"And he was on the ship when Lady Serah was assassinated?"

"Yes."

A fresh wave of murmurs broke out.

Ikane didn't do it. He wasn't like the other pirates. He was trying to help, and here they were condemning him. Just like they were condemning me.

"Did you notice anything strange about Keatep Brendagger at that time? Any unusual behavior?" Goldest asked.

"She had strange nosebleeds almost every night, like she was possessed."

King Sander rose from his throne. "That is not relevant to the accusations. Please stay on topic."

The archduke nodded. "Thank you, Sergeant. You may be seated."

Goldest paced the length of the dais stairs, thumping the scroll against the palm of his hand. "Keatep Brendagger has been in league with the Leviathan pirates all along, leading them into the heart of Roanfire. The question remains, why?" He stopped, turning to me, his red hair glowing. "Death lingers in her wake. Something deeper than treason."

King Sander took one step down from the dais, his long red cloak dragging behind him. "I think we've heard enough." Something dark simmered behind his eyes, like a knife had stabbed his heart and twisted. Maybe he *had* visited me. Maybe he had hoped to spare me from all this, but what I had done made it impossible.

"The evidence for treason is undeniable. Keatep Brendagger has been in the company of a Leviathan pirate, and she did not turn him in," he said.

I looked at the metal cuffs cutting into my skin. Eamon had warned me. I hadn't listened, and I wouldn't change a thing.

"Keatep Brendagger," the archduke said. "For your crime of consorting with a Leviathan pirate, hiding his identity, and secreting him into the castle, you will be branded with the mark of a traitor. You are stripped of all rank and title within Roanfire's borders. Your name shall be known across Roanfire as one of disloyalty and shame." He waved his jeweled hand to a cloaked figure standing beside a brazier.

The shrouded character removed a long metal brand from the coals.

*Let me feast,* Rion said. *Don't let them do this to you.*

*Don't give them any more fuel.*

The soldiers lifted me from the ground as the glowing metal drew closer. I would bear this mark with pride. Pride that I knew Ikane, a man whose heart burned pure. A man who sacrificed everything to bring peace. A man who did more for Roanfire than the overdressed archduke.

I met his gaze. His eyes smoldered, smiling, claiming victory.

The soldier tore my right sleeve, exposing my bruised shoulder, but my eyes remained fixed on Goldest's. He would not hear me cry. He would not see me flinch.

His smile broadened, dripping with malevolence.

The brand hissed against my flesh. My teeth slammed together. But not my eyes. Never my eyes.

My breath pulled through my nose hard. The stench of burning flesh rose through the air. My heart pulsed hard and heavy, each beat threatening to push my body into unconsciousness.

Not in front of him. I knew what he was. He was the one who deserved this brand.

Something wavered in his eyes.

The cloaked figure removed the brand, my melted skin pulling away with it. This was nothing compared to the burning pain Rion inflicted, but the walls spun. No matter how hard I fought, Hala's herbs were fighting harder.

The archduke waved the shrouded figure away. "For the assassination of King Myron, you shall be hanged at—"

"Hold." King Sander raised a hand. "You've proven her to be a traitor, but a king-slayer? Where is your evidence?"

Goldest arched an eyebrow. "She fled the castle. There was blood on her gown. She resisted arrest. She consorted with a Leviathan pirate. What more do you need?"

King Sander's eyes swept across the chamber. "Did I not swear to rule with compassion and respect for truth? Keatep Brendagger was seen fleeing Meldron on the eve of my coronation, but did anyone see her pierce my father's heart with a dagger?"

Hushed murmurs flowed.

"As king, and as the son of a great ruler, I will be certain that we have apprehended the true killer." King Sander approached the archduke, his younger frame boasting authority over the older noble. "You have produced multiple witnesses to account for Keatep Brendagger's treachery but none for the assassination of King Myron."

The archduke's jaw worked. "I have not, as of yet, found one, My King."

King Sander clasped his hands at the small of his back, pacing the steps. "King Myron was a frail man. Anyone who looked upon him would see death near. I was robbed of my chance to say goodbye." He whirled to Archduke Goldest. "You said the blood on Keatep Brendagger's gown marked her as the killer. That it was King Myron's blood."

"I . . . yes, My King."

"From the dagger that pierced his heart?"

"Yes." Goldest's voice wavered.

King Sander tilted his head. "My father was strangled. There was no blood."

Goldest's face grew pale.

My breath came easier, something light pushing through my chest. Flaming feathers, he *had* visited me. He'd found evidence.

"Keatep fled her chambers moments after the king was discovered," Sander said. "She could not have made it from the king's chambers to her own in that time."

"Maybe she persuaded the Leviathan to do it."

"Or you did it before visiting her chambers that evening!"

The gasp of the audience sucked the room dry of sound.

Goldest's mouth clamped shut.

"Two men were discovered in her chambers. One dead, the other severely wounded," Sander said. "You sent them to kill her, didn't you?"

"I did no such thing. Sander, my boy, you've been—"

"I am your king!" Sander roared.

Goldest swallowed.

"Keatep." King Sander turned to me. "You fought back. Where did you injure your attacker?"

I tried to remember his face, the man who had helped me flee the castle. The man who'd packed my bag.

I closed my eyes, running through the scene in my mind. Everything blurred together. I had to remember. King Sander was counting on me. This would seal my fate.

An image flashed through my head.

I'd whirled, rolling onto my back, my sword arching upward.

"His chest," I said. "My sword grazed his torso."

"Which direction? Please be specific."

"Lower right to upper left."

Goldest stepped forward. "That man died from his injuries. It cannot be proven."

King Sander's expression hardened. "That man survived. I call upon Sir Ironshade as a witness."

A hooded figure emerged from behind King Sander's throne.

"Sir Ironshade." King Sander gestured to the young man. "Thank you for stepping forward as a witness. Would you please show the court the injury Keatep Brendagger has described?"

The figure pushed his cloak behind his shoulders. His torso was already bare as if prepared for this revelation. A clean scar stretched from his right hip, rippling diagonally to his left pectoral.

King Sander pointed to Archduke Goldest. "Sir Ironshade. Did that man hire you to assassinate Keatep Brendagger the night of my coronation?"

"Yes." The young man's tenor voice resonated throughout the chamber.

"That is a lie!" Goldest's face grew as red as his hair. "I've never seen that boy before in my life."

"Silence," King Sander boomed.

Goldest bared his teeth, fist crushing the scroll.

The king turned back to Sir Ironshade. "After Keatep fled, what did you do?"

"When I heard the soldiers calling her a king-slayer, I went to King Myron's chambers."

"What did you see?"

"King Myron lay on his bed, face white, eyes wide, lips blue. Bruises splotched his neck."

The crowd murmured.

"And what did you find in his hand?" King Sander kept his gaze fixed on Goldest, daring him to contest.

The young man opened his palm to the king. "This lay under King Myron's fingers."

King Sander held the item up.

A sapphire stone.

It was the missing piece to Goldest's bejeweled neckwear. King Sander had done it. He'd proven my innocence and found the true killer.

Chaotic murmurs rushed across the benches.

Archduke Goldest touched his necklace, his face growing a new shade of red.

King Sander lowered the jewel. "Arrest the archduke."

Soldiers moved in.

"No." Goldest pitched the scroll at a soldier.

The soldier slapped it away and seized Goldest's arm.

"It was her!" Goldest screamed. "She's the one. I have proof. She's a witch. She—"

"Take him away." Sander turned his back to the man.

The soldiers hauled him past me, dragging him to the dungeons.

"You won't get away with this," he cried. "You wait. You'll meet the end you deserve for destroying Roanfire's future."

The doors at the rear of the chamber thunked shut.

"The charge of king-slayer against Keatep Brendagger no longer stands." Sander signaled to the soldiers.

They removed the iron cuffs from my wrists. I sank to my knees, hands bracing against the cold stone.

Finally. No more running. No more hiding. I would never have to say "I didn't do it" again.

"However," King Sander continued, "she *has* been found guilty of treason for consorting with a Leviathan pirate. She shall be placed under house arrest here in the castle. Is there anyone here who will assume responsibility for this woman?"

"I will, Your Majesty." Eamon's voice rang out eagerly as he broke from the masses. His rough, calloused hand gripped my wrist, pulling my arm over his neck. "I will take full responsibility for her."

Sander smiled soberly, an expression I didn't quite understand. "As you should, Eamon Brendagger," he whispered from where he stood a few feet away, placing a hand on Eamon's shoulder. "Tend to her. We'll speak more on the morrow."

Eamon escorted me from the room through a side door, his gait strong, his muscles firm. He smelled of leather and fresh basil, a scent I never imagined on him.

"What have you done to yourself?" he asked. "I kept my end of the bargain, Kea. You were to keep your distance."

I closed my eyes.

"You love him, don't you?" Eamon asked.

My eyes burned. "I do. Feathers, I do."

# CHAPTER 37

# A TRUE
# PRINCESS OF ROANFIRE

The clang of metal against metal carried through the crisp air. Someone bellowed orders. Shouts and grunts followed, the noises too structured for battle.

It was the sound of home. The sound of morning drills. The sound of my past life.

I blinked. Light filtered through the dusty-blue curtains, casting the small room in a haze of gray. The noises came from beyond the single window beside the bed. A table and two chairs sat beneath it. Eamon hunched over the table, his white shirt wrinkled around his shoulders, his arms folded for a pillow. His chest contracted and expanded in sleep.

Stretching, I tested my body. It didn't feel heavy. My muscles moved. Energy soared through me.

I swung my legs over the edge of the bed. A healing ache ran through my thigh. The clean nightdress slipped up my skin, revealing a white bandage. Hala's herbs had been removed.

Eamon stirred. He rubbed his face, pushing his hands through his hair. He blinked at me. "You're awake. How are you feeling?"

"Hungry," I said.

"Then let's remedy that." He stood, his gait steady as he moved to the door. He leaned out. "You there. Bring a meal for Keatep

Brendagger. And don't even think about spitting in it. My eye is as keen as a hawk's."

I stumbled to the window, my bare feet tingling oddly as they absorbed my weight. Catching myself on the table, I pushed the curtain aside. Fire seared my shoulder. I dropped the curtain, sucking air through my teeth. I clutched my arm. The brand.

"Take it easy, Kea." Eamon closed the door. "You've been asleep for five days. Your fever only just broke yesterday."

"Five days?"

He slipped into his chair. "King Sander came to visit you twice."

King Sander? I sank into the seat across from him. "What happened to . . . to the archduke?"

Eamon grunted. "Goldest has been banished from Roanfire. A weak punishment for the murder of a king, especially his own brother. His noble title spared him execution."

My jaw tightened. He'd hunted me for an entire year, chased me across Roanfire for the murder he committed. Eamon was right. Banishment was too good for him.

I reached for the curtain again, pulling it aside. Warm light fell in crosshatched patterns across the table. Clusters of red uniforms filled the courtyard below, warped by the diamond-shaped windowpanes. Formations? Were they leaving?

"They are being sent to Capin," Eamon said. "The Leviathans have overrun every city across Roanfire's shores save Brickmight and Amall. We don't have enough men to drive them back."

The White Fox Resistance could have helped. There were plenty of people ready to fight.

He leaned forward. "Did Ikane say anything to you? Do you know what they are planning?"

I stared at him. "Ikane came to you first."

His jaw tightened, knuckles turning white on the table. "I was not . . . in a good place, Kea. The Leviathans killed my family while I was in Amall rescuing a troubled Leviathan boy. I couldn't . . . I couldn't face him."

I placed my hand on his fist. He glanced up.

"Ikane has done everything in his power to help Roanfire."

Eamon looked pained. "Did you know the Leviathans have claimed Fold as their headquarters?"

Fold? Torquin, Malese, their baby boy. What of Rion, sitting in her tower, overlooking a city of dust and death, waiting for me? Going back to Fold just became impossible.

*I am flattered you think of me.*

*Don't be. If I could, I would let you rot.*

She chuckled. *Your fighting spirit has returned.*

A harsh bang hit the door. A soldier pushed it open with her back, the dishes rattling on her tray.

A soldier, not a servant. King Sander wasn't taking any chances.

She dropped the tray onto the table, the thin broth spilling over the edge of the bowl.

"Thank you," Eamon said.

She saluted him respectfully, turned on her heel, and left the room without a glance in my direction. She hated me. All the soldiers did. With this brand on my shoulder, I could never be trusted.

"Don't mind her." Eamon pushed the steaming bowl toward me.

Where was the meat? The bloated grains of barley? The chunks of carrots? I lifted the spoon, letting the weak broth fall back into the bowl. This wasn't a meal. This was a drop of water to a dehydrated man in the desert.

"Don't look so disappointed. A heavy meal would only irritate your bowels," Eamon said. "King Sander's physician is overseeing every aspect of your recovery. His orders are to begin with light meals every two hours upon your awakening."

I sipped the broth from the spoon, the essence of carrot, leek, and onion warming my throat.

"You'll be happy to know that Ropert has been pardoned," Eamon said.

I swallowed, my heart beating a little faster. "Really?"

Eamon smiled. "He should arrive within a fortnight with the reinforcements from Pedre."

A fortnight? I grinned. That was nothing compared to the year we'd spent apart.

But then my smile faded. I was under house arrest. "Will I get to see him?"

"I'll make sure of it. Now eat."

I lifted the bowl, tipping the broth down my throat.

A knock rattled on the door.

I lowered the bowl, wiping my lips with the back of my sleeve as it opened.

The man's sea-blue eyes lit up, a smile stealing across his perfectly groomed features. "The soldiers said you were awake."

King Sander.

I stood, fist flying to my shoulder in a salute. Too fast. The room tilted. King Sander's image oscillated.

Eamon grabbed my elbow. "Easy."

"Please, sit." King Sander gestured to my chair. "You are still healing."

Me? Sit in the king's presence?

Eamon stepped behind me, pushing my shoulders down, pinning me to the seat.

Sander slipped into Eamon's vacant chair, resting an arm on the table. "How are you feeling?"

"I . . . I've had better days, My King."

"And your leg?"

"It's mending."

His eyes fell on my meal. "Don't let me interrupt. Eat."

I lifted the spoon, dipped it, and took a sip.

King Sander looked up at Eamon. "Would you excuse us?"

Eamon squeezed my shoulder. My heart leapt, wanting to grab his wrist. Me? Alone with King Sander? Was this right? I was a branded traitor.

The door closed.

King Sander leaned forward, his eyes warm. They were just like mine, sea-blue and strong. "Keatep. Do you know who you are?"

I bit my lip.

His smile wavered. "You do, don't you?" He rubbed his face, disheveling his beard. "I've known about you since the day your mother told me we were expecting. I loved you then, and I love you now. You are everything to me. If I could, I would proclaim to all of Roanfire that you are my heir."

"Your Majesty, you don't need—"

"I do." He held up a hand. "I was barely fifteen years of age when you were born. I was betrothed to Princess Lonacheska of the Glacial Empire, but I loved another. My father was furious. He intended to destroy my love and my child."

I didn't want to know. It didn't matter. It was the past, a painful past. He didn't need to relive it.

"I never did find out what happened to your mother. But you, a sweet, innocent babe . . . he couldn't do it. You see? You were the—"

"—first female heir born to the throne of Roanfire in four hundred years," I finished.

His eyes widened. "You know?" He reached across the table, taking my hand. Warmth flowed with his touch. "When Sergeant Gray spoke of the nosebleeds, I knew you were already suffering."

"You know about Rion?"

His brows knit. "Rion Noirfonika?"

"Yes." It was liberating to speak to someone who understood. "She's in my head. She wants to be reborn and needs me to do it. Her ruby lies in the ruins of Fold. That is why nothing grows there. That is why rain never falls. She's draining life from everything around her, gathering power to rise like the Phoenix."

His expression shifted to confusion, almost like he thought I was mad. He *didn't* know. He *didn't* understand what was happening to me.

I pulled my hand from his.

"I . . . I'm sorry. I didn't mean to—"

"Are you talking about the Phoenix Stone?" he asked. "The one depicted on Meldron's library window?"

I looked up at him. "Yes."

"How do you know all this?"

"I discovered some abandoned writings in Meldron's library, though a skilled scribe could make more sense of them. The White Wardent created the ruby for Rion. It was a mistake, and only a princess of the Noirfonika line can destroy it. And only a princess of the Noirfonika line can channel her rebirth. She's taken every princess of Roanfire for the last two thousand years . . ."

"How . . . how long do you have before it takes you?"

Rion was waiting for me. "Not long."

His head hung. "I just got you back." His voice cracked. "What can I do? Anything. Name it."

With his permission, I could make it to the Glacial Empire. Was it worth risking Ikane's life? Rion would take him before I stepped foot out of the castle. There was nothing he could do save give me a taste of the life I would never have.

"I'd like to train with the soldiers again."

His eyes shimmered. He blinked, inhaling through his nose. "I'll see what I can do." His hands pushed against the table as he stood. "Eat, Keatep. Rest. I'll visit you again."

He slipped outside, the door locking.

I turned back to the window.

*You made the right choice.*

The soldiers took advantage at every opportunity to strike when my back was turned. Even under Eamon's watchful eye, I returned to my room bruised and beaten every night.

As a result, Eamon placed me in the care of the castle's blacksmith, Master Lonan. With the Leviathan pirates reaching further into Roanfire, the smithy was overrun with orders. An extra pair of hands were welcome, even if they belonged to a traitor.

With the workshop just beyond the training arena, Eamon could track me while running the soldiers through drills. Under Eamon's instruction, Master Lonan gave me strenuous tasks. Tasks to rebuild muscle. Tasks to challenge my stamina.

I worked the billows until my hands blistered. I cleaned the forge, swept, hauled buckets of charcoal, chopped and towed wood, and topped off containers of brine for quenching.

Master Lonan's apprentices, a pair of brothers, took it upon themselves to make my work as laborious as possible. They hid the buckets and shovels, knocked over my carefully arranged wood pile, and left their workstations littered with scraps of metal.

But it was work. It kept my mind occupied and my body moving.

Smoke billowed from the smithy's chimney, rising to the low-hanging clouds in the sky. My fingers burned as the axe slipped through them, the heavy head splitting the log in two. It was getting easier. My hands were building callouses, my muscles were growing.

I set the fragmented log on the stump, stepped back, and lifted the axe over my shoulder.

The rhythmic clang of Master Lonan's hammer grew faint. Was he out of coal again?

I looked up. He was staring at the gate.

A large troop of soldiers marched into the courtyard carrying midnight-blue-and-gold banners.

The soldiers from Pedre. Ropert.

I lowered the axe. Where was he? His strawberry-blond hair. His tall frame. His broad shoulders. His eyes.

"Hey!" an apprentice shouted. "Get back to work, Leviathan Lover."

I ignored him, scanning the new arrivals, my hand tightening on the shaft of the axe. The soldiers were thinning. He should be here. Eamon said he would be.

There. Something squeezed my chest. His hair. It had grown since it had been cropped, but the mark of a traitor was clear. Soft curls fell across his forehead, brushing his scraggly red beard on his jaw. He was so thin, his gait so weary.

"Did you hear me?" The apprentice grabbed my shoulder, shunting me forward. "Get back to work."

My toes struck a log. I pitched forward, shins colliding with the pile of unchopped wood. Splinters tore into my hands as I rolled into the path of arriving warriors. Soldiers skirted away.

I scrambled to my knees.

A pair of ragged boots planted into the dirt before me, the tip of a soiled stocking peeping through the toe of the right one. Holes gaped in the knees of his trousers. His tunic was near threadbare, exposing thin cords of muscle on his arms. Scabs covered his knuckles.

My eyes rose to his.

Ice-cold shards glowered at me, shimmering, sinking into my heart with the same hatred all the soldiers demonstrated.

Not him, too. I didn't mean for any of this to happen.

"Ropert," I breathed.

"You knew." His voice seethed with betrayal and rage. His nostrils flared. "You knew Ikane was a Leviathan pirate."

"Ropert, there is more to it." I stood, reaching for his hand. "Let me explain—"

He jerked his hand away. "I'll have nothing to do with a traitor."

Whirling, he followed the last of the troops into the courtyard.

I blinked against the burning heat searing my eyes, lip quivering. The sting in my chest was too deep, the cut too wide, the taste too bitter. Hugging my shoulders didn't help. I couldn't breathe.

Warmth slipped into my mind like a forced embrace.

*He will revere you once I have been reborn,* Rion said. *Your form will be glorious and beautiful. You will crush those that shame you now. Guilt will devour their souls.*

A sob tore from my throat, hot tears streaking down my cheeks. *I don't want him to suffer. He's been hurt enough because of me.*

"Brendagger," Master Lonan said. "What's keeping you? My fire is growing cold."

I pushed the tears from my cheeks. But they returned, flowing down the contours of my face, dripping from my chin as I hammered the black log of charcoal into bits.

*Do you love him?* Rion asked. *I thought your heart was stolen by the Leviathan prince.*

What did she know of love? There were so many kinds, each one burning differently. Each one bringing a different light into my life. Ropert's was one of the brightest and rarest. And I'd lost him.

I carried the bucket to the forge, shoveling charcoal into Master Lonan's fire, the intense heat evaporating my tears.

"That's enough. No need to waste fuel." Master Lonan shoved a wedge of metal into the coals. "Well, what are you waiting for? Pump the billows."

I grabbed hold of the iron ring hanging from the rafters, my muscles tensing, sinking, compressing air into the forge.

*Ikane is here,* Rion said.

I paused. *What?*

*He leads the Leviathan Army. They plan to strike within the month.*

She was lying. He was against this war from the beginning. He did everything in his power to stop it.

*Why would I lie to you now? I need you to retrieve me from this garrison before the battle ensues.*

*How? The Leviathans will kill me the moment I set foot in their camp.*

*Do you still have so little faith in me? I've saved you before, and I will do it again.*

My stomach churned, remembering the soldier's grips turning limp against my arms, their hands slipping down as they collapsed.

And Ikane's face, the way he'd looked at me . . . I never wanted to see that expression again.

"Stop! Flaming feathers, Brendagger! Stop!" Master Lonan's tools clattered as he tossed them onto the workbench. "It's too hot. I can't work with this."

My fingers cramped as I pried them from the ring. Sweat slid down my back. My cropped hair clung to my forehead and neck. The heat was incredible, the coals glowing white.

A harsh clap rumbled through the forge. Sparks leapt from a massive crack in the stone.

"Traitor." Lonan whirled, the back of his hand striking my cheek. My head rocked, the sting radiating through bone. "You've destroyed my forge."

"What's going on here?" Eamon appeared.

I staggered to his side.

"This happened because of you. I'll not be doing you any more favors. Look what she's done." Master Lonan jabbed a finger at the cracked forge. "It'll take weeks to repair this damage. She's working with the pirates, I tell you. Destroying my forge is the first step."

"It was an accident," I whispered.

Eamon held up a hand, hushing me. "Lonan. You've petitioned King Sander for a new forge for months. The way I see it, Brendagger has done you a favor."

Lonan folded his arms across his chest. "I don't want her here anymore. Find someone else to mind that whelp."

Eamon gave him a polite nod. "Very well." He took my elbow, steering me away. "What were you thinking, Kea?" he hissed.

I jerked my arm from his hand. "I wasn't . . . I . . . I don't know. My mind was elsewhere."

"Lonan has come to me every evening for the past week, praising your hard work and tenacity. He's even hinted at the idea of taking you on as an apprentice, despite your mark as a traitor. Why, Kea? You have no future in Roanfire's militia. This was a good thing."

I glowered at the dirt beneath my boots. Still the ice-cold shards in Ropert's eyes haunted me. "I saw the soldiers from Pedre."

Eamon let out a deep sigh, running his hand across his groomed beard. "And you saw Ropert, didn't you?"

The tears returned, clogging my throat. "He hates me."

Eamon wrapped his arm around me, pulling me against his side, saying nothing as we walked to the castle. He released me to the soldiers standing by the entrance. "Take her to her room."

They escorted me through the door.

Eamon called after me. "Get some rest, Kea. We'll train this evening."

The autumn breeze rushed through the open window, thick with the smell of dying leaves. Soldiers grunted and weapons clanged below as Eamon's shouts carried across the courtyard.

Ropert was with them. His new uniform hung on his body in a way I'd never seen before, loose and gathered around his waist. I couldn't watch.

Sunlight glowed behind my eyelids, warmth tingling the tears on my cheeks as I faced it. Everything I had fought for was gone. There was nothing left. My future, destroyed. My past, obliterated. It was time to face her, to accept my fate. No matter what I did, death was all that was left.

The lock clicked, and the door cracked open. King Sander slipped inside wearing the same inconspicuous peasant shirt and trousers he had when he'd visited me in the dungeons.

I slipped from the windowsill, saluting.

"No need for that." He closed the door softly. "I heard what happened."

"It was an accident."

"It's alright. That sort of thing happens to the best of us. Master Lonan has cracked three forges over the last ten years. No need for tears." He stepped beside me.

These tears weren't for Lonan. But if I tried to explain, they'd never stop.

"I've been to the library." His blue eyes filled with clouds, a darkness deeper than sorrow overshadowing them. "She's going to take you, isn't she?"

I turned back to the window, looking past the soldiers, fixating on the curtain wall. "I need to go to Fold."

He tore his fingers through his russet hair, turning away from the window. "This isn't fair."

Why was he so upset? We barely knew each other. He was a king, and I was a traitor.

He turned to me. "Do you still have contact with . . . with the Leviathan?"

"I . . . no."

"Could you find him again? Would he listen to you?"

"Why are you asking me this?"

"My counselors want me to send you into enemy territory. They said it would give you a chance to prove your loyalty. They want you to speak to the Leviathan princes, convince them to abandon their quest." He shook his head, fists clenching. "It is a death sentence."

The sun struck the edge of the curtain wall, the hues in the sky shifting. Rion wouldn't let me die before I came to her, and the Leviathans were in her territory. I wouldn't die.

"I'll do it," I said.

His brows rose. "Keatep, I can't ask you—"

"I'll do it."

His mouth clamped shut, eyes brimming with moisture. "But you'll die."

"I am going to die, anyway. I may as well die trying to save Roanfire."

His eyes closed, tears squeezing through his lashes. "You are no traitor—I don't care what they say. Your heart burns for our kingdom. You are a true Princess of Roanfire."

# CHAPTER 38

# ON THE SAME SIDE

*M*ist beaded on my horse's mane, and small clouds pushed from her nostrils. Water collected on my sleeves, dripping onto my trousers. The two soldiers assigned to escort me to the Dead Forest hunched in their saddles, hoods pulled deep over their heads.

Not me. My hood hung at my back, my hair plastered to my forehead. I inhaled the cold, embraced the rain, flowed with my horse's strides. There would be no rain once I reached the Dead Forest. There would be no life.

Here, the trees glistened. Life flowed through them, the rich scent of soil and moss rising from their roots. I would hold on to the breath of the earth as long as I could.

The Dead Forest stood beyond the curtain of life, dry and desolate, a forest of gray stalks reaching for the dull sky.

The soldier ahead pulled her horse to a halt. She tipped her head up, looking at me from under her hood. "You're on your own from here. The Leviathan camp is to the east of the river."

I rode past her, stopping at the edge of the woods. King Sander's letter sat in my belt pouch.

"You have until sundown tomorrow to complete your errand," she said. "We'll wait here."

My heart threatened to crack my ribs. *Rion?*

*The path is clear.*

I gathered one last breath of rain-soaked air. Squeezing my legs, I urged the horse forward. She stepped over the threshold. Dust curled around her hoofs, clinging to her damp skin. The air pushed against my lungs. The rain stopped.

*Come.*

Leaning forward, I kicked my horse's sides. Her muscles tensed.

Dust flew in our wake, snaking through the dead pillars of trees. The faint glow of Rion's jewel smoldered across the sky, a guiding beacon. I was running to my death.

The garrison ruins were a black silhouette on the cliffs, and the tallest tower pulsed with red light through the arched windows. I slowed. Was I doing the right thing? I was about to resurrect a burning tyrant. She would consume Roanfire, turn it into dust and ash, just like the Dead Forest.

I slid from the saddle, boots hitting the dirt.

*I wish you could see how much I value life,* she said. *I have done everything to preserve it, to make it eternal. I sacrificed my own love for the greater good.*

I climbed the stairs to the garrison doors. There was beauty to her words, a humanity I wanted to believe. If I could be with Ikane forever, why wouldn't I do this?

But it felt wrong. This wasn't the way. The White Wardent knew it was a mistake. I was given power to destroy her, like my ancestors.

My footfalls echoed in the barren hallway. I passed empty rooms and climbed crumbling stairs. A tattered curtain hung over a doorway, the place Ikane had nursed me back to health. The place where I'd finally seen how wrong I had been about him.

The spiraling staircase stood at the end of the hallway, red light flowing from her tower of bodies. My feet planted at the base. I never dreamed I'd stand here again.

*Come.* Her voices slithered through my mind.

I couldn't do this. I was sacrificing millions of lives for one man. How did I let her push me this far? I had to fight. I had to do what my ancestors had, even if it meant I would fail.

Red flared behind my eyes, a lightning bolt of fire cracking my skull. I clutched my head, rocking forward, collapsing against the stairs.

*Don't tempt me. I will take him,* she warned.

The fire ebbed. I pushed from the stairs, wiping the familiar sensation of blood from my nose. *How do I know you won't take him after you get what you want? After I can't protect him anymore?*

*You can't protect him now. I choose to let him stay. And I will take him if you don't come to me.*

I took one step up the stairs, then another, bracing against the wall. There had to be another way. I'd trapped her before. I could do it again, couldn't I?

The landing opened at the top of the staircase, red light spilling through the arched doorway. My heart raced, breath shaking.

*I grow impatient.* The crimson glow pulsed with her words, casting ugly shadows on the dozens of desiccated bodies. Fresh ones sent horrid fumes into the stale air.

My mouth went dry.

A child, likely only four years of age, lay withered on the ground near my feet. Her tiny, shriveled hand reached for the stone.

*Come,* Rion said.

There was no way to reach her without stepping on the bodies. And there were too many to move.

I stepped between two legs, something crunching beneath. My boots slipped, and mummified skin peeled away. Standing over the ruby, my stomach rolled, my feet finding space between outstretched hands.

How could such a tiny thing cause so much destruction? Its unblemished surface reflected the shrunken fingers of her victims.

I set my jaw. This was it. *Here I am.*

*Take me to Meldron,* she said.

*Meldron? I thought—*

*I know what you thought, but I have a vision. My rebirth will be the hope Roanfire seeks when there is none. Let the Leviathans come. Let them break down your doors and tear down your walls. We will save Roanfire. We will put an end to all war, to all death.* Her glow dimmed. *I've waited centuries to feel the beating of a heart again.*

If she thought I was going to put that thing around my neck, she was mistaken. And I didn't dare touch her.

Searching the corpses, I found a dusty white kerchief among the heaps of clothing. Throwing it over the glow, I wrapped her inside, plucking the ruby from the ground.

Heavy pelting thudded against the tower's rooftop. Dark spots gathered in the dust through the open windows. Rain, sweet and sharp, brushed the stale air from the chamber.

It was raining in Fold.

My fist tightened around the kerchief. Such a simple act had freed this part of Roanfire from her hold. If only I could crush the jewel between the folds of the fabric, shatter it into a million pieces, turn it to dust. Why couldn't it be that simple?

I stuffed the crumpled wad into my belt pouch, my knuckles brushing against the crisp surface of King Sander's letter. Was there still time? Should I risk finding the Leviathan camp with this curse in my pocket? They were likely to refuse, anyway.

My feet felt heavy as they moved down the stairs. What if Rion was right? What if Ikane *was* here?

*I will not stop you if you wish to see him one more time.*

*Is he really here?*

*He is.*

I swallowed, reaching the garrison's main door. I threw my hood up. Rain pattered against the earth, and muddy streams and pools wound between crumbled stone. My horse looked up as I approached, her ears flicking. She turned, dancing away.

I slowed, my hands outstretched. "Easy now. It's just rain."

Her head weaved, her eyes growing wide.

What was wrong with her? She knew rain. She knew me.

"Come now. We're getting out of here." I clutched her lead. She reared. The leather reins cut into my hand, yanking me off-balance. She bolted into the dead trees.

I curled my fist, easing the sting. It was Rion—it had to be. My horse had sensed the danger. How was I going to make it back in time without a horse?

*This is all your fault, Rion.*

*What are you waiting for? After her.*

Thunder rumbled against my chest. Blue light leapt through the clouds, momentarily revealing the circular shapes of hoofprints in the mud. She was definitely heading for Meldron.

I sagged against the solid trunk of a dead tree, pushing my hood from my head. Rain pattered into puddles and streams at my feet, the ripples illuminated by lightning. Everything was wet. My cloak hung heavy, pulling on my shoulders, soaking through my tunic and shirt. Mud clung to my boots. And to top it off, my stomach pinched. My food was in the saddlebags.

*The Leviathans will make it to Meldron before you do,* Rion said.

*You're not the one trying to keep the mud from sucking your boots off.* I pushed away from the tree.

Something hit my chest. The ground shifted, trees blurring. My back squished into the mud as a colossal figure straddled my body and something cold and sharp pressed to my throat.

Blue light flashed against the man's damp beard and hair. "A wee lass as a spy? How foolish can Roanfire be?" He had the same accent as Ikane. A Leviathan.

His fist clenched my tunic, jerking me to my feet. I held my hands up. "I'm not a spy."

His eyes hardened. The muscles in his neck tightened. He thrust the knife at my chest. I slipped aside, trapping his arm under mine. My other hand shot up, jabbing the center of his neck, the soft tissue giving way. He gagged.

Twisting, I pried the knife from his hand, simultaneously drawing my sword.

He staggered back, holding his throat while I pointed both sword and knife at him.

"I am a messenger. King Sander wants peace."

He cleared his throat, his voice raspy. "You're no messenger. You are a warrior." Steel flashed from under his cloak, the edge of his short sword slamming against mine. My weapon bounced off his, arching for his head. He slipped beneath. A sting ripped across my forearm.

I stumbled away, mud-caked boots making my steps heavy and sluggish.

*He's trying to kill you,* Rion whispered.

*Stop distracting me, or he will.*

He lunged, driving the tip of his sword at my stomach. My blade clanged against his, pushing it away. "I have a letter! King Sander wants—"

A harsh, constricting sensation pressed down on my body. Heat soared through my chest. My ears popped.

The Leviathan froze, his eyes going wide, sword slipping from his grip. Mud splashed my face.

*Rion, no.*

Blue light flashed. The life in his eyes was gone.

He collapsed at my feet.

*I had it under control,* I snapped at her.

*You were losing.*

I slammed my sword back into its scabbard. *Don't interfere again.*

*I told you I would protect you.*

*Don't.*

Crouching, I rolled the Leviathan onto his back. His eyes stared at the sky, hollow and gray. I ran my fingers down his eyelids, slipped his knife into his belt, and set his sword on his chest. A warrior deserved to die with respect.

*Your compassion is your weakness.*

*And your lack of it is disturbing.*

*Are you sure you don't want my help?*

*Yes.*

*Very well.*

Her warmth recoiled.

Had she been that intertwined with my body? My muscles tightened, feeling the true depth of the cold. I pulled my soggy hood up. Icy water dripped down my neck.

"Arne?"

My head jerked up. The voice was muffled by the rain, but it was close.

"Where are you, you lazy dog?"

I pushed my back against a nearby trunk. Two figures moved through the trees, coming closer. I'd gotten too close to their encampment.

Distant thunder rumbled across the sky.

I could use that. I'd wait for the sound to crack then run.

"Arne!" they shouted.

Lightning flashed. I held my breath, listening.

Three, two, one, now.

The rumble masked the sound of my boots sloshing in the mud.

"Over here!" A figure crouched by the dead Leviathan.

I slipped behind the tree, licking water from my lips, heart pounding.

"Someone's here." The ring of swords pulling from sheaths carried through the rain.

I closed my eyes. Maybe Rion could—what was I thinking? I didn't need her. All I needed was thunder and speed. They hadn't spotted me yet.

I sprinted with the next rumble, aiming for the largest trunk in the cluster ahead.

Before I reached it, a shadow whirled from behind a trunk, his forearm slamming into my neck. Boots slipping, my body spun as his arm tightened around my throat, pinning me against his chest. I couldn't breathe.

My nails clawed at his arm.

"Over here," he shouted. "I've got him!"

Shifting my hips, my fist slammed back, hitting my target between his legs. His grip loosened with a grunt. I snatched his arm, twisting it into an arm bar. A pop came from his shoulder.

He roared with the thunder.

I barely caught my breath before more pirates yanked me back. Two Leviathans dragged me into a tree, my shoulders screaming as they wrenched my arms around the crumbling bark.

The pirate who'd initially caught me straightened, dragging a knife from his belt. Rain streamed from his hair as he stepped closer, the knife flashing. I held my breath as the knife slipped under my hood, touching my cheek with cold steel. He flipped the hood from my face.

His brows rose. "Well, what have we here?" He brushed the tip of his knife under my jaw, eyes scanning my frame, lingering on my chest. "It seems tonight is our lucky night, boys. We've caught a wee little plaything."

This wasn't good.

*Are you certain you don't want my help?*

I swallowed, tempted by her offer. "I'm a messenger." I struggled to keep my voice from trembling. "Sent by King Sander."

The Leviathan's head tilted, one brow rising, his lips curling into a smile that made my blood run cold. "So he sent us a little treat?"

He grabbed my belt.

"Don't touch me!" I kicked, my boot hitting his knee.

He grunted as his leg buckled.

The other pirates bore down on me, twisting my arms, wrenching my head, tugging on my clothes.

*Rion!*

Where was she when I needed her?

"What's going on here?" The voice was strong and commanding, a tenor melody with an accent I recognized.

The pirates stopped their assault.

My heart throbbed as I hung between them, tunic loose, cloak sagging to one side. I glanced up. A tall, lean figure stood in the rain, black Leviathan armor glistening by the light of a torch in his hand.

Ikane.

He made no indication of recognition as he stepped closer, eyeing me. "Who is this?"

Alright. I would play along.

"A Roanfirien spy, Prince Ikane," one said. "She killed Arne." He jerked my hair as he said it.

"I'm not a spy." I fought against their grips. "I am a messenger. King Sander sent me."

Ikane glowered at his men. "You didn't think to inform me? Spy or messenger, anyone mentioning the name of King Sander should be brought to me. I decide what happens to them. Not you."

"Aye," they muttered.

"Bring her to my tent." Ikane turned, leading the way.

The pirates hauled me after him.

*What a noble knight.* Rion slipped into my mind, a hint of mockery in her voice. *Not exactly the shining armor you'd expect. Who knows what would have happened if he hadn't come to your rescue?*

*Why didn't you help me?*

*You said you didn't want my help.*

*I didn't need it before.*

*How was I to know?*

I bit my tongue. She knew exactly what I needed.

Ikane wove through the trees, the mist rising from the earth as we entered the Leviathan army encampment. Tents, makeshift shelters, and fire pits scattered throughout the shadows of lifeless trees. Pirates watched as I was marched through the center of camp.

Ikane stopped at a large tent and pulled the flap aside, handing the torch to the pirate with the dislocated shoulder. He pinched my elbow, his grip hard like he feared letting go.

"Leave us," he said. "And I don't want to be disturbed."

He pushed me inside.

The place smelled of him, of leather, mint, and steel. A cot sat in a corner, piled with thick furs and woolen blankets. A half-spent candle glowed on a wooden table, illuminating maps and other instruments—tools of a commanding officer about to wage war.

The tent flap closed.

"Kea." His voice rippled down my spine.

I turned.

His arms engulfed me, strong and warm, his chest solid. My Ikane.

I squeezed. "Ikane." It felt liberating to say his name.

His hands slipped around my neck, running through my cropped hair. "You've been marked because of me."

I reached up, pinning his hands to my skin. I never wanted him to let go again. "I wouldn't have it any other way."

"They didn't hurt you, did they?"

I shook my head.

His eyes slipped to my arm, his brows furrowing. "You're bleeding."

Whatever it was, it didn't hurt. It must have happened when I'd fought the first pirate, Arne. "I'm sorry about your man."

"It happens in war." Ikane pulled back, taking my arm, checking the wound. "It's deep."

My body shook as I sank down onto his cot.

Ikane knelt before me, pulled a box from under the bed, and opened the lid. Healing tools lay inside. He washed the cut, his fingers gentle and strong.

"I don't think it needs sutures," he said.

"Wrap it quick then. I don't have much time."

His eyes met mine, something broken and worried radiating behind them. "Do you really have a message from King Sander? I can't help but think you came for another reason." He paused. "Did you . . . did you destroy the stone? The rain . . ."

I wished I could say yes, and I could see how he thought I had. It never rained in Fold.

"No." I stared at his hands. "But what about you? Why are you here? Why are you leading an army against Roanfire?"

"My brother found me." His grip became stiff, pulling the bandage a little too tight. "Dran. Teilo has taken ill. I've been forced to take his place . . . or they'll kill him."

"He's the brother you mentioned before. The one they threatened when they wanted you to kill the king."

He secured the bandage. "It's happening all over again."

Maybe I could solve this. King Sander wanted peace as much as Ikane did.

My fingers shook with cold as I opened my belt pouch. The edge of King Sander's letter was damp and fragile. I pulled it free. The wadded kerchief pulled with it, and the crimson jewel spilled from the folds, landing with a gentle thump on the earth.

The pattering of rain stopped, an eerie silence filling the tent.

Ikane leapt back, eyes wide, his green-blue irises reflecting her red glow. "Kea . . . what . . . what are you doing with that?"

I couldn't hide it anymore. I leaned over, carefully gathering the glowing jewel into the fabric. Rain resumed pelting against the canvas tent.

"Just like your brothers hold Teilo's life in their hands, Rion is holding yours. I don't have a choice." Wrapping the ruby back into the fabric, I tucked it into my pocket and held the letter out to him. "But there might be a way to help Teilo."

His eyes dashed from my eyes to the paper then back to mine again. Slowly, he reached out and took it.

Unfolding the letter, he moved around the table, tipping it to the light of the candle. His countenance darkened as he scanned the black ink.

"My brothers will never agree to this."

"What?"

He dropped the letter on the table. "Gold. King Sander expects us to retreat to our isles for gold?" He tore his hands through his damp hair. "My brothers will settle for nothing less than Roanfire, the land that should have been theirs. Gold and silver mean nothing to them."

"The story about Simian Ormand," I whispered.

His green eye flashed. "It all goes back to that accursed jewel in your pocket."

I knew. Feathers, how I knew.

"What do we do now?" Ikane asked.

I met his eyes. "We go our ways, fight our demons. I . . . I have to get back before sunrise."

Pain filled his face. "I don't want to do it, Kea. And I don't want to lose you." Moisture enhanced the beautiful glow in his eyes. "I feel like I'm losing everything I love. Everything I've fought for."

Oh, how I understood.

I pushed to my feet, moving around the table, taking his hand in mine. A single tear slipped down his scarred cheek. *No. Don't cry. Please, don't cry.*

My eyes burned now.

I brushed his tear away, letting my hand rest against his face.

"Ikane. Whatever happens, know that I will always love you."

Closing his eyes, he pushed his face into my hand. "Don't go . . ."

Another piece of my heart cracked, clattering against the pile of broken parts mounting inside. Losing Gossamer, the rejection from the soldiers, the ice-cold shards in Ropert's piercing gaze. I shut my eyes, tears pushing through my lashes.

Rion would take him if I didn't do as she said.

"I can't stay," I whispered.

His arms encircled me, pulling me against his warmth. His forehead rested against mine, his breath warm, his lips inches away. If only I could close the gap, be a part of him, seal myself to him. But until Rion left us in peace, until she no longer infiltrated our minds and soiled what could be pure and good, I couldn't.

And I never would.

Rion was going to destroy me. She was going to destroy everything.

I pulled away. "I have to go."

He sniffed, wiping his nose quickly. "I'll take you." He grabbed his cloak. "My men won't miss me until dawn."

A part of me wanted to go alone. I couldn't say goodbye all over again. But if this was the last time I would see him before the war . . . before Rion . . .

I would hold onto him as long as I could.

# CHAPTER 39

# FIT FOR A QUEEN

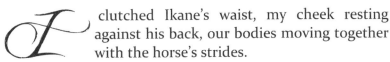 clutched Ikane's waist, my cheek resting against his back, our bodies moving together with the horse's strides.

Ikane had named him. My Leviathan pirate—the man who sailed the seas and hated horses—had named a horse without prompting from me. Recon, short for Reconciliation: Ikane's hope for the future between our two kingdoms.

Pale light touched the sky, the rain shifting to a gentle drizzle. Lush green beckoned us forward, out of the brown and mud of the Dead Forest.

Ikane pulled Recon to a stop. "We're here."

I held him tighter, pushing my forehead into his back. "Why is everything pulling us apart?"

Warmth seeped into my skin as he covered my hands with his. "If it weren't for Rion, would you stay with me?"

"Feathers, yes." What did Roanfire offer me? I was a traitor with no future.

His fingers slipped between my hands and his waist, gently driving a wedge between us. I clung to his wrist, swinging my leg over Recon's back. My boots sank into the mud.

Something moved ahead, a glimpse of red between the trees. The soldiers. They were watching.

"Little Brendagger." Ikane leaned down, his eyes sharp, his grip firm on my wrist. "Do you remember the night on the *Otaridae*?"

How could I forget?

"'Be like the stars,'" he said. "'Never change. Burn constant and strong. No matter where I am, you will be my home.'"

The broken pieces of my heart trembled like they wanted to put themselves together again but couldn't.

*Rion. Please, give me this one thing, this one moment to be alone with him.*

Something gentle flowed from her, a touch drastically different from her usual burn. Compassion?

*I, too, have sacrificed love for the greater good.* She faded away, every burned and charred piece drawing into the ruby. Greens turned brighter. Browns held warmth. And Ikane's eyes, those green and blue gems, glowed like the first time I saw them in Daram.

We were alone. Just the two of us.

"Ikane." I stepped closer, tugging his arm, sliding my hand to the back of his neck.

"I feel it, too." He leaned close, his hand slipping through my hair.

Closing my eyes, I rose up on my toes. Our lips touched, and everything stopped. The world, the chaos, the hatred and anger. This was what my heart needed. The broken pieces pulled together, the cracks sealing, everything returning to the way it should be.

Red invaded.

*No, not yet. Just a little longer.*

Ikane broke the kiss, clearly sensing her. He pressed his forehead against mine. "I love you, Little Brendagger," he whispered.

Pressure built behind my eyes as I scrunched them shut. I hated her. With every part of my being, I hated her.

Ikane's hand slipped away as he straightened, his eyes lifting to the Phoenix soldiers watching from the border. "I should go."

"Ikane?"

He looked back at me.

"I love you, too."

His smile filled with pain. "Three days." He turned Recon around. "We move in three days. Warn your people."

I nodded, my lip trembling.

He kicked his heels, spurring Recon into the mud-riddled forest. My eyes blurred, his back blending with the dead pillars of trees.

I blinked. This wasn't fair. This wasn't right. Centuries of blood and tears had been brought on by the greed of one woman.

All this would have been different if the White Wardent hadn't formed the Phoenix Stone for her.

*You blame me? I've watched people destroy themselves for centuries. They are all the same. They fight, they covet, they take. That will end when I am reborn. None shall stand above another.*

*Except you.*

*They need guidance.*

*They need the truth,* I cried. *They need to know what really happened, why the Leviathans raid. It's because of you, because they knew what you were. What you would do.*

Fire shot through my skull. *I've tolerated your insolence long enough. If you won't respect me, then you will fear me.*

I staggered, my shoulder hitting a tree. Everything burned red.

*I will be your goddess,* she roared.

She would never be a goddess of mine. I would be dead.

As if my thoughts were a warning, her heat drew back, her voices growing softer. *Take me to Meldron.*

I pushed from the tree and trudged to the border where the soldiers waited. My horse was with them. Their backs stiffened as I stepped into the forest rich with life, eyes turning to stone.

"And?" the female soldier asked.

I headed directly for my mount, swinging up into her saddle. "We need to hurry. We have three days before the Leviathans march on Meldron."

*Three days until a new beginning.*

I followed the soldiers into the stable, guiding my horse into an empty stall. My hips ached. The ride had been hard, cold, and long.

The warm smell of hay pushed the chill from my skin. As I

untied my saddlebags, a stablehand appeared. She silently took over, untacking the horse and brushing her down. It stung. I was accustomed to doing it for all my mounts, especially Gossamer. This was another reminder that I had nothing, that I had no place.

"Kea!" The shout came from outside, like subdued thunder.

I stepped from the stall as a broad-shouldered figure charged into the stable.

"Kea, what were you thinking?" Eamon's eyes flashed with rage and relief. His hand gripped my arm, digging into the injury Ikane had wrapped. "Don't you realize you could've been killed or captured or worse? Flaming feathers, Kea. I am responsible for you."

"Didn't King Sander tell you?"

"Only after you'd left." His hand loosened, his voice dropping. "You saw him, didn't you? What did Ikane say?"

I glanced up, scanning the stable for unwanted attention.

Throwing his arm around my shoulders, Eamon guided me outside. "Well?"

"His brothers are forcing him to lead the Leviathan Army against Roanfire. We have three days."

Eamon rubbed his face. "They keep pushing that boy. One day, he's going to fight back. Is it Teilo?"

"You know about him?"

Eamon steered me toward the castle. "They've held Teilo's life over his head for years. The fact his brother still lives is a miracle. It should be an empty threat by now." He opened the door.

"Is it?"

He shrugged. "I don't know."

I stepped into the darkened hallway.

Eamon closed the door. "You said three days?"

"Yes."

His eyes grew distant. "I'd better tell King Sander." He took my arm again but then stopped. He removed his hand, staring down at it. Deep splotches of red covered his fingers. "You're wounded."

"It's nothing." I carried on. What was the point of suturing it? I would be dead in days, turned into a burning nightmare. My body would be mutated into fire, clothed in red, and standing over the people as an inferno raged across Roanfire.

I looked at the blood seeping through my sleeve. What if I

ended it before it began? I was mortal. It wouldn't take much to—

Fire slammed into my skull. My body rocked, falling against the wall.

*I've protected you, shielded you, fought for you, and this is how you repay me? By the eternal lives of the Phoenix, I will not lose to your selfish notion of sacrifice.*

Eamon rushed to my side, taking my hand. "Kea? What happened? Are you alright?"

Her energy turned toward the warmth of his touch, his concern.

She already had Ikane. I'd die before I let her take Eamon, too.

White sparked. I forgot how beautiful and pure it was. Just as beautiful as the stars that night Ikane had—

His words. Did he know what they meant? How deeply they burned?

*Be like the stars,* he'd said. *Never change. Burn constant and strong.*

*What are you doing?* Fire exploded through my skull, engulfing the tiny white spark of hope. Coals burned my eyes and throat. Bones turned brittle, fire spreading through my veins. Smoke clogged my lungs.

*I told you never to touch that light again!*

Warmth trickled down my nose.

"Kea." Eamon squeezed my hand. "Help! Someone, help! Fetch the healer!"

The healer couldn't help. No one could. And that was alright. I didn't need to end my own life. Her unbridled rage would do it for me.

The heat subsided, breath filling my lungs.

She was in my head. She knew my thoughts.

I fell forward, blood dripping from my nose onto the gray stone floor.

Eamon clutched my hand like his life depended on it as his other hand stroked my back then tucked my hair behind my ear. "Kea? Can you hear me?"

I blinked at him. I'd never seen him so worried.

"Just . . . just take me to my room."

As he helped me to my feet, the walls turned.

"Easy." Eamon pulled my arm over his neck. "What's happening to you?"

I held my sleeve to my nose, catching the blood. "Don't worry. It'll be over soon."

My breath fogged the crosshatched windowpanes. Fuzzy shapes of soldiers moved beyond. Some trained, some carried weapons, some lugged bucket after bucket of oil to the crenelated walls. Troops marched through the city, fortifying the outer walls.

The citizens of Meldron poured into the courtyard, carrying what they could on their backs.

Fear flowed with them.

I turned away, hugging the blanket around my shoulders.

My belt hung at the foot of my bed, a corner of the filthy cloth peeking from the leather pocket. She was waiting, savoring the fear, letting it build, letting it consume.

Keys jangled behind the door.

I straightened.

The latch clicked, and the door swung open. Eamon entered, carrying a tray of food. He paused, seeing the untouched meal on the table before me. "Kea." His tone was reprimanding. "You'll need your strength for the battle ahead. Traitor or no, I expect you to fight."

I turned back to the window. Let Rion take my form. Let her feel the pangs of hunger, the sting in my arm, the trembling of my limbs. Let her feel this ache in my chest, the deep gouge in my heart. Perhaps she would not be so eager to have a body again.

Eamon slammed the tray on the table, dishes rattling. "Corporal Brendagger!"

My body reacted, jumping up and saluting.

He smiled. "There's the soldier I know."

My jaw tightened. I wasn't in the mood for this. I sank back to the chair, staring out the window.

Eamon slipped into the chair across from me. "Kea. I know what you are feeling."

How could he? He didn't have a fiery witch in his head, threatening everything he loved.

"I see the broken pieces in your eyes. I see the hole you think you can't climb out of. But I am here, as you were for me. I will not see you waste away as I did."

Was he talking about his drinking? I'd never touch the liquid, even with the pain I felt now. I looked at him.

"You are stronger than me. Your heart is bigger than mine. You've pushed, fought, and overcome. I need that example for my soldiers. They lose heart every passing moment. To see a woman accused of treason standing up against the enemy will inspire them." He leaned forward. "We need you."

I looked at my belt pouch then back at him. "I will be there for you, Eamon."

He leaned back with a sigh. "Now eat."

I reached for the wedge of bread.

"You train with the soldiers today," he said.

I paused. What? They hated me. I was a Leviathan lover. I'd be the appetizer for tomorrow's war.

A knock sounded on the door, then it swung open. King Sander stepped inside, dressed in golds and reds. His eyes were bright with excitement.

He pushed his floor-length cloak aside, waving at the servants that trailed behind him. "Over there." He motioned to the space at the foot of my bed.

Eamon and I stood as the servants hauled a massive sack into the room. Metal clattered inside as they set it on the ground.

King Sander rubbed his hands as he turned to us. "I'm not interrupting anything, am I?"

What was wrong with him? Why was he so excited? The Leviathans were practically at our doorstep.

I bowed. "You are always welcome, My King."

Eamon smiled like he knew what King Sander was up to. "I will leave you. Eat, Kea. You need your strength." He saluted King Sander and slipped out with the servants.

King Sander stepped around the sack, taking my hand. "I assume Eamon has spoken with you? Will you do it? Will you fight and give our soldiers courage?"

"I will do whatever you ask of me."

His grip tightened. "I knew you would. The warrior blood of the Noirfonika family runs through your veins. You've been raised by the most renowned combatant in all of Roanfire." He tugged me over to the sack. "Skill alone cannot preserve you in war. I thought it fitting to bestow a gift upon you, one that complements your heritage." He released my hand. "Go ahead. Open it."

I stepped around the bundle, crouched, and tugged the cords loose. An iron helmet rolled from the opening. It was beautiful. I lifted it from the floor, thumbs caressing the delicate engravings of feathers and flames spreading up the brow.

"This is the suit of armor King Lorand intended to give Queen Damita on her twenty-second birthday. The smithy was never able to deliver it. It has stood in the royal treasury for four hundred years, collecting dust and cobwebs. Today, it will find its rightful place on you."

I looked up. This was too much. "I . . . I'm not worthy."

"Do not say such things." He set his hands on my shoulders. "You are my blood. You are of the Noirfonika line, spanning the birth of Roanfire. This armor is just a reminder of that." He straightened. "Someday, you will be remembered as a hero. The name of Keatep Brendagger will bring hope and light to those who hear it."

I glanced back at the helmet, at my warped reflection in it. He had so much faith in me. So did Eamon. So did Ikane.

I stood. "Rion intends to rise in the heat of battle. I won't survive this war."

His face fell, all excitement draining out of him.

"Will you do something for me?" I met his eyes.

"Anything."

"Only a daughter of the Noirfonika line can destroy the Phoenix Stone. When I am gone, find the White Wardent. Find the letter in the Glacial Empire. And show the next princess of Roanfire the same love and encouragement you have shown me."

Her voices laughed. *You think he can stop me once I am reborn?*

His lips worked, like he wanted to refuse. But he knew. He'd read the letters and journal entries. So he swallowed, his sea-blue eyes glistening. "I will."

The door creaked open.

"Your Majesty." A man with silvery hair stepped inside.

Where had I seen him before? Was he with King Sander when he visited me in the dungeon? Was he in the Judgment Hall?

I blinked. Hala's drugs could have been messing with me then, too.

"What is it, Chanter?"

"Duchess Caitelyn is waiting in the council chamber."

"Oh, yes." King Sander gathered a deep breath, steeling his shoulders as was expected of a king. He stepped around the bundle. "Thank you, Keatep. Roanfire will be forever in your debt."

He and the servant slipped outside, the door closing behind them. I set the helmet on my bed, waiting for the click of the lock.

No lock. No keys.

He trusted me.

# CHAPTER 40

# TWO FRONTS

*D*eep bellowing horns penetrated the thick walls, windows rattling. My eyes flew open to darkness.

They were here.

I tossed the blankets aside. Cold leached into my feet as I moved to the window, reaching for the latch. My fingers were trembling. The window swung open, bitter cold air thrusting against my face, skin prickling.

A sea of blazing torches flickered across the landscape beyond the city walls, bleeding from the trees, as numerous as the stars overhead.

*It begins.* Her voices filled with a gruesome rapture that made my stomach churn.

I looked at the belt hanging at the foot of my bed, a red glow seeping from the seams in the bag.

My heart hit my ribs, each thump shaking my body. I closed the window, moving to the glow. I thought I was prepared, but now . . . what was going to happen to me? What would I become? What would happen to everyone else?

My mouth went dry as I felt the tiny lump of stone. Her red glow burned through the fabric. Queen Damita had been where I was now, overlooking her city, watching the Leviathan pirates destroy her people.

I couldn't do what she did. I couldn't run. I couldn't hide.

I had to face Rion or die.

A hasty knock sounded on the door before it opened.

My fist crushed the wadded fabric, holding it behind my back.

A soldier pushed her head into the room. She didn't make eye contact with me. "The Leviathans have reached the city walls," she said. "King Sander is waiting for you in the courtyard."

"Tell him I'm on my way."

She didn't move.

"What is it?"

"He ordered me to help you with your armor."

Dropping the rag onto my bed, I sank to my knees, pulling the bulky sack from under it. Armor tumbled from the opening. The soldier helped me slip into the breast and backplate, buckling the leather fasteners under my arms. Steel faulds cascaded under the breastplate and down my abdomen like plated shields. Piece after piece slipped onto my limbs as though it had been crafted just for me. Light and flexible, it was a masterpiece.

*It's perfect.* Rion's warm breath traveled down my spine.

The soldier finished the last buckle on my armguard. She stepped back, her jaw tight, eyes hard. I didn't blame her. Why was a traitor of Roanfire wearing armor fit for a queen?

"Thank you for your help," I said. "Go ahead. I'll be right there."

She nodded once, turned on her heel, and left.

I moved back to the bed. It was time. Rion could not be reborn without direct contact with my flesh. Flesh that could burn and shrivel. Just like the corpses in her tower.

*That will not happen to you.* Her glow brightened. *When the time comes, you will feel nothing. Your body will become perfect. It will blossom with fire and gold. It will be the perfect image for the Phoenix Goddess.*

A hollow ache filled my stomach. Was I really going to let her do this? My fingers unfolded the corners of the cloth. Red light filled my room as the ruby was exposed, reflecting on my armor.

*Let me feel your heartbeat.* Her glow pulsed with her words.

My heart thumped unevenly, freezing at the thought of her touching it.

*Delaying won't make this any easier.*

I swallowed, hand trembling as it reached for her. Warmth radiated against my fingers.

*They are waiting for you.*

I closed my eyes and pinched the smooth surface. Heat flowed up my arm, like I'd plunged it into a vat of warm water.

I opened one eye.

My hand wasn't shriveled.

I opened the other.

*There. Is that so bad?*

Swallowing, I slipped a thin leather cord through the golden bail. Eagerness flowed through her as I lifted the ends around my neck. The stone clinked against the armor. Every beat of my heart pushed through the ruby, glowing against the breastplate.

*Will you let me see Ikane again?*

*I am not heartless.*

I tucked the jewel inside the armor. Heat expanded across my chest as if the sun radiated against it.

"Keatep?" The door creaked open. "What's taking you so long?"

King Sander stepped inside, garbed in gilded armor, his helmet tucked under his arm. It was crafted to resemble the head of a phoenix with a plume of red feathers cascading down the center.

The silver-haired servant stood in his shadow.

Sander's eyes shimmered as he scanned me. "It was made for you," he said. "Are you ready?"

I grabbed my helmet. "I am now."

King Sander's gold-embellished cloak dragged behind him as he climbed the stairs, every step in time with the drums from the Leviathan pirates. The red plume of feathers on his helmet swayed, catching the soft glow of morning light. He paused on the wall-walk, turning to me. "Are you ready?"

I placed my helmet on my head.

King Sander stepped up to a notched turret where Eamon waited.

Heat soared against my chest, every heartbeat pulsing with a burst of sparks. All eyes were on me. Every soldier scowled at me from beneath their helmets. Me. A traitor. Speaking for all of Roanfire.

I stepped onto the notched turret. Every bang of the drums shook the wall beneath my boots.

The Leviathan Army spilled across fog-shrouded farmlands, blending into the tree line. Endless. Three crudely fashioned catapults rolled forward, prepped with massive boulders. Phoenix help us.

*I am here,* Rion said.

She may save Roanfire, but at what cost?

A small platoon of Leviathan pirates broke from the masses, approaching the gates. Two took the lead, their black armor resembling the scales of a sea serpent.

I leaned forward. Those swords.

One was Ikane.

He stopped, removing his helmet. He looked up, a stripe of blue war paint running across his eyes. But the green was still there, burning.

The accompanying Leviathan raised a fist. The drums silenced.

"King Sander Noirfonika." Ikane's voice didn't sound the same. It was tight and angry, cutting the air with a sharpness I thought only his swords could deliver. "For centuries, our kingdoms have been at war! For centuries, we've raided and plundered your shores! Today, this feud ends!"

This wasn't him. This wasn't the Ikane I knew.

His green eye flared as he reached up, drawing one of his swords from the scabbards at his back. "Today, we take Roanfire by force! Surrender, and we shall spare the lives of the innocent!"

Those weren't his words. They were forced, rehearsed. His green eye only flared when he was irritated. And he was angry. Angry at his brothers for forcing him to do this.

Sander placed his hand on my back. "Speak to him."

What could I say?

Sander searched my eyes, faith burning through them. He nodded.

Closing my eyes, I inhaled the tense air. All I could do was bolster the soldiers, show them I wasn't afraid, that I was on their side. Opening my eyes, I removed my helmet.

The green in Ikane's eye flickered. He took a step forward.

The Leviathan beside him grabbed his arm, shaking his head.

"You refuse to listen to reason, to hear the truth!" My voice felt weak compared to his. "Both of our kingdoms have been wronged. We've both suffered because of selfishness and greed. Let us change it. Let us talk—"

"The time for talk is over," the man beside Ikane roared. "We take what is rightfully ours today."

My mouth clamped shut.

*Rion. If you're going to rise, now would be a good time, before all the bloodshed.*

*Things are just getting started. Patience.*

She wanted war as much as Ikane's brothers did.

I whirled back to the Leviathans. "Then we fight." My voice held more power. "We stand. We never surrender." A soft hiss echoed across the wall as my sword pulled from its scabbard. I held it high, catching the light of the rising sun on the polished blade. "We are Roanfire!"

The soldiers whispered the call, voices growing louder. They raised their weapons high, chanting. "We are Roanfire! We are Roanfire!"

Ikane's brother spun on his heel, marching back to his men. But Ikane stood silently, the breeze playing with the long strands of hair across his eyes. My heart reached for him, desperate to break through the barrier this war had built between us, to let him know I was on his side.

He looked away, replacing his helmet, and the wall slammed up between us.

I couldn't breathe.

King Sander rested a hand on my shoulder. He nodded, something in his face telling me I had done what he expected of me. It felt wrong. There had to be another way.

The drums resumed, competing with the soldiers' chanting. Sander guided me from the turret.

"Catapult!"

I whirled. One of the massive contraptions towering over the Leviathan army jolted, its arm swinging high into the air. A boulder as large as a wagon hurled toward the city and slammed into a rooftop. Clay shingles, wood, and stone sprayed at impact. The boulder disintegrated.

"Archers ready!" Eamon's voice rose over the chaos. "Fire!"

Arrows launched over the wall, raining down at the tip of the line of Leviathan pirates, not touching a single one.

I paused. Something wasn't right. Their catapult had missed, yet they knew the exact range of our arrows? I glanced at the damaged rooftop again. The boulder had disintegrated like it was hollow, like it had been carrying something inside.

I hoped I was wrong.

Bolting down the stairs, I raced past soldiers through the streets. A trail of rubble mixed with strange fragments of dried mud and straw led to the building. A woman's scream carried through the deserted street as I turned the corner, finding a body slumped at the base of a building, black armor dented, the blue paint on his face smeared with blood.

A pirate.

Two more Leviathans stood over a woman and two children who sobbed over the body of a man lying in the threshold of his home.

Why did I have to be right?

The hollow boulder, the strange fragments, the purposeful miss. The pirates were catapulting over the wall, relying on their steel-like bones to spare them. Why hadn't Ikane warned me of this?

Maybe he didn't know . . .

A Leviathan whirled for me. The other raised his sword to cut down the woman and children.

My fist tightened around my sword—not while I had breath in my body and strength to fight.

I rushed forward.

The pirate swung his sword at my head as I stepped in, limiting his range, catching his arm against my ribs and slamming my knee into his thigh.

The other pirate abandoned his slaughter, moving for me.

I twisted, using the tangled pirate as a shield. The Leviathan's sword slammed into our shoulders, cutting into the leather armor of my captive. His scream mixed with the grinding noise against my ear as the sword bounced off my shoulder plate.

Shunting the wounded pirate into the other, I stepped back, holding my sword ready. My eyes flicked behind them. Thank the Phoenix, the mother and children were gone.

A crack of breaking stone shattered the sky. Screams roared

from the wall. Apparently not all the boulders were hollow.

The uninjured pirate swung at me. I stepped back, the tip of his blade sparking across my breastplate. I deflected the blow as his boot impacted my stomach. The armor pressed against my ribcage like a battering ram, and all air pushed from my lungs as my body hurtled back, slamming into a broken beam.

White sparked behind my eyes, making me almost miss the silver glint of a sword. I spun away, his blade biting deep into the wood where I had been.

I kicked, hitting his knee. He roared as my sword slammed into his exposed torso. Clutching his ribs, he fell to his knees.

My breath came in gasps as I searched the area. Where was the other Leviathan? He wasn't in the crippled building or among the rubble. Had he recovered enough to go after the woman and children?

The Leviathan at my feet dragged his sword from the road, his body trembling in an attempt to rise. He was a determined little rat. I smashed the hilt of my sword into the base of his neck and he collapsed.

I squinted at the darkened alleyways. What could one enemy do, one lone pirate within the walls of Meldron?

What would I do? Hide? Wait for a chance to strike? At what? I'd be much more effective slipping to one of the side gates, where I wasn't expected, and letting the army in from there.

That's where he was headed.

"Brendagger?"

I turned. Ropert stood at the corner, his armor dented and stained with blood. His blue eyes narrowed as he took in the Leviathan at my feet.

"They're catapulting over the wall." I gestured to the fractured pieces of mud and straw. "I missed one. He's headed for the North Gate."

His eyes widened. "Two stray catapults were launched just moments ago."

I turned. "Warn Eamon. We need reinforcements at all the gates."

My legs pumped as I sprinted over the rubble, skidding into a narrow alleyway, exploding onto the main road. Heat soared into my chest as my heart throbbed. My armor tugged on my muscles, the weight growing heavier.

I bound into the empty market square. Queen Damita's stained glass image watched as history was about to repeat itself.

The North Gate wasn't much farther. What if I was too late? What if Leviathans were already streaming into the city?

A blur of steel shot from an alleyway, the sword slamming into the metal faulds shielding my abdomen. The armor shuddered, and a deep ache spread through my stomach. I curled, my body pitching forward. Stone and timber-framed buildings spun, armor clattering as I tumbled into the street. I came to a stop on my back.

A blade raced for my neck.

I brought my sword up. Metal slammed into metal. My shoulders jarred, hitting the cobblestone. A boot rammed into my side, hitting where the armor buckled under my arms. Pain flared across my chest.

*Allow me.* Hot pressure engulfed me, fiery vines surging from my mind. The Leviathan went rigid, his eyes flying wide. His body slumped.

Gulping air, I pushed off my knees, standing. *When are you going to end this?*

*When all hope is lost.*

How many lives would end before she saw fit to rise?

Clutching my sword, I sprinted to the gate. The handful of soldiers standing guard turned in surprise. I wasn't too late.

"The Leviathans are launching over the wall," I shouted before I was close enough to make out their features. "There are seven within Meldron City as we speak."

A tall man stepped forward. My feet froze.

Commander Tamian. His eyes were hard under the rim of his helmet. "Why should we believe a traitor?"

"I don't have time to argue with you." I gasped for breath. "The Leviathans will win this battle if you ignore my warning."

Tamian's jaw worked. "You said seven?"

I nodded, swallowing. "Eamon has already been warned. Reinforcements should be here soon."

Tamian turned to his soldiers. "You heard her. Be on guard. We've already been breached."

My chest ached as I tried to slow my breathing. I looked back, seeing black smoke rising over the rooftops where the brunt of the attack had taken place.

I had to get back.

I threw my arm up, and rock smashed against my armor. The ground shook as I stumbled over fallen bodies and rubble. Black smoke billowed from a smoldering tower, the stench of burning flesh and wood clogging the air. Sparks leapt to the darkening sky. Leviathans vaulted over the destroyed wall, weapons clashing.

They were overpowering us.

"Now!" Eamon roared.

He stood on the wall-walk, his sword cutting down pirates as soldiers strained to tip a cauldron of hot oil over the crenelations. Black liquid gushed down the side, spilling over the gates. Screams erupted.

As I pushed up the stairs, a cry tore through the sky above me, and a body came careening over the edge. Slamming my back against the wall, the figure hit the side of the stairs, slipping to the ground.

I shifted my grip on my sword. *Are we desperate enough yet?*

*Not yet.* Her voices were bright and powerful, like every death filled her with energy. The heat against my chest pulsed, aching deeper and deeper.

My jaw tightened as I sprinted up the steps. A blue-painted face appeared over the wall as I reached the top. I rushed forward, piercing the tip of my sword into his shoulder. He cried out, falling back.

"Brendagger! Down!" Eamon bellowed.

Dropping, I braced my shoulder against the wall. It shook. Stone erupted. Something smashed into my helmet. Ringing tore through my ears as my head rocked to the side, dragging my body to the edge of the wall-walk. The helmet slipped from my skull, plummeting.

Eamon grabbed my arm, dragging me behind the safety of a crenelation.

We pressed our backs against the wall, the entire portion

beside us missing. My heart thundered, heat sparking with each thump. Sweat dripped down my spine. The catapult had nearly taken me.

"Did Ropert find you?" I shouted over the noise.

"I sent trackers into the city," Eamon said. "Ropert is with them. If there are more pirates, they'll find them."

Two Leviathans bounded over the wall. I touched my hip, searching the ground. Where was my sword? Feathers, it must have fallen with my helmet.

Eamon lashed out with his boot, kicking one Leviathan in the knees. She rocked forward, plunging down the side of the wall. Eamon and I pushed off the rock, simultaneously grabbing the second, pulling him back. His legs hit the crenelations. Body tipping, the Leviathan plummeted headfirst over the edge.

"And I gave up drinking for this," Eamon grumbled.

I hung over the wall.

A sea of pirates waited their turn, clambering up the ladders propped against the wall. So many. How desperate did we need to be before Rion stopped this?

A blue-painted face lunged up the wall. Silver flashed. I arched back, the knife cutting air. His legs whipped over the edge, boots catching Eamon's head. Eamon rocked, his metal helmet hitting the ground . . . and he lay still.

Eamon? My heart surged.

The pirate's knife raced for my chest. I had no room to move. The wall-walk behind me was gone, torn away by the catapult. I twisted, fire blasting up my back as my heel teetered on the edge. The knife clanged against my armguard.

I caught the Leviathan's arm, my fist flying at his jaw. His head jarred, but he didn't budge.

His nostrils flared, eyes seething. That was not the reaction I'd hoped for.

I punched again.

He caught my wrist, driving me against the end of the remaining crenelations. The old arrow wound flared as my back arched over the rock, lightning tearing down my leg. The knife sliced toward my neck.

*Rion!*

The Leviathan went rigid, mouth opening, eyes shifting to pain. I twisted, letting his body collapse forward and down the side of the wall.

I gasped the smoke-filled air, waiting for the pain in my back to subside.

"You shouldn't be here," King Sander said.

I turned, finding him behind me, the tip of his sword tainted red.

Wait. He'd saved me, not Rion?

"Neither should you," I gasped.

The silver-haired servant helped Eamon to his feet. Thank the Phoenix, he was alright.

King Sander grabbed my arm, dragging me to the stairs. "Come."

I planted my feet. "I can't abandon the soldiers. Eamon, tell him. I'm needed here."

Blood slipped down the side of Eamon's face under his helmet. "Do what he says, Kea."

My teeth clenched, lips quivering. Just a few moments ago, I thought he was dead. I couldn't leave him.

"Go, Kea." He shoved me toward the stairs. "Get out of here."

My eyes burned as I followed King Sander down the narrow steps, the silver-haired servant trailing behind us. King Sander stopped as a wounded soldier trembled on the steps, an arrow protruding from his thigh.

"Hold on, soldier." King Sander sheathed his sword, reached down, and pulled the man's arm around his neck.

A reverberating boom thundered through the street, coming from the gate. Two dozen soldiers raced for the wrought iron doors, bracing them with wooden posts.

"Keatep," King Sander called from the bottom of the stairs.

Swallowing didn't help relieve the dry taste of ash in my mouth. "They need help."

"*I* need your help." His tone was unwavering.

I clenched my fists. Was there nothing more I could do?

Hurrying down the stairs, I pulled the soldier's other arm around my neck.

*Rion. When will you end this?*

*Soon. Very soon.*

We stumbled through the street, heading to the market square. A woman ran to us, dozens of wounded soldiers moaning from the open door of her home.

Sander handed the injured soldier to her.

"Your Majesty." A soldier came running toward us, blond hair peeping beneath his helmet. Ropert. My breath caught. He was covered in blood, armor scarred with dents and cuts.

He stopped, bracing his hands on his knees, panting. "They . . . they've breached the South Gate."

"Fall back." Sander's voice was weak, like he didn't want to believe what he was saying. He whirled. "Fall back! To the castle! Fall back!"

The beating in my chest intensified as I ushered the droves of peasants and soldiers from the market square into the castle courtyard. Archers lined the castle walls, arrows hissing over our heads, cutting down pursuing Leviathans.

Where was Eamon? Wounded soldiers poured into the market square, but Eamon wasn't among them.

"Soldiers, to me." King Sander stepped onto the edge of the fountain in the center of the market square, towering above the retreating masses.

I pushed forward.

Ropert pressed a sword into my hand. "You'll need this."

I looked up. I needed to see those blue eyes shine, to show that I was forgiven, that he accepted who I was. But his eyes were hard and cold, focusing only on the king.

"Shield formation!" King Sander pointed his sword at the main entrance to the market square.

My shoulder pressed against Ropert's as we took position, parting only to let retreating soldiers pass.

Where was Eamon?

Arrows hissed overhead, slamming into the blue-black wave of Leviathans in pursuit.

There. Eamon's legs pumped, his red surcoat flying. His helmet was missing, and red streaked through his graying hair.

The hot pounding in my chest was too much. I wanted to rush forward, strike down the hoard of pirates trying to destroy one of the few people in my life who still cared. My breath came short, red flashing behind my eyes.

It was almost time. I could feel it.

Ropert pulled on my shoulder, nudging me to make way for Eamon and the last handful of soldiers.

I shook my head. How did I let her push me this far? I was sacrificing millions of lives for one man. One Leviathan prince.

We closed the gap, forming a solid barrier of swords, shields, and spears. The Leviathan Army bottlenecked into the narrow street, slamming against us like the rushing wave of a river hitting a dam.

Bodies pressed against my arms. It was too tight. I couldn't wield my sword. I jabbed instead, thrusting my blade between two soldiers, the tip piercing the soft flesh of a pirate's leg.

This wasn't right. This wasn't the answer. Nothing would change with Rion as the goddess. She hungered for this, for war, for destruction, for the power each life lost gave her. I had to fight. I had to do what my ancestors had, even if it meant I would fail.

Red flared behind my eyes, a lightning bolt of fire cracking my skull. I clutched my head, rocking forward.

*You dare to defy me now? I will take him.*

Something tugged my shoulder, pulling me back. I stumbled from the packed frenzy, blinking at King Sander. There was sadness in his eyes, like he knew.

"You cannot fight on two fronts, no matter how strong you think you are." His voice was soft, unfitting for the surrounding chaos.

My chest burned, and I reached inside my armor. Red light flared. The ruby pulsed with every frantic beat of my heart, flashing against steel.

"Leviathans! On the rooftops!" an archer cried.

A flurry of arrows rained down. Shield bearers swung their shields over the archers along the wall. Black arrows pelted against them, and several archers screamed when arrows slipped by.

A black blur slammed into King Sander's shoulder, wedging between his plates of armor. He grunted, staggering back.

"No . . ." I stood over him, shielding him with my body.

*It's time.*

This was what she had been waiting for? For the king to be injured? Red flared across my eyes.

"The king," I roared. "Get the king to safety!"

Ropert rushed forward, taking King Sander by the arm.

"Fall back! Into the castle!" My voice shook as fire blossomed through my chest, spreading down my arms and legs. "Close the gates!"

Archers launched a new wave of arrows at the Leviathans.

*Stop resisting! You are bringing this pain on yourself!*

Soldiers dashed by me, their crimson uniforms blurring with the red behind my eyes.

I blinked at the gates. Were they safe? Ropert, King Sander, Eamon?

*I will take him!*

My eyes burned, rocks crushing my chest. *Then take him.* My heart shattered as the words came. Ikane. My Ikane. My fearless Leviathan pirate. My wolf.

Her fire ebbed. *What?*

I was just like her. I blamed her for being selfish, for refusing to sacrifice one wonderful thing for the good of the people. For the good of the kingdom. The familiar sensation of blood trickled from my nose as I staggered to the gates.

She should have taken me when she had the chance.

I ushered the last soldier inside.

I'd trapped her before; I could do it again. *I will not be intimidated anymore. I am a warrior. I fight. And I will fight to the death to protect the world from you.*

I pulled the gates, closing the gap.

"Kea, no!" Eamon launched forward, but soldiers grabbed him, hauling him back.

The gates rumbled shut. I heard the heavy wooden plank grind as it slid into position behind it.

I faced the Leviathans filtering into the market square, surrounding me. Rion could burn and torture me all she wanted. She could take away those I loved one at a time.

She would never rise.

*This could have ended in beauty and power! Think about what you are doing!* Rion screamed.

Leviathans raised their weapons.

I closed my eyes, suffocating her red glow in my fist. I would do what Queen Damita did. The world would be safe as long as there were no princesses of Roanfire.

"Hold!"

My eyes shot open.

The Leviathans parted.

Ikane stepped forward, removing his helmet, exposing his rich hair and scarred cheek. His eyes—those beautiful eyes that always brought me back to a summer meadow. How could something so magnificent cause so much pain? I had everything before I met him, and yet everything was empty without him. Empty like the night without a single star.

"Little Brendagger," he breathed.

"Ikane," an unfamiliar voice bellowed.

A man who had to be Ikane's brother shoved through the tightly packed Leviathans. His eyes narrowed as they fell upon me. "What are you doing? Kill her."

"Let it be, Dran," Ikane said.

Dran pushed past Ikane, raising his battle-axe. "Coward. I'll show you how a kingdom is won."

The axe raced for my skull.

Black steel flashed.

Fire surged through my veins.

# CHAPTER 41

# BE LIKE THE STARS

*Keatep? Keatep Brendagger?*

I did not recognize the voice. It was feminine and strong, unmarred by a thousand other voices. It couldn't be Rion. She'd never called me by my name.

Where was I? I felt nothing. No heat. No cold. Nothing beneath my feet or in my hands.

Red. Only red.

Thousands of burning specks blended into fiery clouds. I was one of them, a star, nothing more than a little light among millions of others.

An essence brushed against me, a whisper of strength and formidability. *I feel you. The blood of the Noirfonika line flows in you.*

*Who . . . who are you?*

*Engage while you still can,* the voice said. *You are losing connection to the world, to life, to humanity every moment you're here. Don't think. Don't try to understand.*

Where was "here"? How was I to engage? *Who* was I to engage? I was nothing but a speck. I had no body, no sword, no armor, nothing to ground me.

*I sent you the dreams, but Rion changed them. I never meant for you to get hurt. I needed you to know, to understand. The Phoenix Stone must be destroyed.* The warm essence expanded, a star shifting. Something about it was familiar and tangible. I'd felt her before, been inside her head, heard her thoughts and dreams.

*Damita?*

*Don't interact. You're losing yourself.*

Red energy surged among the stars, collecting them, solidifying them into the glowing form of a woman. Her frame burned, hair roiling into rays of sun, eyes shining white. Her crimson gown rippled with fire. *Silence!*

It was Rion. Her voice was more distinct than I'd ever heard it, but it was her.

Damita's star hovered between us, shielding me with her fragile light.

*Even now, you are a nuisance! I should have used your essence up years ago!* Red flaming energy bolted across the cavern, slamming into the star, a thread of fire piercing her.

Damita's cry echoed. Her pain radiated, ripping across the stars, each one trembling more than the next like they were all connected.

This was Rion. This was her domain, her future. This was what Roanfire would become. Fear was her power, crushing hopes, destroying dreams, ending everything that made us who we were.

Something surged inside, swelling through my soul like the soothing breeze of a warm spring morning. I was a warrior, a protector. I fought for everything I loved and cherished and missed: the solid earth beneath my feet, the gentle air caressing my skin, the warmth of a fire at night, the smell of the sea.

My form flashed white, illuminating her prison, revealing the stars for what they were: frightened souls trapped in a dome of red.

*That's it.* Damita's voice was tight. *That is your power.*

Rion snarled, teeth flashing as white as her eyes. Fire surged from her form as she jerked the burning thread, pulling Damita to her.

Light exploded from my aura. *Let her go!*

Damita had lived in this prison for four hundred years, suffering under Rion's asphyxiating fire, her life cut short only to become fuel for this burning nightmare. She was my blood, my family.

Rion caught Damita's light in her hands, her hollow white eyes burning into me. *I am more than you know. I am life and death. I am everything.*

She was mad.

Damita's light waned.

Rion was consuming her. Draining lives from my world wasn't enough—she devoured them twice over in this prison.

Enough was enough. I had to do this for the future of Roanfire. For King Sander, for Eamon, for Ropert, for Ikane.

I remembered his firm hands, his warm skin, the promise of summer shining in his eyes. *Be like the stars,* he'd said. *Never change. Burn constant and strong. No matter where I am, you will be my home.*

I had to do this for him.

White fire surged from me, pushing against the thick aura of fear.

Rion's eyes narrowed. *I hold his life in my hands.*

*And millions of others,* I said. *You are drunk on them. You do not know the meaning of love, future, or peace. If his life is the price to free Roanfire, then so be it.*

Her hands crushed Damita's illumination. *You brought this on yourself!* She whirled, tugging the end of a thread at her back. It soared through the stars to the ruby's surface, a distant glow of blue light shifting like rolling clouds. Twisting the thread through her fingers, the blue light drew into the prison, turning violet.

Her crimson lips spread into a grin, white eyes burning into me. *He's mine.*

Ikane!

She was taking him. I wanted to close my eyes, shut out the image. I couldn't watch.

I had to let go. I had to focus on everything I was saving, everything I was fighting for. Everything *Ikane* fought for. Mayama slaving away in her kitchen. Faslight and the intense fragrance of the herbs in her little cabin. Eamon's stern look when I resisted. Torquin and Malese in the deserted ruins of Fold. Borwick and Cherry and their dumb sheep. Hala and the White Fox Resistance. The Leviathans and the hope of peace.

My light expanded gradually, falling across the shivering stars like the rising sun.

It touched Rion's fire.

Her flames sputtered, bending away. She flinched, like she'd touched something too hot. *You ignorant child. You do not know what you are doing.*

Her hand shot to the stars, fiery threads piercing them, dragging them to her, each one fueling her with renewed strength. They were endless.

I couldn't contend with her eternal power. It was as foolish as facing the entire Leviathan army alone.

My light faltered.

*No. Don't stop.* A new star approached.

*She fears you,* said another. *You've done more than any of us could have ever hoped. Fight. Hold on to life.*

I knew them. I'd never seen them, but I knew them. They were born of the same blood, princesses and queens of Roanfire. They were with me.

White light flooded the ruby.

Fire spluttered from Rion's throat as her scream tore through the sea of stars. The thread pulling Ikane's blue energy into the stone shifted direction. Red stars shot across Rion's dome. They converged on the ribbon like a beacon, barreling to the surface.

*Stop her!* The lights beside me resisted the pull. *She's escaping.*

Escaping to where?

More and more red stars pulled to the beacon, slipping away, and blue lightning burst from the point where it touched the surface.

Ikane?

Feathers, no.

This was not supposed to happen.

White light surged. I shot forward, streaking past stars and shimmering clouds of energy. Rion had taken enough.

Just a little farther. I could almost touch her.

Her burning eyes grew wide. She gripped the beacon, fire curling around the racing stars, surging to the lightning. A thunderclap reverberated through the ruby.

I shot through nothing, hung in nothing.

Red dissolved.

No. I failed. I thought I had nothing more to lose. Now . . . now everything was gone.

My light receded like a tide. Stars streaked past me. I was falling. Falling through a night sky like the one Ikane had showed me on the deck of the *Otaridae*, through whispering voices of gratitude, through the glassy surface of stone.

Splinters tore through my lungs as air rushed inside. My eyes flew wide.

My body ached, heavy with armor, smarting with bruises and cuts. Ash drifted through the air like black snow. An eerie silence floated with it.

I raised my arm, uncurling my fist. The tiny jewel sitting in my palm no longer burned red. It was blue, like a misty spring morning. She wasn't there.

Gritting my teeth, I rolled to my knees.

My heart stopped.

Bodies. All around me. Circling like the corpses in Rion's tower. Their eyes were wide, glazed over and lifeless.

The sea of death stretched across the market square, into the streets darkened by smoke and ash.

*Rion. What have you done?*

Nothing. Pure silence.

"She's alive!"

The voice came from above. Faces looked down at me from the castle walls, eyes wide. They whispered to one another, smiled, cried, laughed, shook their heads.

It was impossible.

"Little . . . Little Brendagger?"

I whirled to the sea of bodies. "Ikane? Ikane, where are you?"

An ash-dusted figure moved beside me, trembling as he tried to roll onto his back.

Armor clattered as my knees hit the ground. "Ikane." I grabbed his shoulders. He fell across my lap. A crimson streak cut across his old scar beneath his emerald eye. He smiled, reaching up, resting his hand on my cheek.

"You're . . . you're alright." Summer rose in his eyes,

shattering the surrounding horrors.

I pressed his palm against my skin. He was here. Why did it hurt so much to see him? Losing him would kill me, and yet, he shouldn't be here. *I* shouldn't be here.

His eyes scrunched shut. Breath wheezed into his lungs, chest swelling.

"Ikane?" Where was he hurt? My hand flew across his shoulders and neck, checking his side, his chest . . . something warm and wet streaked across my fingers. My mouth went dry as I turned my palm up. Blood. It hemorrhaged through a cut in his black armor in the center of his rib cage. An axe had done this. The weapon of his brother.

My hand pressed against his chest. "You can't die now. I've tried . . . I've tried everything."

His lashes fluttered, a smile pulling on his lips. "I'm a lycanthrope, remember? I'm not . . . not that easy to kill."

A laugh cut through the tightness in my throat. "I believe you."

His eyes closed again, smile shifting to clenching. His hand shot to my arm. Even through my armor, his grip was crushing. "I . . . I feel her. She's burning. Anger."

His face blurred as tears burned down my cheeks. I couldn't breathe as something in my chest broke. I didn't want to believe it. This was my burden to bear, not his. What had I done?

A streak of red leaked from the corner of his lips, running down his cheek. He gasped, each breath pushing a renewed wave of blood through my fingers.

Yet I knew he wouldn't die today. No, he faced something far worse than death.

"I am so sorry, Ikane," I whispered.

He was her new host.

# The Phoenix Host

# ACKNOWLEDGEMENTS

This project has been one that has grown with me over the past two decades. Characters have changed and scenes developed into something more than I could have imagined with the help of family and friends. The Phoenix Host has been through countless revisions—and each new revision drove supporters mad until many said they'd had enough, and "let me know when the book is finished".

But there are a few crazy people who stuck with me.

My husband, Matt. This book would have never made it into print without him. He brainstormed with me, sat with me for hours, watched me cry, tear my hair out, and melt into puddles of doubt. He was always there to lift me up again. From the bottom of my heart, thank you. You are my Leviathan prince.

Trina Tolman and Rachel Kackstaetter, my baby sisters. Oh, how they always brought excitement back to me whenever I lost my drive. They light me up and fill me with excitement when I ask for help with characters.

Tina Marshall, my high-school friend and writing buddy. All our years of sending notebooks back and forth paid off.

My parents. They always supported my dreams and ambitions, providing me with a computer so I could begin transcribing the story from notebook to computer at age fifteen.

I want to thank special people that have come into my life as this project progressed. They have encouraged me in ways they can't comprehend.

My Musketeer-sister, Kristin Ewert. Creative buddy, Brandon Ho. Mr. Brad Scornavacco, head of Scornavacco Martial Arts Academy—his passion for teaching and books inspired me. His training has been invaluable in my life and in my ability to write believable fight scenes. Fellow Authors: Wesley Lowe, Liz Steinworth, Philip Smith, and Marissa Gramoll (who was also my editor.)

And a huge thank you to my brothers, Ruben and Jon Kackstaetter, the tech gurus, who rescued my manuscript countless times from the abyss of my computer's brain.

I need to thank my three beautiful little boys. I am so blessed they have a deep bond and will play happily for hours so I can write. They bring so much joy.

I couldn't have done this without everyone. And I couldn't have done this without the support and encouragement of my Father in Heaven. I have felt his hand as I've worked. The times I tried to pray before writing were the times everything flowed, scenes came together, and inspiration struck.

Thank you to all the crazy people who stuck with me.

This is a dream come true.

(New acknowledgement as of December 2021 to Melissa Frey, my new editor who helped me polish this book for its second refinement and new cover release.)

# ABOUT THE AUTHOR

C.K. Miller is married to a gentle giant, the mother to three growing Leviathan pirates, and adopted mom to a Zimmertieger. (Her diva-kitty, Toph). She is an artist, gardener, martial artist, and health enthusiast.

www.ckmillerbooks.com

C.K. Miller

.

Made in the USA
Monee, IL
09 October 2023

44249039R00236